BEYOND THE WIRE

Books by James D. Shipman

TASK FORCE BAUM

IRENA'S WAR

BEYOND THE WIRE

Published by Kensington Publishing Corp.

BEYOND THE WIRE

JAMES D. SHIPMAN

www.kensingtonbooks.com

KENSINGTON BOOKS are published by

Kensington Publishing Corp.
119 West 40th Street
New York, NY 10018

All Kensington titles, imprints, and distributed lines are available at special quantity discounts for bulk purchases for sales promotion, premiums, fund-raising, educational, or institutional use.

This book is a work of fiction. Names, characters, businesses, organizations, places, events, and incidents either are the product of the author's imagination or are used fictitiously. Any resemblance to actual persons, living or dead, events, or locales is entirely coincidental.

To the extent that the image or images on the cover of this book depict a person or persons, such person or persons are merely models, and are not intended to portray any character or characters featured in the book.

Special book excerpts or customized printings can also be created to fit specific needs. For details, write or phone the office of the Kensington Sales Manager: Kensington Publishing Corp., 119 West 40th Street, New York, NY 10018. Attn. Sales Department. Phone: 1-800-221-2647.

Maps courtesy of Mapping Specialists, Ltd., Madison, WI.

The K logo is a trademark of Kensington Publishing Corp.

ISBN: 978-1-4967-3642-7 (ebook)

ISBN: 978-1-4967-3671-0

First Kensington Trade Paperback Printing: February 2022

10 9 8 7 6 5 4 3 2 1

Printed in the United States of America

This book is dedicated to all the victims of the Holocaust.
May we never forget.

There may be times when we are powerless to prevent injustice, but there must never be a time when we fail to protest.

—Elie Wiesel

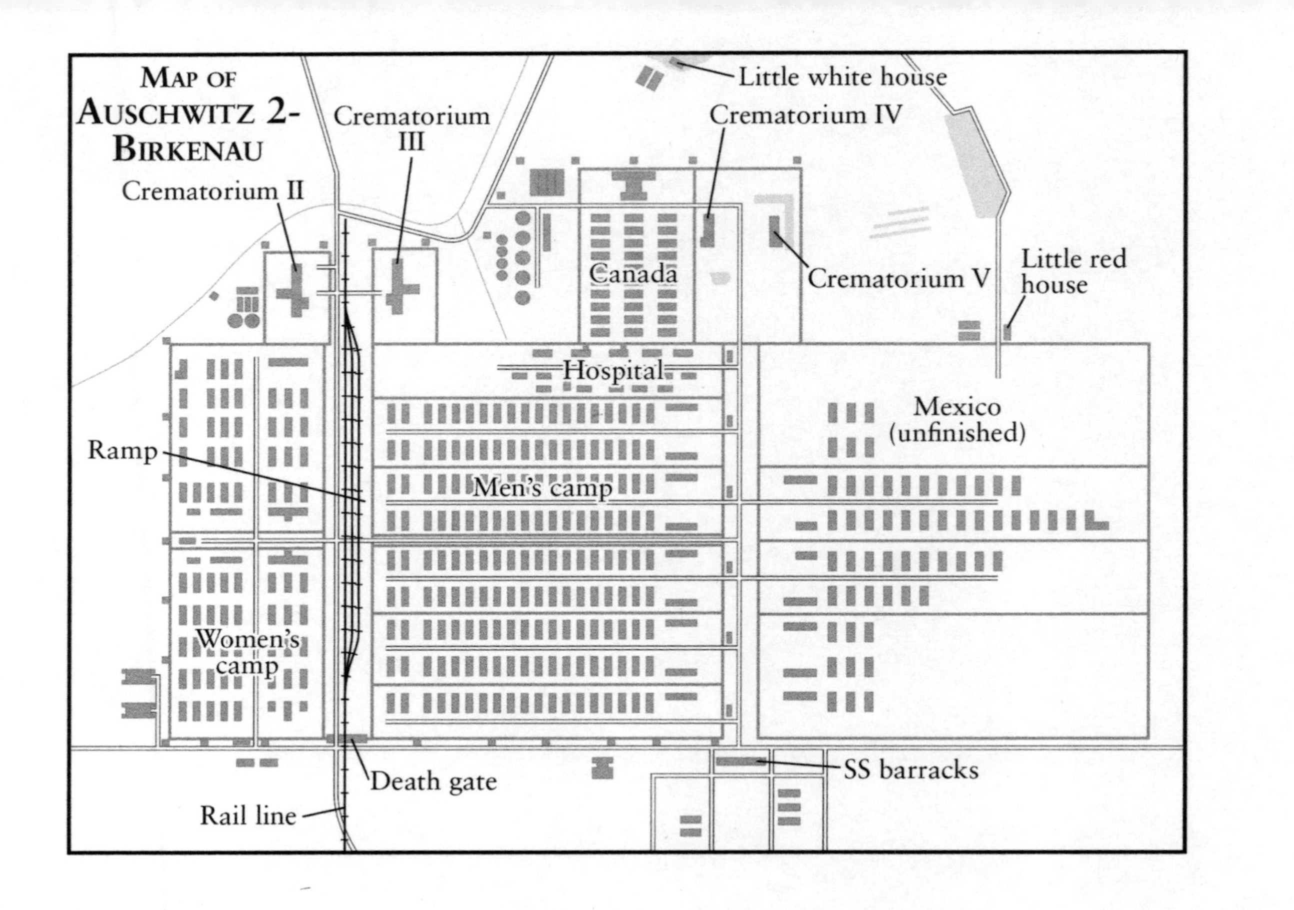
Map of Auschwitz 2-Birkenau
Crematorium II
Crematorium III
Little white house
Crematorium IV
Crematorium V
Little red house
Canada
Hospital
Mexico (unfinished)
Ramp
Men's camp
Women's camp
Death gate
Rail line
SS barracks

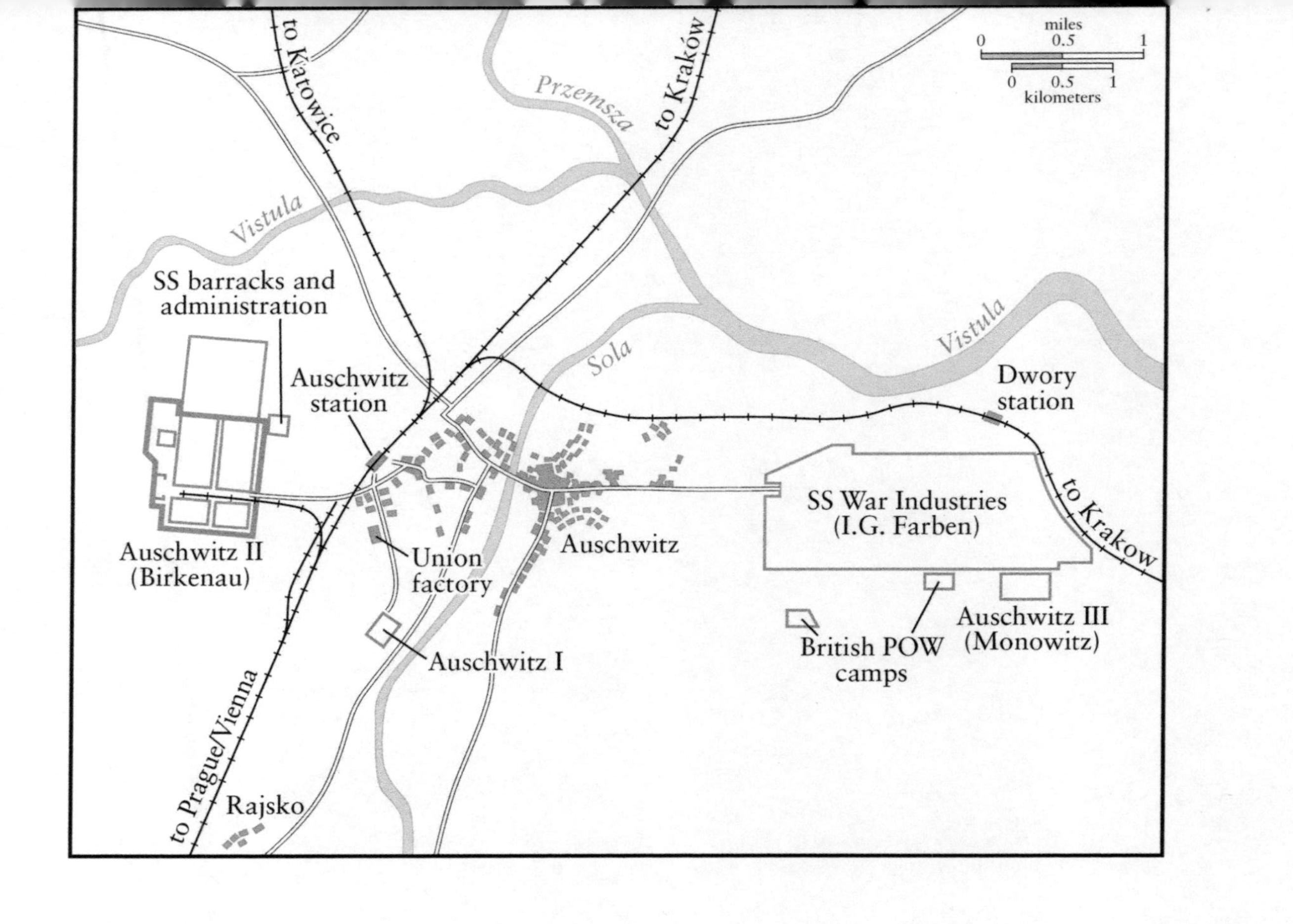
miles
0
0.5
1
0
0.5
1
kilometers
to Katowice
to Kraków
Przemsza
Vistula
SS barracks and
administration
Auschwitz
station
Sola
Vistula
Dwory
station
SS War Industries
(I.G. Farben)
to Krakow
Auschwitz II
(Birkenau)
Union
factory
Auschwitz
Auschwitz I
Auschwitz III
(Monowitz)
British POW
camps
to Prague/Vienna
Rajsko

INSPIRED BY TRUE EVENTS

Chapter 1
The Death Factory

October 1944
Auschwitz-Birkenau

The screams faded. Jakub hunted through the coat of a dead man. He searched with a practiced hand, groping through pockets, fingering seams. He felt something hard. Eyes forward, he tore at the fabric, ripping open a secret pocket. An object fell into his hand, circular and metallic. A watch. He glimpsed a flash of gold. Jakub lifted the jacket, folding it and stacking the fabric on a pile he'd made. With the return movement, he slipped the watch into his striped pajama pocket. He didn't look around for the guards. Taller than the others, he couldn't afford to attract their attention. If one of the SS did catch him it wouldn't matter. He'd never feel the bullet.

He was so thin that his frame felt stretched, his skin translucent like paper. He looked over his matchbook arms swimming in an ocean of sleeves. Jakub reached up and ran his hand over his head, feeling the stubble. He'd possessed a mop of unruly reddish-brown hair, but it was gone, shorn off by the Nazis—

who needed it for the felt slippers of U-boat crews, or some such madness. Another casualty of this hell.

All quiet now. The Zyklon B had done its work. Another thousand candles snuffed out. He shook his head. Mustn't think of that right now. When his clothing stack was head high, he jerked the pile from the bench and stumbled to a nearby cart, easing the cumbersome load inside. If the fabric toppled over, he'd have to start again, and he might get a beating for it if a guard was nearby.

Schmidt was here today. The worst German of all. He looked like a child in his SS uniform. He was missing his upper middle teeth and his words whistled and slurred when he spoke. His cheeks were deeply pocked. When Jakub had first arrived in Auschwitz, he'd felt sorry for the man's unpleasant features. That hadn't lasted long. On the first day he'd watched the SS sergeant shove two workers into the gas chamber—killing them just for fun in a game the Nazi called "the lottery." He played it most days he was stationed here. Jakub wished that Schmidt were all he had to worry about, but amusements were just one of a thousand ways to die.

Up and down the long, narrow undressing room, the *Sonderkommando* labored, each prisoner rushing about, head down, avoiding the attention of the SS.

"Hurry up, you worms!" shouted Schmidt. "There's another group waiting. Get things put away double-quick or I'll send the lot of you in for your own special treatment."

Jakub dashed to another stack, eyes on his feet. The room was nearly cleared out now. He clutched the handle of the cart when he was finished and struggled toward the door. Another prisoner hurried up, crashing into him and nearly knocking him over. It was Tomasz.

"I'm not letting you take all the best jobs," his friend whispered. "Still alive I see."

"I am," whispered Jakub. "But for how long? Only God knows."

Tomasz chuckled grimly. "Always the philosopher. You're still breathing this moment, that's what matters. Tomorrow you could be up the chimney, so why worry?"

"I'm going to survive this," insisted Jakub, gritting his teeth.

"Sure you will, boy, sure you will. If anyone can, it's you. As for me, I'm just trying to live until tonight." Tomasz leaned in closer, looking up at his friend. He wasn't much older than Jakub, but he had the fierce, weathered features of a Warsaw tough. "Do you have anything?"

"A watch. A little money. I couldn't count it."

"The watch any good?"

"Gold, I think."

Tomasz whistled. "That alone will get us through. And a bit more than that."

"How are you fixed?"

Tomasz smiled. "It's been a good morning. I've got three gold coins. Good-sized ones. Old Russian ones I think. A couple biscuits too. I've one for you when we get around the corner." They pushed the cart through a set of double doors and turned to the left. For a few seconds they were unobserved, and Tomasz shoved his hand in Jakub's pocket, leaving behind a lumpy object.

"Thanks, I'm starving."

"Aren't we all, my boy? But we manage a hell of a lot better than those poor bastards in the main camp."

Jakub nodded. "And they hate us for it, and for handling the living and the dead."

"Bah," scoffed Tomasz. "What choice do we have? I don't remember filling out an application, do you? They can get all high-and-mighty about what we must do, but that's not why they dislike us. It's our access to things that help us survive that they hate."

"I'd be dead already without the extra food," admitted Jakub. "Still, that might be better than living like this."

"There you go again, thinking. No good doing any of that in here. It's grab the goods, eat what you can, and trade for a little fun. No point worrying about anything beyond that. A bullet or that gas yonder is just a mistake away."

"Speaking of that, Schmidt's in a mood today."

"Watch that one," warned Tomasz. "He's a snake inside a wolf inside a demon."

"He looks half devil," said Jakub.

"More like a rat to me. But one with a deadly bite."

They reached the end of the corridor and pushed the cart up a ramp to the outside. The undressing room and gas chamber in Crematorium II were located in the basement, necessitating a laborious trip up to the ground floor. They couldn't talk now because there were guards present. They strained at the weight of the thing as they shoved it up, spurred by the shouts and orders of the waiting SS. They reached the top and recovered their breath for a moment as one of the Germans picked at the stacks with a baton. After satisfying himself that there was nothing smuggled inside, he ordered Jakub and Tomasz to load the clothing into a waiting truck. They moved on the double-quick, stacking the articles in the back. Fortunately, the bed was nearly full, so they didn't have to climb in and out. In a few minutes they were done, and they scurried down the ramp with the encouragement of a couple blows to the back from the Germans who screamed at them to hurry.

"I hardly feel them anymore," muttered Tomasz. "The bastards." He leaned closer and whispered, "The Russians will hit these Nazi pricks even harder, I think."

"If they ever get here."

"They will. Have faith. But whether we are alive or just some dust by then, that we will have to see about."

They reached the basement and pushed through the doors to

the undressing room. There was already a new group of arrivals there, starting to undress. Jakub hesitated.

"What are you doing?" Tomasz asked.

"I don't want to go back there. Can't we wait?"

Tomasz looked around. "Too risky. Maybe if Schmidt wasn't there today. But that bastard is looking for any chance." He shoved the cart along. "Let's go. Just a few minutes and they'll be gone."

Jakub reluctantly followed him. The room was crammed with bodies. They were men, elderly, with a sprinkling of young children. Most of them were removing their clothes, unaware of the death that awaited them a few meters away. But there were a few who looked around, fear in their eyes, watching the guards, looking for answers.

"Excuse me," a well-dressed man said, stepping up to Jakub. He looked like a professor, with his thoughtful eyes and peppered hair. "What's going on in here?"

"Nothing," Jakub responded. "It's just a quick delousing and then you'll get your work uniform and barracks assignment."

"Are you telling me the truth?" he persisted.

The man's eyes were searching his, pleading for answers. Jakub turned away, trying to avoid him, but he felt a hand on his arm.

"Please," the man said. "I just want the truth."

"The truth is you better get undressed," snapped Schmidt, who had noticed the exchange and rushed up to them. He looked Jakub over, his lips curling in a twisted grin. "Perhaps you should do the same, Bak."

"I'm working, sir," said Jakub. "This man asked me a question."

"And that one question took all this time?" asked the SS guard. "You're going soft, Bak. Surely there are others who can handle this task more efficiently. I think you better join this gentleman for the delousing, since you've become such fast friends."

"Sir, I—"

"Get undressed!" Schmidt shouted, cracking Jakub on the shoulder with a wooden truncheon. "Looks like you just won my lottery for today, Bak."

"Now, now, sir," interjected Tomasz, sprinting up to intervene. "I've got something important to show you. Something I've just come across."

Schmidt's face flushed with anger. "Watch it, Lis. Unless you want to go with them."

"Sir, I know you're going to want to see this." Tomasz never raised his voice but spoke in a calm, measured tone, almost a whisper.

Schmidt hesitated, staring hard at Jakub. He could feel his heart threatening to explode out of his chest. The guard took a step toward him, his eyes glaring. Jakub thought he would strike him. Instead, he took a deep breath and turned to Tomasz. "Well, what is it?"

"Not something for prying eyes, sir."

Schmidt glanced at Jakub for a moment longer, running his fingers along his jaw as if contemplating something. "Fine. Let's step over to the ramp." He turned back to Jakub. "Get back to work, Bak, before I change my mind!" he commanded.

Jakub rushed to the clothing, folding madly, his hands shaking. The new group of victims was already marching to the gas chamber. He stacked the fabric, keeping his eyes down. He was too terrified to search the stuff for anything valuable. He'd forfeited another life. How many more times could he dodge death?

His friend returned, standing next to him and grabbing a handful of clothing. "You cost me all that gold," whispered Tomasz. "Luckiest thing I've found in a while. I could have bought a whole sausage and a dozen loaves of bread. You owe me big-time."

"Thank you," he managed to say. "You saved my life."

"No, I saved your life *again*," said Tomasz. "You owe me for that as well."

Jakub thought of the old man, of the room full of people who were just here. Their lives were already expiring in the adjacent chamber. "Perhaps I should have gone with them," he said. "Truly, Tomasz, I don't know how much more of this I can take."

"You'll endure all that's thrown at you, until you're out of chances," said Tomasz. "You don't only owe me. Remember what your father made you promise."

"I don't want to think of Papa right now."

"You don't have to. But don't forget, our families are gone. Everything that mattered to us is already up that chimney. You're all I have. You're like a brother, Jakub. The nearest thing I've got left, and I'm not losing you to your brooding guilt. Now get your ass moving! Remember, we've the fence to look forward to!"

The work was done. After a half-hour roll call in the frozen evening air, Jakub and Tomasz marched with the others up two flights of stairs to the attic. Long lines of bunks stretched the length of the room. A single stove burned in the corner, emitting a feeble warmth. This would never have kept more than a portion of the space heated, but the crematorium fires below did just that.

Jakub walked over to one of the narrow windows and stared out past the wire that separated Crematorium II from the main camp of Auschwitz-Birkenau. Row after row of long squat buildings stretched out into the distance. The camp was named Birkenau after the nearby birch trees.

Jakub retrieved a dirty iron bowl from his bunk and marched over with the others to the supper line. A prisoner dished him out a half serving of watery turnip soup and a slice of bread. Jakub returned to the bunk he shared with Tomasz. There was no mattress and no pillow, and they had only a thin blanket to share. He could hardly remember what it felt like to sleep in a real bed. He sat on the edge and was soon joined by his friend.

"Hardly worth the effort, is it?" Tomasz asked, glancing down at their meager supper. He shrugged. "Still, every little bit helps."

Jakub reached into his pocket and pulled out the biscuit. It was hard as a rock and terribly stale, but he dipped the bread into his soup, softening it for a few seconds before he attempted to eat it. Tomasz retrieved a chunk of salami about the size of two fingers. He tore the meat in two and handed some to Jakub. "There you are, my friend. This will sustain you."

Jakub shook his head. "That's for you."

Tomasz laughed. "Nonsense. Share and share alike between the two of us." He slapped Jakub on the arm. "If I don't feed you today, who will I have to bother tomorrow?"

Jakub laughed and accepted the meat. He took half of the piece in one bite, relishing the flavor. He closed his eyes. He remembered his mother's cooking, the Sunday meals out in Kraków cafés, all the wonderful dishes he'd ever eaten. "Thank you," he said.

"Don't mention it. But you're in charge of the main course tomorrow so you'd better get busy. And don't forget, you owe me three gold coins and two lives."

"The gold I should be able to come up with. The lives are a little tougher."

Tomasz leaned in closer. "Speaking of gold," he whispered, looking around to make sure nobody was watching them too closely. "Let's have a look at that watch."

Jakub retrieved the object from his pocket. It was indeed

gold, eighteen karats according to the inscription underneath the dial. The face said *Mido* from Switzerland. The band was gold as well, a thick, flashy affair that likely came off the wrist of a wealthy businessman.

Tomasz whistled. "Some rich bastard must have been holding on to this. That's worth more than my coins, I'll bet."

"You take it then," said Jakub, offering it to his friend.

Tomasz shook his head. "Hide it. I know just who to sell it to. We'll have a feast. We might be able to get ahold of a little booze as well. But I don't have time to organize that tonight. And for God's sake don't bring that to the fence; those Nazi jackals will sniff it out and we'll get nothing for it."

"I don't have anything else except a few zlotys."

"Don't worry, I have you covered. I'll add it to the tab."

"If we make it out of here, I'll have to spend the rest of my life paying you back," said Jakub.

Tomasz shook his head. "No, my boy, a decade should do it." He looked down at their empty bowls. "Enough of this slop. Shall we get going? The fence awaits."

Jakub nodded and set his bowl aside. He glanced around for a moment to make sure nobody was looking, then he tucked his gold watch under the middle of the blanket, smoothing it out so nobody would see that something was hidden there. He stood up, arching his back to try to drive out some of the soreness that plagued his back and limbs. He lumbered forward and followed Tomasz toward the door.

He was blocked about halfway across the attic. Two men stepped out into his way.

"Not now," protested Tomasz. "We've an appointment at the fence."

"This won't take long," said one of them, a thick, muscular fellow with a bullet forehead. "The boss wants a word with young Jakub here."

"Well, Jakub doesn't want a word with him," said Tomasz.

"Let him speak for himself."

Jakub looked at the messengers. They were twice his size. He couldn't push his way through them and he didn't want a fight. "I'll catch up."

His friend hesitated and then nodded. "I'll pay the fee up front. You know which guard. He'll be expecting you."

Jakub watched Tomasz go. He turned back. "All right, whatever this is, let's get it over with."

The men led Jakub back into the far corner of the attic. A figure sat in a lower bunk, conversing with another prisoner. Roch Laska, Jakub recognized him right away. He wasn't much older than Jakub but it was the facial features that set him apart. Even with shorn hair, he was easily the most handsome man in the barracks, his chiseled features accented by a long red scar extending from eye to chin—a bullet wound it was said he'd caught fighting in the Polish army as a junior officer during the German invasion.

"Ah, Bak, so glad you could join me. Won't you have a seat?" He offered the place next to him. The other inmate, seeing the gesture, scurried away.

"No, thank you," said Jakub, on his guard. "I'll stand."

"Your decision," said Roch, shrugging. "Do you know why I've asked you to meet with me?"

"I can guess."

Roch stared up at him for a few moments, rubbing his chin. "You're a bit of a conundrum to me, Bak, I must admit."

"How so?"

"Well, I've brought this topic up before, but I have to try again. Why won't you join us?"

Jakub looked away. He didn't want this tonight. He just wanted to make it to the fence and forget all of this for a little while.

"That's not an answer," said Roch after a while. "I've watched you a long time, Bak. You're a hard worker, brave, kind. You're everything we're looking for. We've already invited you twice, correct?"

Jakub nodded.

"But each time you've refused. It's odd to me. A strong young man like you." He leaned forward. "To be honest with you, there's word going around that you might be a coward, or worse yet, a collaborator."

"I would never work with the Germans." He felt his face flush and his insides burn.

"Don't worry," said Roch, waving his hand as if dismissing the idea. "I've had you checked out. We know you aren't one of *those*. But what does that mean? Are you a coward?"

Jakub bristled. "I'm not afraid. At least not more than anyone else. I just don't see the point of your group. That's all."

"How so?"

"You say you are going to resist the Germans? With what? You have no weapons, nothing to fight with."

"You don't know everything. And we're working on that."

"But there's only a few hundred of us in here. Even if we managed to get ahold of a few pistols or something, it would be suicide to take on the SS."

Roch nodded. "True enough. But there are thousands in the main camp. Tens of thousands maybe."

Jakub scoffed. "Those scarecrows. They're at death's door. At least most of them are. They'd do no good for anyone."

Roch's eyes hardened. "So, we shouldn't try to save them? You think we're better than they are? Why, because we can steal a coin or two and feed ourselves? You don't think we owe anything to anyone else?"

"Look, Roch. I'd join with you if there was a point, but I'm not going to risk my life when there's no chance it will come to any good. I intend to survive, if there's any chance to do so. I haven't joined your group because I think you're going to all get yourselves killed. And for nothing."

"That's your friend Tomasz talking," said Roch.

"I can make up my own mind."

"So, you're just going to keep on taking care of yourself? Waltzing through the camp with Tomasz as if you're on your way to a Warsaw theater show?"

"I wouldn't know anything about that, I'm from Kraków."

Roch smiled. "I see there's no point with you. At least not yet." He shrugged, waving his hand in dismissal. "You can go, Bak. But think about what I said. I understand surviving for survival's sake. But there's more to the world than our own little skins. We owe something to all those little candles we lead into the gas chamber. And to the scarecrows in the main camp. We are the only men here in decent shape. The only ones who could put up a fight. That gives us power . . . and responsibility."

"Power? What power?"

"Even a little freedom is something." He waved his hand at Jakub. "Go on now. Go have your fun. I'm not saying we don't all deserve a little pleasure in this hell. But think on what I said. And don't be a stranger, Bak. I'm expecting you to come around. Think on it, will you?"

Jakub nodded. He walked out and started toward the fence. He tried to summon some excitement, but the joy had seeped out of the evening. Roch's words echoed through his mind. *Resistance*. He looked at the guards, their automatic machine pistols, holding vicious dogs straining at the leash. What could they do against these men of steel?

As he approached the fence, he could tell immediately something was wrong. The guard, Himmel, whom Tomasz was going to bribe, wasn't there. There were two SS here, and Jakub wasn't familiar with either of them. Jakub looked around for Himmel, but the man was nowhere to be found. The guards were eyeing him suspiciously. One of them took a step toward him, mouth half open, ready to question him.

Jakub turned and scampered away as quickly as he could. He expected a shout for him to halt, but none came. He made it back to his building, his heart in his throat. There would be no fence tonight. Roch had held him up too long. He kicked the wall, cursing with frustration. Another day of death and desperation in Auschwitz, and not even the fence to shine a little light on him. He slumped up the stairs to his bunk, damning the resistance and the stupidity of Roch's reckless hope.

Chapter 2
Decisions

October 1944
Auschwitz

SS Obersturmführer Hans Krupp sat impatiently in the outer office waiting for the Birkenau *Lagerführer* to summon him. He checked his watch again. He'd already been here a half hour. How dare Kramer keep him waiting this long! The bastard. He suspected he knew what this was about.

Finally, the *Kommandant* stepped out of the office and fixed Hans with a steely stare. The Birkenau commander possessed criminal features, with squinted eyes and a flat forehead. Hans stood and delivered Kramer the Hitler salute.

"*Ach*, Krupp, come in. I'm sorry I had to keep you waiting." His face didn't look sorry at all. "What can be done about all this paperwork?" he muttered, not putting any real effort into making his excuse carry weight.

Hans followed him into an office in the main guardhouse overlooking the arched "Death Gate." Hans looked out over the rail line that split the camp. At the far end a kilometer away

Crematoriums II and III were partially visible behind the trees. To the left, along the fence line, was the penal company and the infamous Block 25, the "Death Block." To the right of these were the rows of barracks constituting the women's camp. Farther on, across the wide gap of the railroad, and occupying a much larger space, were the men's camp, the Gypsy camp, and the family camp. And beyond them in the far distance were Crematoriums IV and V, along with the buildings where the clothing and personal items of the gassing victims were sorted and collected. This area was called "Canada" by the inmates because of the almost mythical association it had as a place of wealth and treasure.

The rail line itself was the central and focal point of the camp. This was the place where trains unloaded thousands of people at a time. Here they were sorted by an SS officer near the tracks. If he moved his thumb one way, the unlucky person joined the line of about 90 percent of the new arrivals, and would be immediately marched a few hundred meters to Crematorium II or across the tracks to Crematorium III, where they were undressed and gassed. A wave in the other direction and a person had renewed life and would be tattooed and processed into the camp for labor.

Hans thought of this past summer when Kramer had just arrived at the camp. Birkenau at the time groaned under the flurry of activity as the Jews of Hungary arrived and disappeared. Hundreds of thousands of them were liquidated. Nobody knew how many for sure. The new *Kommandant* had been too busy during this harvest to do much administration within the camp, Hans knew, but recently the transports had slowed down and Kramer turned his eyes inward, looking for new objects of his frenetic attention among the German staff.

The office they sat in now was a modest one. A steel desk was pushed against the wall. Cheap wood paneling covered the walls. An oversized portrait of Adolf Hitler loomed above and behind the chair where Kramer perched. The camp commander thumbed through a file folder with Krupp's name on it.

"So, you've been here since 1942 it looks like? *Ja*?"

Hans nodded in answer. "I came when the camp was just getting going."

"You were promoted to head of security in the Birkenau camp in January this last year? Correct?"

"Correct."

"Hmm. A few months before I arrived. To be honest, I'd like to have made that decision myself, but we don't get everything we ask for."

Hans ignored the implied insult. "You came at a chaotic time, sir. What with the Hungarians arriving in droves."

"I doubt you could find a Jew in all of Hungary today," joked Kramer. "Colonel Eichmann did his work well."

"He always does."

"Which brings me to *your* work." Kramer frowned over the paperwork, running his finger down some official report. "Ah, yes, here it is. I want to talk to you about this Edek and Mala escape."

Hans thought this might come up. "What about it, sir?"

"I read the details. A messy business. It seems there were a lot of inmates involved. Prisoners with low numbers. And hints that some of our own men might have helped them."

Hans knew what Kramer meant by low numbers. Each permanent inmate, those who were not immediately gassed, was given a sequentially numbered tattoo. Inmates with low numbers, often a German criminal or non-Jewish Pole, were people who arrived in the camp several years before and had managed to survive the almost impossible conditions in the camp. These men, and some women, now formed a kind of camp elite.

"Well, Krupp? Were SS involved in the escape?"

"Only rumors I'm sure, sir."

"Perhaps. But how did the two of them manage to get so far?"

Hans shrugged. "The camp complex is huge, sir. Some of these prisoners have been around a long time and have garnered quite a bit of influence. Given enough time, it's not surprising what they figure out. And I would point out, sir, they *were* caught after all."

"Yes, they were, but I'm not worried about the last escape, I'm concerned about the next one. You're right about the prisoners. There are far too many of them, and a troubling number who've managed to make it so long. Still, that's a problem we will sort out in the long run. What I'm focused on today is the astounding lack of progress that you seem to have made in infiltrating their numbers."

Hans hadn't expected this. "What do you mean, sir?"

"I'm talking about spies, Krupp. With so many influential prisoners, why don't you have more informants? I don't want to find out about escapes after they happen. I want to catch prisoners before they've even acted. That way, nobody will be tempted to even try it."

"We always have a system of informants, sir. However, they tend to ferret out the snitches," responded Hans. "And they dispose of them."

Kramer's face reddened. "So, the prisoners run things here? Is that it? I don't care what happens to these little weasels. But we need the information. I don't want to hear that they are killing off informants so we can't get what we need. If one dies, secure two more. Good God, Krupp, they are starving and they have no possessions. There is no hope of them ever leaving here. How hard is it to get a few of them to squeal in exchange for a little food or protection?"

"I'll double our efforts immediately."

"Excellent. I'll expect a full report in the next few days, listing all the new contacts and what information you've gleaned from them. Now go, Krupp, I've other matters to attend to."

Kramer didn't even look up or salute. Hans seethed with anger, but he controlled himself and stomped to the doorway.

"And Krupp . . ."

He stopped, turning to the *Lagerführer*. "*Ja*?"

"If there is another escape, it will be your head. Understood?"

Hans nodded and left. Checking his watch, he realized he only had another half hour in his shift. He spat on the ground and headed to the exit. Forget it. He would start tomorrow. He summoned a car and was transported back to the town of Auschwitz, where he had rented a flat. They sped past the downtown market and the brick administration building and former barracks of the smaller Auschwitz I. The driver turned left down a narrow road between squat, low-roofed houses until they reached a two-story structure near the edge of town. His rented flat was on the second floor.

He exited the car and clopped up the wooden stairs on the outside of the building, fumbling with his keys before managing to open the door. The aroma of chicken stew surrounded him. He stepped past the worn sofa, dropping his gloves on the coffee table. A stand-up radio dominated the cramped sitting area, a Christmas gift from his parents. A few books and picture frames cluttered a case. Across the way his wife faced the other direction, busying herself over a pot in the kitchen. A corridor led off to two bedrooms and the single bathroom. The ceilings were low and the light dim. He hated the place, but it was all he could afford.

Hans made his way across the room. "*Guten Abend*," he said finally, putting a hand on his wife's back. She was so petite, his fingers covered most of the space between her upper shoulders. A tumble of blonde curls spilled over them. She didn't turn around. Bracing himself, he asked as cheerfully as he could muster, "How was your day?"

"Every day here is lovely," she said. Her voice, so musical in the past, was forced and brittle. He turned her around. Her pale skin was flushed and her eyes red. It looked like she'd been crying. He felt his heart tearing, but he kept up a smile. *Not tonight. Please not again tonight.* "Oh, come on now, it's not so bad as that. You're not the only wife here at Auschwitz. You said you were going to the market today. Did you see any of the other women we've met?"

"I have to watch our supper," she said, attempting to turn away, but he held her.

"Come now, *mein Liebling*, tell me what's got you all in a huff."

"I can't stand this place," she said, her face contorting in a scowling mask. "I told you I didn't want to come here. It's worse than I'd even imagined."

"How can you say that?" he said, letting go. "You've been here barely a month now. Isn't this better than only seeing me a few times a year?"

She turned back around, not answering him.

"Mmmm, that smells so good," he said, trying a different tack. "Is that chicken? And what is this? Is that a pie in the oven?" He put his hands on her waist. "You've always taken such good care of me."

"Why are you early?"

"I had a meeting." He realized there was no point in trying to cheer her up.

"With whom?"

"The *Lagerführer*."

That got her attention. "What about?"

"I told you that things would change when these transports slowed down. All the chaos that's been allowed would be nipped away."

"What does that have to do with you?"

Hans hesitated. "When is dinner ready?"

"Hans!"

"All right. He's unhappy with the security. He pointed to that escape with the Jewish couple. He seems to think I could be doing more to find out what's going on before it happens."

"I told you that was going to be trouble," she said. "You should have cracked down harder on them. The only thing the Poles and Jews understand is fear."

Hans laughed. "Yes, you'd show them, Elsa. They should put you in charge."

She turned back to the stew. "Are you in trouble?"

"A bit. He told me if there was another escape, he'd demote me."

"Well, that's the end then," she said. "You can't stop every prisoner from getting away from this mess. We might as well go home now."

He heard the hopeful note in her voice. He hadn't expected the conversation to take this road. "It's not so bad as that. Kramer's just posturing, I'm sure. If they fired every security boss for an escape from Auschwitz, they'd have had to let a hundred of them go since the camp opened."

"It doesn't matter what happened in the past. It only matters what this *Kommandant* is willing to do." She turned back to him. "That settles things, Hans. I've told you again and again that I can't stand it here. With your job in jeopardy, there's no point in me—"

"Don't say you're leaving," he protested. "I've told you how much it means to me that you're by my side. This is not . . . an easy camp to work in."

"So you've said, but you won't tell me why." She moved away from him. "That's just another of your secrets. How many more do you think our marriage can survive?"

"You promised we would have a fresh start."

"And you promised me a beautiful home here. Not this drab flat in the middle of nowhere with nothing to do."

He forced a smile. "Things are going to get better," he said. "Please, just stay a little longer."

"Dinner is ready," she said.

They ate in silence, as if the other was not there. Hans was distraught. First these work issues and then the mess at home. There must be something he could do. But what? He picked at his food, racking his brain for a solution. But for now, at least, nothing came to mind.

After dinner Hans moved to the sitting room. He smoked a few cigarettes, mulling the problems over in his mind. Then it hit him, something he'd already considered before, but now the plan coalesced. *Yes, that would solve both problems.* He excused himself and returned to his office in Birkenau. Elsa did not protest. She seemed to prefer it when he wasn't there. He shook his head. He couldn't think about that right now. He didn't bother to call a car; the walk and the fresh air did him good. The more he considered his new idea, the more he liked it. Certainly, this could solve all his problems.

He arrived at his office and immediately picked up the phone. He contacted a friend of his in Berlin associated with SS personnel. He talked quickly, overcoming objection after objection. No, he could not wait a few days. No, they would not need transportation. They only lived a few hours away by car. They just needed authorization for the border. No, they didn't need to worry about uniforms and equipment, he had everything here. Call after call, everything fell into place. He'd worried it would take a week, but he placed a final call at the end of the evening. The most difficult one of all. After a half hour of stern lecturing, he got what he wanted. They would be there in the morning, sometime before noon.

Hans checked his watch; it was nearly eleven. He decided to spend the night here. He picked up the phone to call Elsa, but set it back down. Let her worry about him for once. He worked for another hour more before stumbling down the hall. He found a room with a cot and tumbled into it. He didn't bother to undress or even to find a blanket. He was asleep immediately.

He woke with a start, rubbing his neck in pain from the supporting bars under the fabric. *I'm getting too old for this.* The morning sun stabbed through the window, burning his eyes. He checked his watch. *Scheiße.* It was nearly ten. He must have been more tired than he realized. He called a car and rode home. He was surprised to see a vehicle already parked outside his flat. They'd arrived before him. He'd wanted to be present, but no matter. He smiled to himself, excited to see the reunion.

He opened the door and a frozen atmosphere washed over him. This was not at all what he'd expected. His wife sat on the sofa, her arms around her sister, whose face was buried in her hands. His nephew Dieter sat nearby, staring up at him with something akin to hatred.

"Hannah, Dieter. So nice to see both of you. How did you get here so quickly?"

"How could you have done this to my sister?" asked Elsa accusingly, with fire in her eyes.

Hans raised his hands in the air. "Now calm down. What is it I'm supposed to have done?"

"You transferred me, Uncle," said Dieter. "You took me away from my unit." He unfolded himself from his seat and lurched across the room, unwilling to meet Hans's eyes.

"Now, now, why is that such a bad thing? I thought you'd be happy."

"How could you believe that?" his nephew asked, towering over his uncle. Although he was tall, he weighed considerably less and his face was that of a boy of fourteen or fifteen. He hadn't grown into himself yet. His eyes bulged behind thick lenses. "I've trained with my Wehrmacht unit for months," Dieter said. "I was with all my friends, all my classmates from the neighborhood. I was going to fight the Russians. Protect the Fatherland. Now instead you've robbed me of that future and made me into what? Some kind of a jailer!"

"Now, now, Dieter. Listen to me." Hans took a step toward him.

"I won't!" shouted Dieter. He pushed past Hans and out the door, slamming it behind him.

Hannah stood, starting to go after him.

"Let him go," said Hans. "He'll be back. Maybe it's good that he left." Hans stepped over, taking a seat in a nearby chair. "Hannah. I don't understand what the problem is. We talked last night about things. Sure, at first you weren't convinced, but after I explained the opportunity I could offer Dieter, you said you liked the idea. After all, your boy would be safe here."

"That was before I discussed it with him," she said, her face ashen. "You will not believe the things he said to me. He raged all the way here," she said. "I'm sorry, Hans, but this is not going to work."

"But he's protected here. You know that."

"I admit, as a mother I want to save him from harm. But how can I stop him when he wants to serve Germany? How can I crush his dreams?"

Hans looked over at Hannah. She was exhausted from the frantic night of packing and travel. It was hard to tell they were sisters. She was taller, with auburn close-cropped hair and a sprinkling of freckles on her face. Only the pale skin reminded him of his wife. Right now, her cheeks were anything but white, flushed with an angry scarlet red. He'd never seen her this distraught. He had to calm her down. "Listen to me. You have the right instincts. Trust me. You must overcome his objections. He's living in a fantasy of serving the Fatherland and coming home a hero. But that's all it is—a dream."

She was listening now, and he slowed his words, speaking each with a pause in between so he could emphasize their importance. "There is nothing out there on the front except death. Back at home you don't hear what's going on out there. We are losing this war. Nothing can stop that now. Thousands of men are dying every week fighting the Russians. Do you want Dieter to be one of them?"

"I don't understand why you didn't tell me about this last night!" his wife interjected. "What were you thinking, doing all of this without consulting me?" She was as angry as her sister.

"I wanted this to be a surprise," he said quickly, trying to keep the momentum of the conversation within his control. "I've been thinking about this for a long time now. Aren't you happy to see Hannah? I invited her to stay with us until Dieter is settled. You'll be able to have a good long visit. I did this for you as much as for Dieter."

"I don't think he'll agree to stay," said Hannah. "All the way here he told me he'll never say yes."

"Is that your main objection?" asked Hans. "If Dieter agrees, will you be satisfied?"

"Of course. I feel a little guilty about what you've proposed, but I would be so relieved if he didn't go off to fight." She was calming down now, and it seemed Elsa was doing the same. Hannah leaned toward him. "But truly, Hans, what sort of a place is this? You're always so vague about your work."

"Leave Dieter to me," said Hans. "I'll talk to him now." He rose and strode out of the flat before they could raise any more objections.

Hans found him a few blocks away, standing on a corner. "Let's go get something to eat," he suggested. Dieter nodded.

Hans led him to a café he knew. They were seated quickly, and he ordered tea and some cold meats and cheese. "I haven't had anything yet today," he professed, digging into the breakfast. They made small talk for a few minutes, munching on a little bread. Dieter told him about the completion of his studies and the rigors of his basic training. Finally, Hans got to the point.

"I understand that you want to be with your unit. But why?"

"We've trained together. We are going to fight the Russians together, serve the Fatherland. If I don't go with them, I'll be letting my friends down, letting down Germany. I'll be a coward."

"I can appreciate that it might seem that way, but it's not. What do you think I'm doing here? We in the SS are fighting too, and perhaps in an even more important way than your unit."

Dieter looked up. "What do you mean?"

"You want to fight the enemies of the Fatherland? Sure, they are out there on the Eastern Front. But I'll let you in on a little secret: The worst enemies of all aren't in Russia, they are here. We have contained them, and they are paying for their crimes."

"What do you do here?"

"We keep Jews, Gypsies, homosexuals, and other undesirables. All the scum of the earth. There are other camps out there like this one, but this is the biggest of all. Every day I make sure these criminals are not loose, not working against the war effort, poisoning the home front like they did in the last war." Hans leaned forward. "Anyone can stop a bullet, Dieter. But it takes real courage to do what we do."

He could see he'd caught Dieter's attention. "What do you mean by courage?" his nephew asked.

"The camp is not . . . pleasant. There are things that happen there that no man should see or go through. Your aunt doesn't even know what we are really doing here. She thinks I'm just a kind of policeman or a jailer. But we are doing much more than just that. We are fighting our own kind of war against the enemies of humanity. And it takes more guts to serve here than it does to fight the Russians at the front. Do you have that kind of courage, Dieter? Or should I send you home?" He saw his nephew bristle. He smiled to himself. Young men were so easy to manipulate.

"What would you want me to do?"

"You'd join the ranks of the guards in the camp, but that's not all. I have a secret duty for you."

"What duty is that?"

"If you join us, you will be part of a new operation, and I need someone just like you. You are young and you look like someone that a person could trust. I need you to meet with some contacts I have among the prisoners and to make new ones. I need information about escapes, plots, anything that can be useful for Germany."

"You want me to spy on people?"

"Bah, *spy* is a dirty word. I need you to gather intelligence. This camp is full of criminals and they cannot be trusted. I need someone I can rely on to be my eyes and ears."

"Can I have some time to think about it?"

"Of course you can," said Hans, knowing he'd won. He waved a finger at Dieter. "But this is wartime. You're not on a holiday. I'll give you the day, then you must give me your answer."

"Fair enough."

They rose and he clapped his nephew on the shoulders. "You'll make me proud."

"This is truly more important than serving at the front?" Dieter asked.

"More important and more difficult than you can imagine. Tomorrow you'll know what I mean, but you will be sworn to secrecy."

"Thank you. If you don't mind, I'm going to walk around for a bit."

"That's fine," said Hans. "But be careful. This isn't a tourist town. Make sure they don't mistake you for an escaped prisoner in disguise! You're so thin, you might pass for one!"

Dieter laughed and strolled away. Hans watched him, loving his nephew, proud to have him here.

He arrived back at the apartment a few minutes later. "It's all right," said Hans. "He's calmed down now. I think I know what decision he's going to make, but he wants the rest of the day to make it."

Hannah smiled and even Elsa looked happy. "That's wonderful news, Hans. If Dieter did agree to serve here, that would mean so much to me. And it would be delightful to stay for a month or two and see both of you. It's been so long."

He stepped away and let the sisters continue their conversation. He busied himself with a file, pretending to scan the documents as he listened to them across the room. They were catching up on the last month. Elsa was animated, and joy laced her voice.

Hans was pleased he'd recovered the situation. Today caught him by surprise. He thought his work last night was going to be the only hurdle he would face. He hadn't anticipated Dieter's objection or how that might affect his wife and sister-in-law.

There was a pounding at the door. Dieter must be back already. "That didn't take long," he shouted. "No need to knock, just let yourself in." The door opened. It wasn't Dieter. An SS private stood at the door, an envelope in his hand. He saluted. "Message from the *Kommandant*." Hans took the package and tore it open. The letter informed him that the commander knew about the unauthorized transfer of Dieter Lehmann to the Auschwitz garrison and that he was to come to his office immediately. *The request for transfer is hereby denied.*

Chapter 3
Anna

October 1944
Auschwitz

Anna shivered in her underclothing and bare feet. The temperature was below zero. Her feet were buried in the dirty snow and pain shot up through her legs in waves as her nerves screamed against the cold. She kept her head down, away from the stabbing light and prying eyes.

She hunched over the trough, her stomach on fire, fighting back the nausea as she twisted and turned the coarse fabric in the frigid water. *What was the point?* she wondered. Even if they killed the lice in their clothes, there were thousands more waiting back in the barracks.

She risked a glance at the line of uniforms a few meters away. There were three SS women and a male guard. He wasn't supposed to be here she was sure, but who would stop him? His face was set in a grotesque leer as his eyes moved up and down the line of women moaning and groaning their way through their labors.

"The bastard," whispered her friend Urszula, spitting into the dirty water.

"At least he's only looking," said Anna, careful to keep her head down. If she was caught talking, she might get the lash.

"For now."

"Now is all we have." She'd lived moment to moment for a year now. She remembered her past life as if it was a dream—the apartment in Katowice with her parents and her little brother. Her father was a prominent teacher at a local academy. She'd grown up playing in the park, with dolls and love and family. Then the war came. At first they were left alone, but not for long. Her father lost his job, they were forced to sell much of their belongings for a little bread. There were no more walks in the park. Then the Germans had come. She remembered the explosive clamor of boots on the stairway and a violent pounding on their door. Not even waiting for the inhabitants to answer, the Nazis tore through the entrance, rushing in to seize them. She could still see the German throwing her father from the third story window of their flat.

"Anna, are you listening to me?" asked Urszula.

She shook the past out of her mind. "I'm sorry, what did you say?"

"I said, at least we have someplace to go tonight."

"I don't know if I can make it. My stomach is on fire."

"You'll feel no better if you starve. We need the extra we can get."

"I can't eat."

"Come with me at least," her friend urged. "If you can't keep it down, you could give it to me."

"Leave her alone," said Estusia, another of Anna's comrades. "You're going to get her in trouble with all that horsing around."

Urszula laughed. "And you're not? Tell me, who is taking

the bigger risk? At least I'm risking my life for something to fill my belly."

"It's always about yourself, Urszula."

"Quiet now," said Anna, venturing a glance at the guards. "They're looking our way."

The male guard was looking right at her. She recognized him. Knew him. What was she going to do? Then again, perhaps it was just her imagination.

Her stomach spasmed, ripping her attention away. What if she had dysentery? She'd seen others wither away and die in just a few days from the crippling illness. The slightest shirking of her duties could land her a bullet or a trip to the dreaded hospital. The hospital was death.

"That's enough, you sluts!" screamed the block wardress. "Now get back to the barracks!"

Finally. She wasn't sure she could stand much longer. She gathered her wet clothes in her arms and turned to follow the line away from the wash bins. As they moved away she ventured a final glance at the male guard. He was still watching her. He followed her with his eyes and a crooked smile.

"Never mind him," whispered Urszula. "We'll soon be in a better place."

Chapter 4
Past and Future

October 1944
Auschwitz

The October sun burned Jakub's back as if it were midsummer. The block *Kapo* had assigned him a landscaping *Kommando* today and he was pulling weeds along the exterior of Crematorium II. He was grateful to get away from the gas chamber for a day. He didn't have to reassure people on their way to death. There were no faces to stare into, or false smiles to give. He hated that duty, although worse yet was the disposal *Kommando*, the men who removed the bodies from the gas chamber and transported them upstairs to the cremation ovens. Every time he was forced into this group, he was haunted by nightmares for days.

He was much happier with this landscaping assignment; however, the work out here was backbreaking. Although he was young and had access to more food by far than the average prisoner in Birkenau, he was still much weaker than when he'd arrived at Auschwitz. He'd lost weight, and although in his early twenties, he now moved at the pace of a middle-aged man.

He remembered a summer day a few years ago in Kraków. Before the ghetto, before the war. He was pulling weeds then as well and just as unhappy about it. His sister worked next to him. They fought, complaining that the other one was slacking. His mother brought them tea and some pastries. She smiled down at them. Later she took them to their father's dentist office in the old town. They'd had lunch at an outside café in the huge medieval city square, under the shadow of St. Mary's Basilica. Nobody would have taken them for Jews. They dressed like the upper-middle-class Poles that they were. They hardly even followed the major Jewish holidays. They thought of themselves as Poles first, Jews second. They spoke Polish and German. Jakub and his sister were educated in a Catholic private school. They lived in both worlds.

Then the war came. He remembered their confusion and surprise when they were herded from their beautiful apartment home and forced to march with a handful of luggage to the newly formed Jewish Ghetto in the Podgórze district. It was March 1941. A lifetime ago. Jakub had carried a double share of their meager possessions. He'd walked behind his father and mother, his sister clinging to him. The streets were lined with Poles shouting insults and hurling garbage and food. They'd shared a single bedroom in a ramshackle flat on Krakusa Street with another family of six. There were thirty-four people living in that one apartment that had previously housed a family of four. Food was scarce. Jakub's father performed a little dental work with supplies he'd brought with them, but his medicine was quickly exhausted. There was no way to make money. Months went by as they grew thinner and more desperate—rumors swirling around them of the most wild nature: some saying the Germans had lost the war and the Russians would soon be there; others that the Nazis had defeated the Soviets and that America had surrendered. They tried to find work with one of the German factories, with Madritsch or Schindler, but these jobs were scarce and difficult to come by. They couldn't obtain the essential worker permits that would keep them safe—at least for a while.

Another memory. It was early 1943. The blaring brightness of the morning sun as the doors of the cattle car were ripped open. Shouting voices forced them out into an alien landscape full of barbed wire, low-roofed buildings and swarming SS. Jakub's mother and sister screamed as they were pulled away into a separate line, the women sorted from the men. Jakub held his father's hand. He felt so out of control. His father had always seemed like the center of the world, but he had no power here. There were hands on him. A guard was pulling him to yet another group filled with young men only. He tried to rip the hands off, battling to get back. His father screamed at him, ordering him to stop, to go with the young men. He smiled sadly at Jakub. "You must survive!" he shouted over the milling throng. "For all of us! No matter what, survive!"

His hands kept working at the weeds as he fought back tears. His father couldn't have known what that promise meant. Surviving here meant leading others to their deaths, day after day. Why did he have more of a right to live than the rest of the people? Than the rest of his family did? He felt the anguish and depression wash over him. Perhaps his father was wrong.

Despair threatened to crush him as it so often did. He looked to his left. Fifty yards away was the fence to the main camp. It was electrified. All he had to do was sprint to it and throw his body onto the wires. In a second it would all be over. He'd seen others do it. He longed to die, to put an end to the suffering and the pain. *But you made a promise to him. Survive.*

"Get to work, Jew, or today will be your last!" The voice startled him until he realized it was familiar. A body crashed down next to him. "What are you doing out here?" asked

Tomasz. "It looks like hard work." His friend followed Jakub's eyes and his tone abruptly changed. "Are you thinking of killing yourself again?"

Jakub shook his head, but he couldn't help a smile. "Is it that clear?"

Tomasz shrugged, pretending to weed. "You're a simple young man. Don't feel bad about it. I admire your innocence. I lost mine long ago." Jakub knew Tomasz had been a Warsaw street tough before the war. In the upside-down world of Auschwitz, a former criminal had a far better chance of survival than he did.

"Where were you last night?" his friend asked him. "I wanted to ask when I got back, but you were already asleep."

"Roch delayed me too long. By the time I got to the fence the guard had changed."

"I figured as much," said Tomasz, his hands still moving near the soil. "Well, no matter, we'll go again tonight."

"I don't have anything to pay with."

"Ah, but you've forgotten your gold watch. That's worth the price of admission, and some bread and sausage as well. What did that bastard Roch want with you, anyway?"

"Same as always, he wants me to join the resistance."

"Bah!" said Tomasz, spitting. "That band of idiots. They're going to get themselves killed if they keep playing at soldier, and likely all of us with them."

"You don't think we should fight the Germans?"

Tomasz shrugged. "I hate the bastards as much as they do. But resist them with what? Our bare hands? Even with our extra food, we grow a little weaker every day. And we're the fittest men in the whole damned camp. The rest of them are half dead, or worse. There are hundreds of those SS bastards with machine guns and dogs. We're segregated by electric wire. There are a dozen nationalities here, some of us enemies going back centuries." He clapped Jakub on the back. "Trust me, my boy, if there was any chance, I'd be the first one to sign up to fight. But I'm not going to sell my life that cheaply." He shrugged. "Besides, things aren't so bad here. We have food and shelter, and something to look forward to a few nights a week. And who knows? Maybe the Russians will get here before they kill us all. That's our only real chance. Didn't you promise your father you'd survive?"

Jakub nodded.

"Remember that promise before you join Roch. That's the surest way to get yourself dead." Tomasz rose. "I'd better get back to the cellar before they come looking for me." He turned to Jakub. "Don't forget, my brother, the only real shot we have is to keep up with what we're already doing. Focus on today. Stay alive—today. And remember, there's always the fence."

Jakub continued his work, calmed by the visit from his friend. Tomasz was correct, as always. There was no point in working with the resistance. Joining was simply another form of suicide. He knew there was only a fraction of a chance he would come out of here alive, no matter what he did, but he had to hold on to that chance. He didn't know what he would do without Tomasz. His friend was a criminal, a rogue, someone whom he would have had nothing to do with in his former life. But here, in this hell, he was strength, wisdom, and life.

Now that his mind was settled, he only wanted to finish this day of labor, and move on to the night ahead. But the sun was his enemy, frozen in the sky. He would work away for as long as he could stand it before glancing up again, but each time he did, he felt like there was no movement. His shoulders ached and his back burned. He almost wished he were down there in the basement, telling lies, gathering up the possessions of people who'd been alive a few minutes before. Almost.

Finally, when he thought he couldn't take it any longer, a whistle from his *Kapo* informed him that they were done for the day. Jakub stretched, laboring to his feet, and shuffled inside and up the stairs to the attic. He reached his bunk and retrieved his bowl. He sifted around beneath the blanket to retrieve the watch and was shocked. There was nothing there. He searched again, finally removing everything from the bunk. Nothing. Someone had taken it. He felt his anger surge. He'd clung to this evening as the only thing that would get him through the day. Hour after hour he'd labored, and some bastard had taken it all away from him.

"Who stole it?" he heard himself shout. He was being crazy, reckless. He didn't care. "Who stole it?"

He felt hands on his back. "Quiet now," Tomasz whispered in his ear. "Do you want to get yourself killed?"

Jakub seethed. "They've taken the watch," he whispered back. "They've taken away the fence."

Tomasz chuckled. "Is that all? You're speaking nonsense. Whoever stole it hasn't taken away anything. All they've done is increase the size of your debt."

Jakub turned to his friend. "What do you mean?"

"While you were outside picking daisies, I was in the cellar all day. I've got money and a watch of my own to trade. Oh, it's nothing so high and mighty as the beauty you found yesterday, but it's enough to get us through."

"I can't, Tomasz. I can't take more from you."

Tomasz grabbed his arm with an iron grip. "I told you, boy, you're all I've got. You and that fence. You say you don't want to live sometimes. I make it day by day because I have a purpose. That purpose is keeping you alive and giving us something to look forward to. I don't care if you owe me a million zlotys by the time we're done here. I'm going to that damned fence tonight and you're going with me."

Jakub didn't know what to say. He'd never heard Tomasz talk like this. He nodded.

Tomasz smiled. "Let's go then."

"To the fence? What about supper?"

"This slop? I told you, I have goods to trade. Let's get a decent meal and something for our little friends."

Tomasz led Jakub down the stairs. At the door, an SS guard moved to stop them. Tomasz smiled and stepped up to the German, shaking his hand. The Nazi smiled in return, moving his hand down into his pocket to hide what Tomasz had given him. He opened the door and waved them past.

They walked out into the yard. The sun was down beyond the tree line now and the October air was crisp. The twilight was beautiful. "This place would be nice if it wasn't hell on earth," observed Tomasz. "Still, for us, at least for a little while, it's heaven." He led them to the gate separating Crematorium II from the main camp. The guard here was cooperating too. There was another exchange of goods and quickly they were through. They crossed the rail line and walked along the electrified fence until they reached another gate that led into the men's camp. Tomasz handed some bank notes to an SS guard who winked at him and allowed them to pass. They moved past some of the wooden barracks and entered one of the buildings two rows in. The interior was full of inmates, skeleton thin, staring at them with hopeless eyes as they lay row after row in their bunks. The smell was overwhelming. Tomasz ignored them and moved to the back of the barracks where the block senior's quarters were located. He knocked on the exterior door and they went inside.

Within there were a few tables, bare but set with chairs. "Take a seat," said Tomasz, who stepped away to speak with one of the men nearby whom Jakub recognized as Wieslaw Kieler, one of the camp elite. The inmates in the confined space were largely Poles with low numbers. Men who had come in the first transports to the camp and by wit, cruelty, or luck, had survived to form the Auschwitz royalty. Tomasz seemed to move easily in this crowd. He talked to Kieler and a couple of other men, laughing and joking. After a time, he handed over a wad of zlotys. One of the Poles took the money and stepped over to a cupboard. He pulled out some bread and other items Jakub couldn't see and brought them back to Tomasz.

His friend returned and laid the feast down before him. There were three loaves of bread, a sausage, a tin of oranges, and two small bars of chocolate. "We'll save two loaves and the chocolate for later," he said, "but the sausage and this loaf is for us." He tore the bread into roughly equal pieces and worked his thumb through the middle of the meat, pulling it apart. Jakub bit into the chunk, relishing the flavor, and gulped down the bread in a few bites. The oranges were delicious. He couldn't remember the last time he'd had fruit of any kind. As always, there wasn't quite enough. He was ravenous, and even when they were finished, he was looking around for more, fighting the urge to ask Tomasz if they could finish what he'd held back for later.

When they were done with their supper, they left the men's camp and walked back across the rail line to the gate that led into the women's portion of Birkenau. Jakub knew it was even more dangerous to try to enter here, since there could be no reasonable explanation for the two of them to go inside. Still, Tomasz was as calm as always, approaching two of the SS and chatting with them casually in broken German for a few minutes before handing each one of them a small gold coin. The guards pocketed the money immediately and waved them both through. In a few minutes they were in another barracks within the women's camp, which was abandoned except for a group of tables set up where other influential prisoners sat, both men and women, chatting over bottles of alcohol and plates of food, as if this was some sort of restaurant on the edge of hell.

Tomasz led Jakub to a table that contained a few empty plates. They sat down and Tomasz pulled out their provisions, opening the bottle and dividing up the rations. Jakub looked around. He was shocked to see Schmidt there, a glass of brown liquor in his hand. "Look over there," whispered Jakub. "We have to get out of here."

Tomasz glanced over toward the direction Jakub indicated. He laughed. "You mean old Schmidt? Don't worry about him. He's a pussycat—at least here. He has his own reasons for coming. Look."

A woman in a striped skirt had joined him at the table. She had long raven hair and a pretty face. The SS guard pulled out a loaf of bread and handed it to her. She gave him a crooked smile and started to eat.

"Her hair," said Jakub. He hadn't seen a woman with uncut hair since the day he'd arrived here.

"She's protected by him," Tomasz answered. "That's why her hair is so long. Nobody would dare touch it."

"I see you two have already started," said a voice. Jakub looked up. Anna and Urszula were here. Urszula was tall, with high cheekbones and a sharp nose. She looked like a bird. Anna was the opposite, short and slight, with reddish-brown hair and gray-blue eyes. His Anna. He took her hands, careful not to draw attention. He pulled her to him and kissed her cheek.

"Not here," she whispered.

"You're lucky you two showed up when you did," said Tomasz, laughing. "We were about to eat the rest of our food."

"You wouldn't dare," said Urszula. "That's the only reason we come in the first place."

"I'm no fool," said Tomasz, motioning for the two of them to sit. "But still, this chocolate is almost as tempting as the two of you."

"Chocolate!" Urszula exclaimed. She reached for the bar, quickly unwrapping it and shoving some of the dark substance into her mouth. "I haven't tasted any since before the war!"

Anna reached for hers as well, smiling up at Jakub shyly. To his surprise, she placed the package in her pocket. Jakub watched her. She was so frail, so thin. Only her eyes spoke of an inner strength. They were piercing and full of an icy fire.

"How are things?" he asked.

"I'm still alive," she said simply.

"Well spoken, Anna," said Tomasz. "That's what I keep trying to tell our brooding boy over here. Stay alive day by day. That's all we have to cling to."

Anna took Jakub's hand and pulled him away from the table. She led him down a corridor lined with rooms covered with curtains. She found an empty one and pulled him inside, closing the cloth to give them some privacy. She wrapped her arms around him, looking up at him before she placed her head on his chest. They stood that way for a long time. He noticed she was wearing the perfume he'd found for her. She was warm and he felt the world melt away while they held on to each other. Finally, she took his hand, leading him over to a bunk where they could both sit down.

"Who was that girl sitting with Schmidt?" he asked.

"That's Kamila."

"Do you know her well?"

"I know her. She's in my barracks. She was the wife of some doctor or other in Lvov. She keeps to herself."

"She's with Schmidt?"

Anna looked away, her cheeks flushing. "It's not so surprising. The SS take what they want. A Jewish girl isn't vermin suddenly, when a German man wants something from her."

"And she lets him have her?"

Anna shrugged. "He protects her. Look at her hair. She

gets food, alcohol, cigarettes. She's hated, but nobody will touch her."

"She's sold her soul."

"What happened to you yesterday?" she asked, clearly changing the subject. She took his hands in hers. "I waited for you."

"I was held up by some inmates that want me to join the resistance," he explained. He told her about Roch and everything that had transpired.

"And you told him no?" she asked.

"Tomasz thinks only a fool would join them."

"What do you think?"

"I think I want to kiss you." He moved his head toward hers but she pulled away. "What's wrong?"

"You didn't answer me."

"I agree with Tomasz," he said at last, shrugging. "What's the point? We've no weapons, most of us are ill or too weak to put up a fight. Besides, the Russians are coming."

"I don't agree," she said. "I think you should get involved."

He was surprised. "Not this again. I thought you'd stopped asking."

Anna shrugged. "There has seemed little point in continuing the conversation." She turned to him. "Jakub, I appreciate everything you've done for me. You've given me food, a little protection, something to look forward to. But there's more than that. There's our honor. Our chance to rise up and show the world that we didn't just go like lambs to the slaughter." She stared at him with those piercing eyes. "Or is it enough for you to just survive?"

"It's everything," he said. "That's what I promised my father. To live for all my family that was murdered. Sometimes, even that seems to be too much."

"That's because you're only fighting for yourself," she said.

He scoffed. "How can you say that? Look what I've done for you."

"That's not entirely selfless," she reminded him. "Besides, our worth is not weighed by protecting those we love. Our value as a human is measured in saving a stranger."

"So, you think I should join the resistance? To what end? I'll be caught and killed, and there'll be no more bread and chocolate. Not for me and not for you."

She squeezed his hands tighter. "At least I would know you died for something greater."

He reached in again to kiss her, but she pushed him back. "I can't, Jakub."

"Why?" he demanded, his anger rising. "Because of this? Some silly notion of nobility?"

She shook her head. "I've been ill."

He felt his fury drain away, replaced with concern. "What do you mean, ill? What kind of sickness?" All prisoners in Auschwitz were obsessed with their health. Any malady was usually a death sentence, since there were frequent selections within the camp for the gas chamber, and the doctors in the hospital administered lethal injections to the sick.

"I can't keep anything down."

"Do you have dysentery?"

She shrugged. "I don't know if it's that bad yet, but I've been vomiting too."

"You should have sent word to me. I could have brought you some medicine."

"I've been taking some burnt bread. One of the men in the factory secured it for me."

Jakub bristled. "You have someone else taking care of you?"

She reached forward and kissed him on the cheek. "It's nothing like that. But there are men there that help us as much as they can."

"What are you going to do?"

"I'm going to keep taking the charcoal. It's already been helping."

"Will you come tomorrow?"

"Yes, of course, unless I'm too ill to make it. But don't you worry now. You have enough to deal with. I'm young and because of you, I'm still strong. I'll get through this."

He kissed her on the lips. She kissed him back and he pulled her closer.

"Please Jakub, I can't. I'm sorry."

He felt a twinge of frustration, but he forced the emotion down. She was ill. "I understand. I love you, Anna."

She threw her arms around him, holding him tightly. "I love you too. Please think about what I said. About this being more than just surviving. For you. For us. I'll see you tomorrow. It's getting worse right now. I need to go." She rose, tears in her eyes, and sped out of the room. He thought about accompanying her but realized he would only embarrass her if he tried to follow her to the latrine.

He sat in the room for another half hour, emotions warring within him, then he rose and returned to the camp. He tried not to feel frustrated, but he was. First, he'd missed a night with Anna, then tonight she was too sick to be with him. That was selfish, he knew—and unfair. He thought about her words to him. Was she right about the resistance? Should he join them? Risk the small chance he had of surviving just to prove some other point? He knew what Tomasz would say. That this was philosophical garbage. His mind was in a fog. There was no point in worrying about this now. He had all day tomorrow to ponder things. He left the building and started back toward the main gate.

"Bak, what are you doing over there?" He stopped. He recognized that voice. He turned to see Schmidt, smiling grotesquely, his tongue sticking through his missing teeth. He took an unsteady step toward Jakub, pointing a finger. "I want a word with you, my little Jew."

Jakub was frozen. The SS guard looked up at him, eyes glazed, reeking of alcohol. "What do you think you're doing out of the crematorium, aye? Come with me."

Jakub thought of running, but where was he to go? He fought down his terror and followed the sadistic SS guard into the night.

Chapter 5

The Sick and the Dead

October 1944
Auschwitz

Anna returned to her barracks. There was no use waiting for Urszula. On the way, the fire in her stomach returned and she rushed to the latrine, barely reaching one of the wooden holes before she vomited. She held on to the rounded edges of the hole, her face staring into the foul darkness below. Her stomach heaved again and again but after the first belch of liquid, nothing came up. Her body shook and she fought to control the dizziness in her head.

What was wrong with her? She knew she only had a few days to get better before she was sent to the hospital, or worse. She had to fight this off, avoid the prying eyes of the Germans and her block wardress.

This wasn't the first time she'd balanced on the edge of death. She remembered the labor camp. The hours of backbreaking labor outside in the freezing cold. She was young, fortunate—she endured it better than many of the others. She knew, however, that it was but a matter of time. She was weakening, losing weight. She had always been so thin, frail even. She wouldn't make it much longer.

Her youth saved her and damned her at the same time. She was spotted, removed from her *Kommando* and brought to a special building in the camp. They'd dressed her up in civilian clothes, discarding the striped uniform. She was given more food, her face made up, and then she was shoved into a cell with a bed and a single bare light. It wasn't long before the first Nazi visited, his boots half off before he'd even closed the door.

She'd endured these visits for weeks, months—she wasn't sure how long. Occasionally they brought her a little food or some drink—sometimes only a sharp slap to the face. She'd cried out for death. She'd faded, a little each day. She was sure she was going to die. The thought relieved her—protected her, except for the fraction of her soul that screamed to survive.

One day they'd dragged her from the cell and out into the sharp light of day. She'd joined others, shoved into a cattle car to spend days lurching, starting and stopping on some endless journey. She hadn't cared. She was ready for death. The doors had ripped open and she'd drifted along with the others, hoping this was the end. But she was dragged out again, placed with the younger women, the stronger ones. Death cheated her again.

Here in Auschwitz, of all places, she'd received a new life of sorts. She had been given work inside a building, a little food, a little protection. And most of all, a chance, a desperate hope, that she might avenge her family—no, that wasn't the truth. She simply wanted to inflict some pain—some horror—on a German. Just one. Just once.

Jakub. What would he think of her if he knew the truth? She felt a hot stab of guilt. How could she tell him? He would never have understood. Never have . . .

The pain was subsiding. She opened her eyes and lifted her head a bit, looking around. She was lucky, there was nobody inside. No eyes to betray her. She drew herself up, arms shaking, still trying to clear her head.

She wanted to tell Jakub. Wanted him to know why he should fight. But he was right. She was piling up dangers. It was enough of a miracle to make it each day here.

She couldn't burden him with the past. He was nearly drowning in an ocean of his own troubles. No, she didn't want him to enter the fight because of her. A dizziness overwhelmed her and she set her head against the wood, trying to ignore the wretched stench. She closed her eyes, fighting to maintain consciousness, her arms shaking, holding on until the wave passed.

That's how Urszula found her—she didn't know how much later. "What are we going to do with you?" she asked. She was standing over Anna, still clutching a bit of bread, her eyes filled with obvious concern.

"I'll be all right. I just felt a little ill."

"Too much rich food," Urszula mumbled, stuffing the rest of her bread into her mouth. "It was probably the chocolate." She held her stomach for a second, rocking back and forth. "Still, how delightful, I will risk some pain for so much pleasure. Tomasz promised me more. I told him he better deliver, if he wants any more alone time with me." She laughed, and then returned her gaze to Anna. "Are you going to make it back to the barracks?"

"I'll manage, somehow," said Anna.

"Well, don't be too long about it. It's getting late and you know what that whore of a block wardress will do if she catches us out late." Urszula started to leave and then turned, looking back at Anna. "Do you want a hand?"

Anna shook her head. "I have to make it back under my own power. If I don't, they'll know something is wrong, and then I'll catch it."

Urszula nodded. "Wise, wise words." She took the last bite of bread and turned, walking out the door into the fading light of the evening.

Anna stayed there a few more moments, gathering her strength, then she pulled herself to her feet, her hands still resting on the latrine boards. She took a few deep breaths and then rose, stumbling toward the door. She held the handle for a few moments, and then opened it and marched woodenly out into the twilight.

Chapter 6
Complications

October 1944
Auschwitz

Hans stewed as he waited in the *Kommandant*'s office. How dare this bastard step in and try to destroy his plan? Worse, the camp commander was intentionally leaving him waiting again. He'd sat here for an hour, trying to suppress his fury, while Kramer attended to other matters that he apparently deemed more important.

The door swung open and his superior strolled in, crashing down into a seat behind his desk. He checked his watch and scanned the documents covering his work space. Tapping a pencil on the papers, his eyes abruptly shone on Hans like twin searchlights, scanning his subordinate's face.

"What am I going to do with you, Krupp?" he asked at last.

"Sir, I can explain—"

"I don't want explanations. I want results." Kramer reached into his desk and pulled out a worn pipe. He retrieved some to-bacco from a pouch inside his tunic, tamping it down with the end of his pencil. Flicking a lighter, he drew the flame over the top, sucking in deeply until the brown leaves were lit. Taking a few deep puffs, he returned to Hans.

"If this is about my nephew—"

"This is about you, Krupp. I warned you. I told you to get to work immediately and solve this escape problem. I would expect one of my officers in such a position to move mountains for me. But I came to find you right after our meeting, and you'd already gone for the day, like you were working as some kind of clerk in a shop." He picked up a document on his desk. "Then I get this. A transfer of some nineteen-year-old nobody from a Wehrmacht unit in your hometown to service here. A transfer I didn't request or authorize." Kramer leaned forward. "So, I threaten your job, your future, and you go home for the night and spend your time trying to protect your family?"

"That wasn't my intention, sir, I was—"

"What you were doing, Krupp, is taking your last actions as the security chief for this camp." Kramer reached down and drew up another document. "I'm ordering you back to Berlin. Your transfer will be accompanied by a written evaluation by me." He pushed the document toward Hans. "They can figure out what they want to do with you from there."

"Sir, if you would just give me a moment to explain."

Kramer waved the papers at Hans, but he refused to take them. Frowning, the *Kommandant* dropped them on the desk and took another puff of his pipe. "Fine, Krupp, I'll give you a minute to convince me why you won't be on the first train back to the Fatherland."

"Bringing my nephew here is part of the plan," said Krupp.

"Your master scheme is for a pimple-faced boy to solve your problems?"

"He's young. You're right, he looks like a boy. But that's part of what will make him useful. I'm going to infiltrate him into the camp as a guard. I want him to contact some people I know in there. He will gain their trust—let them know he's dissatisfied with the war, horrified by the conditions he's found here. He'll do them some favors, bring them a little food. Before you know it, they'll be telling him what we need to know."

Kramer frowned, chewing the end of his pipe. "Interesting, Krupp." He nodded. "Not a bad idea. But hardly a solution to the problem."

"That's just one piece," said Krupp hastily, reaching into his tunic to pull out some documents. He handed them to Kramer. "Here is the whole plan."

Kramer took the papers, his eyes darting over the contents. He whistled. "Interesting notions, Krupp. Why didn't you tell me about all of this before?"

"I was planning on setting a meeting. You have everything to deal with. I was waiting for Dieter to get here and become acclimated before I bothered you with the details."

Kramer picked up the orders transferring Hans and held them next to the security plan, as if weighing them against each other. He was silent for a few moments.

"Fine, Krupp," he said, handing back the plan. "You can implement this for now." He opened a drawer, depositing the transfer inside and slamming it closed. His eyes narrowed. "But remember this: Nothing has changed. The same rules apply. If there are more escapes, it will be your job. Someone must pay the price, and it sure as hell won't be me. Now get out." He waved Hans off without a farewell. Hans stomped out of the office, his anger rising.

The bastard! Who did he think he was? The Auschwitz camp system was vast, spanning kilometers in every direction. How could he stop each and every escape from happening? That was impossible. It was only a matter of time before someone exploited a gap somewhere and made their way off. He'd never protect his job that way. What Hans needed was a major coup. He had to uncover a plot, a black market, something big, and crush it. That would assure his place here and even attract the attention of the upper SS administration. Yes, that was the solution.

He arrived back at the flat to find everyone waiting for him. "What did the commander want?" Elsa asked.

"They know about Dieter," said Hans.

"You mean this transfer came directly from you?" asked his nephew.

"It shouldn't matter," said Hans, taking a seat and pouring himself some tea from a tray set on the table. "As security chief I've always possessed latitude to bring in my own people."

"Are you in some kind of trouble?" Elsa asked.

Hans shook his head. "Everything is fine now. I told him what a fine young man Dieter is and convinced him he'll be an excellent addition to our staff. He's agreed to take you on." Hans turned to his nephew. "Which leaves this decision in your hands."

Everyone turned their attention to Dieter. His nephew chewed his lip, still struggling with what to do.

"Well, my boy, what will it be?" asked Hans.

"I was going to war with my unit. With my friends."

"You've said that."

"I have a duty to serve the Fatherland."

"You said that as well."

"What would I be doing here?"

Hans smiled. "The most important service. Keeping the true enemies of our state at bay. Helping me fight the most important war of all."

"Is it dangerous?"

"In many ways, the risks of harm to you are greater than a Russian bullet."

Dieter hesitated. "Perhaps you could show me the camp?"

Hans had truly won him over now. He knew it. He saw the smiles on Hannah's and Elsa's faces. "Yes. I can show you tomorrow. We'll need to leave early. I need to fit you for a uniform and there's other paperwork you'll need to complete."

"What time?"

Hans checked his watch. "Let's depart at five. We can eat at the camp. The food's not half bad either. Sausages, fresh cold cuts, cheese, and bread. All you can eat. Better than those wretched rations you would get in the field. You'll see, my boy, this position has advantages you have only dreamed of."

The hour was late. Elsa made up a bed for Hannah in the spare room and brought out some blankets for Dieter on the sofa. Hans stayed in his chair, puffing away contentedly on his pipe. After everyone was settled, he made his way to his bedroom, changing into his nightclothes and climbing into bed. His wife rolled toward him. Turning off the light, she moved closer, her arms around his waist. *That was a surprise*. She hadn't touched him in months.

"Thank you, Hans," she whispered, kissing his neck. "You don't know what this means to me." He ran his hand down her cheek. He felt the tears.

She kissed him deeply, passionately. They made love for the first time since she'd arrived in Auschwitz. When they were finished she fell asleep with her head against his shoulder. Hans lay awake for a long time, staring at the ceiling, smiling to himself in the darkness.

Chapter 7
Cat and Mouse

October 1944
Auschwitz

Schmidt shuffled along, a bit unsteadily. He paused after a while and turned back to Jakub, a smirk creasing his features. The guard stepped up to him, standing close. Jakub was overwhelmed by the reek of alcohol. "So, my little friend, you still haven't explained yourself. You have no business in here," he said, feigning surprise. "What are you doing outside of the *Sonderkommando*?"

"I was . . . I was checking on medical supplies," stammered Jakub, grasping for an excuse. He looked around desperately for Tomasz but he was nowhere to be seen. Jakub knew that his friend was unlikely to leave now, since he himself had only departed early because of Anna's illness. He felt terror crawling up his spine. What was this game Schmidt was playing? He knew full well why Jakub was there, and how he'd made it to this part of the camp.

"Medical supplies, eh? I don't remember you being an orderly. Why would they send you?"

"They . . . they needed an extra set of hands."

"Liar!" shouted Schmidt, striking Jakub's cheek hard with the back of his hand. He crashed to the ground, his head spinning. He could taste blood in his mouth. He tried to rise, but he felt a boot on his chest. "Stay down there, worm," ordered Schmidt. "I haven't decided what to do with you yet."

Jakub looked this way and that, trying to find anyone who could help him. But who was there to protect him against an SS guard? He had to think, to survive this somehow. "Sir, if I can explain," he started, trying to buy some time.

"There's nothing to explain, Bak. You're out-of-bounds without a pass. You've obviously been smuggling goods in here or carrying messages for your pitiful little resistance. The question is what to do with you." Schmidt kept his boot on Jakub's chest as he ran his fingers along the sharp edge of his jaw, in mock contemplation. "I need some time to think, Bak. But let's not waste time. I believe a little sport will entertain me while I consider your fate."

Schmidt ordered Jakub to his knees. "Now follow me at a hop." Schmidt walked away, strolling along the edge of the fence toward the Death Gate in the distance. Jakub hopped behind him, his knees burning, his legs threatening to buckle beneath him. Schmidt kept turning his head quickly, trying to catch him cheating. Jakub knew if he tried to stand up, or if he fell over, he would be beaten until he managed to scramble back into position. He'd endured this type of "sport" before.

Meter after meter the piercing pain continued. He passed other prisoners who pretended not to see him. Any show of sympathy could land them in the same place as Jakub. He could expect no support.

After an eternity, they reached the arched entrance into Birkenau. Schmidt spoke to the guards at the gate, who turned to Jakub and laughed. They waved them through and Jakub followed Schmidt, still hopping, his head growing dizzy. He looked around desperately, trying to find someone to help him.

He was outside Birkenau, he realized. He hadn't been out of the camp since the day he'd arrived in Auschwitz. He wished he could take a breath, look around and see what was out here, but he couldn't risk a moment. As if on cue, Schmidt turned and stared at Jakub as he hopped the last dozen meters toward a brick building. He wore a mask of disappointed anger, as if Jakub's success at making it this far had only fueled his sadistic thirst.

"Enjoying yourself?" he asked, chuckling at his own humor. "I know what I want you to do for a start, Bak. You're going to clean our barracks." He grabbed Jakub by the neck and dragged him through the door, shoving him hard against a wooden bed. Jakub had never been inside the SS quarters before. He hadn't known even exactly where it was located, except that it was not within Birkenau itself. Now inside, Jakub stared around him in wonder. The floor was immaculate. There were real beds with mattresses and pillows. Lamps sat on bedstands with stacks of magazines and books. These spartan surroundings seemed a paradise on earth to Jakub after his months of sleeping on hard wooden slats, teeming with lice, and shared with multiple men to each cramped, moldy bunk.

Schmidt strode over and retrieved a bucket from the corner. He filled the container with water and a little soap. He carried this to Jakub, and shoved the handle toward him, his other hand holding out a brush. "You'll start with the floors." He slammed the bucket to the ground. Soapy water spilled out, covering Jakub. The liquid was ice-cold and the soap burned his eyes.

Jakub took the brush and dipped it in the freezing water. He scrubbed the floor as hard as he could. His knees burned and trembled from the long sport. He couldn't see from the soap but he worked frantically, trying to avoid the mistake that would give Schmidt an excuse to put a bullet in his brain.

"No, Bak, you're doing it all wrong," Schmidt called. "You don't hold the brush in your hand, you hold it in your teeth."

Jakub, shaking with pain and fear, shoved the handle of the brush into his mouth and bent down, his face against the wooden floor. He moved his head back and forth, the brush grinding his teeth. His jaw throbbed in pain and he tasted blood. His eyes burned with fire. His head spun. He was sure he would pass out at any moment.

He could hear whistling above him. Schmidt had taken a chair and was sitting nearby, watching his torturous labors. "Keep it up now, Bak. Keep it up," he mumbled, half to himself.

The unendurable work continued. Every few minutes Jakub would slide himself forward a meter, more to give himself a moment's respite than because he was making any real progress. He was drawing on his last stores of energy. He knew if this didn't conclude soon, he would pass out. At that point, Schmidt would execute him. He kept fighting for his life, as moment after agonizing moment passed.

Jakub wanted to rest his head against the floor just for a moment. If he could only recover his breath, he'd be able to go on again. *No! If I give in, I'll be dead. I must survive. I promised my father. I must live for all my family.* He pressed on, fighting the seconds.

He felt a hand on his neck. His head was jerked back. Schmidt was leaning over him, eyeing him closely. "Still with me, Bak? I'd thought you'd be ready for a rest by now. Why don't you take a little break?" Jakub shook his head, averting his eyes. He placed the brush back into his mouth and lowered his head toward the floor. A blinding light erupted in his mind. He blinked a couple of times, not knowing what had happened. He was on his back he realized. Schmidt must have kicked him in the face. Blood filled his mouth and he spat it out, gasping for air. He felt hands on him. Schmidt pulled him up, forcing him to his feet. "Let's take a walk."

The guard was going to kill him. He was sure of it. He thought of his family. He thought of Tomasz, of Anna. They'd wonder what happened to him until rumor trickled back into the camp. He didn't want to die. Life in this hell was better than no life at all.

Schmidt shoved him out into the sunlight. He must have been at it all night. He blinked his eyes painfully and lurched forward, the SS guard pushing him in the back to move him along. He marched Jakub through the Death Gate and back along the fence line toward the *Sonderkommando*. A wild hope grew inside him. Was Schmidt going to let him go? They crossed hundreds of meters. Jakub could barely put one leg in front of the other, but he kept going, praying he was correct, hoping the guard had satiated his cruelty for the day. They were two hundred meters away from the gate, then a hundred.

"That's far enough," said Schmidt.

Jakub halted, a bare fifty meters from the fence line. In the distance, he could see some of his comrades busy at work outside Crematorium II.

"Well, go on then," Schmidt ordered.

Jakub took a step toward the gate.

"Not that way."

He froze. What did Schmidt mean? He turned back to the guard, who was watching him with amusement. "That's the gate back to the *Sonderkommando*," he said.

"I know that, you idiot. But since you didn't have a good explanation for how you got through that gate in the first place, I must assume you just climbed the fence. Go on then," he said, pointing to the barbed wire. "If you climbed in, you can climb out."

Jakub was horrified. The wire was electric. It was instant death to touch it. "But, sir, the fence is hot."

"I didn't ask for excuses, Bak. I told you to climb that fence." He checked his watch. "Hurry along now, it's nearly time for my breakfast."

Jakub stood, frozen. So, it was death after all. Worse yet,

Schmidt was forcing him to commit a form of suicide. He took a step forward, and another.

"Much faster, Bak. I have my own duties to attend to."

Jakub felt his heart leap in his chest. The pain was gone from his limbs. He felt a cold calm. This was the end of things. There was no way out. He took more steps. He was thirty meters away, twenty, ten. He stopped five meters from the fence. Try as he might, he couldn't go farther. He labored to breathe. His heartbeats roared in his ears.

"Just a bit more. Another step and you can join your family." Schmidt laughed behind him. Jakub felt a sharp shove and he fell forward, hands out, trying to stop himself from hitting the fence. He froze in midair, his fingers a bare meter from the wire. He felt a tug. Schmidt had seized the back of his shirt and was jerking him back. He heard shrill laughter. "Don't worry, Bak. I'm not really going to kill you. At least not today. Scurry along now, head back to the gate."

Jakub stood still, his emotions a maelstrom. He gathered up enough courage to move and lurched toward the gate. He felt a hand on his throat, fingers squeezing, threatening to cut off his air.

Schmidt drew his head sharply back, placing his lips to his ear, whispering, "I've just done you a favor, and I'll expect payment."

"What do you mean?" he managed to say.

"You'll bring me everything you pilfer from now on. All the gold, jewelry, and cash."

"Sir, I don't—"

"Don't lie to me, Bak, I know all about it. How else would you get through that gate? The food you can keep, but everything else comes to me."

Jakub nodded. He didn't have any choice. But how would he get across the fence again?

Schmidt released Jakub and whipped him around. "That's a good boy. Oh, and one thing more. I'm taking Anna."

He stared at Schmidt in shock. "What do you want with her?"

"I'm going to have her all to myself. At least for a little while." He leaned closer. "But I'll make you a deal. You are not to talk to her for a month. You will not cross the fence. You will not pass her messages. If you do, I'll know," Schmidt warned. "She'll think you've deserted her, and she'll reluctantly fall into my arms. When the month is past you can have her back." He laughed. "Well, what's left of her at least. I'm sure she'll understand when you explain to her what happened, and if not . . ." Schmidt shrugged and released Jakub, shoving him again.

"Now get going. And remember, don't let me catch you here for thirty days. I'll be by every few nights to collect my fee. Now run off, little Jew!"

Jakub stumbled off in misery toward the gate. He made it through and took a few steps within before he collapsed. He heard whistles and the sharp barking of a German voice, before all was darkness.

Chapter 8
The Tour

October 1944
Auschwitz

The next morning, Hans kissed his still-sleeping wife in the darkness and felt his way to the bedroom door. Letting himself out, he found Dieter already dressed and ready. He checked his watch. It was 4:45. Waving for his nephew to follow, he led them out the front door and down the stairs where a car already waited.

"Did you sleep?" he asked Dieter.

His nephew only grunted. Hans smiled; he couldn't rest before his first night in Auschwitz either. No matter, there was no doubt the young guard would sleep well tonight.

The car made its way in the darkness to the Birkenau main gate. The driver dropped the two of them off and Hans led Dieter into the guardhouse and up the stairs to his office. There was an SS private's uniform laid out in a chair near his desk. Hans directed Dieter to the bathroom and waited for his nephew to dress. Hans nodded when he reappeared. He walked around him, adjusting his collar, and smoothing out a crease.

"You look excellent in that uniform," said Hans.

Dieter appeared uncomfortable. No matter, he would grow used to the thing. Hans stepped over to his desk, lifting a black leather holster and belt. The holster held a Luger 9mm pistol. "Put these on," he ordered. "It's unloaded for now, but I'll get you ammunition tomorrow."

Dieter complied. Hans made some tea while his nephew filled out pages of documents. When he was done, Hans scanned the contents, making a few corrections. "That should get us started," he said. "Let's get moving."

Hans walked Dieter through the upper and lower guardhouse. He made introductions before they left the main gate and stepped into the camp. He handed his nephew an overcoat to protect him from the cold air. Even in October, the morning was near freezing.

They stepped out and walked along the rail line heading into the camp. The spur split into three lines with two next to each other and the third veering off somewhat to the right. The tracks ran in a straight line for five hundred meters or so before merging back together in the distance. At present there were no trains on the rails. Hans marched Dieter about a third of the way down on a wide gravel pathway.

He drew Dieter's attention to the fences on his left. "This is the women's camp," he said, pointing to a series of long, low brick barracks past the fence line. Even as he said this, emaciated women in striped dresses were wobbling out of the barracks and starting to assemble for roll call.

"*Mein Gott*, they are so skinny," said Dieter, his face turning a pale white.

"*Ja*. That's true," said Hans, shrugging. "We try to keep them decently fed but there is only so much food available. If it weren't for the damned Russians, we would have so much more. But the Bolsheviks push us at every turn, and we must devote so much for our soldiers at the front. Surely you'd agree that our fighting men must receive food first."

"Of course," said Dieter, although his voice trembled.

"Also, on this side are the penal barracks for those who are in punishment. You can't see them from here though, they are all the way in the back. I'll show those to you later." He turned completely around and pointed to the fence on the far side of the train tracks. "On the other side, past the electric wiring, are the men's barracks and a separate section for Gypsies. There was a family camp here too, just over there," he said, pointing to a line of barracks, "but it was cleared out in July."

"What do you mean cleared out?" asked Dieter.

"I'll be able to show you how that works in just a few minutes," said Hans. "Ah, look what's coming in. How delightful. This is perfect timing."

In the distance, past the main gate, a train could just be made out. The engine, belching black smoke, loomed closer with every moment. The locomotive passed slowly through the arched entranceway into the camp. The screech of the brakes tore through the crisp morning air. Shouts erupted in the distance as SS guards scrambled out at various points, some moving toward a building a few hundred meters farther along.

"This is excellent," noted Hans, clapping his hands together in excitement. "Come, let me show you what we do here. But prepare yourself, Dieter. This is not for the faint of heart."

The train slowed, chugging past them. An SS guard hung out of the driver's door, his eyes darting left and right. As the train lurched to a stop he jumped down into the gravel. There were a dozen SS in the area now, as well as men and women dressed in the striped uniforms of prisoners, with short clubs in their hands.

"This is the unloading area," explained Hans as they drew nearer. He pointed at an officer nearby dressed in a white coat. "That one is a doctor," Hans explained.

"For the sick?" asked Dieter.

"Sort of. To sort out the sick in any event, and others as well."

"What do you mean?"

"He selects those who are unable to labor effectively, from those healthy enough to work."

"How many are picked for employment?" asked Dieter.

"*Employment.* I like that word. I'll have to remember that. In terms of your question, it depends on where they are from," said Hans. "If they arrive from a well-fed area, France or Holland for example, maybe as much as twenty percent. If they're from Poland, maybe ten. But the rules are always the same. Usually it's just the young women and men. It also depends heavily on the needs of the camp. The Hungarian Jews were in fantastic shape. Before they arrived here, they'd been virtually untouched by the war. But despite that, there were just too many coming in this past summer. The trains arrived faster than we could deal with them. So, for the most part, we sent them all straight away for special treatment."

"What is special treatment?"

The door to the first cattle car was torn open, revealing a packed jumble of bodies. There were at least a hundred people inside, their eyes blinking, fear and disorientation drawn on their haggard faces. The smell from the car was overwhelming, and Dieter gagged.

"Don't worry, you'll get used to that too."

The SS screamed, ordering the people out. The inmates in their striped uniforms rushed forward, ripping people out of the car.

"Who are they?" asked Dieter.

"Prisoners, just like the rest of them. But they are leaders. We call them *Kapos*. Most of them are Poles. There's even a German or two. No Jews though."

"*Mein Gott.* There are children in there!" shouted Dieter.

"Keep your voice down!" ordered Hans. He turned to his nephew. "Yes, there are children—we bring everyone here as a family. You must understand, we try to handle everything as humanely as possible. At first, we used to split them up and send the children in separate transports. We thought that would be easier on the parents and the children, but it wasn't. So, we started sending them all together. Trial and error you know."

"And this is supposed to be better?"

"Don't worry, it's only for a few minutes. Before they are sorted. See, look," said Hans, pointing back to the SS doctor in the white physician's tunic. "Dr. Mengele is conducting the work today." He directed Dieter's attention to a handsome officer in his midthirties who was carefully examining the crowd as it passed him. With a jerk of his thumb he would direct a person out of the line. "He's one of our best. Very efficient. All this is over in no time."

"What happens to those who cannot work? Are they taken to a different camp? Where do the rest of these people go?"

"Come on," said Hans. "Let me show you the rest of the operation." Hans led his nephew around the front of the train and crossed the tracks. They walked along a long straight line of fencing until they came to an opening about midway through the camp. "There is much to see this way. I want to show you Canada."

Hans led the baffled Dieter down the road between the two men's camps. "Immediately to your right is a space where we were keeping some of the Hungarians," said Hans. "And to the left is the men's camp proper."

"What is this used for?" asked Dieter, pointing to the wide pathway they were walking along.

"Sometimes we bring the arrivals this way to some buildings farther on," explained Hans. "But this is also the route to the sorting lots and one of the ways to the hospital." They moved to the end of the camp. Just past the fence line there were new barracks that appeared partially constructed.

"Is that Canada?" asked Dieter.

"Would you believe it, it's called Mexico. That's an extension to the camp we were building to accommodate additional arrivals. They've stopped work on it though. We've processed so many units already, and what with the Russians growing close, I don't know if it will ever be finished now."

They turned at the fence and walked along the northern edge of the camp. As they passed a set of buildings to the left, Hans pointed them out. "This is the hospital section. There are hundreds of inmates there at any given time." After a few minutes more they reached a cluster of barracks separated from the rest of the camp. "This is Canada," said Hans, as they cleared the gate. "You won't believe it until you see it."

They entered one of the buildings. Inside there was a hive of activity. Dozens of prisoners worked away at tables piled with clothing. They were picking up each individual piece and running their hands over the contents, searching the inside and out before carefully folding the item and stacking it in a pile. "The incoming people hide things inside their possessions," he said. "Food and medicine but also gold, silver, money, and jewelry. We let these prisoners eat the food for the most part," he said. "Unless it's a large quantity. Then it must be turned over to the kitchen."

"What happens to the valuables?"

"They are to be turned over strictly to the Reich," said Hans. "You wouldn't believe the amount of wealth that has come through here. Millions of Reichsmarks in goods. Auschwitz has helped Germany finance the war." He stepped closer and placed his hand up to his mouth. "That's not to say that a piece or two doesn't find its way into other pockets."

Dieter's face paled. "You aren't saying you steal from the Fatherland?"

"Keep it down," said Hans, putting his hand on Dieter's shoulder. "It's not stealing. It's an investment for the future. I'm not talking about wholesale plunder, mind you. I'm saying a little here and there. No matter who wins this war, Dieter, times are going to be tight. You're a young man. When this is over, you'll go home and settle down with some nice girl. You will marry, have children, there will be a house to buy. I'll make sure you have a good start. And if we lose—"

"How can you say such a thing!" Dieter shouted this and Hans looked around. The prisoners were all watching them now, along with an SS guard who eyed them suspiciously.

"I told you to keep your voice down," ordered Hans. He stepped closer to Dieter. "Don't worry about that right now. What I'm telling you is that either way, I'm going to make sure you have a future. A few diamonds, a little gold. It's easy to carry and easy to hide."

"What if we're caught?"

"In Auschwitz, for us, there's no such thing as *caught*. Everyone accumulates a little. We are all taking care of each other. You've joined the SS, Dieter. No matter what, we are coming out of this war as a brotherhood."

They left the barracks. "What's in the rest of these buildings?" Dieter asked, pointing at the rows of structures in Canada.

"More of the same," said Hans.

"So much? But where does it come from?"

"All of these transports," said Hans. "We sometimes get a few trains a day. You should have seen this place over the summer when the Hungarians came in. Tens of thousands of people at a time. Like I said, we couldn't handle the volume."

"And you take the clothes from all of them and issue these striped pajamas?"

"There's one more place I have to show you. Remember, I told you this is a difficult camp, that the work we are doing here is important, but more challenging even than fighting the Russians."

"I still don't understand what you mean."

"You will. Come with me."

Hans took Dieter along the north end of the camp, then turned and headed back toward the rail line. When they reached the tracks, they crossed and turned right, heading west until they moved beyond the barracks to two large buildings, one to their right and one to their left. Hans led him toward the building to their left. This structure was nestled behind a row of trees, set apart from the women's camp with its own separate electric fence and enclosure. They passed through the gate, the guards saluting Hans, and headed into the perimeter of the building.

Within this space, there was a long line of men shuffling toward a ramp leading downward to a wide set of double doors. They walked around to another entrance on the ground floor and Hans led Dieter to a set of steps leading to the basement. He stopped him at the entranceway. "I want to remind you that you are sworn to secrecy about this camp."

Dieter nodded. "I understand."

"You need to prepare yourself."

"Prepare for what?"

"In your training they told you about combat. About death?"

Dieter nodded.

"Prepare yourself, Dieter. This is death."

Hans and Dieter arrived at the flat an hour later. Dinner was already on the table. Elsa and Hannah greeted them at the door, their eyes hopeful, smiling and welcoming them back. Dieter pushed past them and rushed to the bathroom. They heard choking and gagging inside.

The smiles melted to fear. "What happened?" asked Elsa.

"I showed him the camp," said Hans, stepping over to the table to take off a bit of bread. "Not everything is easy there."

"What did you do to him?" Hannah demanded.

"I didn't do anything. He was in no danger. Some of the camp is . . . difficult."

His wife stared at him. "Why haven't you ever acted like that? You don't tell me anything about your work."

"I'm used to it," said Hans. "You weren't here when I first arrived. By the time I brought you out I'd settled into things. Trust me," he said, munching on the bread. "He'd see things on the front just as bad. At least here he doesn't have to hold his best friend's guts in his hands while he dies in his arms. Here he won't be shot, or blown up, or bayoneted to death. He'll get used to things and then he'll settle in just fine."

The toilet flushed and Dieter stepped out, his face pale. He wiped the back of his uniform sleeve against his mouth. His mother rushed over to him, putting her arms around his shoulders. "Are you all right, my son?"

"I've never seen anything like that," Dieter whispered.

"Careful, Dieter," Hans warned. "Remember your oath."

"What have you gotten him into?" Hannah repeated, turning to him with eyes flashing.

"Exactly what I told you when I called," said Hans. "I'm saving his life and protecting him. More than that, I'm building his future. Beyond that, I can't discuss the activities inside the camp."

"They're murdering them in cold blood," blurted Dieter, stumbling to a chair.

"Dieter! I warned you."

"What are you talking about?" Hannah demanded.

"I'm sorry, Uncle, but oath or not, I can't stay quiet about this." He turned to his mother. "It's a murder factory in there. They lead the people like sheep into a basement and then they gas them until they're dead. Thousands at a time. These aren't soldiers I'm talking about, or prisoners of war. They are just people. Mothers and children." He put his head in his hands. "I can't do it, Uncle. I can't go back there. I'm sorry."

"Dieter! You cannot tell them this. You're going to get us all killed!"

Elsa looked at Hans in horror. "Is this true? Are you killing women and children in Auschwitz? All this time?"

"Bah. He's exaggerating."

"No, I'm not. He took me to a building where they force people to take off their clothes. Then they herd them into a long narrow room and gas them. After, they throw the bodies into a crematorium connected to the same building. It's a death mill. I've never imagined anything like it." Dieter gagged again and put his hand to his face, fighting back another round of nausea.

"You *are* killing people!" shouted Elsa. "How could you have brought me here and never told me any of this?"

Hannah stood up. "Dieter, pack up your things. We are going."

"I'm coming with you," said Elsa, beginning to rise.

Hannah stepped over to Dieter, reaching out a hand to help her son to his feet. His nephew rose and they stepped toward the guest room to pack, his wife following behind them.

"Stop, all of you!" ordered Hans.

They hesitated.

"Look at me!"

As one they turned to face him.

"You're all going to grow up right now!" he shouted. "You've been living in a fantasyland—safe and secure on the home front. Well, let me tell you the truth!" He turned to Hannah. "You think you can walk out of here and take Dieter home? Do you know what they do to deserters? They'd arrest him and he'd be dead before the week is out. You can't just undo what I've done."

"I'm not without connections," Hannah retorted. "We didn't ask for this transfer, you shoved it on us. I can get him returned to his unit."

"To what end?" he demanded. "Pick that pathway if you can. He'll be dead in a month on the Eastern Front. We've lost this damned war!" He could see them flinch. "I know it's treason to say it, but all the men in uniform know it's true. We haven't had a chance in a year. Hell, in two years. The Russians are crushing us. We have thousands of men facing millions. The Soviets are a steamroller and they are crushing us. We cannot defeat them."

"The Führer promises miracle weapons," Dieter mouthed.

"If he had them, he would have used them long ago!" shouted Hans. "Trust me, boy, there are no miracles coming, I promise you that. The Russians are killing thousands of Germans a month. Before this is over, we'll have lost another million men on that front." He turned to Hannah, his hands out in supplication. "Please, be reasonable. It's murder to send Dieter there."

"At least if I'm fighting them, they can shoot back," said Dieter. "At least they would be men I would be fighting."

"We aren't killing women and children here. We are disposing of *Jewish* vermin. They are enemies of the state! They stabbed us in the back at the end of the last war and they'll do the same to us in this one. It's not only Jews we deal with, but Gypsies, homosexuals, all the disease of the Earth. We are killing them not only for Germany but for the world."

"They are still innocents," said Hannah, sounding a little less certain.

"They are what they are. I'm only following orders. But I'm following them in a safe camp, where there are no German casualties. Nobody is killing my comrades or my men. Dieter will be safe here. No matter what, he'll survive the war. He'll live through this, and I'll help provide for his future."

"By stealing from the dead!" said Dieter. His nephew took a step toward Hans, raising an accusing finger. "The killing isn't all of it. They loot gold and diamonds from the clothes of the victims. It's all supposed to go to the Fatherland, but your husband is pilfering some of it along with the other guards."

Elsa flushed red with anger. "You're stealing from Germany?"

"I told you all to grow up," said Hans dismissively. "This war is almost finished. When it's truly over, the Russians are going to take everything. All that will be left will be what valuables can be hidden. We must have resources to trade, to barter. I've provided for our future," Hans said, turning to his wife. "I'm trying to prepare for Dieter's too. The Russians won't get here for a few months. There's enough time for Dieter to save up for his life as well."

Hans walked past them and locked the front door. He turned and stood in front of it, barring their way. "Now, here is what we are going to do. All of you are going to stay calm, and you're going to face reality—right now. You are all going to stay here. You are going to keep your mouths shut. Dieter is going to serve the rest of the war with me. You are all going to live with what I must live with. We are going to secure what we can. When the Russians get close, we are going to get back to our hometown. We will survive this war, and we will get through what happens after. Together."

They stared at him, faces pale, anger creasing their faces, but they made no further effort to leave. Let them hate him. He would keep them alive. It was all he could do.

Chapter 9
The Future

October 1944
Auschwitz

Jakub tossed and turned in agony. In his fevered dreams he remembered the first day he'd seen Anna. He was standing at the fence line staring into the women's camp. There she was, in a group of girls clustered together. She was pale-skinned and frail. Her face was fair, but by no means beautiful. Even at a distance her piercing blue eyes drew his gaze. The next day he'd thought only of her. Tomasz teased him mercilessly. Finally, his friend had revealed that if Jakub wanted to meet her, it could be arranged.

That first time through the fence was harrowing. Jakub didn't know Tomasz well then. He was risking everything on a wild gamble that the guards would accept a bribe from an inmate. Why wouldn't they just take the gold and then turn them in? Or simply shoot them on the spot? But they did take the coins without comment. They'd whisked them through, and Jakub found himself in the women's camp.

Tomasz had set off for some privacy with Urszula, leaving Jakub alone with no idea what to do. He could see Anna in the distance. She was by herself, sitting with her back against the outside wall of one of the barracks, dipping a spoon into a bowl. The problem was he had no idea how to approach her. For a month he'd handled the dead, but he hadn't the first notion of how to start a conversation with the living. With a woman. Still, he had to do something. He'd risked his life to get through the fence. And there was no future. Today could be his last alive. If he ever wanted to talk to this girl, he needed to do it now. Screwing up his courage, he ambled cautiously over to her.

"Good evening," he said when he drew nearby.

She looked up in surprise, nearly spilling her soup bowl. She tensed like a cornered animal, her eyes wide with terror. "What are you doing here?" she asked.

"I'm . . . I'm from the *Sonderkommando* just over there," he'd explained.

"How did you get here?"

"We paid the guards to get through. I came here . . . well, I came here to meet you."

She eyed him without a change of expression. She rose cautiously and then turned away, starting to leave.

"Wait," he said, taking her arm. She jerked it away.

"Don't touch me," she hissed.

"I'm sorry. I just want to talk to you."

But she wasn't interested. Without looking back, she sped away, turning a corner. Jakub was left standing by himself, enduring the mirthful stares and mumblings of a group of female inmates nearby.

He'd come again the next day and the next. However, after the few words that first time, she wouldn't even speak to him.

Tomasz took to teasing. "Why bother with her?" he'd ask. "There are plenty of others, far prettier—and more appreciative." He gestured toward his girlfriend. "Why don't you let Urszula here find you a proper prize?"

"It's her or no one," said Jakub.

"Suit yourself." Tomasz laughed. "If you want to waste your precious time on an ungrateful little wretch, I guess that's your business."

So he'd persisted for weeks, enduring her rebuffs. She would not take it, so he left it for her friends to make sure she received the food.

"I don't understand you," said Tomasz. "Such a waste of your time."

But he continued to try. A month passed and one day she did not turn away. He had approached her and to his surprise she reached out and took the offered food. Her hand was trembling, he noticed.

"Thank you," she said. "What is your name?"

"Jakub."

"I'm Anna."

They walked together and spoke for a few minutes. She kept her distance from him, her eyes darting this way and that as if searching for escape routes. She was just eighteen, a schoolmaster's daughter from Katowice. He didn't ask today, but eventually he learned her family had perished in the gas chambers of Crematorium II, the very building where Jakub lived and worked. This day she would not talk to him long. "You should forget about me," she said. "There are many others who would appreciate this. Thank you again."

She'd hurried off without even saying goodbye. He came back the next day, not sure she would even talk to him again, but she accepted the bread without hesitation that time. Each day she would talk to him a little longer.

"Why do you waste your time with her?" Tomasz asked him another time. "Two months and she won't touch you. Are you mad? Every day here could be our last."

Tomasz was right. There were no guarantees about tomorrow.

The next day she walked with him as usual. He decided to take her hand. She shuddered and pulled away, darting off without saying goodbye. He came back the next day and the next, but she was not there. On the third day she appeared. She took his bread and, on their walk, he felt her tiny hand in his palm. She wrapped her fingers in his and they moved on, not speaking. He could feel his heart pounding. That day she told him about her family, and when he left, she wrapped her arms around his neck and kissed his cheek. He had found something in this hell to cling to.

"He's starting to come to."

Jakub heard the voices from far away. He didn't want to wake up. He'd been having such a pleasant dream.

"Someone turned quite a trick on him." Jakub recognized the voice. It was Roch. He opened his eyes. He was in a bunk. Faces stared down at him, including the resistance leader.

"Ah," said Roch, smiling, "it looks like our patient is coming around at last."

"How long have I been out?" he asked.

"Most of the day," said Roch.

Jakub felt pain throbbing all over his body. He struggled through the fog of his mind, trying to remember. He saw that smirking face, the torture, and the threat. Panic coursed through his veins. *Anna!* He had to do something. He tried to rise but he could only move a few centimeters off the bunk before he felt dizziness overwhelm him and he sank back down.

"You're far too weak to go anywhere," said Roch, placing a hand on Jakub's forehead. "Now tell me what has happened to you."

"Schmidt," Jakub managed to mutter.

Darkness creased Roch's face. "I might have known. What did he do to you?"

Jakub relayed everything that had happened: the beating, the bribery, and his demands of Anna. When he was finished, Roch didn't say anything for a few minutes, instead staring at Jakub with a great sadness.

"You're lucky he left you alive," Roch said at last.

"I have to get to Anna," said Jakub, trying to rise again. "I have to stop Schmidt."

"We can stop him, together."

"How?" asked Jakub. "It has to be right away. He'll go to her tonight."

"That can't be helped. I'm not talking about today. I mean we can stop him by fighting. We can punish all of them—when the time is right."

Jakub's anger flared. "When? A week from now? A month? What happens to Anna between now and then? I have to get to her today."

Roch placed his hand back on Jakub's chest. "I understand how you feel, my friend, but remember where we are. Who we are. Schmidt is a god here. He has power over life and death. He can go where he wants, when he wants. The only way to stop him is for us to secure power ourselves. We are getting close to the day when we will be able to do something about Schmidt. About all the rest of them. But it's not *this* day. I must ask you to be a little patient. You can help us, Jakub. We need your help."

"Be patient? And what happens to Anna in the meantime? How many times will Schmidt rape her before the appointed day when we will finally do something about it?"

Roch looked at him, a deep sadness in his eyes. "Yes, you're right, she may suffer. But she's alive. How many are not? A hundred thousand? A million? My wife and my little baby girl were gassed in this very building. They are gone forever, along with your family, and everyone else's. We have a chance to do something about this, Jakub, but you have to trust me." He leaned over him. "Will you join us? We have important work to do."

"I don't know. Right now, all I can think about is Anna. I must figure out a way to get to her. To warn her."

"There might be something we could do. It's possible we could get someone through to warn her," said Roch. "If I can, I'll let you know. Will you think about my offer? You're bright and brave, Jakub. The guards are used to you bribing your way around Birkenau. We have plans for you. And they cannot wait."

"Thank you," said Jakub. "Yes, I will consider your request. Can you write down a message for Anna from me?"

"Of course," said Roch, drawing out a slip of paper and a pencil from his pocket. "What do you want to tell her?"

Jakub told Roch what he wanted to convey. The resistance leader wrote it down and then departed. Jakub laid his head back down. He had to recover. He must clear his mind. It was a glimmer of hope that his message might reach Anna, but it wasn't enough. How was he going to save her?

"That fool can do nothing for you." He recognized the voice immediately. Tomasz lifted his head up from the upper bunk across the way. He'd apparently listened to everything.

"He said he'd try to get a message to her," said Jakub.

"I heard. There's a pretty big emphasis on *try.* How would he do it? What connection does he have? Have you ever seen Roch at the fence?" Tomasz jumped down and sat at the foot of Jakub's bunk. "I told you before. He's an idealist. He can offer you nothing but dreams. He will deliver nothing to you but a bullet when his ridiculous plot is discovered."

"What am I supposed to do then?"

"Let me take care of it, of course."

"How?"

"I'll go tonight and talk to Anna."

"What good will that do?"

"I'll warn her to stay away. But that's not all. I'll pass a little gold around to the other guards. They don't want their supply to run out. They'll intervene with Schmidt. Trust me, monster that he is, he can be reasoned with. A little pressure in the right direction and our sadistic sergeant will back off. Don't you worry about things. Let your old friend Tomasz take care of anything. Only promise me you won't join that pack of idiots. When Roch comes back, you tell him no."

Jakub lay in his bunk, barely able to move. His body throbbed in pain and his mind reeled, flashing through scenes of Schmidt and Anna. He had to get to her, to warn her. But what could he do?

Nobody had promised him a complete solution. Tomasz was sure he could bribe their way out of the situation. That would work if everyone played along, but what if one of the guards refused? Even if the other Germans were willing, would Schmidt comply? Regardless of what Tomasz thought, Schmidt did things his own way, and the other guards were afraid of him. Would Schmidt forgo a chance to toy with Jakub, to inflict the pain on him he so enjoyed, just for a little gold? Did he even need any more money? There were so many valuables available in the camp and he already had a promise from Jakub to turn over everything he collected for the next thirty days. Tomasz's offer was genuine and it might work, but Jakub couldn't rely on it as the only way to save Anna.

Roch's promise was even less secure. He wanted Jakub to consider the good of all the prisoners over his own personal interests and to recognize their inherent helplessness in Auschwitz. Roch was right, of course. Concern for all the prisoners was a noble objective, and the resistance naturally did have severe limitations on what they could accomplish. But Jakub *had* defied the Germans in his own way. He'd paid them money and valuables and they had broken their rules for him, letting him into the women's camp over and over to visit Anna. Jakub had to do something, and although Roch led the insurgents in the

Sonderkommando, in this, he seemed to have far less power than Tomasz, or even Jakub for that matter. His vague promise, to "try to get somebody to her," did little to satisfy Jakub's fears.

A plan formed in his mind. A dangerous scheme on several levels. He turned it over and over, looking for weaknesses and risks. Of course, there were many. But when in hell, nearly every choice leads to the fire. He decided he had to try, had to risk friendships and life to get to Anna.

Tomasz checked in with him a little later. Jakub was already sitting up by that point, stretching his limbs, battling the racking pain. He was bruised everywhere and his body so riddled with agony that he was unsure he could even stand.

"Take it easy," Tomasz admonished as he stepped over to the bunk. "You shouldn't be moving yet. Take another day. We can cover for you."

Jakub nodded but didn't answer.

"Have you thought about what I said to you?" Tomasz asked.

"Yes."

"Well?"

"Your plan makes sense. It's the best we can do. I trust you, Tomasz. I want you to try to save her."

Tomasz smiled and patted Jakub on the back. "I knew you'd come to your senses. Those fools in the resistance talk a big game, but you saw that in reality, there's nothing Roch or any of them can do for you except get you a ticket to the gas chamber."

"Can you go tonight?"

Tomasz nodded.

"I don't have anything to give you."

His friend laughed again. "What is new, my friend?" He reached into his pocket and pulled out a gold necklace and a wad of zlotys. "Here's my take from today. I'll spread this around and we'll get things taken care of."

"I can't repay you."

"What is new? Don't worry about that. I told you before, you can pay me back after the war. So we add another decade," he said, laughing.

Tomasz moved closer. "Now listen, Jakub, you have to take things with the resistance carefully. Don't tell them no outright. You need to convince them you are interested. If you don't, there's no telling what they might do."

"What do you mean?"

"You haven't been around as long as I have. These things get out of hand sometimes. They may mark you as a spy."

That rattled him. "I would never work for the Germans," he insisted.

"I know that, but they don't. And it might not matter. They kill snitches here, even those they just think are spying. I've seen it happen, and I haven't always been sure they were correct."

Jakub hadn't considered that. If Roch thought he was playing some kind of secret game . . .

"Don't worry about it," said Tomasz. "Just tell him you need time to consider things. If they start pressing you, I'll step in. They aren't exactly afraid of me, but I don't think they'll cross me either." He stared intently at Jakub. "Nobody should."

"You're a good friend, Tomasz."

"That I am," he said, clapping Jakub on the shoulder. "Now get yourself back into your bunk and get some rest. I'm leaving soon for the fence. I'll take care of things and make sure your Anna is protected." He shook his head. "What you're willing to do for that girl. I'll never understand it. Are you sure you don't want to use this as an excuse to pick another woman? There are far prettier girls who would do so much more for so much less."

Jakub shook his head and started to respond.

"No need to lecture me," said Tomasz. "I gave up that battle long ago. If it's Anna you want then it's Anna we shall protect. Whatever your muddled reasons."

Jakub squeezed his hand. "Thank you," he said.

Tomasz left a few minutes later. Jakub waited another hour until he was sure his friend would have departed for the fence. When he thought enough time had passed, he lifted himself back up and slowly, painfully, set his feet on the floor. Using the bunk as a support, he pulled himself to his feet. He drew himself up, gasping at the agony tearing through him. He took a single step, then another, and shambled forward.

He made it to Roch's bunk minutes later. The resistance leader was sitting there, finishing a bowl of soup. He looked up at Jakub and smiled. "I see you're up," he said.

Jakub nodded.

"Have you thought about what I said?"

"I have."

"What is your decision?"

"I'm going to join you, on one condition."

Roch smiled. "What condition?"

"You said you could try to get somebody to Anna. I want that attempt made tonight."

"Jakub, I said I would try, but it will take some—"

"Tonight, or it's no deal."

Roch stared at him, color filling his cheeks. Jakub was sure he would rebuke him but after long seconds he nodded. "We will make the effort."

"How will you get somebody through?"

"I can't tell you that," said Roch. "Not now anyway. But perhaps later, when—"

"When you trust me?"

Roch smiled. "We've been betrayed before."

"Tomasz told me that. He said he's not sure you were right."

"Your *friend* Tomasz thinks lots of things," said Roch.

"What do you want me to do?" asked Jakub.

"With what?"

"The resistance."

Roch looked at him. "Nothing right now. Go back to your bunk and rest up. We'll make sure you are not disturbed tomorrow or the next day. We'll meet again when you're healed, and I'll tell you what I have in mind."

"All right. But you have to get somebody through tonight."

"If it can be done, we will do it."

Jakub nodded and stumbled back to his bunk. He collapsed on the hard wood, gasping for breath. It had taken all his energy and power to make it across the barracks. He couldn't do more tonight. He tried to stay up, to wait for Tomasz or Roch to return, but he'd done too much. A dizziness spun through his mind. He fought the feeling and tried to rise again, but he was too weak, and against his will, he was soon fast asleep.

Chapter 10
A Surprise in the Dark

October 1944
Auschwitz

Anna shuffled through the mist, trailing a line of skirted skeletons as they marched the two kilometers to the factory. She shivered in the frozen morning air. She was ill. Her stomach twisted and turned, and she feared she might be sick again. If she threw up, the *Kapo* would assuredly send her to the hospital—a death sentence. *I will not be sick*, she willed herself. She forced a step, and another, keeping her eyes on the girl in front of her. They reached the village and marched through the middle of the street. The shopkeepers were just opening their stores. An occasional owner would stare in their direction, stepping back as if they were riddled with disease. Some of them were, she knew.

Ten minutes later they stumbled toward the barbed wire gates of the Union Factory. SS guards with machine pistols perched at the entryway. One of them restrained a German shepherd that barked and snarled, lunging at them. The guard laughed, making some joke to the man who stood next to him. Anna didn't catch the words.

They shuffled through and were led into the factory. Long lines of inmates were already at work at the machines. Anna took her place, lowering herself onto a hard stool in front of a pile of fabricated tools. Nails stabbed her insides.

Her friend Estusia Wajcblum took the seat next to her. She was a girl of about eighteen, with dark hair and frail features. They were barracks mates and they knew each other from months working side by side. Gradually they'd become friends, and confederates. Closer than her and Urszula, who worked in a different *Kommando.* Now Estusia's face was as twisted as Anna's stomach. Not out of pain, but in concern.

"What's wrong with you?" Estusia whispered, her eyes forward and fingers busy polishing a tool.

"It's nothing."

"You're a terrible liar. Your skin is as white as the snow."

"It's my stomach. I can't stop the pain."

"Have you been sick?"

Anna nodded.

"Diarrhea?"

"Yes, and the other direction. I think . . . I think I'm going to be ill again right now."

Estusia looked around. "Go quickly. I'll watch things here."

Anna nodded and sprinted to the latrine. She barely made it to a wooden hole before she retched loudly. Her stomach churned and bucked, spilling liquid into the foul darkness below. She fought back the pain, but the spasms continued. Her head spun. She grabbed the edges of the crude bench, struggling to maintain consciousness. After a few minutes the heaving ceased. Her breath sputtered in ragged gasps. Anna dropped to her knees and closed her eyes. She tried to ignore the wretched stench of the place as she labored to regain her strength. She had to hurry. The SS regularly patrolled the bathrooms, on the lookout for shirkers. If she was caught like this . . .

"Well, well, what do we have here?"

She recognized the voice. Blinking a few times to fight away the pain, she opened her eyes to see Kamila, perched above her, hands on her hips. Schmidt's favorite had a cigarette dangling from her lips and her face wore a cynical smirk. "Too much breakfast, is it?" she asked.

"I'm fine."

"You don't look fine. You look ill. Perhaps I should notify our guard. I'm sure he would make sure you were well taken care of."

"Kamila, please."

"Please, is it?" the woman asked, her mouth twisting in a smirk. "You've never given me the time of day before, but now you want a favor?"

"Just leave me alone."

"I'll leave you alone, all right," she said, turning to leave.

"How can you betray your own people?" hissed Anna.

Kamila turned back to her. "*My* people? Do you mean these wretches out here? What have they ever done for me? You don't know how they've treated me, do you?"

"All of us have suffered."

"At least you have people to bear it with you." She stepped closer. "Let me tell you my story. My husband was a doctor in Kraków. We had two little ones, a boy and a girl. We were happy, wealthy, respected. Then the Germans came. The ghetto came. We were shoved into that hell with everyone else. That was fine, but our neighbors took delight in our fall. They gave us the worst food, the most decrepit accommodations."

"I'm sorry, but—"

"My husband turned in on himself. I had to fight to keep us alive. Then the trains. My little ones were torn from my arms when we arrived. Dead. They're all dead." Kamila spat on the pavement. "No matter, they're better off than me. You'd think I had suffered enough. But no, I'm still the *rich woman* from Kraków. Nobody will talk to me or give me the time of day. So, what choice did I have? I turned to Schmidt. I still had my looks. My last treasure. He's a shit all right, but he treats me better than all of you. He gives me food, cigarettes, protection." She scowled at Anna. "I haven't betrayed my people. They've betrayed me. I do what I do to survive." She started to turn.

"Don't go," said Anna. "I understand. I'm sorry you've been treated this way."

Kamila turned back, her face twisting in a knowing smile. "You're sorry because for this moment I have power over you. No other reason."

"Leave her alone," said a sharp voice. Anna looked up. Estusia was there, standing in the doorway, fists clamped to her sides, her face in a rage.

"I was just leaving," said Kamila.

"You'll leave all right, and you'll keep your mouth shut."

Kamila looked back and forth between them for a few moments. "Fine," she muttered at last. "Have it your way." She pushed her way past Estusia and stormed out of the bathroom.

Estusia rushed to her side. "Are you all right?"

Anna nodded.

"Don't pay any attention to that witch," said Estusia. "She has a lot of gall coming in here and threatening you."

"I don't know if she really meant it."

"Anna, you're too kind. That woman is a demon."

"She was rejected. By all of us. She lost her children and her husband."

"She's sleeping with an SS guard!" said Estusia.

"Does she really have a choice?" asked Anna. "She takes the food and the protection as the price for all the pain. Is she really any different than the rest of us?"

"She's different all right. And she'd sell your life for a single ersatz cigarette, and don't you forget it!" Estusia took her arms. "You must listen to me. You must never trust her. She will be out to get you now."

Anna nodded, but she wasn't sure she believed it. She felt a deep sadness for Kamila, and guilt. Hadn't she ignored the woman along with everyone else? She'd been warned on her first day to avoid her, and she'd done so, never trying to talk to her about Schmidt and his "protection." Of anyone here, she could have shared her story . . .

Anna closed her eyes; she mustn't think about that now. She had so little time and there were things she must do today. Her stomach felt a little better. She hoped the nausea would stay away, at least for a while. She couldn't afford to draw attention to herself with so much at stake. And she had to look presentable for Henryk. Estusia helped her to her feet. She squared her shoulders, took a deep breath, and prepared for the rest of the day.

A few minutes later, Anna slipped back to her workstation. She spent the next couple of hours polishing the machined tools in front of her, scraping off the little metal imperfections from the rough tooling. She hated these slivers that would lance into her hands, burying deep inside her fingers. She'd grown used to the infections, the pain, but she dreaded the labor. Still, things could be far worse. Here she had to work hard, and the walk each day was long, but they were inside. It was relatively warm and the effort, while tedious and tiring, was not backbreaking. She thought of the women in the brick gangs, carrying exhausting loads of materials for construction in the freezing cold. These women quickly became scarecrows, dying in a few weeks.

And there were men here. Prisoners just like they were. The men looked after the women, bringing them food, protecting them as well as they could against the guards and the worst of the labor. If one wanted to survive, one must have a protector.

She felt a hand on her shoulder. She turned and her face flushed. Henryk was there, looming over her, his muscular frame visible even under the loose, worn pajamas. She stared into his coal-colored eyes for an instant. They burned with amusement and something more. She started to turn away.

"Don't," he whispered.

She glanced up and down the line of busy inmates. "The guards—"

"Won't bother me."

He was right, of course. The Germans respected Henryk both for his size and because he spoke fluent German. He was a Polish Jew of German ancestry. He'd grown up near the border with the Reich. Because of these things, the guards often turned a blind eye to Henryk, so long as he wasn't too reckless.

"Eat up," he ordered, handing her a biscuit.

She took a bite, and another. Her stomach churned and she had to fight down the urge to throw up again, but she knew she needed the sustenance. She finished the biscuit and he handed her another.

"For later," he whispered. "And now, what do you have for me in return?"

"Henryk, I'm not feeling well."

He laughed. "Always something with you, Anna." He shrugged. "Very well. Is there anything else I can do for you today?"

"You know what I need."

He looked around. "Why bother? You can't eat that stuff, and really, what good will it do in the end?"

"I have to have it."

Henryk's eyes lit up. "Is it that important to you?"

"Come on now," she protested. "You've supplied it to me so many times. Don't be like that."

Henryk whistled and stroked his chin in mock consideration. "You're right, I have. Maybe I should have held out for a little more. Perhaps those tiny baggies of powder you need so badly have been the key to your heart all along."

"Henryk," she said sternly. "I won't bargain with you. Either give me what I asked for, or I won't speak with you again." She felt the hot guilt, the shame, but she pushed it down. She had to have this.

He put his hands in the air. "All right, all right. But I can't give it to you for free. I'll need a kiss."

She hesitated. "There are people all around us."

His eyes lit up. "I'm more than happy to find us somewhere that is more private."

She breathed in deeply. "Fine. You may kiss me on the cheek."

He smiled, leaning down.

"The powder first!" she demanded.

He looked around again, more carefully this time. "Very well." He reached inside and drew out a fragment of handkerchief tied in a tight little ball.

Anna grabbed the lump quickly and drew it down into a hidden seam on the inside of her dress. She felt the thrill of the thing as she did it. Henryk watched her appreciatively and whistled. "Let me put that away for you next time and I'll bring you double," he whispered.

"Stop joking around, Henryk," Anna responded with irritation. She turned back toward her work.

"Uh, uh, uh. Don't forget the kiss."

"Fine. Quickly then."

He reached down and pressed his hot lips against her cheek. She bristled and squirmed, trying to pull away. She had intended for this to be quick but he held on to her shoulders, his hand moving down her neck toward her breast.

"Stop it," she hissed, ripping away from him.

He laughed and drew himself up. "That's a down payment," he said. "If you want any more of this, you'll have to pay more. This is dangerous for me and the price is going up."

She didn't respond, turning to focus on her work, picking up a cloth to polish one of the tools in front of her. She heard Henryk laugh one more time and then make his way down the line, striking up a conversation with one of the other men as he did so.

Anna made sure the lump was firmly in the hidden pocket beneath her dress. It would be disastrous if it fell out and was picked up by a German. The hours ticked by endlessly. She kept an eye out for the guards. They hadn't performed many inspections inside the factory, but still, she had to be prepared. What she was hiding was death for her.

Finally, the workday was over. Under the screams of their guards, the women filed out of the factory and into the frigid evening air. It was already dark out and Anna flinched before the biting wind, yearning for the barracks and the hot soup that awaited them when they reached Birkenau. Later, she would get to see Jakub. There would be more food and some time together. Her stomach felt better tonight. With any luck they could steal away and find a few minutes to be together. She thought of Henryk again. What was she going to do about him? Perhaps it didn't matter. They were almost ready. Maybe they wouldn't need any more.

She walked hand in hand with Estusia. Her friend's bony

fingers gave her a fraction of warmth and they were able to support and balance each other. The market in Auschwitz was already closed. Lights shone from houses and the smell of warm bread and cooking dinners wafted out toward them. Anna wanted to run toward one of those houses, to steal or beg something to eat, to plead for help, but she knew it was instant death to rush out of the line. Besides, most of the inhabitants here were German transplants, who would as readily kill her as give her any food.

They moved on out of the town and away from the damning smells. They were in complete darkness now, trudging through slush and cold, each relying on the motion of the woman in front to keep orientation and direction.

A half hour later they approached the entrance to the camp. Anna's hands and legs ached with pain, but she felt a surge of energy as they arrived at Birkenau. In a few minutes she would be back in the warmth of the barracks. She'd made it.

"Line up for inspection!" She heard the words in German, and she froze in fear as she worked out the translation. Not today of all days. Somehow, she'd managed to be lucky in the past. They'd never performed a search when she'd smuggled in a package before.

She felt her body shiver. Her hands trembled. The SS were already there, just a few people ahead of her, flashlights out, patting down the first woman in line. Other guards were stepping out of the darkness and striding down the line. She had moments to act, if she wasn't already out of time.

A guard passed and searched Estusia, directly behind her. Anna glanced back. The German was busy, his hands passing up and down her friend's dress. He would be done in a few moments. She spun around and reached down, pulling the hem of her skirt up and retrieving the little ball of fabric from the hidden pocket. She dropped the skirt and keeping her eyes forward, clawed at the ball, digging her fingers into the cloth. Seconds passed. Nothing was happening, she couldn't find the opening. Her heart tore through her chest. They were going to catch her.

At last her thumb ripped through the material and she could feel the grainy substance beneath. Her fingers pulled and she turned the little ball inside out so that the powder poured out of the opening and onto the ground. Keeping her eyes forward, she crushed the substance into the snow and mud with her foot. Feeling the cloth to make sure there was nothing left in it, she let the fragment drift from her fingers.

Rough hands seized her, running over her dress; a stabbing white light shined in her eyes. Fingers groped over her breasts and down her waist. The guard felt roughly between her legs, searching uniform and skin. He looked at her and grinned. The brightness receded and he was gone. She was left shivering in the darkness.

Shouts. The line moved again. Anna stumbled forward. Relief spilled over her. She'd made it! She'd lost the precious gunpowder but that didn't matter. It was such a small amount and they'd labored for months to smuggle the stuff in. She could bring more tomorrow. She'd figure out some way to coax Henryk into helping her without giving in to him. She thought of the barracks, the warmth and the coming soup. She smiled to herself. It was good to be alive.

"Anna."

She froze. Schmidt had appeared out of the darkness, that crooked smile on his face again.

"I'm so glad I've found you," he said silkily.

"I'm late for supper," she said. "Please excuse me, sir."

He put a hand on her elbow, starting to draw her away from the line. "No, little one. Not that way. I have a much better night planned for you."

Schmidt dragged her into the darkness, into the nightmares of her past. She screamed, a fire bursting inside her. She clawed at the guard, trying to rip her hands free, but he held on to her with a granite grip, the smile curling on his face. Schmidt struck her hard on the top of her head, again and again. She fought a tornado of dizziness, but she was overwhelmed and she gave way to the darkness.

Chapter 11

Desperate Measures

October 1944
Auschwitz

Jakub awoke abruptly. He was stunned, confused, unable to function. He heard a knock on the wood frame, and he looked up. Roch was standing over him.

"How is our patient this evening?"

He struggled, trying to remember what had happened to him. "What do you mean, evening?"

"You've slept a night and a day. Don't worry, you needed it, and we made sure you were not disturbed. How do you feel?"

"Numb."

Roch laughed grimly. "I feel that way every day. I'm talking about your body. Are you recovering?"

Jakub nodded. "A little." He started to rise.

"Don't move," Roch ordered. "We'll bring your supper. Tomorrow I'll make sure you are assigned light duty. We need you to recover as quickly as you can."

"Thank you."

The leader looked him over for a second. "Aren't you going to ask about the other thing?"

Jakub blinked, trying to remember what Roch was talking about. Then it hit him. Anna! Schmidt! "Did you—"

"We got a message through the gate."

"To Anna?"

"I don't know. Our man was able to pass it on to one of the female *Kapo*s last night. That's all I know for sure at this point."

Jakub started to object. "A *Kapo*, they are—"

"Don't worry. She's trustworthy. She won't betray us."

Well, at least that was something. No matter what else happened, he hoped Anna knew that he hadn't betrayed her. That Schmidt had orchestrated this. Perhaps she could even avoid the German entirely. Could she hide from the SS guard? Jakub had no idea how much power Schmidt had in other parts of the camp. He'd seen him many times in the women's camp, but that was always in the vacant barracks where the elite gathered. Did he have free rein to go wherever he wanted? To turn the barracks upside down in search of Anna? It was difficult to say, but Jakub hoped there would be some limits on the man's power. He couldn't just waltz into a barracks and drag Anna out, could he? After all, relations between the Germans and their prisoners was officially *verboten*.

"Are you listening to me?"

Jakub cleared his head. "I'm sorry, what?"

"I was saying that there is a reason we want you healthy. We have something for you, and it can't wait long."

"What is it?"

"I'll tell you when the time is right. Tomorrow night, after supper, I will come find you." He knelt down to Jakub, looking around before he spoke. "I won't lie to you. It's dangerous."

Jakub nodded. "I'll be ready."

Roch took his hand. "Rest up, my friend." The leader looked around for a moment, making sure nobody was nearby, then he leaned closer. "Oh, another thing. There's a new guard in our midst. A kid really. He appeared this morning. Tall, red hair, you can't miss him."

"All right."

"That's not why I'm telling you. He's been talking to prisoners, asking questions. We think he's some kind of plant. We're trying to learn more about him but that's all I can tell you for now. He's very young. He might be sympathetic, and if so, we might be able to use him at some point. But we can't afford to be betrayed, so for now, stay away from him if you can."

Jakub nodded. "Thank you for telling me."

They shook hands and the resistance leader departed. Jakub closed his eyes, pondering this new information.

"Still relaxing, I see." He heard Tomasz's voice a few minutes later. "What did that Boy Scout want from you?"

"The same as always."

Tomasz laughed. "They tried to play that same game with me at first, but I told them no. They persisted for a bit but they finally gave up." He leaned closer. "I have news."

"About Anna?"

"Yes."

"What news?"

"I managed to make it through the fence last night. It was late. She's safe."

Jakub half rose. "You saw her?"

"No, but I've guaranteed her protection."

"How?"

"I told you, a little wealth here, a little there. These Germans act like they are above it all, but it's just like Warsaw. Everyone wants their fat little fingers in the pie."

Jakub breathed deeply. "That's a relief." He genuinely felt that. Tomasz's assurance was even more comforting than Roch's. He'd seen his friend work wondrous miracles, and he was as good as his word.

"Can I go back through the fence soon? I want to see Anna."

Tomasz shook his head. "I don't have confirmation yet that Schmidt will fully cooperate."

"But you said—"

"Anna's safe. That's what I know for now. But you might not be able to come back through for some time—maybe the full month."

"How will I know if Anna truly is safe?"

"You can trust me, my boy. I always look after you. I'll tell you more as soon as I know something. Hopefully I can get you through quicker, but if not, a month is only a month. I'll still need what you collect, by the way. Schmidt will want to be paid off in any event, and I have other wheels to grease. Get as much as you can. The more you give me, the more I may be able to speed things up."

Jakub nodded. He wanted to ask more but he knew there was no point. He would just have to wait and see what happened. At least on Tomasz's end.

"Are you coming to work tomorrow?" his friend asked.

"Yes. Roch promised to get me some light duty."

Tomasz nodded his head approvingly. "Good boy. Dangle your help out there like a piece of string and get what you can out of Roch. That's using your wits. I'll turn you into a regular rogue if I can have a bit more time with you."

"I'm afraid we're out of time."

"That's been true since we got here. It's all borrowed time now. But you've got along pretty well living on credit. If you can owe me a million zlotys, perhaps fate will keep lending days to you as well."

Jakub smiled and clapped his friend on the shoulder. "I don't know what I would have done in here without you." He wanted to tell Tomasz about Roch, but he knew he couldn't.

"Well, I've got to get going," said Tomasz. "There's a fence to go through and the lovely Urszula to placate. I'm telling you, my boy, you might want to forget Anna. These girls and their demands! They're hardly worth it."

Jakub forced a laugh. "You may be right. I'll do my best to keep the money flowing. I'm not sure how much I'll be bringing in tomorrow."

"No matter, every little bit helps. Besides, we could be up the chimney before then. I'm off, boy. But don't worry, I'll check on you when I'm done. And remember," he said, waving a finger at him, "dangle the string with Roch, but don't let them get their hands on you."

Tomasz departed, leaving Jakub alone with his thoughts. Anna was safe. At least that was something. But a new idea was just beginning to form.

He rested that night and returned to work the next day. Good to his word, Roch convinced a *Kapo* to place Jakub on cart duty. All he had to do was wait at the top and assist prisoners in moving stacks of clothing from the carts to the back of the truck. The other prisoners, knowing Jakub had been ill, did most of the lifting themselves. He was desperate for news of Anna. Tomasz had returned from the fence the night before, but he didn't know anything further. Anna was nowhere to be seen.

What could he do? His friend had assured him all was taken care of, but could Jakub be sure? Could he wait a month, not knowing what had happened to her, unsure that Schmidt was truly keeping his word, and wasn't visiting her every night . . . ? He didn't even know if Anna truly had word of what had happened, of why he wasn't coming. He had Roch's and Tomasz's assurances, but there was no confirmation.

He turned his new idea over in his head. He thought through the risks, the consequences. He decided he had to try it, even if he threatened everything else in the process. The day seemed to drag on forever, but eventually they were called to supper. Jakub sat with Tomasz, half listening to his friend's stories of adventures in the Warsaw streets before the war. Eventually his friend left for the fence. Jakub knew he was supposed to meet Roch, but he had something else he had to do first.

The battle still raged inside him. He was being reckless, he knew. Did he need to take this risk? Between Tomasz and Roch, they had assured him that Anna was safe. She was warned and protected. Why not be patient and see what happened? Like Roch said, *We are helpless in Auschwitz*.

He shook his head. He couldn't do nothing. If there was a chance to help her. A chance that Tomasz and Roch had failed. He had to do more. Jakub rose from his bunk and looked around, making sure nobody was watching. Fortunately, this part of the barracks was currently deserted. He reached under his bunk, his fingers moving along the crude wood. He groped in the corner formed by the end of the bunk. For long moments he couldn't find what he was looking for. He feared someone had discovered his hiding place, but his fingers closed in on cloth. He pulled the sack off the little hook he'd fashioned and drew his hand back up to his waist.

He looked down. The fabric fragment was tiny, no bigger than a midsized coin. He tore at the strings, his fingers fumbling until he was able to open it. He upended the sack and three diamonds rolled out into his hand. This was all the wealth he possessed in the world. His secret last valuables to be used in the last extreme to bargain for his life. He rolled the diamonds around in his palm and then slipped them into his pocket.

He took some steps toward the door, keeping an eye out for Roch or any other prying eyes. He slipped down the stairs and reached the landing below. His first barrier. A guard stood at the outside entrance, making sure nobody left or entered the building. He knew the man, he'd worked with him before.

"*Halt*," the German ordered, eyeing Jakub with interest. Normally Tomasz handled this transaction, but he was sure the guard didn't care who offered up valuables. Jakub reached into his pocket and retrieved one of the diamonds. He held his hand out to the soldier. The guard glared at him for a moment and then took a step forward, his hands fumbling for his belt. Something was wrong. Jakub waited for the man to draw his pistol, for the shouts of alarm to bellow from his mouth, but the German was merely pulling up his trousers. He stared at the stone in Jakub's hands for a moment and lifted it out of his hands, holding it up to a nearby light. The Nazi turned back to Jakub. "*Was?*" he asked.

Jakub motioned to the door.

The guard stared at him then shrugged, tucking the diamond into his pocket. "*Ja*," he said. "*Schnell.*"

Jakub had won. He moved past the German and out into the falling light. He had two diamonds left. He had to pray that the rest of his plan would work.

He shambled toward the gate, fear coursing through him,

crossing the interminable distance to the gate. Normally he thought nothing of this, but today the fence seemed a kilometer away. He reached into his pocket, taking another diamond between thumb and finger.

He made it to the gate. The guard had turned and was watching him closely now. He pulled the diamond out and handed it to the guard, who looked around quickly to make sure nobody was watching before he slipped it into his pocket. The guard opened the gate and waved Jakub through. But that wasn't what he wanted. He spoke in his broken German, asking a question. The man looked surprised and he asked a question in return. Jakub nodded. The SS shrugged and stepped through the gate, leaving another guard to watch him.

The guard returned a few minutes later in the company of another. It was the tall gangly youth that Roch had told him about. The young man looked at Jakub with curiosity, the two other guards watching them as well. Jakub introduced himself. "We need to talk," he said.

Jakub returned an hour later in search of Roch. He found the resistance leader near his bunk, huddled around a few other prisoners. He moved toward the group but felt hands on him, holding him back.

"Where do you think you're going?" asked a gruff voice from behind him. Someone must have been on the lookout.

He saw Roch look up quickly. His face shifted from concern to a wide smile. "It's all right, he's with us." Roch beckoned Jakub over and introduced him to the other men. Then he motioned for them to depart so they could speak privately.

"You're late," he said, his eyes searching Jakub's.

"Yes, sorry. Tomasz wanted to talk to me and I couldn't get away."

"You haven't told him anything about this?" Roch asked.

"No, of course not. He just was offering to contact Anna for me."

"He could be helpful there," Roch agreed.

"Did you hear whether your message got through?" Jakub asked.

Roch shook his head. "I don't know that yet, but I should have that information in the next couple of days. I don't know why it wouldn't have, the *Kapo* we gave it to is reliable." He looked Jakub over. "How are you feeling?"

"Much better. Thank you for protecting me the last couple of days."

"Of course. I would have wanted to even if you didn't join us. Are you feeling well enough to walk a bit? Our little project requires you to travel some distance."

That caught Jakub's attention. The entire camp was only about a kilometer square. That meant something outside Birkenau. "I'm well enough."

"Good. What I'm about to tell you is top secret. You should tell nobody about this, especially Tomasz."

"Why not Tomasz?"

Roch hesitated. "Let's just say he's not one of us."

"But you said *especially not*."

"It's nothing. Just a precaution. Can you agree to those terms?"

Jakub nodded, his heart racing as he waited for the information.

"All right. I'm trusting you with something significant. We have an outside contact we want you to meet up with."

An outside contact. "Who is that?"

"He's a Pole, not a Jew. A member of the Armia Krajowa and we've been communicating with him for the past few months."

Jakub whistled. "The real Polish resistance. Where is he?"

"He lives in the village of Auschwitz." Roch reached into his shirt and retrieved a small piece of paper. "Here are directions to his house. Memorize those and then destroy the paper."

"Do you have a message for me to give him?"

"On paper? No. It's too dangerous. I'm going to trust you with our biggest plan."

Jakub couldn't believe Roch was telling him this. Why him? Why so quickly? "What is the message?"

"We need the AK to be ready to act in five days."

Jakub was shocked. What did that mean? "What's in five days? What are we going to do?"

Roch looked at Jakub as if weighing something in his mind. He turned his head this way and that, making sure nobody was close by, and then he leaned in, his lips almost touching Jakub's ear. "We are going to revolt."

"Revolt! What does that mean?" asked Jakub.

"Quiet," Roch warned him. "It means just that. We've been planning this for some time. We have weapons. Some explosives and a few pistols. When the time is right, the Poles are going to attack the camp near our crematorium. We will kill our guards and then together we're going to liberate the camp."

Jakub couldn't believe the plan had progressed this far. He asked a question while he tried to gather his composure. "Where did you get the weapons?"

"We've stolen a couple of pistols from the SS."

"And the explosives?"

"Gunpowder, taken from the Union Munitions Factory. Gram by gram."

"That's where Anna works."

"I know. She's one of our operatives. Did you not know?"

Jakub was stunned. Anna was involved with the resistance. Another complication. "No, she never told me."

"Brave girl, that Anna. And smart. She probably didn't want to put you in danger by telling you."

"She's been encouraging me to join you for months."

Roch nodded. "That's Anna all right. Like I said, smart girl."

"I don't understand. Why do you want me to go? You have so many other members. I'm just joining. How could you even trust me?"

"I'm well aware of the risk. Perhaps the biggest I've taken since I've been here. There are many against it. But we are out of time—and after all, you have been connected with Anna. You're right that we have many members, but none with your special skill set."

"What skill?" Jakub asked. "I don't know how to do anything."

"Oh, but you do, my boy. You know how to do the one thing that we have almost no experience with. You know how to get in and out of those gates. You've been through a hundred times, Jakub. I've been watching you for a very long time. Sure, we've been able to do it as well, but only now and again, and at great risk. We've had men killed trying to get through. But not you. You and Tomasz pass through every night as if you were taking a stroll through the park. This message has to make it, and I think you have the best chance of reaching our contact."

"And I'm expendable, too, aren't I?" asked Jakub, the thought occurring to him suddenly. "If I'm caught, you haven't lost anyone critical to the plan."

"You're wrong there," said Roch. "We've had two men captured at the gate. Neither have returned. We live in constant fear that they will talk under torture, and everything will be exposed. Assuming they are even alive. By telling you the plan as well, I've just added to the risk." He flicked his pencil in his fingers. "But I'm not worried about you. I've known there was something different about you from the moment we met. You're our best hope in this, Jakub. I'd like to give you more time to heal, but we're short on that commodity right now. Will you go?"

Jakub thought of the considerable risk. *Traveling outside of the gate*. It was one thing to bribe a guard into the women's camp. It was another to leave Birkenau itself. There were prisoners out there, of course. Many *Kommandos* worked beyond the camp itself. But they had passes, and German guards that made it obvious to anyone they met that they were *supposed* to be there. He would be traveling alone. There was no place to hide. If he was caught, he would assuredly be tortured for information. And when they were done with him, he would be executed. *Still*, it might not all come to that. He did have a layer of protection now, after all . . .

But the risk was substantial. He might be shot in the woods, or on the road to Birkenau. The Germans might not bother capturing him. Would he take that risk to be on the deep inside of this? The whole plan sounded insane. What would a pistol or two do against the combined might of hundreds of guards? Even if they succeeded, where would they go? But this information was priceless. And on the other hand, what if the revolt was successful? He'd never had any real hope of survival here. Like everyone in the camp, he clung to a vague fantasy of liberation, but he knew deep down that he was going to die. If the Russians ever did get close, the Germans would kill them or move them to another camp farther from the front lines. This plan sounded like madness. Still, if the Poles were going to help them, it might just work. Either way, he had to know.

"I'll do it," he said at last.

Roch smiled, slapping his leg. "I knew I was right about you."

"When do I leave?"

"Tonight." Roch retrieved a cheap pocket watch from his shirt and checked the time. "A half hour from now."

"All right. I'll be back then," said Jakub. "I've got a few things to do before I leave."

A half hour later Jakub was hurrying through the barracks to get back to Roch's bunk.

"Where are you going so fast?" asked Tomasz. Jakub froze, surprised to hear his friend's voice.

"Nowhere. I thought you were still at the fence. Did you see Anna?"

Tomasz shook his head. "Still nothing. I swear that girl has disappeared."

Jakub started to protest.

"Now don't get yourself into another of your fits. I told you, I've taken care of it. I don't know why she's not about, but she's not with Schmidt. I saw him eating a meal with Kamila." Tomasz laughed. "I don't know what was wrong, but she seemed mighty angry with him. It's a joy to watch an SS sergeant endure a tongue-lashing by a Jew."

Jakub didn't care about that. He only cared about Anna. "I need to know if she's all right."

Tomasz smiled in understanding. "I know you do, my boy. Tomorrow night, I'll try to see if I can find her. I wouldn't mind nosing around her barracks in any event. To be honest with you, I'm getting a little tired of Urszula. Lately she's demanding more and giving less. I may have to look for a new one. Maybe someone a bit younger."

"You do that, my friend. And please try to find Anna if you can. Tell her what happened. Tell her I'll see her soon."

"I will."

They shook hands and Jakub turned, beginning to walk away. He was late now.

"Oh. Jakub."

He turned back. Tomasz was eyeing him with a grave expression. Jakub's heart froze. "Give Roch my best."

"Tomasz . . . it's not what you think. I can explain."

"It's exactly what I think it is. You went against me. You betrayed me." Tomasz shook his head. "And for what? To join that pack of idiots and get yourself killed? I thought we were brothers, that we trusted each other, told each other everything." Jakub could see the pain in his friend's face.

"We do. I have. I just—"

"You just wanted to be a hero after all. You think my way of doing things is wrong? You think I'm some kind of criminal? Is that it? That bribing is below you?"

"Please, Tomasz. It's not that, it's just that—"

"Don't worry yourself. I'll give Anna your best and I'll tell her you'll probably never see her again. That you're going to go and get yourself killed. I can't believe you didn't listen to me."

"Tomasz, wait. Let me explain!" But his friend had turned and was marching quickly away. Jakub wanted to go after him, but he was already very late. He took a deep breath and turned to begin his mission.

Chapter 12
Descent into Nightmare

October 1944
Auschwitz

Schmidt marched on through the dark. His iron grip wrenched Anna's wrist, forcing her to stumble along, trying to keep up.

"Please, sir," she begged, knowing there was no escape. "Please, I haven't done anything wrong."

"Not yet," he joked. "But we will soon remedy that." His head was darting this way and that, looking for something. "Ah, here we are," he said, pulling her toward a darkened barracks. He kicked open the door and dragged her inside, throwing her to the ground. She could barely make out his outline in the blackness of the room. She was freezing, and her body trembled with more than cold. She was back at the labor camp, all the horrors were closing in on her again.

"Please." She managed to whisper the word.

"I appreciate the sentiment," he said. "You'll get far by being polite."

"What about Kamila?"

"What about her?" he asked. "She has her purpose. But I'm a connoisseur of many different tastes and delights. I've been watching you for a long time, little Anna."

"I don't want to," she said.

"Not yet," he said, his form drawing closer to her as she lay crumpled on the frozen floorboards. "But you will. There is much I can do for you."

"I have protection already."

"Hah!" he scoffed. "Do you mean that fool Jakub? Well, don't worry about him, we've made an arrangement."

She felt the fear fill her. "What do you mean?"

"He sold you to me for a pack of cigarettes and a bottle of cognac."

"You're lying."

"I'm afraid not, my pretty. It was his idea. Frankly, I would have paid quite a bit more for you, but he didn't even bargain very hard. He said he was tired of your little charade and it was time to move on."

She heard the words but she couldn't believe them. She knew he had to be lying—but her past crowded her mind, filling her with doubts.

"I see you're not so sure of yourself after all," said Schmidt. He was kneeling down now and she felt a hand on her leg. "Forget about Jakub. He's just a boy. A powerless nothing. I, on the other hand, can give you so much more than a little bread. I can get you all the food you want, medicine, a release from work."

"Kamila works."

"Does she?" he asked, laughing again. "Oh, she marches out with all of you each day, but have you ever seen her doing anything at that factory of yours?"

Anna didn't know. She didn't work closely with Kamila.

"I see you're thinking about things," whispered Schmidt,

drawing closer to her. "Forget your foolish Jakub. He's already forgotten you. Think of your future, of your life."

He loomed over her, his head drawing toward hers.

Anna turned and vomited on the floor, her mind reeling, her stomach heaving.

Schmidt drew away. "Disgusting!" he shouted. "What the hell is wrong with you?"

"I've been ill," she whispered, fighting back the bile in her throat.

He prodded her back with his boot, silent for a moment as if considering something. "You disappoint me, Anna," he said at last. "I was offering you everything."

"I'm sorry," she whispered, fighting for time. "It's not your words, I'm just ill."

"Well, I cannot help you then," he said at last. "It's off to the hospital for you."

"Please, no!" she turned, grasping at his feet, trying to stop him.

"There's nothing to be done for it. This is out of my hands. I'll send someone for you." He put his head down near hers again, whispering, "But don't you worry, Anna, I'll be sure to tell Jakub how sweet you were. I wouldn't want him to feel that he'd sold me a broken whore. I'll visit you tomorrow, if you survive the night. Who knows, if you improve, you might still benefit from our little arrangement."

Schmidt rose, laughing to himself as he marched out of the barracks.

Anna lay there in a pool of her own vomit, waiting for the guards to come and take her to the hospital. She thought of Jakub, fighting down the tears. She waited for death.

Chapter 13
The Journey

October 1944
Auschwitz

Jakub waited in the darkness amidst the trees, without movement. He shivered in the freezing night air but he didn't dare move. He was sure his clothing would betray him. The fabric was too pale, and with even a breath of light, it would surely stand out against the tree line.

This was only the second time he'd ever been outside of Birkenau—the first being the fateful trip to the SS barracks with Schmidt. This trip was very different. He was alone, unguarded. As he waited, an emotion sparked, growing until it filled him: He could escape. He could leave the camp and everything behind him, and attempt to make his way—somewhere, anywhere. He fought down the urge. He was alone, with no food, no weapon, exhausted and in a prisoner's uniform. He wouldn't make it ten kilometers before he'd collapse. He also knew that his sense of freedom was an illusion. Somewhere out there, God knew where, there was an outer fence that surrounded the greater Auschwitz complex. He was outside Birkenau all right, but there was another barrier he would never make it through on his own.

Besides, he couldn't leave his friends, leave Anna. He had made a promise and he had to keep it. His father's voice warred with him in his mind even as he reached this conclusion: *Escape, survive, no matter what. You are the last of us.*

The minutes ticked by endlessly. He wasn't sure how late it was, but he knew he had to be patient. This would be dangerous enough when people were settled in for the night. He couldn't risk traveling when there was the chance of encountering someone, anyone, on the road. He drew a little bit of dry meat that Roch had given him from his pocket. The piece was pitifully small but it was all he had to sustain him. He bit off half of it and gnawed at the stuff, chewing slowly to try to make it last. In a couple of bites, he'd already eaten half. He wanted the rest but he resisted and shoved the rest back into his pocket. He would save it for the return journey, if there was such a thing.

He thought of Anna. He wished he was with her right now, sharing a meal, talking. He wanted to find out everything she'd done with the resistance, to share with her what he was doing for them now. That there was a glimmer of hope for the future. Of course, she wouldn't approve of everything he had done . . .

Finally, when his feet were frozen and his head drooped in exhaustion, he deemed it was time to proceed. He took a cautious step, then another, his shoes crunching loudly in the snow. If anyone was out there, they would hear him.

He moved on, skirting the edge of the woods, avoiding the road. He strained his eyes, struggling to pierce the darkness. He hoped there was nobody left out here, but of course Auschwitz was never unguarded. He could chance across a lonely outpost, or a patrol, and that would be the end of him.

Time passed. The trees continued on and on. He kept moving, battling the impression that he was on some hellish treadmill without an ending. Lights. He saw first one, then another, flickering in and out among the trees. At last he was approaching the village. He must not be more than a few hundred meters away now. He felt excitement and relief, mixed with a rising fear. The town would surely be guarded. Only caution would get him through, along with luck.

He stepped farther into the trees now, moving into the forest a few yards with the hope of concealing himself from a chance encounter near the road. This made the going more difficult. He was so tired. Damn the strength these bastards had taken from him. When he'd arrived at the camp he could have run back and forth from Birkenau to the town a dozen times over. Now each step was agony.

The little collection of houses took shape through the branches and the brush. He could see a dwelling up close now, a single light flickering on the porch. Smoke drifted out of a chimney. Jakub thought of the fire inside. He would give everything to stand in front of a stove, warming himself, feasting on a full supper and drinking hot tea. He shook his head. Mustn't think of such things. He had to concentrate. The smallest mistake and he'd never return to Birkenau.

He reached the edge of the trees. More houses were visible, no more than fifty meters away now. He closed his eyes for a moment, thinking about the map he'd memorized. He had to make it past the first few lines of houses. This was the most dangerous part of his journey. If he was going to be spotted, it would be in the next few minutes. He felt his heart thumping hard, the pulse rippling through his temples. *Go, Jakub, in a few minutes you'll be warm and safe, or it won't matter anymore.*

He stepped into the field, shuffling through the slush toward the houses. He was exposed out here. The snow around him seemed to glow. There was no cover. If anyone was looking this way, they would see him instantly. He was thirty meters away, then twenty. He was sure he would be spotted. The first house was ten meters away, then five. He reached the edge of the building. He leaned his hands against the shingles. He pressed himself against the frozen wood, resting for a moment, catching his breath. He'd made it—at least this far.

He moved on, trudging along the roofline of this first house. The snow was half melted here into a thick slush that seeped into his shoes, adding to his misery. He reached the corner of the house.

A growl. The horrid noise was right behind him. He rotated his body slowly. A German shepherd was perched there, a meter away. The thing was a monster, its head almost to his chest. Teeth bared, mouth half open. The dog barked, a thunderclap in the darkness. Jakub put his hands up. "Quiet now," he whispered.

The shepherd lunged, drawing closer, nearly biting him. The dog barked again, snarling and growling. The animal would leap on him at any moment and the clamor had to be calling the Germans down on him.

There was only one thing he could do. He reached into his pocket and pulled out the dried meat. The remaining chunk was the size of a small coin. He waved the food back and forth in front of the dog. At first the shepherd ignored it, snarling at him with bared teeth, but the dog began sniffing and quieted down, its head following the food as Jakub moved it back and forth in front of the animal. Drawing his arm behind him, he hurled the meat as far as he could. The canine rushed after it, hurling itself through the slush in pursuit of the meager treat.

Jakub ran as fast as he was able. No need for caution now. He had to get as far away from the monster as possible. The encounter had certainly awoken people in the village, and he expected to see SS closing in on him from every direction. He passed a second row of houses and a third. He wasn't trying to reach the meeting place anymore; in his terror he'd lost his orientation. He just wanted to escape before the dog came rushing back to kill him.

"Get over here!" He heard the sharp command in the darkness. He was caught. He looked up. A man stood on the porch of a nearby house, a shotgun in his hand. "Now, you fool!"

Jakub realized he was speaking Polish. He rushed forward, his desperation giving him new strength. He tumbled up the steps and fell forward, collapsing into the arms of the Pole. He was dragged rapidly inside and he hit the floor hard.

"Quiet now!" the man commanded. "Not a word!" The figure sprinted away. The lights inside the house were extinguished. Jakub lay there, exhausted and freezing, waiting for the Germans to come. He was dizzy and waves of nausea poured over him. His whole body shook. Outside he could hear shouts in German, the barking of the dog. He tried to rise.

"Don't move," whispered the man. "They're hunting you."

"Who are you?" asked Jakub.

"I'm Marek Pankiewicz, your contact." Marek looked him over, his lips pursed and his features creasing into a frown. "You've made quite a mess of things."

"I ran into a dog."

"Yes, I heard," said Marek dryly. "Everyone in Auschwitz heard." He turned his head toward the door. "Quiet now, they're growing closer."

Jakub craned his neck, straining his ears. He could hear footsteps. A flashlight flared through the window, streaking across the far wall. A rapid thud crashed against the door. They were here.

They remained frozen in the darkness as the harsh knocking continued. Jakub knew there was no place to hide. He was too weak to move and even if he could flee into another room, the slush, mud, and water he'd left all over the floor would betray him. They were going to be captured.

The door thudded again, the edge moving inward. Someone was pressing against the wood, trying to force their way in. Marek stared at the door as well, moving his shotgun up and aiming the double-barreled weapon.

The Germans whispered outside, apparently debating something. There was a shout from farther away and an answer from near the door. Boots clambered off the porch and receded into the night.

"They've gone," said Jakub.

"For now," said Marek. He set the shotgun down on a table and strode into another room, returning a moment later with some towels. "Help me clean up this mess. They may be back any second."

He handed Jakub a cloth and they set frantically to work, mopping up the slush and mud from the floor. They had to work in the dark, and Jakub feared they would leave some traces behind, but they did their best and continued soaking up the wetness until the floor was merely damp. Marek stepped across the room and reached down, pulling the edge of a carpet and dragging it until it covered the entranceway. "That will have to do," he said. He took a deep breath and turned back to Jakub. "We've been fortunate so far, but it may not last. We've got to get you well hidden. Follow me."

Jakub rolled over onto his stomach and pulled himself to his knees. His body cried out in pain but he willed himself to his feet. Once he was up, he followed Marek through the house, moving slowly with his hands in front of him, out of fear that he would crash into a wall or some furniture. They reached the back of the house and Marek unlatched a door. He took a step in and down, then another. Jakub moved after him, feeling his way. They were climbing down some stairs. "Close the door behind you," Marek ordered. There was a grinding metallic click and a flash of brightness as Marek ignited a lighter. Jakub blinked his eyes several times. They were in a narrow staircase leading down into a basement.

They reached the bottom and Marek moved across the space, the flickering flame bobbing up and down. He paused and hunched over what looked like a bench, fumbling with something in front of him. Jakub felt his fear rising again. Was this really their resistance contact? What if he was a German spy? He breathed easier when he saw that Marek was lighting a lamp. He covered the container and turned it up until the entire cellar was illuminated. A few jars sat atop some crude wooden shelves. The bench contained a jumble of rusted tools. A sack of something sat bunched in the corner. The ceiling was low, less than two meters. The entire room lay under a thick layer of dust.

"Won't they see the light?" Jakub asked.

Marek shook his head. "No windows down here. Plus, our voices will be muffled. We should be safe here to talk."

Jakub shivered and stamped his feet. He glanced into the corner of a room where a coal stove sat. "Any chance we could light that?"

"No, that we can't do. The Germans will be looking for smoke from the chimneys in town. It's late, near three o'clock. Very few people would be up. Smoke would be suspicious." He took off his jacket and moved toward Jakub. "Here, take this."

Jakub accepted the coat gratefully. He pulled the fabric on, fighting the weight. The cloth swam on him, like he was a boy trying on his father's jacket.

"You're so thin," Marek said.

"I'm better off than most," said Jakub.

"How so?"

Jakub explained his position in the *Sonderkommando*, his access to extra food and other items not available to the general population in the camp.

"How terrible to have to work with the damned," he said. "How can you stand it?"

"There is no choice. I work or I'm dead."

"Perhaps death would be better."

"When all you have is life, you cling to it, whatever the cost."

"You're right," said Marek, "I am in no place to judge."

"I have something for you. A message from Roch." Jakub explained the plan, and the request for action.

He whistled. "I had no idea things were this far advanced. Five days?"

"That was the message. Can the resistance out here be ready at the same time?"

"For an attack on the camp? I don't know. This is a significant operation. When I last was in contact with Roch, I thought we would have longer. We may need more time."

"Are you joking?" demanded Jakub. "We aren't at a spa. There are people dying by the thousands every day!"

"Keep it down!" demanded Marek. "They'll hear us."

"If we are ready in five days, you need to be too. I don't care what it takes. We've waited long enough." He took a step toward Marek. "Whatever the cost, get your people together and make it happen."

Marek shrugged. "You're not the only people with problems. We've had plenty of our people killed. Not only fighting the Germans, but arrested in their beds, betrayed by friends and family, tortured to death over days or weeks. I'll do what I can, but I can't promise five days."

Jakub stared at him for a moment before responding. "Have you had your entire family taken away from you and gassed to death? Have you watched mothers having their children torn out of their arms? Have you worked for fifteen hours a day with nothing but a bowl of watery turnip soup and some coffee to sustain you, while Germans stand by, whipping and beating you, waiting for any excuse to put a bullet in your head?"

Marek didn't respond. He watched Jakub, his mouth opening a couple of times. He turned and motioned toward the floor. "You can stay the rest of the night here," he said, pointing to a couple of empty sacks of flour. "I wish I could offer you better. We'll find a way to get you back to the camp in the morning."

There was nothing more Jakub could do. He watched Marek climb up the stairs, flipping the light off behind him. Jakub hobbled over to the corner, kneeling and picking up one of the sacks. The material was coarse and gave off a stale stench, but it was better than nothing. He lay down on the cold ground and covered himself with the sack, shivering in the darkness. He thought there was little chance he could rest, but his body gave out on him. He was exhausted and already so frail. After a few minutes he was fast asleep.

He was awoken violently to a clatter. He didn't know where he was at first. When he realized his surroundings, his heart thrummed. He was captured! He could hear the boots tearing down the stairway. He rose feebly, but what could he do? He had no way to defend himself. A figure turned the corner, a flashlight in his hand, the light shining painfully in his eyes.

"It's time to get up."

Jakub exhaled in relief. It was only Marek.

"What time is it?"

"Nearly eight."

Jakub was shocked he'd slept that long. He thought he would toss and turn fitfully in this freezing basement, but it felt like he'd just shut his eyes moments ago.

"Is it safe to leave?"

Marek shrugged. "Who knows? You didn't tell me your plan to get back to the camp."

"I was intending to find a *Kommando* coming through town toward the camp and try to join it without being seen."

"Well, you're in luck. There've already been several that have come through, and I'm sure more are on the way. There are always gangs sent into the town to scavenge bricks and wood from some of the abandoned houses."

Jakub rose, pulling himself to his feet with some difficulty. Marek reached down, helping him up.

"Follow me."

Jakub climbed slowly up the stairs and back into the front room of Marek's house. He could smell coffee and the scent of cooked eggs.

"Get something to eat in the kitchen before you go."

Jakub nodded gratefully and stepped around the corner. There was a small table with two chairs. Two plates were set, each containing two fried eggs and a little bread. Coffee steamed out of a cup in front of the plate. He sat down and grabbed at the eggs, not bothering to use the fork placed out for him. He crammed the still hot food into his mouth, the yolk running over his fingers. He licked greedily at the yellow liquid. He hadn't had an egg in years, since early in the war. He paused to take a drink of the bitter coffee and then grabbed the chunk of bread, sopping up the remaining yolk on the plate and gulping down the food. It wasn't enough. There was never enough. But he felt much better.

"Eat mine as well," said Marek.

Jakub looked up, shaking his head. "I can't," he said. "That's yours."

"I insist."

Jakub grabbed the second plate and wolfed down the food. He was done in less than a minute. He wiped his face with the back of his hand and sat back in his chair, sipping on the coffee. Now, for once, he felt full.

They sat there for a half hour or so, neither speaking to the other, lost in their respective thoughts. Finally, Marek stood, looking out the window.

"Ah, I see another of your groups is setting to depart back to the camp. You'd better join them while you have a chance."

Jakub nodded, looking out the window and gauging the distance between him and the *Kommando*. The dangerous part would be leaving the house. It was possible the Germans were still searching for him. If he was spotted among the houses and away from the main thoroughfare, he might be taken in for questioning. The line of men in striped pajamas was a hundred meters away. He turned, putting his hand out to Marek, who took it.

"Take care of yourself, Jakub. And be ready."

"We will be."

He took a deep breath, opened the door and lurched forward, his eyes darting around, seeking any threats. He took a step off the porch, and another. His nerves crackled as he stomped forward. He'd moved twenty meters, passing the next row of houses, then another. He could see the prisoners now, a few steps away. He stumbled into a group of them, nearly knocking one man over.

"Careful," the inmate hissed. He looked up, frowning. "Where did you come from?" he asked suspiciously.

"Shut your mouth," Jakub whispered back.

The man stared at him for a moment, his mouth half open. He dropped his head. "Well, take this at least," he mumbled, extending his hand toward a wheelbarrow full of bricks and lumber.

Jakub moved around gratefully, taking the handles. He lifted the cart up, grimacing at the weight, and joined the line of men who were already forming up to return to Birkenau. He stumbled and pushed, fighting the heaviness. How did they do this day after day and survive?

They moved out, step by step leaving the village of Auschwitz behind them. They moved along a road dotted with a few farms before they entered the birch tree forest from which his home camp derived its name. As they reached the camp, Jakub feared he would be recognized as not belonging to the *Kommando*, but the Germans let them through without a question, obviously wishing to return to the warmth of their guardhouse. A few minutes later he was back inside the men's camp. The other members of this *Kommando* were queuing up for some coffee after they stacked the building supplies. Jakub dropped his load off and then set the wheelbarrow against one of the buildings. He waited a bit longer and then slipped away, heading toward the gate out of the men's camp.

A half hour later Jakub entered the ground floor of Crematorium II. He hesitated in the entranceway, closing his eyes and taking a deep breath, then he plunged forward in search of Roch.

He located the leader in the basement. He was pushing carts of clothing up the ramp. The man nodded to another prisoner to take over for him and then, after making sure of the location of the guards, he motioned for Jakub to follow him upstairs into the attic where they could talk in private. When they'd checked through the barracks to make sure there was nobody nearby, Roch started asking questions.

"So, you made it safely to Marek?"

"I don't know if *safely* is the right word, but I'm here."

"Tell me what happened," said Roch.

Jakub relayed the harrowing trip to Auschwitz and back. Roch's eyes widened and his face morphed into a mask of concern as he listened to the story.

"I'm sorry, Jakub. I knew it would be dangerous, but we had to get to him."

"I understand," said Jakub. "I'm glad you sent me."

"What was his answer? Will they be ready for us in five days?"

Jakub nodded. "He didn't want to at first, but I convinced him we couldn't wait. They'll be ready."

Roch smiled. "I knew I picked the right person to go. You have a strength about you. A will to survive this that I've rarely seen in others."

How did he know that? What did Roch see in him that he didn't see in himself? How much more did Roch see? A new worry. He would think about that some other time.

"I have another important job for you," said Roch. "Something I need to have you accomplish tomorrow or the next day."

"What is that?" Jakub asked.

"Inside the men's camp, near the main gate, there is a barracks that is being rebuilt."

Jakub nodded. "I know it. The one with the partially collapsed roof?"

"Exactly. Inside that building there is a crude workbench that was constructed as a table to hammer things, cut boards, and so on."

"What of it?"

"The bench was really built for another reason. Under the top boards, there is a hollowed-out area. You have to pry the nails out and remove a few of the boards to reach it."

"What's inside?"

"A full SS uniform and a pistol. A loaded pistol."

Jakub whistled. "How did you secure that?"

"I have some friends in the camp who do the laundry. They held back a piece of uniform one item at a time over a few months. Nobody complained, just assuming the items had been misplaced."

"What about the weapon?"

"The pistol was more difficult. But there's a work crew that cleans the SS barracks. One of the men crept into the armory and took the pistol and some ammunition."

"It's miraculous they weren't caught."

"Agreed. But what matters is we have a full uniform and a weapon. When the time comes, we'll outfit one of our better German speakers with it. It might mean the difference between accessing a gate peacefully or having to fight for it."

"When do you want me to try to retrieve it?"

Roch smiled at him. "Not today. I'll get you light duty again and then you can get a night's rest. Do you think you could get through tomorrow?"

"I'll need something to give the guards."

Roch nodded. "We'll take care of that."

"I'll go tomorrow then."

"That will be a great help. We've got a meeting tonight, after supper. I'd like to see you there. Report to the head *Kapo* for now, he'll assign you duties for today. I've already talked to him so he knows what to do."

Jakub shook his hand and then headed back down the ramp. He was surprised to see Tomasz there, pushing another cart. He tried to call out to him but his friend stared stonily ahead, as if he couldn't hear him.

He felt his heart wrench at Tomasz's rebuff, but he couldn't deal with that right now, his mind reeling from all he'd heard. *A pistol and a uniform, hidden in the men's camp*. That was something for him to chew on. Could he risk it? He was supposed to be reporting to the *Kapo* now. It would have to wait, he realized.

He reported and was assigned the task of sweeping out the attic. He set to work, moving among the empty bunks, taking his time. Normally this was a job of no more than an hour, but he'd been given the whole day. There was plenty of time to recover and to mull things over.

He thought of Anna. He wanted desperately to see her. To hear from her, anything. But Tomasz wasn't talking to him, and if Schmidt caught him trying to enter the women's camp . . .

No, he had to be patient. In the coming days he would see Anna, one way or another.

What to do about the new information, though? He felt the hot guilt lancing through him again. He shook it off. This was Auschwitz. He thought of Roch, a sadness filling him. He returned to his sweeping, the bristles ripping against the floor as he whipped the handle this way and that.

The day passed slowly. He was alone in the attic, tired and confused. He let his mind wander, thinking about the past, dreaming that there was no war, no ghetto, no trains to hell. Evening came and the prisoners filtered up to their bunks, picking up their bowls and lining up for their soup. He spotted Tomasz, but the man wouldn't look at him. He wanted to confront him, to explain, to tell him everything, but he let the moment pass. Jakub ate nothing. He sat on his bunk, staring out at the others, these comrades of his, whose lives hung by a string.

It was time. He stood up and made his way to the corner of the attic, finding Roch there with a few of the men. The leader looked up and smiled at him, waving him over.

"Jakub, good to see you." He turned to the others, filling them in on Jakub's journey the night before.

"So we're going in five days," said one of the men.

"Four now," said Roch. "Jakub is going to fetch the other uniform and pistol tomorrow. With that, we'll have three pistols along with twelve grenades."

"That doesn't sound like much," the man said.

"It should be enough," said Roch. "The other *Sonderkommandos* will all act with us. We're going to take the four crematoriums simultaneously. We'll do it just after midnight, when the guard is lightest. After we secure our own areas, we'll attack the women's camp, along with the men from Crematorium III. The other groups will hit the men's camp. We'll have help from inside those sections as well. Finally, the Poles will attack the SS barracks. The Germans will be scrambling, trying to wake up, attacked from several directions. With any luck, we'll have the camp in our hands before they've even had time to react."

"And what if we don't have good luck?" someone asked.

"Then we fight and we take as many of them with us as we can."

"How many Poles will Marek have?" Jakub asked.

Roch shook his head. "I don't know. Less than a dozen, I'll bet."

"A dozen against hundreds of SS," said Jakub. "How can we win?"

"That's why we're hitting them in the middle of the night. By the time they are up and reacting, we should have dozens of weapons and thousands of prisoners in revolt."

"We're going to take terrible casualties," said Jakub. "Even if we're successful."

Roch nodded. "That's likely. But what other choice do we have? If we do nothing, we're all going to die. At least with this, we have a chance, and we'll get a chance to kill some Germans as well."

Another prisoner approached. Jakub started to block him. "Don't worry, Jakub, this is Pawel. He's with us."

Pawel hurried up, glancing at Jakub. "I need a word with you, sir," he said to Roch.

"What is it?"

"Bad news."

"What is it now? Reduced rations? Another selection? Let them do their worst, they only have five days."

"That's the problem sir. We don't have five days," said Pawel.

"What do you mean?"

"We've been betrayed. The Germans know something is up, and they know it involves the *Sonderkommando*."

"How did you find this out?"

"One of our sources in the women's camp, a low number, heard it from a guard."

Roch turned to the group. "We may have to move our plans up."

"There's no time," said Pawel. "They're going to kill all of us first thing tomorrow morning."

Chapter 14
The Plan

October 1944
Auschwitz

"You've done well. Better than I believed you could do."

Hans sat in the camp commander's office, enjoying this moment of triumph. He'd succeeded beyond his wildest expectations. By taking risks, and with a little luck, he'd uncovered and would soon foil the most significant plot in Auschwitz's history.

"You pull this operation off correctly and I'll be recommending you for a promotion in rank, and a commendation."

"Thank you, sir. And my men?"

"By your men, do you mean Dieter?"

Hans laughed. "Among others."

"I suppose that is appropriate. What do you have in mind for your nephew?"

"I'm not sure he's made for Auschwitz. He's a sensitive young man. I had hoped to keep him in the camp for the remainder of the war, but . . ."

The commander nodded. “This work is not for everyone. Still, with this operation wrapped up successfully, I’m sure I can find something for him in Berlin.”

“Would it be too much to ask for a bump up as well?”

“I’ll consider it. Frankly, Krupp, I’ve never seen anything like this.”

Berlin. A promotion. It was everything he’d hoped for. Of course, he would rather keep Dieter here. There might be more opportunities for advancement. But moving him to a place of safety would have to make Hannah happy. And if Hannah was happy, Elsa would be as well. He and his wife would be alone again but he would have done everything he could for her family. It would be a new start for the two of them. And under those circumstances, being alone might be the best thing for them.

“What time is the operation commencing?” he asked.

“Before dawn,” said Kramer.

“Why not now? I could have the men in place in an hour.”

Kramer shook his head. “Too many men are already home for the night. But they’ve been briefed, and we’ve spread the word. Beyond that, I don’t want to raise the attention of the prisoners. There’s no rush. The *Sonderkommando* isn’t planning on moving for another few days. They’ll be storing up energy, their guard will be down.” He shook his head. “No, tomorrow will be best. We’ll run them out of their bunks. They’ll be tired, confused. They won’t have time to respond.”

“Will you just liquidate the leaders?”

“No. The whole *Sonderkommando*. It’s time to liquidate them anyway. We can pull a fresh set off an incoming train.”

“It’s a bit of work to train a new set,” said Hans.

“A necessary evil. It’s good for the guards too. They grow too complacent. Cracking down on a new group toughens them up. And we rid ourselves of these messy relationships that tend to form between our guards and the prisoners. Like Himmler said, *Every German has a favorite Jew.*"

Hans nodded. "I'll assemble the men in the morning and get everything prepared for Crematorium II."

Kramer shook his head. "I want all four *Sonderkommandos* taken down."

Hans looked up in surprise. "We'll be spread pretty thin."

"You should be fine if you hit them before dawn." He looked over his glasses at Hans. "Really, Krupp, this isn't an operation against armed men. They are a bunch of starving prisoners, unarmed and asleep. A half dozen SS per building should get the job done."

"It'll be a lot to train up four new groups of *Sonderkommando* at the same time. Usually we spread the liquidations out, so each group trains a new one before we send them up the chimney."

Kramer nodded. "I agree, but it's unavoidable. Besides, it's long past due. We should have liquidated these men midsummer, but the rush of Hungarians delayed things a bit. The last thing I needed was an incompetent *Sonderkommando* when we were grilling tens of thousands a day. But now—"

"I understand, sir. Don't worry, I'll take care of it," said Hans. "Do you want me to stay overnight and work on the logistics?"

Kramer stood. "No, Hans. Go home and get a decent meal and some sleep. Tell that nephew of yours congratulations from me as well. I'll see you here before dawn."

Hans arrived home for dinner a half hour later. Dieter was already there, along with Elsa and Hannah. They were all smiles. His wife stepped up and put her arms around him, kissing his cheek. "I'm so proud of you," she said.

"It wasn't me," said Hans. "You can thank your nephew here."

"I didn't do anything," said Dieter. "It was—"

"You were part of things," said Hans, clapping him on the back. "And I have news for you."

"What kind of news?" asked Hannah.

"Commander Kramer is going to recommend Dieter for a promotion. And he's going to try to find something for him in Berlin."

"How wonderful!" said Hannah. "But why Berlin?" she asked.

Hans looked at Dieter. "This is a tough camp. I'd love to keep you here, but I know you would prefer a different station."

Dieter returned his look, his cheeks flushing. "Uncle, I will do my duty. You don't have to send me away."

"I told you I wanted to find a good job for you, a safe duty, and something that would move you forward for after the war. That just happened, and now you have a chance for a spot in Berlin. With that posting, you'll be in the center of the action. I have a few connections at headquarters as well. A couple of calls and I'll get you on staff with a colonel, maybe higher. You'll be far back from the front and you'll be doing important work."

Hannah stepped forward and put her arms around Hans. "I can't tell you how thankful we are," she said, kissing his cheek. "And I . . . I want to apologize. I know we weren't very grateful when we arrived. Or frankly, since. But you were right and we were wrong. You've protected us and you've given Dieter a future he would never have had otherwise."

"Think nothing of it," Hans said, beaming inside. "I told you I would do everything I could for him, and for the family."

"Let's celebrate," said Elsa. "I have a little chicken left and some bread." She moved away and opened a cupboard, pulling out a dusty bottle. "And this," she said, showing them a bottle of Cognac. I've been saving this for when we won the war. But if Hans is right—"

"Don't worry about that," he said gently.

"Well, no matter. Even if we were going to win someday, I would still want to open this now. I can think of no better reason to celebrate."

They spent the night feasting, drinking, and laughing. Hans hadn't seen Elsa like this in years. She was almost like when they had first met, her face shining, teasing with him. She held his hand under the table and her warmth filled him with joy. This was everything he'd wanted. Promotion, safety for Dieter, and his wife back in his life.

They stumbled into bed a few hours later. He was a little drunk and it was far too late. He knew he would suffer for this in the morning, but he didn't care. He'd needed this so badly. After all these years, he had his life back, his family, his wife.

She moved under the covers to kiss him. There was an urgency to her actions, a passion he hadn't experienced since everything fell apart so many years ago.

Later, as she curled up against him in the darkness, his mind drifted to that past.

He remembered their early marriage, the poverty and the struggles. That hadn't mattered to either of them. They had each other. They looked forward to a family, a future. He'd won a position in the SS and started moving his way up quickly. Her father, who'd disapproved of the marriage from the start, was forced to admit that his daughter had chosen well.

They'd had a child. Frederick. The apple of his eye. They would raise him in this new Germany, a child of the Third Reich. He was blonde and blue eyed like his mother. A perfect little Aryan child.

One morning he'd gone in to admire his son before work. Something was wrong. His face was blue. His skin cold. He'd died in the middle of the night—not even two. They'd mourned

Frederick's death. The light had gone out of Elsa then. Their friends and family were supportive. They encouraged them to have more children. They'd tried for a year before they went to the doctor. There were tests. The news came back one day: There would be no more little ones. Elsa faded slowly away. She lost her fire and her love, turning in on herself. She only showed emotion now for her sister, and her nephew, who became a kind of surrogate child. The only one she would ever have.

He'd drifted away from her after that. With his new position in the SS, he was admired in those pre-war years. He met a woman and had an affair. That lasted for a few months, but they still lived in a small town. Someone sent an anonymous letter. They'd stayed married, but nothing was ever the same between them.

Then the war had come. Hans was almost thankful to get away. But as the months turned into years, he longed for the old Elsa, for their love. He wanted what family he could have. He'd brought her to Auschwitz, hoping that time had healed some of the wounds. It hadn't. She was cold, distant, angry at being uprooted to this miserable little village in the middle of nowhere. His personal life mirrored his professional one, which was eroding as well. If only there was something he could do.

Then the crisis. His job and his career were ending. He'd had a desperate flash of insight, as if from God. He could save his future, his wife, and his nephew all at the same time. How strange fortune was, to bring him victory at his moment of ultimate defeat. He smiled to himself, his hand resting on Elsa's back. He closed his eyes, dreaming of his future, their future.

He was jerked out of sleep by his alarm clock. He rose and dressed as quietly as he could in the darkness. He expected he would have to wake Dieter, but his nephew was already there in the front room, munching on a little of the bread from the night before. Hans watched him for a moment in the semidarkness. Should he order him to stay behind? This was grim work ahead. It was one thing to lead unsuspecting civilians to their death. It was another to push a *Sonderkommando* into the gas chamber. There would be screaming and pleading. They might have to execute a few of them outside to get the rest to comply. No, he would need him. They were stretched too thin already. Besides, Hans thought, he'd gone through this himself. It wouldn't hurt Dieter to face a little more difficulty. It built character. No, this was good for the young man. He would have him tag along.

"Are you ready?" he whispered.

Dieter nodded.

"Is there any more bread?"

"A bit."

"Bring it with you. We'll have it on the way."

A car appeared. They drove in silence to Birkenau. They arrived a few minutes later, whisking through the main gate. A line of SS was already assembled, machine pistols in their hands, ready for action.

Hans and Dieter stepped out, his nephew moving quickly into the line where he was handed an automatic weapon. Hans located Sergeant Schmidt, who would be leading the operation in Crematorium II. He didn't really like the man. He enjoyed his work too much. He was like a cat, toying with his victims. It wasn't professional and it created problems with the prisoners. The man also had a taste for Jewish skirt. Still, he'd earned this privilege.

"Are you ready?" he asked the sergeant.

"Yes, sir."

"I want you to take Crematorium II yourself. That's the heart of this thing."

"I'll take care of everything personally, sir."

"And take my nephew with you."

Schmidt raised an eyebrow. "How involved do you want him to be?"

"I want him to see it, but don't put him in the thick of things. I'd prefer he not have to shoot anyone himself."

"I understand, sir," said Schmidt, smiling wryly. "So, you expect some resistance?"

"There always is. And this group was ready to revolt. Be prepared for anything, Sergeant. This isn't the usual liquidation."

"Don't worry, sir. We have it handled. How soon until we have replacements?"

"Kramer didn't share that with me. But a few trains are coming in today. We should be able to cull out enough units to form a new group."

"Will you let me make the selection?" asked Schmidt. "These doctors are good at spotting the healthy ones. But they don't know men the way I do. I know just the kind we want for the *Sonderkommando*."

Hans considered that. "It's an unusual request but I think I understand. Which doctor is on selection this week?"

"Endress, I think."

Hans nodded. "I'll talk to him. I'm sure he won't mind."

"Are you coming with us?" asked Schmidt.

"Negative. I've got a briefing with Kramer. I want to finish up my report on how the intelligence was put together. Please find me as soon as you're finished. How long do you think it will take?"

"They'll all be dead in an hour, sir."

"Excellent. Good work, Schmidt. I'll see you in a little while."

Hans smiled at Dieter and then returned to his office. He made it there a few minutes later and fixed himself some tea. He set to work on his report, choosing his words carefully. He put a little music on so he could relax. He loved Mozart. As he hummed along, he considered how to craft the document. He had to give credit where it was due, but he wanted to emphasize certain aspects of the operation to place himself and Dieter in the most positive light, without overtly appearing to do so. In the distance he heard the pop of a pistol, then another. Things were progressing.

He heard footsteps in the hallway. He checked his watch. Kramer must have arrived. He was early, he noted with a little irritation. He hoped he wouldn't be disturbed until Schmidt had reappeared.

There were more footsteps outside. These were moving rapidly. He sighed and looked up from his report, listening to the echoes. Why were there so many people rustling around at this hour? There was a loud banging at his door.

What now?

"I need to come in," said a voice.

"Enter," said Hans, not looking up. "What do you want?" he asked at last.

"Sir, I need you to come with me immediately. There's been a problem."

Chapter 15
A Surprise at Dawn

October 1944
Auschwitz

They spent the night in the attic of Crematorium II, debating what to do.

"All of our plans have gone awry," said Roch, coming full circle after hours of debate. He looked up at Jakub again, his eyes sharpening. "You're sure you didn't talk to anybody?"

"How can you even ask that?" said Jakub.

Roch shook his head. "I'm sorry. But someone has turned against us." He scratched at his chin. "Unless . . . Is there any way that the Germans might have discovered Marek?"

Jakub shrugged. "There's no way to know that. But they'd already searched the night before and they never came inside his house."

"Were you spotted leaving?"

"No. I don't think so. If I was, wouldn't they have arrested me immediately?"

"Likely. That's likely. I think we have to assume that Marek is still safe, and that he's not the source of the information the Germans now have."

"How do we know they have anything new?" asked Jakub. "This might just be a routine liquidation of the *Sonderkommando*. We know that was coming at some point."

"That's possible," said Roch. "But the timing is too coincidental. We have to assume that someone tipped the Germans off to our plans."

"It doesn't matter who betrayed us, or even if we were betrayed," said Pawel. "The question is whether we can do anything about it."

"You're right, Pawel," said Roch. "We'll have plenty of time to sort out the traitors if we survive this. Right now we have to figure out what to do." He scratched his chin, thinking the problem over. "We have to warn the others," he said at last.

"Is there anything I can do?" asked Jakub.

"Do you think you could get to the other *Sonderkommandos*?" he asked.

"Bah, it's the middle of the night," said Pawel. "They're not going to let him out of here."

"Do you have another plan?" Roch asked. "We have to attempt something."

"I could try," Jakub said. "But I don't have anything else to bribe the guards with."

"Will you make the attempt?"

Jakub hesitated. What did he have to lose? And if he was caught . . . "Yes," he said. "If you can get me something to pay off the guards with."

Roch motioned and another prisoner rushed up. He whispered into the man's ear and a few minutes later he returned with a wad of zlotys. Roch turned to Jakub. "This is the entire savings of the resistance," he said. "We were storing this up to try to obtain another few weapons, but we're out of time."

"When do you want me to go?"

"Now. We don't have a minute to lose. Get word to each of the *Sonderkommando*."

"What if I'm not able to make it to each of them?"

"Do your best. Anything you can do will be progress."

"All right. I'll go now then."

"You're a good man, Jakub. I wish we'd had more time to work together, but sometimes that's not what God has in store for us."

Jakub nodded and turned to leave.

"One last thing."

Jakub's blood froze.

"Go with God, my friend."

Jakub darted away, his emotions a maelstrom. He considered waking up Tomasz. He wanted to clear the air, but there wasn't time. If they made it through this, they would sort things out. If not, it wouldn't matter.

He walked down the stairs and came to one of the entrances to the crematorium. He put his hand in his pocket and clutched the zlotys. He pulled some of them apart, prepared to bribe the guard at the door. He was surprised to find there was nobody there. That was odd. The doors were always guarded at night. Perhaps the German had stepped away for some reason?

He moved out past the building and toward the inner gate into the camp. There would be two SS here. He prayed he knew them and they were used to "cooperating" with him. He wished Tomasz was here. He moved closer. Sure enough, there were two guards here, machine pistols hanging from their shoulders.

"*Halt!*" He heard the command and he froze. A light was flashed in his eyes. "*Ach*, Bak." He was in luck. He recognized the voice. It was one of his regulars. He greeted the man and stepped forward slowly. Jakub explained in broken German that he wanted to get into the men's camp. He reached into his pocket, peeling off some of the zlotys and reaching them out to the guards.

The guard looked at the notes and then spoke rapid German to the other guard. They talked back and forth, their voices rising, as if in some kind of argument. Jakub tried to suppress his fear. He could not follow their conversation. Finally, the first guard turned to him and shook his head. Eventually Jakub understood. Nobody was allowed through the gate. It was *verboten*.

Jakub pressed, trying to hand the cash to the guard, but the man pushed him back. The other German screamed at him and pointed his machine pistol. Jakub raised his hands in the air and stepped slowly backward, keeping his eyes on the guards. When he was about ten meters away, he fled. When he reached the door of the crematorium, he ripped it open and ran inside, collapsing on the ground. He gasped, battling for breath, trying to calm himself down.

"It's all closed up," said a familiar voice. He looked up. Tomasz was standing over him.

"Nobody is getting in or out. A fire is coming. I told you not to get mixed up with those fellows."

"Tomasz, I can explain—"

"No need to tell me anything," said Tomasz, his voice strained. "I don't want to be let in on any of your little secrets. You'd better hurry along now and report to your master. I'm sure Roch will want to give you a treat."

"Tomasz. There's something you need to know. In the morning—"

"In the morning we'll all be dead. Yes, I know. The whole camp knows, Jakub. So much for your big secrets." He looked at Jakub sadly for a few seconds. "You should have stuck with me, my boy." He turned and stomped into the darkness.

"Tomasz!" But his friend was gone. There was nothing he could do right now. How did he know about the liquidation?

Had someone in the attic tipped him off? Or had the Germans? He was so well connected. It didn't matter, he realized. Even with this knowledge, Tomasz was in the same position they all were. He just wished they could have worked through things before the morning.

Jakub thought of Anna. He wanted desperately to see her, just one last time. But he probably never would again. Unless he was lucky . . . He thought bitterly of Schmidt. The bastard had robbed him of his last chance to see her. He was sure the man was relishing that thought. It was just the kind of game he liked to play.

Jakub caught his breath and then climbed the stairs back to the barracks. Snores and coughs thundered through the room. Almost everyone was asleep. Despite Tomasz's words, the men seemed largely unaware of the fate that awaited all of them in the morning. He moved past row after row of bunks until he arrived in the far corner of the room, where Roch was perched with the others. The leader spotted him and his reaction told Jakub he already knew he'd failed. Of course he would know. He'd only been gone a half hour at the most. Not enough time to make it to the other *Sonderkommando* and back.

"What happened?" he asked.

"I was stopped at the gate."

"They refused your bribe?"

Jakub nodded. "It was a regular too. He wanted to take it, I could tell he did, but he argued with the other guard and then refused to let me out. It looks like nobody is going through the fence."

Roch's eyes moved up and down his face.

"I'm sure you did your best," he said at last. "There is nothing we can do. We can't warn the others. We're all on our own."

They waited out the remaining hours before dawn. Roch was stunned at first at his news, and Jakub was afraid the man had given up, but he quickly recovered and turned to preparation for the morning.

"We have one advantage," said Roch. "We know they are coming."

"What good is that going to do?" asked Pawel. "We are what? Twenty resistance members? We have two pistols and a few grenades. Against the SS?"

"We are going to fight," said Roch. "We are lucky. We are on the edge of the camp. If we can overpower the guards and make it through the outer gate, we will be free."

"Free," scoffed Pawel. "We won't be *free*. "We'll be prisoners of the greater Auschwitz camp. We still will be inside the fence line, with more SS to get through. Even if we breached the outer gate, what then? We are weak, unarmed. We have no clothes. The Germans will be rushing in reinforcements. We'll be slaughtered."

"We're going to be slaughtered in the morning, anyway," said Jakub.

Roch nodded. He stepped over and clapped Pawel on the shoulder. "You speak the truth, my friend." He turned to the group. "Let's be honest with ourselves. What real chance have we ever had? Nothing more than a sniff of a future. Even if the entire camp had risen, the Germans would have come in their thousands with tanks and airplanes to hunt us down. We are not an army. Most of us would have been killed or recaptured. But a few might have escaped them. We would have fought them."

He stood straighter now. His eyes on fire. Jakub felt the defiance washing over him. "We have the same chance now. We can overcome the guards. Take some prisoners. Perhaps kill some of them. If we make the gate, we can rush into the woods, look for some isolated houses, seek out food, supplies, perhaps more weapons. Then we can worry about the outer gate. Some of us might make it through. And if even just one of us survives, all of this will have been worth it."

Jakub nodded, admiring Roch. He'd never heard him like this. He'd known the man for a long time now, but only from a distance. Roch wasn't talking about earthly pleasures. About doom, death, and fate. He wanted to defy these things, even for just an instant of time. He was right. If they were going to die, they should go out with a fight, even if they didn't make it. Even if nobody on the outside ever learned about what they had done here. His thoughts were conflicted though. Was this his only way out?

"What do we do next?" asked Jakub, trying to mask his emotions.

Roch smiled at him. "We prepare. I have a plan."

A little later Jakub lay in his bunk, wide awake. Roch had sent everyone back to pretend they were sleeping. He went over everything in his head again. The room was pitch-black. Dawn was still some time away.

He heard shouts below, followed by the clatter of boots on the stairway. An electric tension ripped through him. They were here. The lights flipped on abruptly and the pounding cadence of German rang down on them. Jakub blinked, his eyes burning from the light. He could hear rustling all around him, men shuffling out of their bunks, murmuring to each other. Most of them didn't know what was coming. Roch had deemed it too risky to tell the others.

They were ordered downstairs and the men moved together, whispering, some linking arms. Nobody resisted. Jakub could smell the terror of his brothers. The Germans had never woken them up like this before. Anything out of routine in Auschwitz was to be feared. The unusual was often the end.

They were herded down to the basement, to the dressing area. Jakub saw Schmidt there, along with a half dozen other guards. All armed with machine pistols. He recognized Dieter among them. He tried to make eye contact but the guard was looking the other way. He glanced over and saw Tomasz, standing a few meters from him. He was staring straight ahead.

Ignoring Jakub. Tomasz always had a plan. What did he intend to do? Or had he given up? His friend had always joked about going up the chimney. Perhaps he thought it was all over and there was nothing he could do.

Schmidt screamed for the *Sonderkommando* to be quiet. "Listen up," he ordered, switching to Polish. "You've been ordered to give the gas chamber a thorough cleaning," he said, his eyes dancing.

"All of us?" shouted someone skeptically.

"Well, it's a big job," said Schmidt. "And we want it done correctly."

"You're going to kill us!" shouted another prisoner in the crowd.

"Now, now," said Schmidt. "There is no reason to be afraid. This labor will only take a little while. Then you'll be on to your next assignments."

"And what if we resist?" the first man asked.

Schmidt smiled. "All the better." He whipped his machine pistol around and fired a burst into the prisoner's chest. The sound was thunderous in the narrow confines. The man fell backward into the arms of the others behind him. Another inmate fell with him. The Germans raised their weapons and screaming rocked the chamber.

Death was here.

Chapter 16
The Chamber

October 1944
Auschwitz

The basement of Crematorium II erupted in chaos. The smell of burnt powder stung Jakub's nose and the smoke scorched his eyes. Men shoved each other and scrambled away from the Germans, from the entrance to the gas chamber. The screams of the wounded added a hellish encore to the scene.

Jakub sought out Roch, but he couldn't see him amidst the jostling throng. This wasn't the plan. They had intended to shoot first, but Schmidt had acted too quickly. Now, in the smoke and the chaos, how could the resistance members possibly respond together?

He finally spotted Roch across the room, rushing toward the wounded, grabbing men and trying to rally them. Jakub glanced at Schmidt. The guard was standing, smoke still wafting from his machine pistol, a fixed grin on his face as he relished the mayhem around him. The other guards were nearby, weapons raised but not firing, protecting their commander.

Dieter was there too, but his arms were at his side. The young guard's mouth was open and his face was a mask of fear.

Jakub started toward Roch. He had to get closer. The order to return fire had to be mere seconds away, and he had a part to play—if he chose. Despite his efforts, he could make little headway. The crush of bodies was incredible, and he was trying to fight his way upstream, as the prisoners fled away from the Germans to the far side of the room. He felt hands on his arms and a familiar voice.

"Where do you think you're going?"

He looked up to find Tomasz there. "Leave me alone!" he demanded.

"There's nothing but death that way!" Tomasz shouted.

"We're all going to die if we don't fight them," said Jakub.

"Who's been telling you that?" said Tomasz.

"They're going to kill us all."

"Stay with me," said Tomasz.

Jakub hesitated. What was he saying? He turned his head back, looking at Tomasz for a moment. He twisted hard, pulling his arms away. "I have to go," he said. "Come join me!"

Tomasz's face was sad and he glanced toward the Germans. "I'm sorry, Jakub. But I'm not going that way."

"I have to!" shouted Jakub.

Tomasz tried to take his arm again. "Please, Jakub," he pleaded. "You've got to stay with me." His voice was almost a whisper.

"I'm sorry," Jakub said, ripping away from him. He rushed into the crowd, shoving first one man aside then another.

He made some progress against the tide. He steered toward Roch but he was still meters away. The leader had reached the wounded men by now and was leaning down, trying to help them. What was Roch thinking? They had no time for that. It was almost too late. Jakub chanced a glance at Schmidt. The guard still had that self-satisfied smirk on his face but it couldn't be long before he herded them into the gas chamber.

Jakub reached the front of the men. He could move quickly now. He turned to his right and sprinted forward. He was less than ten meters away from Roch.

"Bak!" He heard the voice and he froze. "Bak, come here." His heart sank. Turning slowly, he saw that Schmidt had focused on him. The guard's grin was turned up and his eyes were fixated on him like an eagle locked on to his prey.

"Now, Bak!"

He turned and moved slowly toward Schmidt, his hands in the air. The guard took a few steps forward, meeting Jakub out of earshot of the rest of the Germans. He leaned his head in and moved his lips close to Jakub's ears, speaking in Polish.

"Do you know what is going to happen to you today?"

Jakub didn't answer.

"I'll bet you do. You were always the wise one. Let me tell you something else before that happens. I just wanted you to know how sweet Anna has been. Oh, she resisted at first, but then she gave in. She doesn't even want to see you again."

"You're lying," Jakub whispered back with gritted teeth. "You were bribed not to touch her."

Schmidt laughed. "Do you think I care about bribes? We split up your money among ourselves and laughed about it," he whispered. "Did you truly think you had power over me?" He threw his head back and laughed. "I just wanted you to know the truth before you die. But don't worry. Anna will be in good hands. At least until I'm done with her. Then I'll escort her to the gas chamber myself. Tonight I'll tell her what happened to you. Although I doubt she'll care."

"You're lying," Jakub repeated, but there was a hollowness to his words. What if Schmidt was telling the truth? He'd assumed he'd saved Anna from the Nazis, but how could he know? He looked toward Dieter but he was still frozen, eyes fixated out into space above the crowd.

"I don't believe you," he whispered.

"Yes, you do. Because you know I'm telling you the truth. Now go, little Jew."

Schmidt shoved him and Jakub fell back, crashing into some of the other men. He wanted to find a weapon, to go after Schmidt, but there was no time, and he was sure if he charged Schmidt he would be shot down long before he reached the man. Knowing he only had seconds left, he rushed to find Roch.

Jakub reached the resistance leader. He nearly slipped. Looking down, he saw the growing pool of blood on the floor. Roch was kneeling, his arms around the inmate. The man was already dead. There were two more down near him, both with gunshot wounds.

"Roch!" he whispered, trying to get the leader's attention. Jakub reached down and shook his arm, finally getting him to look up.

"We have to do this now!" said Jakub. He could see the intense sadness in Roch's eyes. "We have no more time," he said.

He was afraid for a moment that Roch was beyond caring, but he saw recognition in his eyes. The leader nodded and pulled himself to his feet.

"Block the Germans from seeing me," he ordered. Jakub moved around so that Schmidt and the others could not see what he was doing. Reaching down, Roch felt around on the man's body. Finding what he was looking for, he reached inside the man's shirt and retrieved a 9mm pistol. The handle and barrel were coated with sticky red liquid. He handed it to Jakub.

Jakub took the weapon, his skin revolting against the tacky warm substance coating the handle. "What now?" he asked.

Roch looked around. There were a few more resistance members clustered near them, although most were lost in the jumble of the crowd.

"Now we act," said Roch. He reached into his own shirt and drew the other revolver.

"Where are the grenades?" asked Jakub.

Roch shrugged. "I don't know," he said, looking down at the pistols. "We are going to have to depend on these."

This was hopeless. They had two pistols against six Germans on the alert and armed with automatic weapons. Jakub turned, beginning to raise the weapon. If he was going to die anyway, he wanted to take Schmidt with him.

"Not now," hissed Roch.

Jakub turned back to him. "Why not?"

"We're too far away," he said. "We need to get closer."

Jakub slipped his pistol into his pocket. He turned to face the guards. They were still watching the mad scrambling in front of them but it seemed Schmidt was satiated now. The sergeant turned and whispered something to the other Germans, who fanned out to his left and right. They began shouting for the prisoners to move into the gas chamber itself. Jakub turned to Roch, who nodded toward the doorway. Surely, he wasn't suggesting they step inside?

But that was exactly what Roch intended. Without another glance at Jakub he moved toward the entrance of the death chamber, as other men followed him. They shuffled slowly, woodenly, as if most of them accepted what was about to happen to them. Jakub followed the mob, confused but not knowing what else to do.

He stepped into the killing room. The ceiling was low. The space extended thirty meters to the far wall. Pillars stood like sentinels guarding the space. They were hollow and surrounded by wiring. There was an unholy aura about the place, as if the hundreds of thousands of men, women, and children who had perished in this very room were crying out for vengeance.

Jakub sought out Roch, who had stopped about a third of the way into the chamber. He was surrounded by a few other resistance members now. They'd regrouped after the chaos of the undressing room. Perhaps that's what Roch had intended. They could attack the Germans now, if they hurried.

"Just wait a moment," said Roch.

What could he possibly be waiting for? Almost everyone was in now. Jakub could already see Schmidt at the door, hurrying along the last few stragglers. Roch was watching the sergeant intently, his mouth half open as if he was going to give the order to attack.

"Roch, we have to—"

"Just a second."

"They're going to shut the door!" insisted Jakub.

"They won't without—"

Schmidt stepped out of the chamber and slammed the door shut. They had waited too long. They were going to die here, without a fight.

Jakub stared at the ceiling, waiting for death to come.

Chapter 17
The Lockdown

October 1944
Auschwitz

Anna lay in her bunk, pressing against the woman next to her for warmth. It was still some time before dawn. There was no blanket, no mattress, no pillow. Coughing filled the room. She could hear crying and praying. The sounds of the night in Auschwitz.

Her stomach was still on fire. She felt the waves of nausea creeping up to her throat. She fought down the feeling, her mind a wretched agony, trying to determine what to do after the hell she'd experienced the last couple of days. Worst of all, she didn't even have Urszula to talk to. To her surprise and sorrow, her friend had been transferred to another part of the camp while she was away.

The hospital. She was sure she was a dead woman when Schmidt had taken her there. What had come next was as unexpected as anything that had ever happened to her. She was so sure she was going to be killed on the spot, but somehow she'd been saved. *Saved for what?* she wondered.

Where was Jakub? The thought passed her mind for the thousandth time. How could he abandon her at this moment of crisis? The brittle scrap of hope she'd clung to these many months had been torn from her. She'd given everything to him. He'd supported her, made this hell she lived in bearable, survivable. And now he had abandoned her, just like Schmidt said he had.

She remembered him pursuing her. She hadn't wanted a protector. She would never give her body to someone again simply for a little food. She would rather die. He'd persisted, and over time she had decided to give him a chance, to spend some time talking to him, learning about him. They'd walked and talked. He'd lost all his family, of course, just like her. He told her about his past, and although they came from different cities, they might have grown up in the same family.

He wanted more than friendship. She knew that. He was the right kind of man. A man she could spend her life with, have children with. But there was a condition she would require, no matter what—Auschwitz or no Auschwitz. She told him about it one day. To her surprise, he said he'd expected it of her. He asked a few questions and then he agreed.

And so it was, that one day, in an empty portion of a barracks in the women's camp, Anna and Jakub had married—the ceremony performed by a rabbi. He'd had to bribe the guards to look the other way. It must have cost him dearly. She'd loved him for it, and for his commitment to her when it would have been so easy to find someone else who would do everything he wanted for a loaf of bread. He'd told her he didn't want anyone else and he wouldn't want her any other way.

They had lived that way, as secret husband and wife, separated by the wires, existing in a hell that could take either or both of them in an instant. She'd carried on with her smuggling. It was a terrible risk but she had to do something for the chance of freedom. She'd kept it from Jakub, knowing he would join in his own time as well. That was the kind of man that he was.

Then her world had fallen apart. She was pulled aside by that monster Schmidt. Taunted about Jakub. He had forsaken her, the guard informed her. Jakub had sold her to Schmidt and would not be coming back. How could that be true? She didn't believe it, but in this inferno anything was possible. She had learned this information right before the real nightmare began. Now she faced the horror of her future without Jakub, without her husband. Was he really gone forever?

She had to do something, had to know. What about Tomasz? She had seen him from a distance, walking back toward the fence. She'd called to him but he'd kept moving, as if he couldn't hear her or had chosen not to. In her weakened condition, she'd been unable to reach him in time.

She had to track down Jakub's friend. That's what she would do. She would talk to Tomasz and find out what was going on. She would tell him about Schmidt, about the trauma and terror she had undergone since she last saw Jakub. Surely Tomasz would take care of things. He always did. A calmness washed over her for the first time in days. She just needed to hear from Jakub. To tell him what she'd been through and find out, she prayed, that Schmidt had lied to her, that something else was stopping him from coming. Yes, Tomasz was the answer.

First, she would have to make it through another day. Her sickness was worse. She'd barely made it through her workday yesterday. She didn't know today if she even had the strength to walk all the way to the Union Factory, let alone to labor there for fifteen hours. She steeled herself. She would survive. No matter what it took, she would make it there this morning and she would work all day. She would keep her back straight and her eyes on her duties. She would survive until they returned tonight, and then she would seek out Tomasz and tell him what was going on.

She felt the fire in her stomach again and this time she knew she couldn't fight it down. She rushed out of her bunk, out of the barracks and to the nearby latrine. Reaching the open hole that served as a toilet, she fell to her knees, gagging and heaving as she vomited violently into the foulness below. She felt like she was going to die.

Anna made her way back to her bunk. In the darkness she decided what she must do. She had to write to Jakub. Even if he had deserted her, she needed to communicate with him one more time. There was so much to tell him about what had happened to her. She tried to go back to sleep but her thoughts were racing. She gave up on any more rest and instead concentrated on forming a message for him, the words burning themselves in her mind. She felt the tears streaming down her cheeks. When she was done, she was sure she had to write the real message to him.

But how to get it to him? She could wait until tonight and try to track down Tomasz. She would do so if nothing else came up. However, there were always men coming into the camp. Carpenters making repairs or building bunks. Orderlies bringing medical supplies to the women's hospital. She had never tried to communicate with these men, but perhaps she could convince one to carry a message for her. She wasn't sure about the logistics of getting into the *Sonderkommando*, but perhaps one of them had access and would be willing to help her? Yes, she would try that in the morning before they left for the factory. If she didn't see anyone then she would wait for Tomasz tonight. Either way, Jakub would hopefully have her message by the end of the day. She was terrified of what he might reply. But she had to know.

The barracks grew imperceptibly brighter. Dawn was near. She steeled herself for the morning. She would need a miracle to walk all the way to the factory. She would have to seek out

Estusia, who perhaps could help her if she faltered. *One more day*, she willed herself. She must concentrate on the hour, on the minute. She'd carried herself through the camp this way. Those that looked too far ahead or, God forbid, too far into the past, were already dead.

In the distance she heard a crack, then another. Gunshots, she realized. These weren't unfamiliar sounds in Auschwitz, but rarely before the prisoners were properly up and about. She felt a rustling next to her, and a rising symphony of whispers played through the building as the women wondered out loud what might be happening out there in the camp.

Minutes later the block wardress flipped on the lights and in her German-laced Polish, ordered them out of bed. Estusia was there, a smile on her face. "How are you this morning?" she asked Anna.

"I'm well."

"You're far from that. But don't you worry. I'll be with you every step today. I'll make sure nothing happens to you."

"Thank you," said Anna. "There is something else I need."

"What is that?"

"Do you still have a little paper?"

Estusia's eyes narrowed. "You're not writing to that dog?"

Anna nodded.

"I won't allow it. Let him perish in his own stew. He doesn't deserve to hear from you ever again."

"I have to, Estusia. Please, I know you don't understand, but I must tell him what's happened. Just so he knows."

Estusia thought about that for a moment. "You're right," she said at last. "The bastard deserves to know what has happened to you. Let him take that up the chimney with him when they shove him in the gas chamber one day."

"Estusia, please."

"I won't apologize. I will bring you some paper," she said. "For you, not for him."

"You're a good friend," said Anna. "More than I deserve."

"In here, we must all help each other. We're treading water in an ocean of death. We must fight to keep our heads up."

"Mine is already under." Anna laughed grimly.

"None of that talk," ordered Estusia. "We will get through this too."

"You may, but I don't see a future for myself anymore. I have a death sentence."

"There are always solutions."

Estusia brought Anna a little slip of paper and a pencil. "I'll bring you some breakfast in a minute. Hurry up now and write what you need to send to him. Keep an eye out for the wardress. At best she'll confiscate your note. At worst . . ."

"I'll watch for her."

Anna took the paper and leaned over the bunk. Her stomach burned and she had to lean her head against one of the supports for a few moments, fighting down another round of nausea. She finally was able to concentrate and she began writing, the words flying onto the paper. She remembered everything she'd written in her mind early this morning, and by the time Estusia brought her "breakfast," which was no more than a cup of lukewarm barley coffee, she was already done.

"What are you going to do with that?" asked Estusia.

Anna told her the plan.

Estusia shook her head. "It's too dangerous to approach someone you don't know. Better to wait for Tomasz."

"I don't want to wait," insisted Anna.

Estusia looked as if she was going to argue with her, but apparently decided against it. "Be careful then," she said. "And you'd better hurry. We'll be leaving soon."

Anna set aside her cup of coffee, untouched, and pulled herself to her feet. She shuffled forward, first one step, then another. She looked around, making sure the block wardress was nowhere nearby. She reached the entrance and stepped out into the crisp morning air, her body cringing from the cold that seeped through her thin dress. Clouds pressed the sky, releasing a misty rain on the camp.

Anna was surprised. Usually by this time there was already activity, groups of women marching here and there to work assignments, the odd male or two carrying a pass and moving supplies into the camp. But the outside was deserted. She heard the sharp cry of a woman's voice and she looked up. An SS guard was sprinting up to her, shouting and pointing back at the door. Anna, surprised by the intensity of the woman, stepped back inside. The door was slammed shut behind her.

"What's going on?" asked Estusia, moving up to Anna.

"I don't know," she said.

"What did the German want?"

"She ordered me back into the barracks. There's something going on. There wasn't anyone out there," said Anna. "It's like the camp was deserted. No women, no men."

"A lockdown," said Estusia. "I wonder if those shots we heard earlier have something to do with it."

Anna's plan had failed. At least for now. Nobody was coming into the camp or leaving. She'd heard of these lockdowns before, which might last for hours, or even days. For now, she was isolated and trapped. There would be no way to reach Jakub.

Chapter 18
For This Moment

October 1944
Auschwitz

Screams. Jakub's mind reeled. They were in the chamber of death and the door was closed. Friends clung to one another. He'd played out this moment in his mind so many times. He'd always expected to end up here, that this moment would be the end of him. He knew the death would be agonizing, twenty minutes spent gasping for air, fighting against the cyanide gas that would fill his lungs. He glanced at the square fenced pillars, waiting for the Nazis above to drop the cylinders of prussic acid down through the traps above. He closed his eyes, praying, thinking of his parents, his siblings, his darling Anna.

The moment didn't come, at least not yet. He heard a shouting and a beating on the door. Something had stopped the Germans from moving forward. He opened his eyes, looking around.

And then he saw it. This was why Roch had waited. Amongst the sea of striped prisoners, he spotted a dash of green. One of the SS was inside with them. He'd lost his cap but Jakub recognized the glasses, the boyish features. It was Dieter.

"Pull him away from the door!" shouted Roch. "They won't kill us as long as he's in here!"

Jakub wondered if that was true. What was one more dead human to the Germans? Would they care if one of their own was lost?

But Roch was correct. The door opened and Schmidt was there. He brandished his machine pistol and screamed at them to release Dieter. But the young guard was ten meters or more into the chamber, and he was surrounded by a press of inmates who were shouting at Schmidt, arms waving, blocking his access.

Schmidt fired a burst into the crowd. Several men fell, the gunfire deafening in the confined space. Screams filled the aftermath, and smoke obscured Jakub's view.

"Now!" Roch screamed. He and Jakub and Pawel pushed forward, shoving men out of the way trying to reach the front of the chamber. There was a scuffle ahead. Some prisoners had crashed into Schmidt and were battling with the guard. The machine pistol fired again, this time at the ceiling. A prisoner ripped the weapon out of Schmidt's hands. The sergeant broke free and sprinted out the door. The prisoner rushed to the threshold, shoving his leg into the doorway, preventing the Germans from closing them in again. He raised the machine pistol, fumbling with the weapon, and fired a few rounds.

Jakub reached the front. He could see the undressing room now. Schmidt was nowhere to be seen and must have escaped. He looked over to the man holding the weapon. It was Tomasz.

"My friend, you've saved us," said Jakub.

His friend looked stunned. His face was ghost white and he opened his mouth a couple of times as if to speak, but the words wouldn't form.

Roch stepped up and clapped Tomasz on the back. "Jakub's right," he said. "You're a hero, Tomasz. I didn't think you had it in you."

Jakub clapped his friend on the back as Roch removed the weapon. "That was the bravest thing I've ever seen anyone do," he said. "Thank you, Tomasz."

Tomasz still refused to speak, staring out the door where Schmidt had made his escape.

"We don't have time to stand here!" Pawel shouted. "What are we going to do now? They'll be back any second!"

Roch looked around, getting his bearings. "You're right," he said. He handed the machine pistol to one of the men. "We need to get out of here and secure the undressing room." He turned to Jakub and Tomasz. "Bring the wounded out. Jakub, give your pistol to Pawel here." The leader looked out over the crowd, cupping his hands so he could make himself heard. "We're going to fight them! If you have a weapon, guard the entrances! Everyone out of the gas chamber while there's still time! Move!"

The men shuffled forward, streaming around Tomasz and Jakub, who were assessing the wounded. One man was dead and one was wounded. The injured inmate had a gunshot to the chest and blood pumped out of an angry hole in frothy scarlet fountains. The prisoner's back was arched, and his limbs shook. His eyes were wide open, staring through them to the ceiling. He screamed as he writhed in agony.

"What are we supposed to do with him?" asked Tomasz. "I'm no orderly."

"I don't know," said Jakub, looking down in dismay at the man.

"There's nothing that can be done," said Tomasz. "I don't think he even knows what's going on. He won't last long. Look," he said, pointing down. The man's body shook even harder and he started to choke. He gave a violent jerk and the air in his throat rattled, then he was still. "Let's go," said Tomasz, rising and moving toward the door.

"What about his body?" asked Jakub.

"No time for that. Besides, there will be plenty more of those before this is over. Unless we are very lucky, we will all be back here before long, if our SS friends out there don't just blow up the whole building and be done with us."

"They were going to kill us anyway," said Jakub. "At least now there's a chance."

"If it weren't for your glorious leader, none of this would have happened," said Tomasz.

"What do you mean?"

"Why do you think they're liquidating us?" said Tomasz. "They have spies everywhere. They learned about this pathetic revolt and decided to take action."

"How do you know that?" asked Jakub, keeping his expression blank.

Tomasz shrugged. "There's no other explanation. Now let's get out of here and join the others. You've dragged me into this thing so I might as well make the best of it."

"It's good to have you with us," said Jakub. "I never wanted you to feel betrayed by me."

"Not betrayed, my boy. Just disappointed. I always knew there was a hero lurking inside you somewhere. I've done my best to stifle it, but I guess it was going to come out at some point, no matter what."

Jakub didn't feel like a hero. "You're the man of the hour," he said. "You took Schmidt's weapon. You nearly killed him."

"Nearly isn't going to be good enough," said Tomasz. "We haven't seen the end of Schmidt." He turned and gestured for Jakub to follow. They moved out of the gas chamber and into the undressing room. Inmates milled around in the confined space, forming up in little circles and talking to each other. Jakub scanned the crowd until he spotted Roch.

"There he is," said Jakub.

"You go ahead," said Tomasz.

"You're not coming with me?"

"I'll join the fight but I'm not going to take orders from Roch."

"What is it about him that you don't like?"

"I don't know exactly. Maybe it's because he was an officer," said Tomasz. "Part of the establishment. Part of everything I hated in Warsaw. Hell, he might as well have been a policeman. Go along now. I'm not mad at you. Not anymore. You tell me what the plan is, and I'll help as best I can."

Jakub shook his hand. "Thank you, Tomasz. Thank you for everything."

"Sure thing, kid. Now go figure out how we're getting out of this."

Jakub left him and waded his way through until he finally reached Roch. As he neared the group, he caught the eye of Dieter, who was sitting on the floor, mouth gagged and hands and feet tied. Dieter's eyes were filled with fear, and he stared questioningly at Jakub. He hurried his pace, turning his head away. He couldn't deal with that right now.

Roch looked up from what he was doing and saw Jakub. He motioned him over, a grim grin on his face.

"How are the wounded?" he asked.

"Dead," said Jakub. "There were only two hit. One was already gone when we got there. The other was dying. What are we going to do? Are we going to try to escape the camp?" he asked.

Roch shook his head. "We've been talking about that. I don't think we're going to make a run for it yet. Although, there's no way to get word to our Polish friend in Auschwitz village, or to others in the camp for that matter; everyone in Birkenau must know something is going on by this time. Our brothers and sisters in the camp will join us if we can hold out long enough. With any luck, Marek will hear the noise too, or he'll learn about what's going on from rumors in the town. So, we've got to stall for time. We need to take the rest of the building. If we control the whole structure, we can wait this out and see if the camp rises. If it does, we won't need to run, we can fight."

"Fight? Do you mean with these two pistols?" asked Jakub incredulously. "There must be a few hundred guards. They'll overrun us in minutes and kill us all."

"We have the machine pistol also," said Roch. Then he gestured to Dieter. "And we have him. With any luck they'll hesitate to put a German life in danger by a hasty attack. If they take time to plan something more intricate with hopes of saving our SS friend here, then there is more time for the other cells in the camp to join the fighting. If everyone rises, we'll overrun the guards and take Birkenau. It should take them some time to organize. We've caught them off guard and it's early. We should have a couple hours before they can even get their full force into position."

Jakub wanted to believe Roch, that there was some chance they could capture the camp, but it seemed like some kind of madman's dream. He thought they should escape while they had a chance.

Roch noticed his expression. "It is what it is, my friend," he said, as if reading his mind. "Don't worry about tomorrow. Don't even fret about an hour from now. Live for this moment."

"Why?"

"Because, Jakub. Right now, in this very moment, you're free. We're free. No matter what else happens, we've fought those bastards and driven them away."

He was right. It struck Jakub like a thunderbolt. For the first time since the war had begun, more than five years ago, he was not living under the thumb of the Nazis. They'd controlled his life at home, in the ghetto, and now here, more than ever. But right now they had no power over him. Right now he was free.

Roch nodded. He gave Jakub the pistol back. "I want you to have one of these," he said.

"Why? There are others who know more about fighting."

"Because I trust you," said Roch. "I knew from the start that one day you would join us, and that you would help save us when the time came."

The words sliced through Jakub. He nodded, forcing a smile. "What are we going to do now?" he asked.

"We're going to take the rest of the building."

"How?"

"You and I will lead a group up one stairway, and Pawel with the machine pistol will lead the other group. We'll take that guard with us, directly behind us. If we encounter any resistance, we'll show him to them. Hopefully they'll back off. If not, we fight."

Jakub nodded. Roch turned and explained the plan to the rest of the resistance group. They, in turn, circulated quickly through the undressing room, passing on information until everyone knew the plan.

"We're ready," said Roch at last. One of the men pulled Dieter up violently. He reached down and untied the guard's ankles. Jakub avoided the German's eyes. He was thankful the young man's mouth was gagged.

Roch waited a few more minutes until the inmates had closed in, pressing near. "Are you prepared?" he asked Jakub.

Jakub checked the pistol, making sure the safety was off. He nodded.

"Let's go then," said Roch, turning and moving quickly toward the staircase. Jakub followed, his weapon aimed over Roch's shoulder. They scrambled up the first flight of steps where there was an abrupt 180-degree turn. Roch wanted to reach the second landing before the Germans would have time to prepare. This was the most dangerous moment. If there was a guard above, weapon at the ready, he would assuredly kill Roch as soon as he turned the corner.

The leader didn't hesitate. Outpacing Jakub, he tore around the corner and kept going. There were no gunshots. Jakub made it to the turn and moved up to the second flight. Roch was already near the top. Jakub stomped up the stairs and reached the landing. He expected gunfire but there was nobody there.

Roch moved quickly around the space, darting in and out of the bunks, looking for Germans as more men moved up. In another minute he was back. "It's empty," he said.

Pawel appeared, confirming the same news. Roch took a deep breath. "The building is ours!" he shouted. There was a tremendous cheer. Jakub clapped and laughed. He felt a slap on his shoulder and turned to see Tomasz there, smiling in approval. Jakub couldn't believe it. They held the building. Now there was a chance.

He heard a shout. An inmate was at the window, yelling and pointing. Jakub rushed to the window and his heart fell. In the distance he could see the fence line. The perimeter was full of SS, standing just outside the wire, weapons at the ready. There were at least a hundred of them. The SS had organized quickly. They were about to attack.

Chapter 19
Course Changes

October 1944
Auschwitz

Hans hurried out of his office and down the stairs into the camp. He jogged after the messenger who was sprinting ahead along the rail line, heading for Crematorium II. Of course, it had to be this *Sonderkommando*, he thought. He couldn't afford problems in any of them, but if something happened to Dieter . . .

He still didn't know what the issue was. He hoped it was nothing—just an overreaction by one of the guards. He reached the end of the rail line a few minutes later and moved toward a cluster of men who were huddled near the gate leading into the perimeter of Crematorium II. There were dozens of SS here now, with more running in from every direction. What in the hell had happened?

Sergeant Schmidt was there, his arm wrapped in a towel. Blood was soaking through and the guard's features were warped by a grimacing combination of pain and anger.

"Schmidt, what's happened?" he asked.

"We moved in to conduct the operation," said the sergeant. "Everything was going according to plan. I had to shoot a few of them."

Hans nodded. "As we discussed. So?"

"That seemed to work well and we herded them into the gas chamber. They were worked up, as I'm sure you can imagine."

"That's no surprise," said Hans. "They knew what would be coming next."

"That wasn't the problem. Somehow, in the confusion, one of the guards ended up in the chamber with them."

"What idiot allowed that to happen?" Hans was furious.

"It was . . . it was your nephew, sir. I'm sure he didn't realize what he was doing. It's perfectly understandable. He just started the job, after all."

Hans felt an electric surge course through his body. Dieter in the gas chamber! "What did you do next?"

"Well, we couldn't liquidate them under those circumstances," said Schmidt.

"Of course not."

"So, I opened the door back up. I was in the process of extracting your nephew when some of the bastards grabbed me. They wrestled my gun away. I had no choice but to retreat. One of them fired at me. I thought I was a dead man but fortunately he only hit me in the forearm."

"Where is Dieter now?"

Schmidt avoided his eyes. "I don't know, sir. He didn't come out."

Hans felt his hands shaking. He controlled his anger. "Is he dead?"

"I . . . I don't know, sir. I don't think so. When I retreated, he was fine. I can't imagine they would kill him. He's a hostage, their best chance for cutting a deal. I knew you wouldn't want anything dangerous to happen, so I ordered the rest of our men out of the crematorium and we retreated to here. After that I called a general alarm and sent someone to find you."

Hans knew that if it was anyone other than Dieter, he wouldn't hesitate a moment. He would order the men to attack immediately and if the hostage was killed, so be it. But what was he going to do now? The *Sonderkommando* controlled the crematorium and had at least one weapon. He needed to think about this.

"Good work, Schmidt," he said at last, more out of something to say in front of the men than with any real feeling. The idiot should have made sure no guards were inside the gas chamber. He should have kept Dieter away from the most dangerous activity. But could he truly blame Schmidt? Hadn't he decided to send his nephew in to give him a little more experience? He cursed himself for that decision. Now he had a hell of a mess. He couldn't afford to let these Jews resist him for any length of time at all. If Kramer arrived and learned what was going on . . . By the same token, he had to get Dieter out safely. What was he going to do?

"Schmidt, go get that looked at," he said. "I'll take things over here. As soon as you've received medical attention, I want you back here. No more than a half hour." The guard nodded and strode away, flanked by two of his men. Hans loathed Schmidt but the man knew everyone in the camp. He knew the personalities of the *Sonderkommando*, who the resistance leaders were, or at least who they might be. He would need the man's insight to make sure he had the best plan possible.

After Schmidt departed, Hans considered the tactical situation further. He needed to get into the crematorium quickly, with a minimum of fuss. He needed a diversion. He considered things for a while and came up with a plan. He gave orders for the guards to gather as many men as possible. He wanted a concentrated force at the gate.

"What about the other *Sonderkommandos*?" one of the men asked.

"They don't know what's going on. Continue with the liquidation. Pull a few men from each one of those groups and get them here as soon as you can." Hans knew this would leave the other units undermanned, but he had no choice. He needed all his forces here.

Schmidt returned a half hour later, as ordered, his hand wrapped in a tightly bound bandage. He still grimaced and Hans noticed approvingly that it did not appear the man had taken anything for the pain. He needed the sergeant's mind clear.

The men filtered in, until he had at least a hundred guards present, all armed with machine pistols. He moved the men into position to his left and right, surrounding the crematorium on two sides. He wanted his force visible, so the *Sonderkommando* knew they were preparing for an attack.

"What's the plan?" asked Schmidt. "It looks like a general assault."

Hans shook his head. "That's what they're expecting now, and what I want them to think. We'll never get into the crematorium without casualties," said Hans. *Or without risking Dieter's life.* "I want you to take a small team. We'll let you in on the far side of the fence and you can approach the building from over there," said Hans, pointing to his left. "There are fewer windows there and we'll make lots of noise over here with machine-gun fire to keep their attention. I want you to get in quickly, neutralize the resistance, and rescue Dieter."

"If he's still alive."

"Yes, if he's still alive." Hans couldn't think about the alternative. If he lost his nephew it would be the end of him. The end of his marriage, his career. Everything would be gone. He sent Schmidt to assemble his team and he stepped away from the men, pacing back and forth as he waited to hear back from the sergeant that he was prepared to proceed.

"Krupp, what's going on here?"

Hans froze. Kramer was here. Why wouldn't the bastard stay in his office and let him do his job?

He turned to the *Kommandant* and put his best face on. "A small problem, sir," he said. "Nothing we can't handle. We're just mopping things up now. I can report it later to you if you'd like."

"Not later, now. What's the issue?"

"Very well. The *Sonderkommando* in Crematorium II became somewhat unruly when they were forced into the gas chamber. They fought back and Sergeant Schmidt decided to call a tactical retreat out of caution. We are preparing to move in and eliminate them right now. All of the other *Sonderkommandos* are being liquidated as we speak, according to the plan." *He hoped to Gott this was true.*

"You have to be joking," said Kramer, his face reddening. "Your men couldn't handle the simple task of herding a few starved and unarmed Jews into the gas chamber?" He looked around. "Well, I suppose it can't be helped. But get this done, Krupp. I want this wrapped up before noon, do you understand?"

Hans nodded. The *Kommandant* stormed off and Hans took a deep breath. He'd been afraid Kramer might stay and take a hand in the operation. That was all he needed. He returned to the problem at hand.

The sergeant returned a few minutes later. He had four men with him. Hans recognized all of them, some of the best men in the camp. "This is your team?" he asked.

"*Ja.*"

"Is five of you enough?"

Schmidt nodded. "It should be, sir. Any more than that and

they'll certainly spot us. It's going to be tough getting in there without attracting notice in the first place."

"Don't worry about that," said Hans. "When you're ready, I'll have some of the men spray the side of the building with fire. That should keep their heads down, at least for a minute or two. Move fast."

"Yes, sir. And if I succeed?"

"You'll be richly rewarded."

The sergeant departed with his fire team, moving along the fence to the left and into the tree line that separated the main camp from the crematorium perimeter. They would have to cut some of the fence to get through. He'd already ordered the electricity shut off this morning. He wasn't pleased they would have to damage some of the wire, but no matter, it wouldn't take that long to replace. They should have it back up in the early afternoon, before they selected a new *Sonderkommando*. Hans relaxed. This was going to work. The Jews weren't soldiers. When he fired at them, they would assume it was the main attack. They would take cover, at least for a little while. They wouldn't expect an attack from another direction. Once Schmidt was inside, the inmates would be stunned by a sudden, violent attack. The Jews should surrender, and Dieter should be captured unharmed. Assuming he was still alive and the Jews didn't do anything unexpected.

Hans watched Schmidt's team move into position in the distance. He turned to one of the guards, preparing to give the order to attack. He closed his eyes for a moment, saying a quick prayer that his nephew was still safe, and that God would protect Dieter.

A horrific explosion rocked his ears, jolting him out of his meditation. The roaring sounded like the tearing of linen. He looked up, expecting the crematorium in front of him to have devolved into an inferno. But the building was untouched. He cranked his head, searching wildly, and there in the distance he saw it. To his right, about half a kilometer away, a cloud of black billowing smoke was filling the sky. *Oh no*, he thought. He heard the shouts of men rushing up to him, begging for orders, staring in shock at the distance. Hans didn't know what had just happened, but one thing was sure, no matter what happened with Dieter, that black cloud was the end of his career.

Chapter 20

A Flicker of Freedom

October 1944
Auschwitz

Jakub stared at the mass of SS. There were more approaching by the minute and they were spreading out with weapons drawn. He turned to Roch, who was also looking out the window. "What are we going to do?" he asked his leader.

"We're doomed," said Pawel. The burly man stepped forward, dragging the captured SS guard with him. Jakub could see the fear in the young man's eyes. He had a black eye. In the chaos, someone had struck him. "The bastards are going to kill us all," said Pawel. "We can't win, but let's at least take this little shit with us."

There were murmurs from several of the prisoners. Another man stepped forward and kicked Dieter in the stomach, doubling him over. Shouts of "Kill him!" erupted from the crowd.

"No!" screamed Roch, staring fiercely around him. "We need

him as a hostage! Nobody will touch him again." He stepped forward, pulling Dieter away. He turned to Jakub. "Look after him," he ordered.

He shoved the guard to Jakub. The young man was a few centimeters taller than him but was so thin he could have passed for a prisoner in the camp. Jakub endured the glares of the other prisoners, his own mind a storm of emotions. *Why me? Of all the people that Roch could have chosen.* He kept his eyes averted from Dieter, but he felt the guard's gaze on him, trying to make contact. He had to find some way out of this.

Roch returned to the window and was watching the gathering of forces. "They're going to come at us soon," he said. "I want that machine pistol at the stairwell. I'll stay at the window with my weapon. When they storm us, I'll take a shot or two at them to try to keep their heads down and slow the attack. When they get inside the building, we must wait until they're near the top of the stairs. When they are almost to the top, hit them with machine-gun fire. Just short bursts, and don't waste any shots. If we can kill one or two and force them to retreat, we'll have more weapons to fight them with."

Despite the strength in Roch's voice, Jakub felt the leader knew they were doomed. Even if they somehow retrieved another weapon or two, what were four guns against a hundred? Still, what choice did they have? He tried to concentrate on the coming battle, keeping his grip on Dieter but refusing to look at the man. What should he do? Could he turn the guard over to someone else? There had to be something. Then he remembered. He had the other pistol. "You there," he said, calling to another member of the resistance. "Hold on to this guard. I need to help Roch at the window."

"What help can you give?" the man asked skeptically.

Jakub flashed the pistol.

The prisoner nodded and moved forward, pulling Dieter roughly away.

"Remember what Roch said," Jakub warned. "No harm is to come to him."

"So long as there's hope," said the man. "But if we are losing . . ." He made a motion of wringing a neck.

Jakub nodded. "Aye. If we're losing."

Jakub turned and moved away, breathing a sigh of relief. He made it to the window and looked out. There were even more SS now and they were massing to attack. He looked at his weapon, checking the safety again. He would follow Roch's lead and try to preserve ammunition. He wasn't sure he would be able to hit anything. He'd never fired anything in his life.

A thunderous explosion erupted in the early morning air. Jakub stared out, his eyes darting left and right. Had they brought artillery in to aid in the assault? And then he saw it, in the distance, a rising cloud of fiery blackness against the gray clouds. He watched for long seconds and then a wild yell escaped his lips—a shout of joy he couldn't contain. He heard the sound echoed in all the men around him. There was fighting in the camp. They weren't alone. Either other inmates were revolting, or the Poles had heard the early gunshots and were attacking the camp. A desperate happiness coursed through Jakub. There was a chance.

The SS below seemed entirely disoriented by the explosion. Most of them had left the fence and were standing in small groups, watching the smoke, ignoring the *Sonderkommando* behind them. Jakub moved over to Roch, who was watching with the same excited joy that he was feeling.

"What does it mean?" he asked.

"It means somebody else is fighting them." The leader turned to Jakub. "Do you realize how this changes things? We aren't going to die here after all. There's no way that this signal can be missed, either by the rest of the camp or by the Poles in Auschwitz. Now we must wait. In a few minutes there will be groups all over the camp springing into action. We just have to hold out here for an hour or so, then we should be able to go on the offensive. Look," the leader said, pointing out at the SS. "They are already scrambling away. The threat of an immediate attack is gone."

"For now," said Jakub.

"Yes, for now. But we must pray it is forever. There's a chance now, my friend. With a little luck, we'll be greeting our Polish friends at the gates of Birkenau before this day is through."

Was that possible? They'd seemed near death just a moment before. Could they truly rise up and take the camp? He imagined large numbers of them, armed, battling the Germans, pushing through the fence line and into the women's camp. He saw Anna there with the other women, cheering for him, running into his arms and together making their way with Roch and Tomasz through the outer fence line, and then into the woods. Safe and free. Whatever happened from then on didn't matter. They would have escaped the dreaded camp, defeated the Germans. They would have a real chance at life. He thought of his father's words to him, the promise he'd demanded. To survive. The notion had seemed little more than a delusional fantasy, but now there was a real chance. But that would leave the problem of Dieter . . .

He felt a hand on his shoulder and he was pulled around. Tomasz was there, whispering in his ear. "Come away and talk to me," he said.

"I can't," he said. "I've got to watch things here. I have one of the pistols."

Tomasz laughed. "You're not going to stop them with that

little toy. Besides," he said, looking out at the milling confusion, "I agree with Roch for once. They won't be back at us, at least for a little while." Tomasz turned and moved away, walking through the bunks and motioning for him to follow. Jakub hesitated for a moment and then stepped away from the window to find Tomasz.

"You have to come with me," whispered his friend when they had found a place to be alone.

"What do you mean?"

"This is doomed. All of these men are going to die."

"But the explosion. The camp is rising."

Tomasz spit on the floor. "You're following that fool again. Listen to me instead." His friend looked at him with intense eyes. "You've trusted me since you came here, Jakub, and I've never done you wrong. You must trust me now. There isn't going to be an uprising. You're listening to a fantasy. The Germans are distracted for a moment, and only for a moment. The only chance we have is to get away from here. If we can make it to the gate, we can find some of my contacts. I can talk to them, bribe them. I'm confident they'll let us pass."

"Tomasz, they came this morning to kill us. You were in the chamber with us. They aren't going to let you go. Our only chance is to stay here and fight."

"You're wrong," Tomasz said, shaking his head. "There was no time this morning. Now there's a pause. The Germans will take a little while to regroup. If there's any chance of us surviving, we've got to get away from these fools and make our way to the Germans."

Jakub couldn't believe his friend's words. What possible chance was there in that? Still, in one part of his mind, the doubts were rising. This was a conversation they'd had many times, as Roch had attempted over the months to recruit Jakub.

All of Jakub's lingering doubts about the resistance were

cropping up again. He had been a hairsbreadth from death this morning. Yes, they had survived, but the Germans were lined up outside and could soon regroup and assault the crematorium. Tomasz had an alternative plan. His friend had never let him down, and while it seemed impossible that the Germans would allow them to survive, he'd seen Tomasz work miracles with the Germans many times in the past.

But could he leave Roch and the rest of the men to their fate and only save himself? His father's words echoed in his mind as they always did in moments of crisis: *Survive*.

"Jakub, I know you want to do the honorable thing, but we have little time," said Tomasz. "I want to save you but we must move now." He tugged at Jakub's arm.

"I can't," said Jakub, gently pulling his arm away. He saw the sadness in Tomasz's eyes.

"Go with God, my friend," Tomasz said. "If there's any way I can save you, I will." He darted out the back of the barracks. Jakub watched him for long moments. Had he just walked away from his only chance of survival?

Jakub returned to the window, where he found Roch watching and waiting. He made his way over to the leader, who looked up at him and smiled. "Jakub, my friend, I wondered where you had gone," said Roch. His voice was joyful somehow, amid the tension. The leader looked out the window and smiled grimly. "Those bastards still don't know what to do. They don't realize that the end has already begun for them. I hope they enjoy their last moments as the hunters, instead of the prey."

Jakub was caught up in his leader's enthusiasm. He saw that Roch was right. The Germans were still milling about. Nobody seemed to be in charge. He'd never seen them like this before. They were always so strong, in total command, with death at their fingertips. Jakub realized they were human. These Germans, under the right conditions, were no different than he was. That meant that they could be fought, and possibly even beaten. The smoke in the distance had grown even thicker in the sky. Someone out there was fighting with them, and others might join them soon. Perhaps Roch was right after all. They merely had to wait and see what would happen.

Chapter 21
Disaster

October 1944
Auschwitz

Hans moved back and forth among his men, shouting and commanding them to return to the fence. He didn't know what to do, but he could only think of saving Dieter. If his own career was over, there was no point in trying to solve the problems out there somewhere in the camp, under that smoke. They would sort themselves out. He had to rescue his nephew, the closest thing to a child he would ever have, and the last chance of saving his marriage.

He grew increasingly frustrated. The men were not listening. The black, billowing cloud was too much for them, and they only wanted to group up with their companions and discuss what happened. Hans moved into the huddled bands, screaming at them to obey, slapping a few across the face to get their attention. Slowly, first one group, then another, turned their backs on the smoke and returned to the fence line.

Hans moved up and down the row of men, repeating the orders from earlier. It was essential that they wait for his command, he stressed, and that they keep up a constant stream of fire on the windows, to keep the prisoners' attention away from Schmidt and his fast attack team. He would have to track down the sergeant also, and make sure he was still following the original scheme. Everyone seemed rattled by the explosion, and he had to keep the assault team focused to assure Dieter had the best chance of surviving.

He started down the line toward Schmidt, only to find the NCO moving toward him through a pocket of guards who were still grouped up. Schmidt gave him a crisp "Heil Hitler," which Hans returned.

"What's going on over there, sir?" Schmidt asked, pointing to the fiery black cloud in the distance.

"I don't know yet," said Hans. "There's not time to investigate."

Schmidt appeared surprised by this. "But, sir, we have almost all the men here."

"That's correct. We're proceeding with the assault."

Schmidt shook his head. "We can't. We have to get over there and find out what's going on."

"No," said Hans. "We're going in now." He started to move away but Schmidt blocked him.

"Listen, your nephew is not going anywhere. I know those Jews in there better than you do. If they've already killed him, then there's nothing we can do. But they haven't. I'd bet my career on it. Their leaders are too smart. They'd keep Dieter as a hostage, only to be killed at the last desperate moment. If we don't attack the building, they're not going to touch Dieter. The danger isn't there," he said. "It's over there." The sergeant pointed at the black clouds behind Hans.

"You've heard my order."

Schmidt's face took on a shrewd turn. "You think your career went up in smoke with that explosion, don't you, sir?"

Hans grew angry. "How dare you say such a thing. Now listen, Schmidt—"

"It doesn't have to be that way," said the sergeant. "If you follow my plan."

"Explain yourself. And be fast about it."

"Nothing like this has ever happened in the camp before. You uncovered this revolt before it even started. You told the commander. He had the choice to bring in more troops, to reinforce you. He chose not to. You've done the best with what you have. I would back you on that, sir. All the way."

What was Schmidt saying? *He would back him?* What possible difference could Schmidt's word have? Then again, the sergeant had an oversized reputation in the camp. He was respected for his ruthless and sadistic manner. If he stood up to the commander for Hans, that might go a long way in exonerating him.

"That's right, sir, I can help," said Schmidt, as if reading his thoughts. "But not if this gets out of hand. We need to get our forces over there right now. We need to beat Kramer there, for God's sake, and we need to stop whatever is happening and capture or kill those responsible. If we move quickly, when the *Kommandant* arrives to see what's going on, we will have the situation contained, and you can report you've stopped the attack."

"He won't listen to me," said Hans.

"Leave that to me. Order a few men to stay here in place. That will keep this *Sonderkommando* from doing anything other than sitting in their barracks. Let the Jews spend a few hours exhausting themselves, trying to figure out what we are doing. When we've handled the first problem, we can move over here and we'll use the same plan as before, but it will work even better because they'll be tired, their reflexes and their guard will be down."

Schmidt had a point. The sergeant was thinking more clearly than he was, Hans realized. Perhaps the situation wasn't so hopeless after all. With a little luck, and with the sergeant's help, he could save Dieter and his career. He just needed a little more time to prepare. He looked thankfully at the man. He'd never really liked Schmidt, but he'd always respected his cunning and his determination. Right now, that was exactly the right combination of traits to save the situation.

"You're right, Sergeant. Thank you for having the courage to tell me."

"Think nothing of it, sir. But now, with your permission, I'll rally the men and get them over to the explosion."

Hans nodded. "Go ahead, Sergeant. And, Schmidt, if this works the way you've planned, there will be plenty of reward for you."

Schmidt beamed. "It will work, sir. Trust me." The sergeant darted off, calling out to the men, and ordering them past Crematorium III toward Canada and Crematoriums IV and V beyond. The entire action took less than five minutes. Schmidt left five men to guard the perimeter of the gate leading to Crematorium II. Hans could see the Jews watching from the attic. He saw the looks of confusion on their faces. Schmidt was right. They would wait and they would do nothing. If these leaders were as smart as the sergeant thought, then they would certainly keep Dieter alive. It's what he would do. If not, well, it wouldn't matter under those circumstances whether they'd attacked now or later. All would be lost. He closed his eyes and said another prayer, that his nephew would be safe, that his career would be saved, and that they could liquidate these vermin by the end of the day as he'd so carefully planned. When he was done, he felt much better. God was on the side of the Germans, after all.

A half hour later, Schmidt returned to report the situation at the site of the explosion. He looked exhausted and his cheeks were smudged black from the smoke and ash.

"What happened?" Hans demanded.

"It was Crematorium IV," said Schmidt, coughing out the words one by one as he tried to gather his breath. "The Hungarians."

Hans nodded. Crematorium IV was manned by a *Sonderkommando* made up of Hungarian Jews. "What did they do?" he demanded.

"They blew up the building. Well, most of it anyway. We can't get close enough yet to investigate. It's too hot in there and we keep hearing popping sounds. I don't know if there are some men still alive with weapons in there, or if it's just the fire."

"How could they have blown it up?" Hans asked incredulously. "With what?"

"We don't know, sir. We may never know, unless we can capture some of them alive."

"Have any of them escaped the perimeter?" Hans asked.

Schmidt shook his head. "None to my knowledge, sir."

Hans exhaled in relief. "Good. If we capture prisoners, that will be just fine, but the key is to avoid any escapes. Do you understand me?"

"Of course, sir. I understand completely. With your permission, we're going to storm the position as soon as the heat of the fire dies down somewhat. In the meantime, we will keep our men all around the perimeter. Nobody will make it out."

"Excellent," said Hans. "But how many men will you need? I don't want to delay the attack here any longer than necessary."

Schmidt thought about that for a second. "No more than thirty, I would think."

That would leave seventy or more for the attack on Crematorium II. "Good. Get the men situated and then send everyone else back as soon as possible. I don't want you to stay for the attack on Crematorium IV. As soon as the fence is secured, bring the other men back and get into position for your assault here."

"Yes, sir." The guard turned to execute the command.

"And, Schmidt, excellent work."

The sergeant grinned and sprinted off to follow the orders. Hans couldn't believe his fortune. Schmidt was right. Having secured this situation and prevented any escapes, it looked more like the successful repression of a major revolt than a botched negligence on Hans's part that allowed for escapes. Now if only Dieter was alive and could be extracted safely.

He motioned for a couple of the men to follow him, and he moved off into the fenced pathway that cut through the middle of the camp. Here and there as he trudged through the camp, he saw other men staring out at him from windows. Prisoners from the main men's barracks. He saw the fear and the dejection in their eyes. Word was already spreading. Whatever plan was afoot in the camp was being foiled this morning, and they knew it. He congratulated himself on ordering an immediate lockdown on the rest of Birkenau as soon as he'd received word that something was wrong. That was forward thinking and it had assured that no other attacks would occur in Birkenau, or if they did, they would be swiftly put down. *Except the Hungarians, of course*. But with that exception, the rest of the camp was quiet. The downside of this strategy was they would not flush out the other little resistance groups right away, but no matter, after this was over there would be plenty of time to bring in some of the men for interrogation. He would make them sing, and he would put an end to this foolish rebellion.

"Krupp!" He heard the shout just as he reached the rail line. He wanted to move away and avoid the confrontation he knew was coming, but he had no choice. He turned to see his red-faced commander storming up, tailed by a group of administrators.

"What the hell is that?" Kramer demanded, pointing in the direction of Crematorium IV.

"There was an explosion, sir. The revolt was more widespread than we first believed. The Hungarian *Sonderkommando* resisted our efforts to liquidate them this morning. They blew up their building."

"What do you mean, they blew it up?" shouted Kramer. "How the hell did they manage that?"

"We don't know yet, but don't worry, we've got the situation contained."

"You mean you've saved the building?"

Hans hesitated. "No, sir, they destroyed it. But we have the *Sonderkommando* surrounded."

"You have the *Sonderkommando* full of defenseless men and behind an electrified fence surrounded?" asked Kramer sarcastically.

"Sir, we were spread thin. This is a much bigger revolt than we'd anticipated. I was concentrating on Crematorium II."

"I'm not so concerned about what you've been doing this morning," snapped Kramer. "Although that leaves much to be desired as well. What I care about is how you've let this camp plan a rebellion right under your nose. What in the hell have you been doing the last few months? Drinking and sleeping with that slut of a wife you have in Auschwitz?"

Hans flushed with anger. "I don't ever drink to excess, sir, and no matter what you have to say to me, you won't say that about my wife."

"I apologize, Krupp. You're right. That was out of line and insensitive. She's your wife and you should be able to spend time with her. As a matter of fact, I'm going to make sure you have as much time with your wife as you desire."

"What do you—"

"You're relieved of command, Krupp. Immediately."

"But, sir, we're in the middle of—"

"You're in the middle of losing my camp to me! I've had enough of your incompetence! You're to report to your office and remain there until I've sorted this mess out. Then I'll deal with you."

The commander stomped off, trailed by his group of lackeys, the last of whom shot Hans a smug grin as he passed. Hans stood at the rail line, staring after them, stunned. Then he turned and stomped off toward the Death Gate looming over the open arch of the camp.

Chapter 22
The Waiting Game

October 1944
Auschwitz

Jakub watched out the window of Crematorium II as the SS moved rapidly away from the fence line and toward the fire in the distance. In a few minutes they were out of sight, except for a handful of guards who spread out, weapons fixed on the crematorium.

"They're boxing us in to prevent an escape," he said.

"Let them," responded Roch. "That plays right into our hands." He scanned the windows, peering out into the distance toward the other segments of the camp. "Is there any other sign of resistance yet?" he asked.

"Negative," said Jakub.

"Don't worry, there will be."

Jakub wondered whether that was true. He thought of Tomasz. He'd tried to see if his friend had made his way out to the fence, but their view was blocked out toward the trees. He hoped he'd succeeded, and somehow worked a miracle to save his own life. Should he have joined him? The thought tore through his mind again, shaking his conviction. *Survive*. His father's voice echoed through him. Had he just walked away from his best chance in order to follow Roch? Was his leader the well-meaning but naïve fool that Tomasz claimed he was?

"We should interrogate the German," said Roch abruptly.

Jakub was jolted out of his thoughts. "What good would that do?"

"Probably none. But he might know something." The leader turned and started toward the bunk, a dozen meters away, where Dieter was sitting, still gagged and with his hands tied, surrounded by inmates watching him closely.

Jakub hurried up and took Roch's arm. "You're needed here," he said.

Roch turned back. "I don't think so. There should be plenty of time before they get back."

"The men need you," said Jakub. "Why don't you let me question him?"

The leader hesitated, considering this thought. "That's a good idea, Jakub. Loan me your pistol so I can give it to another of the men to watch the window. Question this guard and find out anything you can. Ask about how many men they have in the camp, is there any artillery, do they have reserves nearby. Anything you can find out."

Jakub nodded. "I'll take care of it," he said.

He returned to Roch a half hour later.

"Well?" the leader asked.

Jakub shook his head. "Nothing much of importance. He started in the camp a few days ago, apparently. He was supposed to be observing things and getting used to his duties. He doesn't even know the names of the other Germans. I'm afraid he's not going to be of much help to us. That's probably why he was caught in the gas chamber in the first place. He didn't know what he was doing."

Roch sighed. "Well, I wasn't expecting the information to solve all our problems, but I was hoping it would give us a little advantage. Maybe I should talk to him as well."

"There's no point," said Jakub. He turned Roch's attention to the window. "Any sign of fighting in the camp?"

"None," said Roch, turning to scan the horizon again. "I don't understand it. There should be something by now. We have another dozen cells out there in Birkenau. Even if the SS stopped a few of them, one or two should be fighting by now. And where are the Poles?"

"Perhaps they aren't coming," said Jakub. "Maybe that explosion was it, and we are alone now."

"Nonsense," said Roch. "Keep the faith, Jakub. They'll come."

Another hour passed and the conditions in the camp appeared to be the same. Jakub noticed the smoke in the distance seemed to be dissipating. He felt a sinking, numb detachment. Roch still looked hopefully out, insisting more attacks would come at any moment, but Jakub was starting to lose faith. He saw glances from other men as well, even some of the resistance members. The mood of optimism and hope was fading.

Finally, Jakub couldn't take it anymore. "Sir," he said, walking over to Roch. "I think we have to consider the possibility that the revolt is over."

Roch wouldn't meet his gaze. He paused for a second and then shook his head violently. "We have to be patient," he said. "I know they will come."

"I think Bak is right," said Pawel. "What if there is no big rebellion?"

"Then we're dead," said another.

"You were already dead this morning," said Roch.

"That was then, and this is now," said Jakub, as gently as he could. He turned to Roch, taking a step toward him. "You know I respect you above all others," he said. "But there is no sign that anyone is coming. Look outside," he said, pointing. "The guards haven't returned yet. We have time to escape, to get out of the camp."

"And leave everyone else?" said Roch. "Give up taking the camp? God gave us a miracle this morning. He must have done that so we could fight and free Birkenau." Roch turned his head back toward the fence. "You're right, there are only a few SS out there. If the camp won't come to us, then we must go to the camp."

"What are you saying?" asked Pawel. "You're not suggesting we attack Auschwitz by ourselves! With what? Three weapons and a pinch of ammunition? A few hundred unarmed prisoners?"

"We can do it," said Roch. "Look out there at the fence facing the women's camp. There are only two guards there. We can overwhelm them and force our way through."

"So we can add thousands of starving women to our ranks?" Pawel asked. "I'm sorry, Roch, but you're speaking madness. Our plan required attacks from multiple places, all at the same time, early in the morning, when the guards were half asleep and unaware. We never counted on fighting alone, against an alert and full contingent of SS. That's impossible, and you know it."

"Like I said, we are already dead."

"But right now, we're alive," interjected Jakub. "And we have a second chance. You're right that there are only two guards watching the fence into the camp, but look the other way," he said, pointing to the west. "There are two guards there as well, and that way there is freedom."

Roch scoffed. "Freedom? That leads nowhere but into the greater Auschwitz camp. There's still an outer cordon and God knows how many SS out there. We don't know the area, have no idea where to go. Without the help of the Polish resistance, that way is the surest death sentence of them all."

"We don't know that," said Jakub. "We know if we stay here it's suicide. Out there, at least there's a chance."

"Jakub, you have to trust me," said Roch. He looked around. "You all have to trust me. Haven't I earned that from you? I've risked all with you, fought for you, coordinated this attack for months. Please," he implored.

"You're too close to this," said Pawel. "We do respect you, Roch, but our lives are the only things we have left. If we must relinquish them, then so be it, but we don't want to spend them cheaply."

"I understand," said Roch, bowing his head. "Do me this favor. Give it one more half hour. If there is no action in the camp, or from the Poles by that time, then I will lead us out. Although I don't believe it is our best course of action, I can see that the will of the men is to take a chance at escape, however impossible. I will make that attempt with you."

The men murmured in approval. Several stepped up and shook Roch's hands vigorously. Jakub was quiet. He liked Roch but he didn't agree with him. What would a half hour do for them? He would love to break into the women's camp, to get to Anna and liberate the others there. But he knew it was madness. He agreed with Pawel. Roch was too close to this. He'd allowed his desperate desire to free the camp to cloud his grip on reality. Jakub was sure that nobody would come in the allotted time. This would leave them with a reckless flight into the unknown, the Germans closing in from every direction, with no maps, no provisions, no friends. He thought of Tomasz again and the chance he'd given up. *Survive*.

The time passed with no new action in the camp. Roch kept looking at his watch and back out the window, his face growing somber as the minutes ticked by. The half hour expired, and he took a deep breath, turning to the men. It looked like a part of him had died in the intervening time.

"I was wrong," he said. His voice shook. "I'm sorry, men,

but I believed the revolt would happen. My faith in our organization, in the people involved, was too great. I've put all our lives in greater danger. But I'm ready to lead us out of here," he said at last. "I understand if you want someone else to guide us."

"No!" came the shouts from a dozen voices. The men dashed forward. "You must lead us," the prisoners demanded.

Roch smiled, tears streaming down his face, overwhelmed by this show of confidence. "I will take us out," he said. "And if there is a way to freedom out there, I will find it for you."

There was a cheer and for a few moments Roch couldn't make himself heard. "Quiet now," he ordered. "Here's what we are going to do—"

"They're coming!" interrupted a voice from near the window.

Jakub looked out, half expecting to see a mob of striped prisoners, weapons in hand, storming the gate to their compound. But that's not what the man had meant. He saw to his terror that the SS was returning, weapons at the ready, marching double-quick as they spread out on the fence to the left and the right. There were more than fifty of the men. Fifty weapons against four. They were trapped and it was too late to escape. The revolt and their lives were over.

He could hear the word echoing in his mind again as his eyes took in the disastrous scene around him, but this time the word was delivered in Tomasz's voice. *Survive.*

Chapter 23

A New Plan

October 1944
Auschwitz

Hans sat at his desk, his eyes watching the camp and the dwindling smoke of Crematorium IV in the distance. *Relieved of my position*. He couldn't believe it. If he'd just had another few minutes, he could have moved his men into position and taken Crematorium II. By the time the commander had arrived, he would have squelched the entire insurrection, captured or killed the remaining inmates, rescued his nephew, and he would have stopped the greatest revolt in the history of Auschwitz. He would have had Schmidt's backing and even though Kramer did not like him, he would have almost assuredly been forced to concede that Hans's actions had saved the day.

Instead, through the chances of fate, he had arrived at the rail line at the exact moment Kramer was coming by. Even if the *Kommandant* had arrived mid-attack, just a few minutes later, then Kramer would have been forced to wait and see the results. Instead, Hans was now removed and taken out of the action. The assault, which was almost assuredly going to succeed, would be credited to Schmidt, or more likely to the commander himself. Hans was finished.

There had to be something he could do. But what? He'd been ordered here. He was not to leave. He sat for a few minutes, mulling the question over and over in his mind. He finally rose and picked up his overcoat from the hook. Whatever the risk, he knew he had to go back. If his career was already over, then disobeying this order to remain in his office would have little additional impact. If there was any chance of saving his future, he had to be there, where the action was. Beyond that, Dieter was in there. If something was going to happen to him, *if it had already happened to him*, then Hans had to be there. He would never forgive himself otherwise.

He left the building and moved out along the rail line. He was a full kilometer from Crematorium II, and the building was masked by a row of trees along the line at the end of the women's camp. In the distance he could see figures scampering around. He strained his ears, listening for the *tat-tat-tat* of machine-gun fire, expecting any moment for the assault to commence.

He crossed half the distance to the far fence, three quarters. He still didn't hear any gunfire. What on earth were they waiting for? His hopes rose. Although he had no faith that he would be redeemed, at least he would see the attack, would share the moment of success or failure.

He approached the fence line. A cluster of men stood near the intersection of the two fences that ran west and south, forming one angle of the perimeter of the crematorium compound. Hans spotted Kramer. The man was scanning the building with binoculars, while turning now and again to shout an order to one of the men. The guards were spread out on both sides of the fence, weapons at the ready. Groups of men were huddled near the gates into the compound, preparing to attack. Hans scanned the tree line, looking for Schmidt. He couldn't see the man. Why was the main body of guards preparing to attack from here? This would result in a face-to-face gun battle with the barracks. The plan had been changed, he realized. Kramer had ordered a general attack! Hans had to do something, he knew that in such an assault the guards would quickly take the building, but that this would assuredly result in Dieter's death.

"Prepare to attack!" ordered Kramer.

"Wait!" shouted Hans. The commander turned abruptly. His face afire.

"What are you doing here, Krupp?" he demanded. "I ordered you to stay in your office."

"You can't attack them that way!" insisted Hans. "You'll lose Dieter! I had a plan for the assault that was going to work!"

"I've seen your schemes, Krupp," said Kramer dismissively. "And they all end in failure. This assault will take the building quickly, and with a minimum of casualties."

"What about Dieter?" Hans demanded.

"He is one man," responded the *Kommandant*. "He's probably already dead, but if he isn't, that's on your head, not mine. I'm not going to risk more men on a limited assault just so you can pull your family member out alive. The little prick shouldn't have been there in the first place!"

"Sir! Don't do it!"

"Take this fool into custody," Kramer ordered. He turned back toward the fence. "Commence the attack!"

Orders were given and, as one, the guards at the fence raised their weapons, spraying the windows with gunfire. The assault teams stormed through the gates, charging hard over the open grass toward the crematorium doors. Hans saw the flash of weapons at the windows. One man fell, then another. The first team reached a door, one of the men ripping open the handle and throwing a grenade inside. There was an explosion.

"Get that idiot out of here!" he heard over the clamor. The guards holding Hans pulled him back, turning him from the battle.

"Please, sir!" he shouted. "At least let me stay."

"Get that bastard back to his office and keep him there!"

Hans was torn away, one man jabbing an automatic weapon into his ribs. He tried to struggle, to escape their grip. He felt a thudding crash against his temple and saw a flash of light.

Chapter 24
The Assault

October 1944
Auschwitz

The Germans rushed through the gates, the lead members sprinting toward the building as they fired wildly with their machine pistols. Jakub watched the attack unfold from the window, darting his head up now and again to glance at the situation outside even as bullets shattered their windows and rattled off the ceiling and walls. Several inmates lay near him, writhing in agony, blood spurting from fresh wounds.

Roch stood next to him, firing his pistol coolly, ignoring the gunfire that filled Jakub with such terror. He took careful aim between each shot, and Jakub could see two SS already down within the fence line. Amidst the terror he felt a wild surge of excitement. He'd never experienced combat before and the adrenaline pumped through his veins. More than that, they were fighting the Germans! They'd already won a kind of freedom this morning, no matter how fleeting. Now they were doing more, battling these monsters who had taken everything away from them and this morning attempted to extinguish their lives as well. He heard himself shouting a wild yell of defiance. He wanted his own weapon, to fire back at the Germans, to kill one before they took the building and they were all killed or captured.

The Nazis reached the building. The gunfire grew in intensity. An explosion rocked the floor beneath their feet. A grenade or some artillery he couldn't see, Jakub thought. There were wild shouts, in Polish and in German. Jakub knew they would not be able to hold out very long, but at this moment he didn't care. Let them come, they'd fought them, they'd taken a few of them before they were dead.

"We have to make a run for it!" Pawel shouted, ducking his head, screaming for Roch's attention.

The leader looked at him and then back out the window. He shook his head. "It's too late!"

"There's still time," insisted Pawel. "Look out there. There's only a handful of guards at the outer fence. If we storm it, we could battle through the gates and escape the camp!"

Roch fired his pistol again. He seemed caught up in the battle, on fire with the ecstasy of resisting the Germans. "It's too late!" he repeated. "They're already below us! We have to make our stand here!"

Jakub shook his head, trying to shake his emotions loose from the dazed euphoria that gripped him. What was Pawel saying? Escape? Was that still possible? He turned to Roch, flinching as a particularly close bullet sent glass fragments crashing by his head. "Is he right?" Jakub asked. "Is there a chance?"

Roch pulled the trigger again but nothing happened. He was out of ammunition. He fiddled with the weapon, searching for more bullets, then shoved it into his pocket, eyes darting here and there. He seemed a man possessed.

Jakub stepped over to Roch and grabbed the man by the

front of the shirt. The leader fought back, striking Jakub hard in the face with a fist. He aimed another blow, but Jakub moved in closer, refusing to let go. "Listen to me!" he demanded.

"What is it?" the leader said at last, his eyes blinking and his breath coming in gasps as he appeared to pull himself back from the brink.

"Can we escape?"

Roch shook his head. "I don't see how we could," he said, staring at Jakub with compassion in his eyes. "There are Germans everywhere now. They're downstairs already. We'd never make it out of this building. Even if we did, they'd be hot on our tail when we left the camp. There's no point in trying. I'm sorry, Jakub," he said softly. "Better to let it end here. We've done everything we could do. But the bulk of the camp never rose."

Survive. "We have to try!" demanded Jakub. "We owe it to our families, our friends, to everyone who died here. We have to see if there's any chance at life!"

Roch smiled. "That's right, Jakub. You try. You lead them out of here. You can do it. I'll stay behind and keep the Germans busy."

"No!" screamed Jakub. "That's not good enough! I trusted you! I put my life on the line for your plan, your leadership! We all did! You owe it to all of us to try! The men won't follow me! But they will follow you! We need you, Roch! Lead us out of here! Let us be free of this hell, even if it's just for a little while!"

Roch listened as if dazed. He closed his eyes, considering Jakub's words. Finally he nodded. "All right, Jakub. You've earned that. I guess everyone has. Whether I believe it or not, if you want to try, and you still want my leadership, then I'll do what I can to get us out of here." Jakub could see determination creeping over Roch's chiseled features. His eyes narrowed and a crease of concentration appeared on his forehead. "Get all the men together near the back stairwell!" he ordered. "We'll have to rush them all at once. If we move quickly and don't stop, we'll surprise them and there's a chance we can break through to the outside. But that's only half the problem. Once we get out, we'll have to rush the gate even faster. If we hesitate at all, they'll catch us in a crossfire in the open space before the fence. When we reach the gate, we'll take down the guards, take their weapons, and then move through the gate. The armed members will have to stay at the entrance until everyone is through, and then use their weapons to keep the Germans delayed for a while, otherwise we'll have them biting at our heels."

"Where will we go once we get out?" Jakub asked.

"I don't know yet," said Roch. "We'll have to trust to our luck. We'll need to keep under cover and try to make our way to the outer perimeter. If we can get there quickly enough, we will do the same thing—rush the gates and overpower the guards."

It sounded impossible. Perhaps Roch was right, perhaps there was no way this would work.

Roch smiled at Jakub's expression. "Yes, my friend. We'll most likely perish out there, long before we make it, if we even get out of this building. But you're right, I owe it to you to try."

Jakub grasped his hand. "I know you can do it, Roch."

"Spread the word."

Jakub moved quickly among the other men, explaining the plan and asking others to pass the information. He stepped over wounded, ignoring their pleas, and dodged bullets and flying glass. Eventually everyone was aware of what they were going to attempt, and most of the men had assembled near the stairwell, with a few remaining at the windows to keep the Germans at the fence busy.

"What are we going to do with him?" one of the men asked, holding Dieter by the shoulders. He gave the SS guard a shove and the tall youth stumbled forward, barely keeping from a fall.

"We should finish him," said one of the men.

"We're out of bullets," said Roch.

"That's not the only way to end a man. Look at the skinny duck, I bet I could wring his neck easy enough."

Roch thought about that, weighing the issue. "He still might come in handy," he said. He turned to Jakub. "Bak, I'm putting you in charge of the prisoner."

"Why me?" he asked.

"You've interrogated him. You know a little about him now. More than I do, in any event. Besides," he said, smiling, "I trust you."

Why had they captured Dieter, of all the guards in the camp? He found himself wishing that one of the men had acted, and simply disposed of the guard during the fighting. What if he did it himself now? They would be running soon. There would be chaos. What if something was to happen to the guard during that time? But he knew the answer to that question. He could never kill someone in cold blood. And with his bare hands . . . No, if Dieter was to go along with them, it was best that Jakub was the one to keep in control of him.

Jakub stepped up and took Dieter's arm. His eyes caught the guard's for a second. He nodded and turned toward the group. At least he believed the man wouldn't resist him. He, of all people here.

Roch moved to the front. The wild firing continued below them. There was screaming everywhere. The air was thick with the smell of blood and the acrid burn of gunpowder. Roch looked over all of them for a few moments. It seemed like he was going to make a speech, but he must have decided against it. Brandishing his now useless pistol, he waved it once at the men and then turned, scrambling rapidly down the stairs. Others followed, screams rising in their throats as the group jammed into the bottleneck.

The gunfire increased, as did the shouting. Jakub, near the back of the group, had no idea what was going on. He had Dieter in front of him and he was pressing on the guard's back, pushing the group forward. They were a dozen meters from the door, five meters, then they finally reached the entrance.

The stairwell was smoky and dark. Someone had shot out the light above, or perhaps the Germans had cut the power. The sound of gunfire here was deafening, and Jakub's ears roared. Hands were pushing him from behind now and if he hadn't been pressed by the bodies in front of him, he would have surely fallen headfirst down the stairs. He kept his grip on Dieter, at this point more to keep his own balance than to secure the prisoner. The movement in the darkness was glacial, and Jakub was afraid they'd failed, that the Germans were waiting below in force, mowing down the men as they turned the corner at the bottom of the first flight of stairs.

The press of bodies continued. Jakub could barely breathe. His heart roared in his chest, ringing in his ears. The stench of gunpowder mixed with the sweat of the mass of men wedged in the stairwell was almost enough to make him retch. Whether his eyes were open or closed, he could see nothing in front of him. Every few minutes he would slide down another step. He fought to keep his grip on Dieter in the chaos and the press of bodies.

Finally, they reached the corner and rotated around. He could see now, a dim light shimmering through the smoke. The mass lurched forward more quickly, and he soon reached the bottom of the stairs.

The scene here was chaos. Bodies lay everywhere, with at least a dozen inmates dead or wounded. The ground was slick with blood and the salty, thick odor of the stuff added to Jakub's misery. Screams mixed with the roar of machine-gun fire. He moved forward, expecting to be hit any second, using Dieter now as a kind of shield as he maneuvered the guard through the mass of arms and legs, and pushed forward toward the door.

The battle raged around them, but there was not a mass of

Nazis nearby as Jakub had feared. He shoved forward, heading more by instinct than line of sight, in the general direction of the door that was closest to the outer fence. A man fell next to him, then another. He knew he was going to be hit, but he pressed on, battling for that door. The object was the only thing left in his life, the only purpose he had remaining. If he made it there, then life would begin again. He would try to make it to the fence, or beyond. For now, there was only the door.

Agonizing step after step, he moved forward. His ears rang so loudly now he could no longer hear the gunshots or the screams. His eyes burned so that the scene in front of him was blurred and confused. At least there was a little room to move here, unlike the sardine-like press of the stairwell.

Before he knew it, he was there. The precious portal. He pushed Dieter ahead, through the opening and out into the morning—the light from the overcast sky hurting his eyes after the darkness of the stairway. Blinking, he made out the chaos in front of him, striped forms running, hands waving. More bodies in the grass. In the distance he could just make out the fence and a handful of SS firing at the mob of his comrades charging them. Even as he watched, the first men crashed into the gate. There were intense screams as the *Sonderkommando* members grappled with the guards for their weapons, fighting with a superhuman strength born of desperation and nothing to lose. Jakub shouted in support of them, pushing Dieter forward into a half stumble, half jog as he tried to close the distance to the melee.

Bullets flew in every direction. He knew there were Germans to his right, firing at them from the fence that paralleled the end of the rail line. Men dropped near him, even as he struggled forward. He might be hit in any instant, but he battled onward and others ran with him, struggling for their freedom.

The guards at the gate were overwhelmed. Jakub could see some of his comrades, now with arms, returning fire at the Germans. The fence loomed above him. He reached the gate, shoving Dieter through the throng and out of the perimeter. He was free. He was outside Birkenau without permission, fighting the monsters who had controlled every aspect of his life. They hadn't truly escaped, there was another outer fence to the overall Auschwitz complex of camps, but he felt power and excitement coursing through his veins. He heard the shouts of joy and the clapping of his fellow inmates. He saw the joy and the tears on their faces as they battled through, waving their fists at the Germans who were shooting wildly now, dodging and moving for cover as the few *Sonderkommando* members with weapons continued to shoot at their captors.

Most of them were through now. Jakub was appalled at the number of men dead and dying between the fence and the crematorium. But there were many more through the gate. He saw Roch, a machine pistol in his hands now, firing away at their enemies.

A lone prisoner sprinted out of the building, rushing toward the fence. He dodged bullets as the Germans, in their fury, tried to mow down this last upstart Jew. The man moved to the left and the right, scrambling over bodies. It seemed impossible he would make the gate. But he kept going, and by some miracle he rushed through and slammed into them, arms out, head down, his back heaving in exhaustion. He looked up and Jakub was shocked. It was Tomasz.

Chapter 25
The Chase Begins

October 1944
Auschwitz

Hans regained consciousness halfway back to his office. The guards were dragging him along and he pushed them aside, wobbling on his feet for balance before he started moving, one step at a time, toward the Death Gate. He spat on the ground, refusing the help of his escort, as he stumbled away. He was losing everything, with no hope of redemption. Several times during the long trip back to the administration building he turned, trying to find some way past the soldiers, but they refused to allow him. After the third attempt, one of the men drew his weapon and aimed it at his chest. He had no choice but to comply.

In the distance behind him he could hear the roar of gunfire and he knew the attack had begun. He was nearly driven mad by the reality that his nephew was back there, and he had no control over trying to save him, in fact was not even allowed to witness the attempt. He could only hope and pray that Schmidt could still get into the building and secure the rescue before somebody killed Dieter.

He stormed through the door and up the stairs into his office. He opened the door and stepped to his desk. The nightmare grew worse. There was a message on his desk that he had company waiting outside the camp for word from him. Steeling himself, he hurried back down the stairs, trailed by the guards, and out the back gate of the camp. His wife and sister-in-law were there, waiting anxiously.

"Hans," Elsa said, rushing toward him. "Thank God you're okay. What's going on out there? Where's Dieter?"

"There was an escape," he said. He looked meaningfully at the guards, who lowered their eyes and did not comment.

"An escape?" Elsa said. "You're trying to tell me that the billowing black cloud you can see all the way from our flat came from an escape?"

"Calm down now," said Hans, his hands pressed outward. "One of the buildings had a fire as well. We have contained the situation and we are in the process of capturing the prisoners. The whole thing will be over in the next hour or so."

"Where's my Dieter?" asked Hannah.

"He's involved in the operation to bring in the inmates," said Hans. "I should be doing the same. I just came back for a few minutes." He stepped forward, putting his hands on his wife's shoulders. He could see the fear there. "Don't you worry now, my dear. Dieter is fine. You and your sister should go back to the flat. Make us a nice dinner. We'll be home tonight and we can all celebrate."

He was lying to them but what could he do? If he saved Dieter then they would return in the evening and his nephew would be all right. That's all that mattered. They would be angry at him for deceiving them, but if his career was truly over, it wouldn't matter. What would come would come. If

Dieter was dead, well, so much the better that they didn't know at this point what danger he'd allowed his nephew into.

They argued with him for a few more minutes, but he kept repeating the same things over and over to them. In the end, they agreed to leave. He'd calmed them down, assuring them that Dieter was in no danger. He hoped they would be calm at least for this day. If things had gone poorly, it would be the last true peace any of them would ever know.

They said their goodbyes and then Hans returned to his office, rushing to the window to stare with binoculars out at Crematorium II. The trees were blocking his view, and other than a few SS moving here and there, he could see nothing. Still, there were very few Germans near the fence and this was likely a good sign. That meant that they'd already taken the building. If the *Sonderkommando* hadn't acted too hastily, there was a chance Dieter had survived and all would be well. Perhaps the commander had been correct after all? Hopefully a fast assault had overwhelmed the pitiful defenses before the prisoners had time to act.

Hans felt a fraction of warmth inside. If only Dieter was all right. There was even a chance that Schmidt could intervene on his behalf. He'd been willing to advocate before, and now that the dust had settled on the operation, the commander might be in a more conciliatory mood. Yes, things would certainly improve when this unpleasant event was finished. Could he still save both his job and his nephew? If Dieter survived, he would certainly receive a commendation after his bravery during the battle. Hans nodded to himself. All was not necessarily lost.

Wasn't there some way he could get back to the action and see what was going on? He paced the office, staring through his binoculars again and again. He turned in frustration to his guards.

"Can't you take me back there?" he asked. "The commander was hasty. There may be men to interrogate. Men whom I know."

One of the guards shook his head. "I'm sorry, sir, but orders are orders."

"Damn your orders!" Hans shouted. "You mark my words, when this is over, I'll be returned to my position. Look out there," he said, pointing to the crematorium in the distance. "The operation is already finished. If I am back in the commander's good graces, I'll remember that you refused me today."

He saw the looks on their faces, but they didn't move and he knew they wouldn't. Faced with incurring either his wrath or the commander's, Hans knew who would prevail.

Hans returned to the window. There was more movement out there now. A lone figure was jogging toward them along the rail line. The man was overweight and he huffed and puffed as he ran along. Hans recognized him—one of the regular guards in the camp. He wondered why he was returning to the administration offices in the middle of the operation, and why in such a rush? A few minutes later the man reached the building and Hans heard him rustling up the stairs and down the hallway. He was surprised to see the guard stop at his office and give the Hitler salute, which he returned.

"What is it?" Hans demanded, curious to see what was going on.

"The *Kommandant* wants to see you immediately."

"Why?" Hans asked.

"He didn't say, but you're to come now."

Hans nodded. He rose and moved toward the doorway, fixing both guards with a knowing glance. *If I'm returned to my position, you will both suffer.* He followed the guard down the stairs and out of the building. Moving along the rail line, he again asked what this was about.

"The *Kommandant* instructed me to find you, and to reserve answers to questions for when you arrived."

An icy fear arose in Hans as it occurred to him what might have happened. *Dieter is dead.* Why else would the commander summon him onto the scene after banishing him to the office?

That had to be it. His nephew was gone, and the commander was doing him the courtesy of allowing him to see what had happened in person. He quickened his pace. He dreaded what he would see, but he had to know.

They reached the tree line a few minutes later, the guard trailing far behind him, winded from the kilometer-long trip. Hans ignored him, searching the scene in front of him. He didn't understand what he was seeing. There were guards standing outside the building and he could see through the windows above that green-clad figures were moving back and forth through the structure. They had taken the crematorium. But that wasn't what was confusing him. What he didn't comprehend were the men moving through the trees and along the road outside the outer fence line, beyond Birkenau itself. What were they doing there? Why would they need to be in such force outside the camp? Had there been some kind of attack? He looked around and spotted a cluster of men. Schmidt was there and in the middle of the huddle Hans recognized the commander.

Kramer met his eyes at the same time, and motioned Hans over to them. He tried to read the look on the commander's face but he'd never seen it before. The features were ghost white, with red splotches at the cheeks. He looked terrified and furious at the same time. Kramer had a reputation of unflappability and he wondered what possible event could have created that reaction.

"Get over here, Krupp!" the commander growled. "Everyone else, give us some space."

The other men cleared out. Schmidt gave him a mischievous smirk, but Hans did not know how to read that. "What is it, sir?" he asked. "Is Dieter dead?"

The commander was confused for a moment. "Your nephew?" He shook his head. "No, not that we know of. His body wasn't inside the building."

"Well, where else would he be?"

"They fought their way out of the camp."

Hans was stunned. "What? How is that possible?"

"We attacked from both sides of the interior perimeter. It never occurred to . . . to us, that they might try to break through the gate and out of the camp. They fought like lions. We killed quite a few of them, but many more have escaped. They're out there in the woods somewhere."

"Do you have men in pursuit?"

"We do. But . . ."

"But what, sir?"

"Look, Hans, you know I've never quite approved of you."

Hans nodded.

"I'll be honest with you. I wanted my own man in your position from the moment I got here. Perhaps I've been unfair about that. You've done a damn good job with the men. There have been a few escapes, but nothing significant. You learned about this revolt and you nearly prevented it. Now I have maybe a hundred escapees out there. You're the only man who knows all the guards. You've been here a long time. You know the area, better than I do. What's more, I don't know what else might be planned in the camp. I need to stay here and make sure the rest of the inmates are kept under control. In the meantime, I need you to take back over, track down the prisoners, and bring the bastards back."

Hans was flabbergasted. "I . . . of course I will, sir. How much of a head start do they have?"

The commander looked at his watch. "No more than half an hour."

"Which way were they going?"

"We don't know for sure. But they started out by heading southwest."

"I'll get going right away."

"Thank you, Krupp. You go get those prisoners and get your

nephew back. If you do this right, he'll have his commendation, and you'll have one too."

"Yes, sir," said Hans, executing a crisp salute. He turned and moved away, calling to the men, giving individual orders for a few of them to gather the rest. He sent two men off to bring up more ammunition, as well as rations, lights, everything they'd need for the next twenty-four hours. He had dozens of square kilometers to search. He knew he would succeed. He was going to rescue Dieter and bring these vermin to justice. God was smiling down on him.

Chapter 26
Escape

October 1944
Auschwitz

Jakub moved with a pack of inmates through the birch trees. They'd escaped the camp just a few minutes before and all the men were moving as quickly as they could, battling to put a little distance between themselves and the Germans. For some reason, their enemies were not pursuing them as they had expected. The shouts and the gunfire had receded until it was a dull thudding in the distance.

Dieter was still in front of him, the man moving along with the rest of them, propelled forward with an occasional prod to the back. Jakub looked around at those running with him, trying to find Tomasz among the fleeing forms. What had happened to his friend? Why was he bleeding? He wanted to find him and ask those questions, but he knew they had to keep moving. As they retreated, he could see the mass of men beginning to slow down. The conditions in the camp, even with their special access to extra food, had worn them down far below the physical condition they had when they'd arrived in the camp, and their bodies were betraying them now. Jakub knew they had to keep moving, as quickly as they could, but he was exhausted, and Dieter seemed to be drained as well, with his hands bound. He kept stumbling and losing his balance.

Men started to drop off, first singly, then in groups. Jakub kept moving, another twenty or thirty meters, but his legs were giving out. He ordered Dieter to stop and then he collapsed on the ground. The German tumbled down next to him. Jakub pulled himself up against the base of a tree, his breath coming in ragged gulps. He shut his eyes as his head spun, and he tried to recover. He heard footsteps and he turned, expecting an SS guard to charge out of the trees, but it was another inmate, moving toward him. The man fell down a meter away. It was Tomasz.

"My God, my friend, what happened to you?" Jakub managed to mutter in between breaths.

It took Tomasz a moment to reply. "I made it halfway to the fence, when the SS started shouting at me. I recognized one of them and told him I wanted to leave, that I had money to pay. The bastard took a shot at me. I turned and sprinted back as fast as I could. The Germans were already beginning to rush at the building. A bullet ricocheted off the wall and grazed my forehead," he explained, running his finger over the bloody mess. "It hurts like the devil." He turned and looked at Dieter. "I see you brought the guard along. The new one. How did you get stuck with him?"

"Roch put me in charge of him. I interrogated him earlier. He wouldn't tell me anything." Jakub didn't want to talk about Dieter. He wasn't sure even Tomasz would understand. He still didn't know what to do with the guard. He'd hoped the young man would be killed in the attack or would have broken free and escaped. Anything to get him away from the group. Barring that, he realized it was best the man stay with him. He just hoped he'd keep his mouth shut. If he didn't . . .

"Where is your fearless leader?" asked Tomasz, looking around.

Jakub was grateful his friend had changed the subject. "I don't know. I haven't seen him since we ran away. He had set himself near the back, to guard our escape."

"Of course he did," said Tomasz, spitting bitterly into the dirt. "Such a Boy Scout."

"He did his best," said Jakub, a trifle defensively.

"They always do. But the man is no realist. And dreamers don't just risk themselves, they are good at getting everyone killed. I remember his type from Warsaw. Not my friends, but others who thought they could fight, thought they could lead the Poles to victory over the Germans. They ended up corpses in the street, those who weren't betrayed by collaborators long before their foolish plans bore any fruit."

"You thought you could make it through with bribes," said Jakub. "Your plan didn't work either."

Tomasz looked sharply at him and then grinned. "True enough. But by then, the die had been cast. I still haven't given up on that plan. You watch, it might save us yet."

Jakub was about to inquire as to what he meant, but he stopped when he saw Roch moving among the trees toward them. His leader was limping, and he used a crooked branch as a cane to support him as he walked. A bloodstain radiated out from his left, although Jakub could not tell how bad the injury was, or what might have caused it. Despite the injury, Roch's face exuded warmth and confidence, as if he was on a casual Sunday stroll before the war. He stopped and talked to the men, his head nodding, and he helped them stand up and hobble forward as he gathered all the remaining *Sonderkommando* members. Eventually they all clumped together, most men still slumping on the ground and against the trunks of the birch trees. Jakub looked from man to man. They were spent. It seemed impossible that they would be able to go any farther.

Roch was about to speak when he saw Jakub. His face broke

into a greater grin and he hobbled over. "You made it," he said. "And you brought the prisoner out. I've been looking for you all this time and when I didn't see you, I feared the worst."

"Tomasz made it too," said Jakub, gesturing at his friend. Roch looked over and nodded.

Tomasz laughed. "He's not quite as happy to see me as he is you, Jakub."

"I thought you'd gone," the leader said with a neutral tone.

"No such luck for you. I tried to get out but our Nazi friends had other plans for me. So I guess I'm getting to join this little adventure. I hope you have a plan, Roch, because while many people have made it this far in escapes, very few are able to get beyond the outer fence."

"I wish I knew exactly what to do, but I don't. I thought we would have taken the camp before we left. I also thought we'd have help from our Polish friends."

Tomasz scoffed. "I don't know who is more unreliable, the so-called Polish resistance or the fools back there in our camp."

"You never believed in us, Tomasz. Of course, you've never tried to help anyone—except yourself."

"Ask Jakub here. I've done plenty for him."

Roch nodded. "You found a plaything to run the fence with. That's not the same as trying to save lives, to fight our enemy."

"I lived and I helped Jakub live. And we'll see how far your big plans get us. Your revolt is assuredly going to get us all killed."

"Please, both of you, stop," implored Jakub, hobbling into position between them. "There's no point in casting blame right now. The Germans are going to be closing in on us. If there's any chance for us to survive, we must keep moving somehow. We need a place to flee and then we must figure out some way to get through the outer fence. At least the rest of you do."

"What do you mean?" Roch asked.

Tomasz laughed. "You say you know this boy, but you don't understand the first thing about him. He wants to go back for that girl of his." He turned to Jakub. "That's it, isn't it?"

"Yes. I don't want to leave Anna behind."

Roch looked sadly at his friend. "You can't go back, Jakub. There's no chance you could save her."

"I don't have to go back," he said. "It's daytime. She's probably at the factory by now. I just have to figure out how to get there and then some way in. It can't be as well-guarded as the camp."

"We don't even know where that factory is," said Roch.

"I do," said Tomasz. "I've seen it. I've seen most places around here."

"It doesn't matter," said Roch. "We can't go traipsing through the village and beyond just so we can liberate your woman. Some of these other men have family in the camp. I know they'd all want to liberate them if we could. That's one of the reasons I was trying to free all of Birkenau. But that plan has failed." He put his hand on Jakub's shoulder. "Let's face it, my friend, we've little chance of making it out ourselves. We must fight for that chance. I'm sorry, but we have to stick together, and just like when the trains arrived for us the first time, we must leave behind our loved ones if there is any chance to survive."

"For once I agree with him," said Tomasz. "I know you love this girl. I've told you many times that I don't understand why, but I've accepted it's true. Still, that is beside the fact. If we are going to make it out of here, it's just going to be this group. It's terrible, Jakub, but it's what we must do. Remember your father's words."

Survive. He knew what his father would say about Anna. He would tell him if there was any chance to save her, then he must do it, but not if it was impossible. And Jakub knew there was no realistic way to rescue her from here. The guards would be on high alert. They would be armed to the teeth and there would likely be extra security everywhere they went. Not only that, but the Germans would soon be in pursuit. They had to keep moving, and with a single purpose, to find a place to breach the outer gate. He thought of his Anna. Being truthful to himself, he'd never expected either of them to survive. If she was free and had a chance to escape, would he want her to give up that tiny hope on an impossible quest to liberate him? Of course not. He would want her to try to make it, no matter what. That was the only answer and it was the truth that faced him squarely now, as he heard advice from his two closest friends. No, they were right, and his father was right. For his family, for their future, he had to escape if there was any chance. He squared his shoulders, tears running down his face. He nodded once in acceptance.

"That's my boy," said Tomasz. The former street thug turned to Roch. "So that's settled. Now what is your plan to get us the hell out of here?"

Roch turned to Tomasz. "You said you've been around most of Auschwitz. What way should we go?"

Tomasz stared at the leader for a second, then his face broke into a wry grin. "I didn't think there would be a day when you would ask me for advice."

"I don't know why you say that," said Roch. "We've wanted your help since the beginning. You just wouldn't give it to us."

"Fair enough." Tomasz stared out among the men, rubbing his chin for a few moments as he considered their predicament. "These boys of yours are in tough shape," he said at last. "The best chance we would have would be to head north and try to cross the Vistula. But they'd never make it across without a bridge, and those will be well-guarded in any event. We could try to skirt the camp to the north or south, and head east toward the town, but that seems like a dead end too. There are a number of sub-camps in that direction, and we'd probably only find ourselves sandwiched between our pursuers and the Germans in town. No, to have any chance, we should head south. They won't expect that, I don't think. The rail line heads that way, and we might find a train we could smuggle onto, or at least a place where we could fight our way out through a gate a long way from the camp. But I'm not going to lie to you," he said. "We'll be marching for kilometers, and I don't think many of these boys will make it."

Roch looked around. "They're going to have to try." He turned to address the group. "Men, this is not the way I had hoped our revolt would go. I wanted the entire camp to rise. I wanted to win freedom for everyone in Birkenau, and for our revolt to be the beginning of a liberation of this part of Poland. Instead, we were betrayed. Instead, many parts of the camp and our friends outside were caught off guard and were not able to join us.

"We could have taken that as the end. We could have stepped into the gas chamber and let fate take us away, as it has taken so many of those that we love. Instead, we chose to fight. We've killed and wounded some of those that have tortured and murdered us. Our brothers across the rail line fought too, and they caused damage to the camp, and kept the Germans away long enough for us to form a plan and escape. We are free now, even if it is just for a few hours.

"I know you are all exhausted. I know it would be tempting to stay here and rest. But the Germans will be here soon. If we are going to have any chance to escape them, we need to leave now, before they make contact with us again. I've talked to Tomasz, whom you all know. He's familiar with the outside parts of the camp from his long time in Auschwitz and Birkenau. We've agreed that we are going to head south, away from the camps, away from the river. We are going to follow the rail line and look for a weak part in the fence where we can battle through and make our escape."

He paused and looked at them. There were barely a hundred out of the two hundred who had woken up this morning in their barracks. Some had wounds. All of them were at the limits of their endurance already. "I know you are tired," he said. "But we must find new energy to escape them, to fight them. If we stay free, if we stay alive, we will have avenged the deaths of all of those we loved. We will carry on for them, because they cannot carry on for themselves."

There were muted murmurs of approval. Jakub looked around and saw the hope in the men's eyes, the renewed energy. Even as he watched, men were beginning to pull themselves up and stomp their feet, taking deep breaths, preparing for the coming trek. This was what Jakub had long admired about Roch. The man was not perfect. He'd seen that. Perhaps, as Tomasz said, he was naïve and too optimistic. But he believed, and he kept on fighting, long after everyone else was ready to give up.

Roch returned to the group and Jakub. "I wouldn't want anybody else leading us," Jakub said.

The leader smiled. "Thank you, Jakub. That means a lot to me." He motioned at Dieter. "Do you mind keeping the guard with you? We should probably interrogate him again at some point, but right now, we don't have time."

Jakub reached down and pulled the young man up on his feet. He was surprised to see blood trickling down the guard's hands. He realized the cloth tying his wrists had badly chafed the skin. "Is it okay to remove these?" he asked Roch. "I'll keep him in the middle of the pack."

Roch looked down at the hands, concern spreading across his features. He thought about it for a moment and then nodded. "I don't see why not," said Roch. "He can't go anywhere. And truly, if he did, does it really change our chances very much?"

Jakub reached down and fumbled with the tightly knotted

cloth. His fingers were clumsy in the cold. His shoulders and back ached and he grimaced at even this simple effort. But soon he had the binding loosened and he unwound the cloth. He tucked it into his pocket. It was possible he would need it again.

Dieter ran his hands over his trousers, removing the blood, then rubbed his wrists, massaging them over and over. He looked up at Jakub and stared at him with a questioning look on his face. Jakub looked away. "*Danke*," Dieter whispered.

A sharp crack broke the subdued silence. A scream ripped through the woods as one of the men slumped against a tree, blood spreading out from a wound in his back. The men shouted and turned this way and that, looking for the source of the attack. They'd waited too long. The Germans were here.

Chapter 27
An Unforeseen Problem

October 1944
Auschwitz

Anna stared out the window with a cluster of women, watching the frantic anthill of SS activity out at the rail line. Their barracks was in the second row of buildings in the women's camp, so they had only a very limited field of view, but it was clear that something major had happened from the number of guards rushing back and forth along the rail line.

"What do you think is going on?" asked Estusia.

"I have no idea," said Anna. "But it's significant. I've never seen anything like this the entire time I've been here, have you?" There were murmurs of agreement. Anna wished she could go out, but their block wardress had strictly forbidden it and a few SS guards were stalking the women's camp, assuring that everyone sat tight in their barracks.

"Whatever it is," said Estusia, "it must involve the crematoriums."

Anna's blood froze. "Why do you say that?" she asked.

"Because the guards are all heading that direction. If this involved the men's camp, we wouldn't see them running up and down the rail line, would we?"

Estusia was right. Whatever was happening had to involve the west end of the camp along the rail line, and the only structures down there were Crematoriums II and III. Her friend nodded for her to move away from the group and Anna did so, joining her near her bunk, a few meters away. "What is it?" she asked.

Estusia looked around, making sure that nobody was nearby. "What if it's the revolt?"

"There's no way," said Anna. "That's still supposed to be days away."

"I know," said her friend, whispering as quietly as she could. "But what if something happened? What if there was a problem and they had to speed things up?"

"We would have received word, wouldn't we?"

Estusia shook her head. "Not if there wasn't time. Maybe the Germans discovered something, and attacked the *Sonderkommandos*? Wouldn't that explain the gunfire this morning?"

"There's gunfire here all the time."

"I agree. But not usually multiple shots all at once, and never followed by a lockdown of the camp. The only explanation for the freeze is that something is happening that the Germans are trying to control. That, and the location they all seem to be moving toward, points to some crisis in the crematoriums, doesn't it?"

Anna nodded. "You're right. It doesn't make any sense, but you're right." She moved even closer. "What should we do?"

Estusia thought about that for a moment. "I'm not sure, but I think we should get the rest of the group together."

"Is that wise? Right in here? During the day?"

"I don't know if we have a choice," said her friend. "What if we have to take action? We've got to be prepared."

"I agree, let's get them together. We can meet here again."

Anna and Estusia dispersed to collect their friends. They were back a few minutes later. Estusia had brought Roza Robota and Ala Gertner. Anna found Regina Safirsztajn. Roza was a woman with strong, defiant features peering out from some raven stubble. She was their leader, and the woman who risked the most, smuggling their collected gunpowder to a contact in the men's camp. She was scanning the barracks now, head cocked, eyes darting about the room.

"Why have you called us here?" she demanded. Her voice was quiet but steely.

"You've seen what's going on out there?" Estusia asked.

"Of course," said Roza. "How could it be missed?"

"But have you thought what it means?"

Roza peered at Estusia, her lips pursed. "What do *you* think of it?"

Estusia looked around again to make sure nobody was near, then she launched into a hushed explanation of what she and Anna had talked about.

Roza nodded her head. "I think the same. But what are we to do about it?"

"Shouldn't we be ready?" said Anna.

"And how would we accomplish that?" asked Roza. "It's not our job to be ready. The men are supposed to come to us, remember?"

"But that plan has changed," said Anna. "They may need our help. Don't we have anything we could fight them with?"

Roza shook her head. "We don't. Well, I guess that's not quite true. We have one bomb we've fashioned from a metal container and a little gunpowder. But what good would that do? If we were lucky, we might take down our block wardress with it but then what? There's no way we could fight our way to the fence. And even if we could, you've seen all the guards running that way. We'd be moving into a massacre."

"Roza's right," said Ella, who, even with a shorn head, reminded Anna of a movie star. "We can't fight our way out of here."

"But shouldn't we at least be ready?" asked Anna. "If we had the bomb, and if we were all together, we could move quickly if the men do fight their way into our section of the camp."

"It's risky to stay here," said Roza. "There are already eyes on us. That bitch Kamila, for one. Don't look her way, but she's watching us. It won't be long before she sets the block wardress on us. If we had the bomb, there might be a search."

"Where is it?" Anna asked.

"Nearby and safe."

"Is it close enough that we could retrieve it if things start to escalate?" Anna asked.

Roza nodded. "There should be time." The leader looked around again, her hand scratching her cheek as she seemed to consider things. "Here's what I think we should do. Let's get back to the windows. Don't stay together. If things settle down, we'll go on with life as if nothing has happened. But if we see fighting in our part of the camp, we'll regroup here. I'll get our bomb, and if Kamila or the wardress tries to stop us at that point, I'll blow them to hell."

Screams erupted from near the windows.

"What is that?" asked Anna. "Are the men coming?"

"Quiet," said Roza. She turned and moved swiftly to the window. The leader peered out for a few moments and then waved them over. Anna moved as quickly as she could to Roza. She tried to see out the window but there were so many women in front of her, and she was one of the shortest in the barracks. She moved to the left and right, trying to find an opening. And then she saw it, letting out a gasp. An enormous column of black smoke was billowing up toward the sky.

"What is it?" one of the women asked.

"I don't know," said Roza quietly, "but it looks like one of the crematoriums to me."

Estusia stepped up and slid her arm into Anna's. They stood that way for a long time, watching in silence as the blackness filled the sky.

A few minutes later Anna's cell regrouped near the barracks.

"What does this mean?" she asked. "Are they coming? Should we get the bomb?"

"Quiet about that!" Roza ordered. "Give me a second to think." The leader looked back toward the window; her head craned as if she was trying to listen for something. "I don't hear any shooting," she said at last. "I don't know what that explosion means, but if the men were coming for us right now, we would hear something. I don't think anything has changed. We should sit tight and see what happens for now. Does anyone disagree?"

None of them disputed Roza. "What should we do then?" Estusia asked after a time.

"The same as before," said Roza. "Let's spread out and keep an eye on things. If you see men in the camp, or if there is more shooting, let's come back here and talk about it."

The group separated. Anna and Estusia returned to the window they'd stood by earlier. The smoke still billowed up from behind the nearby barracks. They couldn't see any SS now, even patrolling the women's camp. They stood there, watching, for what seemed an eternity. Anna closed her eyes, praying she would hear gunfire, that she would see Jakub and the others fighting their way into the camp, coming to save them.

Time passed. Her stomach rumbled. She felt a stabbing pain. She didn't want to leave the window. She tried to fight down the nausea, but she felt it leaping up into her throat. She was going to be sick. She gagged, turning and running away, jostling another inmate out of the way who stopped to see if she was all right. She rushed out of the barracks, knowing she was risking her life, and sprinted to the latrine. Anna tore the door open and stumbled to the long row of open toilets, throwing herself to her knees and vomiting violently into the foul-smelling opening. Her whole body shook and her stomach heaved as wave after wave of spasm twisted her insides. Finally, she was finished, and she lay over the toilet, ignoring the foul and dirty structure, gasping for breath as she fought to recover.

"That's quite a spectacle you're causing there."

Anna heard the voice and couldn't believe it. Why would she be followed here? She lifted her head. Kamila was there, standing over her, lips curved into a smirk.

"What are you doing here?" asked Anna.

"I should be asking you the same thing," said Kamila. "But I know your secrets, all of them."

"I don't have any secrets."

"Liar!" retorted Kamila, taking a step toward her. "I've been watching you for a long time. First you wound that foolish boy around your finger, then you did the same with my Schmidt. Now you're threatening all our lives with your foolish little plot."

"I don't want anything to do with Schmidt. He's the one who . . ."

"Shut your mouth! I don't believe you." She stepped right next to Anna and moved her head down close. "But we'll get to that in a second. For now, tell me about the plot."

"I don't know what you're talking about . . . You're mistaken."

"Then why were you asking Roza about a bomb!" she asked in triumph. "You're a lying little slut, Anna. You're lying to me about the plot, and you've lied to me about Schmidt." Kamila reached and grabbed Anna's jaw, jerking her head so they faced each other, only a few centimeters apart. Anna struggled, trying to fight free, but she was too weak under Kamila's iron grip. "Tell me the truth about Schmidt. I want to hear it out of your mouth. When did you start wanting him? When did you trick him into sleeping with you?"

"I don't want him. I've never touched him. It's not what you think."

"I saw him leading you off!" she screamed. "Don't lie to me, you whore." Kamila twisted Anna's head and shoved it down the toilet hole into the darkness below. Anna gagged and fought. She couldn't breathe and she coughed and sputtered, her eyes burning. Kamila ripped her head back out of the hole. "Now tell me the truth or I'll hold you down until you're gone."

"I didn't sleep with him. He did pull me aside. He told me that Jakub had sold me to him. He said that Jakub was never coming back and that I was his from now on. He tried to touch me but—"

"What a wild story. Look at you. You can't even protect yourself against me. You could never—"

"You're right, I couldn't have fought him off. I was ill. I vomited, so he didn't touch me. He sent me to the hospital instead."

"Liar!" Kamila screamed. She shoved Anna back into the latrine and held her there. She clutched her head with hands like a vise and soon Anna was running out of breath. She struggled to catch some air. She was blacking out. Kamila ripped her back out and twisted her to face her. "Tell me the truth. The next time I shove your head down there you won't be coming back!"

Hands seized Kamila from behind. The woman struggled, trying to rip free. She let go of Anna and clawed at the fingers wrapped around her neck. Her face contorted and turned an ugly purple. Her feet kicked and scraped against the ground. For a minute or more she struggled, and then her body contorted and stiffened. Her mouth gave out a gurgling rattle and Kamila slumped to the ground. Estusia was standing behind her, her face scarlet, tears streaming down her face. "Are you all right?" she asked Anna, her breath coming in ragged gasps.

Anna nodded, staring at the lifeless form at her feet. "She was going to kill me."

"She won't hurt anyone. Not anymore."

"They're going to execute us for this," said Anna.

"Not if they don't know who did it. We have to get out of here as quickly as we can." She stared down at Anna. "Can you walk?"

"I think so," said Anna. Estusia reached out and helped her to her feet. She was dizzy and her legs shook, but she was able to maintain her balance.

"Let's get out of here," said Estusia.

Anna stopped her friend, turning her around to face her. "You saved my life," she said. "I will never be able to repay you."

"You don't owe me anything," said Estusia, smiling. "You've risked your life for others."

"We all have."

"That's why we have to stick together, no matter what."

Anna pulled Estusia to her and held her for long moments, tears streaming down her face.

"What a tender moment you're having," said a voice.

Anna's veins turned to ice. She looked up to see the block wardress, Mira, there, a rubber truncheon in her hand. The woman was staring at Kamila on the floor and then back at both of them.

"Wait," said Estusia. "I can explain."

The wardress removed a whistle from beneath her striped dress and began blowing it violently, the piercing shriek of the thing tearing through the morning air.

Anna and Estusia looked at each other, the doom washing over them. They were caught, and there was nothing they could do but wait for the SS to come and arrest them.

Chapter 28
The Chase Continues

October 1944
Auschwitz

Hans had immediately sent men to the west, north, and south in an attempt to track down the escaped inmates. An hour passed and he'd grown anxious. What if the Jews had battled through the outer gate and were already gone?

He heard shots fired in the distance. He listened closely and realized it was to the west. He had twenty men with him and he motioned for them to follow as he darted away from the fence line, hurrying into the trees. He paused now and again, listening for more gunfire, but he didn't hear any. Hans pressed on, his stress growing. What if this was a false alarm? Perhaps one of his men had fired at a wild animal, or even just out of fear.

A few minutes later he ran into some of his men. There were ten SS here, spread out among the trees, machine pistols at the ready. He strained his eyes into the woods, looking for the tell-tale striped cloth among the branches and the white spotted tree trunks, but he could see nothing.

"I heard shots," Hans said, addressing the corporal in charge of the group.

"*Jawohl*," he said.

"Did you see anything, or is this a fool's chase?"

"We made contact, sir. We could have moved in, but you ordered us to remain in position. They're out there. Not far off." He pointed in the distance. "Look. Just there."

Hans followed the finger. He couldn't see anything at first.

"On the ground," said the corporal.

Then he saw it. The striped clothing. A figure two hundred meters out, lying prone, face up, not moving.

"You killed one."

"Yes, sir."

"Good shooting, Corporal."

"Thank you."

"But where are the rest of them?"

"They moved off, but not far I think, sir. Even when we attacked them, they were hobbling away. They can't make it far." The corporal looked at the reinforcements. "Do you want me to take the men in and nab them, sir?"

There was the question. He had the Jews right where he wanted them. They were exhausted and he had a full force of men. Capturing the lot of them would take less than an hour, he was sure. But how to do it without Dieter being killed? If he was even with them. That thought tortured him again. They hadn't found his nephew's body in the crematorium. That meant he was likely with this group, but he couldn't guarantee it. He needed the best plan possible to assure his nephew would survive, assuming he was out there. But could he risk the escape of these men when they were so close, just to save Dieter?

He shook his head. "Not yet," he said. "Let's move forward and inspect that body."

The corporal eyed him for a moment as if he wanted to disagree, but he merely nodded and motioned to his men. They advanced, weapons at the ready, spread out, darting from tree to tree. Hans smiled to himself. He'd taught these men those techniques. Combat training. The last *Kommandant* had thought it a waste of time, but Hans always felt it might come in handy one day, although he'd had in mind a future defense of the camp against the Russians, not a threat from within Birkenau.

He motioned for his own men to follow, and keeping about twenty meters behind the first group, Hans rushed forward, sprinting from tree to tree. The birch trunks were too skinny to give real cover, but it was far better than nothing. What if the Jews hadn't fled? What if they'd set an ambush? He knew the *Sonderkommando* had some weapons. He shook his head. That should make no difference. His prey was a pack of civilians, beaten down, half starved. They'd been lucky to get this far. No, they wouldn't put up much resistance when he finally closed the net.

A few minutes later they reached the body. Hans had hoped the man might still be alive, that he could interrogate him and learn their plans, but he was met with an open mouth and wide eyes, staring fixedly up into the heavens. "Look for any weapons," Hans ordered.

One of the men did, but shook his head after a few moments. "Nothing, sir."

"Search the immediate area," he ordered. He didn't expect to find anything, but he needed time to think. What if the prisoners did make it through the outer fence? He'd never see Dieter alive again. Perhaps the corporal was correct. If they attacked quickly, they might bag all of them now. If he was lucky, they'd be too panicked to act against his nephew. He weighed the risks. The man was right, better to get them now, whatever the consequences. He would have to pray that when the fighting was over, Dieter would still be alive.

He called the corporal over. "Here's what we're going to do," he said.

"I've found something!"

Hans heard the call and turned. One of the men moved quickly through the trees, waving a scrap of dirty paper. "What is it?" he asked anxiously.

The man moved up, excitement on his face. He handed the paper to Hans, who stared down at the single word scrawled hastily on the note. It said simply: *south*.

"Should I send the men after them?" the corporal asked.

South. Did this change things? Now he knew where they were going, if the note wasn't a piece of clever subterfuge. No, he knew that he had someone among them willing to leave this note. Could he use this information to increase the chances that Dieter would survive?

South meant the rail line. It also meant the Jews were not heading toward the outer fence, at least at this point. That meant he had time, an opportunity to plan. It meant that at least for now, Dieter was not in danger of being taken away.

"No, Corporal. We're not going after them just yet. Instead, here's what we're going to do . . ."

Chapter 29
Flight to the Gate

October 1944
Auschwitz

Jakub stumbled through the woods, part of the shuffling, shambling, gray-striped herd. Dieter was still in front of him, and he kept a hand on the back of the guard's tunic, making sure he didn't move too far ahead. His chest was on fire as he gasped for breath; his legs were weak and threatened to buckle beneath him. He could see the struggles of his fellow inmates. They were at the end of their endurance.

But they'd been lucky so far. Again, the Germans had made contact but had not pressed their advantage. Surely if the Nazis had pursued them immediately, they would all be dead or captured by now. But by some miracle, their enemy was still hesitating. Roch was leading them away as quickly as the poor men could travel. First southwest, then turning directly south to skirt Birkenau on their left. They were blessed with the protective cover of the birch trees, but Jakub wondered how long their luck could hold out. Worse yet, how much farther could they move without a rest?

As if confirming his fears, Jakub saw the horizon in front of them beginning to thin out. A few hundred meters farther, they abruptly reached the end of the woods. A field stretched out before them, an uneven pasture with overgrown brush, leading to a farmhouse a half kilometer away. Roch reached the boundary first and held up his hand for the mass to halt. Men threw themselves down on the ground, eyes closed, chests heaving. Jakub, with Tomasz's help, pulled Dieter down and positioned him with his back to a birch trunk, then he turned and motioned for Roch to join them.

"What do we do now?" Jakub asked.

Roch looked out among the men. "We rest."

"And after that?" asked Tomasz. "I'll bet we won't be getting any hospitality from that farmhouse."

Jakub scanned the horizon, looking for any cover, but the field extended for a kilometer or more in both directions. Other than the brush, which was no more than waist high, there was nothing to hide behind. When they left the woods, they would be exposed.

"We could wait until darkness," Jakub suggested.

Roch searched the clouds for a moment, then shook his head. "It's early afternoon at best. I don't know why the Germans aren't right on our heels, but there's no way we'll escape their notice until nightfall. We're going to have to risk it in the open."

"No way we make it across there without being spotted," said Tomasz.

"You're the one who suggested we move south," responded Roch.

"I still think it's our best chance," maintained Tomasz. "But what do I know? Like I told you, I think this is a fool's errand."

"There's nothing to be done about it," said Roch at last. "Let's face it, it's a miracle we've made it this far. We should all be dead in that gas chamber. If God wants us to escape, then we will make it. We have to have faith that if we've made it this far, he'll guide us through this field."

"Shall we try it then?" Jakub asked.

Roch smiled. "Yes, my friend, we shall have to try it."

"I disagree," said Tomasz. "Whatever the risk, we should wait until darkness."

Roch shook his head. "The Germans are too close."

"Nonsense," said Tomasz. "We are two or more kilometers away from our original position in the woods. They were not in visual contact with us when we turned south. They will have to send men in every direction. There's every chance if we take a good defensive position here, then we will avoid detection. We still have a few guns. The Germans will be spread out. If we do run into them, we should be able to fight them. If the group was small enough, we might end up with more guns, and more prisoners as leverage. The worst that would happen is they force us out into the field. We'd be no worse off than we are right now. That's what we already face."

Roch considered those words for a few moments. "No, Tomasz, it's too risky. If they find us here in force, we'll be done. We'd never make it across those fields with Germans on our tail. They would mow us down like wheat. We'll have to risk it now."

"Suit yourself," said Tomasz, shrugging. "You're probably right. Besides, the choice is die here or die there." Jakub's friend stomped off a few meters.

"What if he's right?" asked Jakub.

"He well might be," said Roch. "We are faced with impossible scenarios. But I must follow my instincts on this. If there are Germans waiting for us in that farmhouse, and we have Germans behind us as well, then we're done. Better for us to just face what's in front than to be sandwiched between them and caught in a crossfire. Let's spread the word. We'll leave in a few minutes."

Roch and Jakub moved among the group, telling them the plan. The men reluctantly pulled themselves up and shambled toward the tree line. Roch positioned himself as always, in the front of the group, taking the biggest risk. Jakub assisted Dieter to his feet and moved him to the middle. If there were Germans out there, he didn't want their only hostage to be killed by a chance bullet.

Roch gave the signal and they pressed forward out of the woods. Jakub expected shots to greet them immediately, but he heard nothing but the rustling of the high grass as they stumbled out into the field. They were three hundred meters from the farmhouse now and Roch led them on a path veering to the right of the structure and toward a cluster of trees another kilometer away.

They made a strange sight weaving back and forth as they struggled to make progress over the uneven, frozen ground. Here and there a man would fall, hitting the ground with a grimace. Others would stop and help him up, and they would continue on their way.

Jakub scanned the horizon, looking for the farmer, for waiting Germans, for anything that would betray them. He was sure that the alarm would sound, but the farmhouse loomed closer, filling the horizon, and there was nothing. Perhaps it was a miracle? Perhaps the structure had been abandoned? That would explain the tall grass and the uneven field. Could it be that, as Roch had stated, God might be protecting them?

They drew even with the house, passing the structure fifty meters or so to their left. It was an old, squat structure with yellowed brick and a rounded, thatched roof. An ancient barn stood behind it, perhaps another fifty meters away from the house. Jakub could hear cows mooing within the structure.

Abruptly there was a woman's voice shouting out in German. Jakub could see her, standing on the back porch, pointing toward them as she turned and shouted through the door. She was middle-aged, wearing a light-colored peasant's dress, her gray hair pulled back into a severe bun. Her face wore a mask of surprise mixed with anger.

A man appeared next to her, a little taller. He wore trousers and a white peasant shirt covered by a brown vest. He was balding and he looked at least fifty. He stared at them for a moment and then turned and rushed back into the house, only to appear a few moments later with a shotgun in his hands.

"Run!" shouted Jakub, pushing Dieter forward. The mass of men hesitated as others turned to gawk at the porch before the jumble of bodies pushed forward, breaking into an awkward jog. As Jakub watched, the man raised the gun and took aim. The farmer fired and he saw the flash of the muzzle followed a second later by the thunderous retort of the weapon. A prisoner nearest the farm shouted out, his body jerking. He stumbled forward a few more steps and fell, screaming in pain. Several men moved to help him as the rest of the group pushed forward, moans of anguish emanating from them. The farmer took aim again and Jakub grimaced, waiting for the next shot.

But it was not to be. Pawel had moved to the side of the pack and raised his machine pistol. He fired off a burst of rounds at the farmhouse. It didn't appear that he hit the man or woman, but they fled into the house in terror. The wounded inmate, who had a sprinkle of bloody holes on his back, did not appear to be badly hurt, and with the assistance of two other men, moved away as quickly as he could from the house.

In a few minutes they put another hundred meters between themselves and the porch. Jakub looked back several times, but the man and woman did not appear again. They were clearly not used to being fired on and wanted nothing further to do with the prisoners. Of course, they would be immediately reporting their position to the authorities. Jakub wondered whether such a remote farm would have a telephone. If they did not, there would be a delay before the Nazis in the camp would know the position of the *Sonderkommando*, but if they did . . .

They finally reached the safety of the trees. Roch led them

along the eastern portion of the woods, so they could keep an eye on the rail line that was visible a kilometer or so in the distance. The terror of the attack at the farm kept all of them moving for another hour or so, but eventually the men began lagging and Roch called for a halt. They had been fortunate to not run into any more Germans.

Jakub slumped down next to Dieter and Tomasz, his breath coming in rapid gulps as he tried to slow his heart down. He was more physically exhausted than he'd ever been, and he was unsure he could go much farther without an extended rest. He was also starving. They hadn't eaten anything all day and they had no provisions. Worse yet, his throat burned with an agonizing thirst. They would need water soon, or they would be unable to go any farther.

Roch appeared, moving along, talking to clumps of men. He was hobbling, Jakub noticed, and he wondered how the man even had the strength to stand. He'd always looked up to Roch, but now he had more respect for him than ever. The leader saw Jakub and smiled, limping over to him.

"How are things, my friend?"

"Just wonderful," Jakub joked.

"And how is our German guest?"

"Still along for the walk," said Jakub, but then he turned serious. "We need water, food, and rest. What are we going to do?"

Roch's face darkened. "True enough. I'd hoped we could get something from that farm, but the residents didn't seem to approve of us being there. We need water more than anything, but we haven't come across any streams, or a well. I suppose I'll need to send a few people out to see what we can find."

Jakub started to rise, but Roch shook his head.

"Not you. I need you to guard our guest."

Jakub was secretly relieved. He didn't know if he truly had the strength to search for water. But he wanted to do his best and he'd been willing to try. Roch left them and gave orders to a few of the other leaders, who left in several directions. Jakub slumped back against the ground, his eyes staring at the top of the trees. He wanted desperately to fall asleep, but he knew he had to keep an eye on Dieter.

Minutes passed. Jakub floated in and out of consciousness. He saw the gas chamber, Schmidt's smirking face, his parents as they were led away at the rail line by the jerk of an SS doctor, and most persistent of all, the face of Anna, sad, tears running down her face.

"Jakub!" He heard the voice abruptly and he looked up. Roch was standing over him.

"What?" he asked groggily, trying to remember where he was, what he was doing. Then he recalled his duty. Dieter! He sat up, but the guard was still there, sitting, legs crossed, watching him. Tomasz lay next to him a meter away, snoring lightly. "I'm sorry, Roch. I must have fallen asleep."

Roch looked like he was going to lecture him, but his face softened. "We're all exhausted. Just try to stay awake, all right?"

Jakub nodded.

"Come. We've found water, and it's not far."

Dieter rose first. He moved over to Jakub and extended his hand to help him up. Jakub looked up into his eyes, wondering why this Nazi was giving him such a gesture. Was it one human helping another out, or . . . ?

He ignored the hand and rolled over onto his stomach, pushing himself up onto his knees, then with one foot and another, he stood up. Stepping past Dieter, he moved to Tomasz and prodded his friend with his foot. The Warsaw street thug mumbled and opened his eyes.

"We've found water," said Jakub.

They moved out a few moments later, Dieter in front as always, Tomasz walking next to Jakub. They moved about two hundred meters deeper into the woods. Jakub wasn't sure what direction they were truly heading. As they stumbled along, he thought he heard the sound of rushing water. Soon his thoughts were confirmed as they approached a stream running through the woods, sunk down below steep muddy banks of about two meters. Men were already down in the water, squatting at the edge, dipping their hands violently into the channel as they quenched their thirst.

"Go ahead," said Tomasz. "I'll watch our friend for a moment."

Jakub moved thankfully forward and worked his way awkwardly down the slope. Halfway down, he slipped and tumbled into some undergrowth. Thorns tore at his hands and clothing. He grimaced from the pain, but he pulled himself up and stumbled to the water. Washing the blood from his hands, he cupped his palms and lifted the freezing water to his lips. He'd never tasted anything better. Even in the cattle car on the way to Auschwitz, when they'd gone a day without water, he hadn't felt this thirsty. He lapped the water up for long seconds and then, with Tomasz's help, he pulled Dieter down so his friend and the guard could drink as well.

Jakub stretched and stood up. He looked at the sky, which still seemed bright enough, but the light was already dimming under the trees, he realized. It must be late afternoon, turning into evening. They had to hurry, or they would never find where the rail line and the fence intersected.

Roch must have realized the same thing, because he ordered the men to get moving. Everyone was reluctant to leave the water and to end the rest, but under their leader's strict words, the mass began struggling up the far bank. Jakub hopped over the stream, which was fortunately no wider than a meter, and he helped Tomasz and Dieter do the same. They climbed up the bank and moved back into the woods, with Roch always in the lead.

An hour later the sky above was darkening. Visibility in the woods was so dim that they were having difficulty seeing where they were going. Roch ordered the group to tighten up so they did not lose anyone. At last he ordered another halt and asked the resistance members to convene, to discuss what to do next. Jakub left Dieter with Tomasz and joined the meeting.

"I don't think we can go on tonight," said Roch, when he had them all together. "I don't know how much farther the fence line might be, and I don't think we can keep stumbling along in these woods." There were mumblings of agreement but also of discord.

"I don't agree," said Pawel. "Our best chance, if we have any chance of getting out of here, is to keep moving before the Germans are fully organized. We can't attack the gate in full daylight, so that means we would have to wait another day. If we do, they will surely be waiting for us with reinforcements not only from the camp, but probably from outside. We could end up facing hundreds of our enemy, and that gives us no chance at all. I don't like it any more than you do, Roch, but I think we have to trust to our luck now, while we have time on our side."

Roch looked at Jakub. "What do you think?" he asked.

"I want to stay here desperately, but I agree with Pawel. We need to go while we can. If we can't find the fence, well, we're no worse off by searching all night for it. But if we do locate it, we can storm it while it's manned by just a few Germans. If we have any chance of getting out, we have to take it."

Roch asked for a few more opinions, some supporting Pawel, some supporting Jakub. Then he thought about things while they waited in silence. "We'll try it tonight," he said at last.

Roch ordered them up again. Now they moved much more slowly, hands out, many holding each other's arms as they felt their way through the pitch black of the forest. In this strange limbo, time ceased to have meaning, and moments might have been an hour or more. Jakub concentrated on keeping ahold of Dieter with his left hand and Tomasz with his right. He took tentative step after step, listening closely to try to keep up with the group as they moved through their surroundings.

Then, in the distance, he thought he could make out a pin-prick of light, then another. A few more steps and he was sure. There was light out there. The dots flickered and darted, disappearing as they wove through the trees, but the lights grew closer and their number grew.

They reached the end of the trees. They were standing near another field, this time of what appeared closely-cropped grass. In the distance, Jakub could see the rail line extending along until it reached a building. From the top of the structure, a searchlight blared into the darkness, the eye flailing this way and that through the field they would have to cross. Even from this distance they could hear voices, the echoes of many men. They had reached their destination, but it was held by the Germans in strength.

Chapter 30
Problem at the Gate

October 1944
Auschwitz

"What do we do now?" Jakub asked the resistance leader as they stood on the edge of the woods. They couldn't make out the number of Germans out there, but there had to be at least twenty, judging by the noise they were making. The searchlight slashed relentlessly across the open field they would have to cross.

Roch shook his head. "I don't see how we can get through, even if we rushed them," he said. "That searchlight will catch us before we're halfway across. They are already alert, and we'd have incoming automatic fire from multiple locations. I ran into this kind of situation during the war. You can't charge a defensive position of prepared enemy over an open field with our small group. If we all had arms, yes, but we're basically without weapons. We can't do it."

"Brilliant," said Tomasz. "So we've marched around the countryside, now what? Do we walk over with a white flag and ask for forgiveness?"

"We wait and we think!" snapped Roch in return. "And I'd remind you that you recommended this direction. I need a few minutes to consider this." The leader sat there for a while, staring out over the field, straining his ears, his head slightly cocked, trying to gauge what was out there. Finally, he turned back to the assembled group. "We have no choice. We need to stay here until morning. At first light, we will make our way to the west and try to find another gate along the fence. We can't make the rail gate work."

"I disagree," said Tomasz. "We should surrender."

"So they can murder us?" retorted Roch.

"They'll murder us out here. I told you, I have connections. If you let me lead the negotiation, perhaps I can work something out for us."

"There's no chance."

"That's not true, Roch. Out here in this forest there is no chance. In there I see possibilities. Sure, we might all be killed, but then again, we might not be. I just have to get in front of the right people. In my humble opinion, we've a better chance throwing ourselves at their mercy than waiting for the Nazis to find us. I can use this guard here as leverage. They have to want him back."

There were some murmurs of approval from others in the huddle. "Maybe we should give Tomasz a chance," muttered one of them.

"No way," said Roch. "You're all out of your minds. The only thing waiting for us back at Birkenau is that gas chamber. If we have any chance to survive, we've got to get past that fence. You must trust me. We need to wait until the morning, and then get out of here before they find us."

"Suit yourself," said Tomasz, stomping off. Jakub tried to

stop him, but his friend pushed past, leading Dieter a short distance away. Was Tomasz right? He did have connections in the camp. Could he use the guard as a negotiation tool along with bribes to save their lives? That seemed unlikely, but he'd seen Tomasz pull off miracles with the Germans. He felt his doubts about Roch creeping up again. He hated himself for it, but as much as he admired the man, he'd seen him be wrong several times now. Tomasz, on the other hand, had done so much of what he said he would accomplish. He was cynical, distrustful, the opposite of Roch in every way, but which one of them was right?

Roch watched the man leave, shaking his head slightly with a sad expression on his face. He turned back to the others. "All right, here's what we are going to do. We are going to keep a tight watch tonight. I want men on duty in shifts of four hours. We need people stationed fifty meters into the woods in all directions. I'll watch the field. If anything comes our way, run back and notify me. We have to keep the Germans off us until first light." He looked at the group. "I need three men for the first shift. Who will volunteer?"

Jakub raised his hand along with a half dozen others. Roch glanced at him. "Not you, Jakub. I need you to keep an eye on Dieter."

"Tomasz is watching him."

"I need you to do it."

"All right. I'll stay here."

"Good man," said Roch. He turned and moved off into the darkness to give additional orders to the men. Jakub moved over to Tomasz and sat down near Dieter, who was leaning against a tree, his eyes half closed. Watching the young man, Jakub could feel his own eyes growing heavier. He was so tired. He wondered how he would have the endurance to remain awake tonight and guard Dieter. Could he find someone else besides Tomasz to watch the SS man for part of the night?

Could he trust anyone else with Dieter? He realized he would never make it until morning. When Tomasz returned, he would have him share in the duties of watching Dieter. He was certain that Roch was only being cautious in refusing to allow his friend a part in guarding their prisoner.

Tomasz returned a short time later. He looked around, making sure Roch was not nearby, then he slumped down next to Jakub, moving close so that nobody else could hear.

"We need to make a run for it. You and me."

"What do you mean?" Jakub asked, surprised.

"Look around us," said Tomasz. "These men are exhausted. Hell, a third of them are wounded, or so weak they can't go any farther. The Germans are close to us and they'll soon be bringing up the rear. We're going to be caught and when we are, they're going to massacre us."

"I thought you didn't believe in escape," said Jakub. "You've been advocating turning ourselves in."

"That still might be the best course. All I know is that we're doomed either way if we stay here. I've been thinking about things. The Germans are never going to let us all live, regardless of any bribe I could make. You saw the smoke in the camp. They've been made fools of. They are going to want to make examples, lots of them. Roch and his men are going to be those examples. If we don't get away from here, we'll be part of that too. I don't think I'll be able to get anyone to listen to me in the heat of their anger. But, if we escaped, just you and me, and hid for a few days. Then we'd have a chance."

"A chance to surrender again?"

Tomasz shrugged. "Maybe. Or to escape. Listen, Jakub, we've made it farther than I thought we'd ever get. I didn't think it was possible, but now we're just one fence away from getting out of here. I say go off on our own, find a place to hole up, and then we'll take a shot at getting through the outer fence. If they catch us, then you let me do the talking. I know it sounds hopeless but, hell, it's a far better chance than we have here."

"And we just leave everyone?"

Tomasz smiled at him. "I knew it would come to that. You're a good man, Jakub. I've always respected that about you. I'm sorry, my friend, but yes, we leave everyone else here. It's the same awful choice we faced when they dragged us out of those cattle cars. We either fought to survive, or we went with everyone else to our deaths. Remember, we didn't create this inferno, the Germans did."

Jakub closed his eyes, feeling the conflict twisting inside him. Tomasz was certainly correct that their present position appeared hopeless. They were beaten down, wounded, exhausted, and the Germans were closing in on them. Many of these men wouldn't be able to go much farther. If the Germans, now in any force, found them, they would not be able to get away.

But could he leave Roch? Could he betray the man who had believed in him, who had fought to free all of Auschwitz? What about the promise to his father? He knew what Roch would say. Fighting to free the camp was enough. Now they would need to stick together, no matter what. Was he right? Or was it true that fighting had been enough, and now, at the end, if a man had a better chance alone, or with a few men, was it fair to all stay together?

"Well, what will it be?" Tomasz asked after a while.

"Let me think about it for a few more minutes," said Jakub. "Will you watch Dieter for me while I rest my eyes?"

"Of course I will, my friend."

Jakub closed his eyes to rest. He already knew what he was going to do.

A shout jarred him out of his sleep. Tomasz was there, pulling Dieter to his feet. "What's going on?" shouted Jakub.

"The Germans are here!" yelled Tomasz.

The men were shouting, pushing against each other, running in every direction in the darkness. Jakub could hear the clipped bellow of German and, more ominously, a thunderous barking. "They have dogs with them!" he warned.

"I know it!" said Tomasz. He grabbed Jakub by the shirt. "We have to go, now!" His friend started to take off, but Jakub held him back.

"We have to take Dieter!" he said.

Tomasz turned. "Why? He's no good to us now."

"He's a hostage," said Jakub, thinking as quickly as he could. "Like Roch said, he might come in handy if it comes to negotiation."

Tomasz paused, thinking about it for a moment before he nodded. "You're right. Grab him and let's get the hell out of here!"

Jakub rose and took Dieter's right arm. Tomasz took his left. Oddly, the man gave no resistance but instead followed along with them, even with the Germans so near. Perhaps he feared he would be killed now by someone? Perhaps he thought going with Jakub and Tomasz was his best chance at survival. He might have been right.

They wove through the darkness, pushing past scrambling figures. Tomasz shouted and shoved, making his way through and back toward the tree line.

"We can't go out there!" shouted Jakub.

"Of course not," said Tomasz, "but we need the light to see by."

They reached the line and Tomasz turned to his left, moving them along, just inside the trees. His friend was right, with the exposed night sky and the distant light from the gate, there was just enough illumination to allow them to see where they were going. Of course, they would be lit up against the field if any Germans were approaching them from the woods, Jakub realized, but at this moment, they had to take their chances.

Tomasz tore along, speeding up into a dash. Jakub and Dieter struggled to keep up with him and they kept having to twist and turn to avoid trees and some of the heavier undergrowth. Dieter stumbled and fell. They pulled him to his feet and continued. Then Jakub did the same. But Tomasz was unshakable, leading them with firm direction and a steady foot through the darkness.

The woods bent to the north. They had no choice but to follow them, as they battled to put distance between themselves and the mass of screaming and barking behind them.

"We're heading back toward the camp!" Jakub shouted between steps.

"Nothing can be done about that!" responded Tomasz. "We've got to get out of here before we're nabbed with the rest of them. In the morning, there will be a chance to get our bearings, and then we'll see what happens!"

They kept moving. The sounds faded in the background until it was no more than a dim clatter of undistinguishable sounds. Tomasz pulled them to a stop, and they all fell to the ground, breathing heavily. "I think we've made it," he said.

Jakub nodded, unable to catch his breath. Again, he had to admire his friend's strength, his single-minded determination at self-preservation. He thought of Roch and his heart twisted. He'd left his friend behind. But had he really? What choice did he have at that moment when the Germans were on them? Wasn't it every man for himself? And what about the decision he was contemplating when he'd shut his eyes? No matter. What was done was done now. He was still alive for now, and with Tomasz there was at least a fighting chance they would make it. He knew in his heart that while he admired Roch, Tomasz was a pure survivor.

"Let's go," said Tomasz. Too soon. His friend was already up and helping them to their feet.

"Can't we wait just a minute longer?" implored Jakub.

Tomasz smiled. "If I could let you, I would. But we must be off. The Germans will have rounded up the group by now, but they'll be sending out patrols looking for any that might have gotten away. This guard here will be conspicuously absent from their count, and they'll certainly be looking for him. No, we must keep going. Don't worry, we'll find a good place to take a rest. There's a place I am going to try to find. I've never been there, but I've heard of it."

They kept moving through the darkness. They were completely alone now. An hour or so later they came across the field and the farm they had passed before. "Carefully now," warned Tomasz. "We can't be seen here."

They ambled through the field, step by slow step, trying to remain utterly silent as they passed back through the pasture, keeping as far away from the farmhouse as they could. They were in luck. The farmer and his wife seemed to have already gone to bed. A dog barked inside, but that must have been a regular occurrence because the lights did not turn on. Soon they were past the house and they increased their pace through the field. They reached the trees a few minutes later and were able to take another rest.

"We can catch our breath here," said Tomasz. "Not forever, mind you, but for a good while." He looked up at the sky. "I don't see any signs of dawn, but it can't be too far away."

They rested for a half hour in the darkness. Jakub strained his ears, listening for any sound that might indicate the Germans had followed them. There was none. The night was peaceful, and it felt so strange to Jakub that a couple kilometers away, his camp sat in an open field, swallowing humanity in greedy bites day after day. How could there be such tranquility so close to hell itself?

Tomasz nudged him with his foot a little later. They all drew to their feet silently and started off again in the woods, Tomasz continuing to lead them unerringly toward some destination only he was aware of. Soon Jakub felt the strange nothingness of the forest again as they marched deeper into the woods, arms out to avoid low branches and trunks. He looked up into the sky now and again, expecting morning to gradually come, but it was still deepest night.

Tomasz stopped them abruptly. "We're here," he said, sounding relieved. "I didn't know if I could find it or not."

Jakub strained his eyes and could just make out a clearing and what looked like a dumpy single-story house. "What is this place?" he asked.

"It's a little cottage not far from Birkenau that I've heard about. I've never been here, but I knew it was in the woods out here somewhere. If it still stood."

"What if someone lives in there?" whispered Jakub.

Tomasz chuckled. "Not likely. Let's go and investigate." He led them forward and they moved cautiously into the clearing. The house was no more than a dozen meters from the woods. They reached the porch. Jakub noticed the house was painted white, and seemed to glow with an eerie sheen like a ghost in the darkness. He felt terribly uneasy about the place for some reason, and he kept looking this way and that, as if spirits were passing by and through him.

Tomasz led them up onto the porch and then he fumbled with the door, which was fortunately unlocked. He led them inside. The interior was pitch-black. All the windows had been boarded up or painted over. There was no furniture. The interior was freezing and Jakub shivered in his thin pajamas. It felt far colder inside than it had out in the woods.

"Something's wrong with this place," he said quietly, more to himself than to Tomasz.

"It's not a house. At least it isn't any longer." Tomasz moved over to the wall and he pushed his hand through a swinging square wooden latch on the wall. The square was big enough for a large bucket to be passed through. "This was where they dropped the cyanide in," he said.

"What are you talking about?" asked Jakub.

"This was one of the original gas chambers in Auschwitz. Nothing like the factories they built later. This is the little white house. They killed thousands here before the main camp was ready. There's another one out here, too. Closer to Canada, I think. The little red house."

Jakub sucked in his breath. He was in another killing center. He'd started today in a gas chamber, and he was ending it there as well.

"Let's get some sleep," said Tomasz, pulling himself down.

Jakub lay down in the darkness, trying to close his eyes. He was exhausted but he couldn't shake the feeling that the room was full of his brothers and sisters. He heard the echoes of their pleas, their screams, a whole people fading away.

Chapter 31
Mira

October 1944
Auschwitz

Anna stared in horror at the block wardress. She clutched Estusia's hand, not knowing what to do. The wardress, Mira, had a whistle in her teeth and took a deep breath, preparing to blow it again.

"Stop!" shouted Estusia. "Can't we talk about this?"

"Talk about what?" Mira asked. "You've murdered Kamila—Schmidt's favorite. When he finds out, he's going to kill half our barracks, me included."

"You hated her," said Anna. "Everyone did."

"That's beside the point. I'm not going to lose my life over some lovers' quarrel."

"What do you mean?" snapped Estusia.

"I'm not blind!" said the wardress. "Nor deaf. It's well known that Schmidt has taken on a new lover." She looked pointedly at Anna.

"I'm not with Schmidt," she insisted.

"Nonsense. You went off with him. At night," said Mira. "What were you doing? Discussing the weather?"

"He forced me to. Besides, nothing—"

"Forced or willing, he's marked you as his own," said Mira. "It's the talk of the women's camp elite. Certainly, *she* knew it," she said, pointing at Kamila's body.

"He didn't want her anymore," said Anna. "He told me that much."

"Do you think that will matter to him?" said Mira. She shook her head. "I can't risk it. I've got to turn the two of you in." She reached for her whistle again.

"Wait!" insisted Estusia. "What if we can make other arrangements?"

Mira's eyes narrowed. "What sort of other arrangements?"

"You know who Anna is really with," said Estusia.

The wardress nodded. "Yes, that young buck from the *Sonderkommando*. Jakub, isn't it?"

"You know what he has access to," said Estusia. "Food, gold, jewelry. Everything you would need to make your life even better."

"I don't need more food," said Mira. "We get plenty. But the rest of it—I'm still listening."

"We can get you some of Jakub's valuables," said Estusia.

The block wardress stared at both of them, her eyes shrewd. She lowered the whistle a few inches. "Not some," said Mira. "All."

"Fair enough. We'll give you everything he brings her."

"I can't, Estusia—" said Anna.

Her friend turned on Anna, eyes on fire. She shook her head. Turning back to Mira, she continued talking. "Everything it is."

Mira stood and stared at them for a few moments, looking at the body. "Fine then. I'll keep your secret. At least for now. But I'll expect payment. Daily payment. If you miss even a single one, I'll run to Schmidt, and you'll have to explain all of this to him. Now listen, you little sluts, get your asses back to the barracks and keep your mouths shut. Even with my cooperation, there will be an investigation. You've just made a lot of heartache for me. It better be worth it."

"Don't you worry," said Estusia. "It will be."

They moved past Mira and out into the morning light, heading quickly back toward their barracks.

"What have you done?" Anna asked when they were out of earshot. "You've killed us both. Jakub isn't coming again. Schmidt told me—"

"You believe Schmidt? We don't know that."

"What if he was telling the truth? He hasn't come in days. And now with what's happening in the camp . . ."

"No matter what, we will just have to figure something out. We were dead back there. At least I've bought us a little time."

She was right, of course. Although Anna couldn't see any way out of this, Estusia's quick thinking had given them a day at least to figure out what to do. They reached the barracks a few moments later.

"Let's get the girls together," said Estusia when they were back inside.

"No," said Anna. "I don't want to involve them. This is my problem."

"You heard Mira. If we don't deal with this, they'll execute half the barracks before they're done. We've got to get a plan together on how to pay her. And what to do if Schmidt does come looking for Kamila."

Anna nodded. Her friend was right again. They gathered the resistance cell over the next few minutes and they met again in a private portion of the barracks. Anna was too rattled to talk, so Estusia explained the situation. Roza's eyes widened more and more as the story went on, until they threatened to pop out of her head.

"Why did you have to kill her?" she asked at last.

"I didn't have a choice."

Anna nodded in agreement. "She was in a craze. Estusia had no option."

"I'm sure you're right," said Roza. "But this is a new complication. We're supposed to be in a revolt in a few days' time. Assuming that"—she gestured toward the west end of the camp—"hasn't derailed all of our plans."

"I'm sorry," said Anna. "I'll take care of this myself."

"No," said Roza. "Estusia is right. This is something we're all going to have to deal with." Their leader closed her eyes for a few minutes, mulling over the issues. She looked like she was going to speak several times but stopped herself. Finally, she opened her eyes. "We have to assume the plan is still on," she said. "That means we have to bide for time. What did you do with the body?" she asked.

"It's still there in the latrine," said Estusia.

"Where's Mira?"

"She's in there too."

"That won't do us any good," said Roza. "We can't leave the body where it is. Mira has to know that as well." Roza turned to two of the women. "Go to the latrine. Try to avoid being seen. When you get there, I want you to pull up some of the boards and then shove the body down into the filth. That should buy us a few days, unless they happen to clean it out in the meantime."

"What about Mira?" asked Anna.

"She shouldn't stop us. She knows we've got to hide the body, otherwise they'll be after all of us before the end of the day." Roza turned to the women. "If Mira is there, explain our plan. She'll understand what has to be done."

The women hurried to follow Roza's orders. "That will solve the problem of the body for a while," said Estusia. "But what about the bribes?"

"Is there any chance Jakub will be coming tonight?" Roza asked Anna.

"There's no way for me to know," she said. "He hasn't come since Schmidt pulled me aside. I don't know what's happened. I don't believe Schmidt, but he said Jakub wouldn't come, and that part at least has been true."

"I agree with you that Schmidt is a liar and can't be trusted," said Roza. "Still, that doesn't help us if Jakub isn't coming. We'll have to assume there is some reason he's not able to make it here. Whether voluntary or otherwise. Besides," she said, glancing again at the window, "we don't know what's going on out there. We're on lockdown, and that could last for days. We have to assume that he won't be able to make it here for a long time to come."

"Then what are we going to do?" Anna asked.

"You'll have to get things from Henryk."

Anna was shocked. She wasn't even aware that Roza knew about her friend in the Union Factory. "I can't do it," she said.

"You don't have a choice."

"Please, you don't understand. I've been able to put him off with smiles and things so far. But he's become more aggressive, more insistent. And that's for a little food. If I ask him for gold or money, he's going to want much more."

"You'll have to give it to him," said Roza. "There's nothing else to be done."

"She's right," said Estusia. "At least about Henryk. But it doesn't have to go that far. You can pass him a note about what you need and then meet up with him in the bathroom. Get the item from him and then I'll show up and interrupt things."

Anna nodded, hating the deception. "That might work, but how does that really help us? That buys us one day. We need five."

"Estusia is right," said Roza. "Let's figure out tomorrow, and we'll try to come up with a better plan after that. So much could happen. Jakub could come back. If he doesn't, perhaps we can slip a note to his friend, that Tomasz. He might be able to help us."

"Yes. That's possible," said Anna.

The girls returned, hurrying back through the long barracks to their meeting spot. "It's done," said Ella.

"Was Mira still there?"

"Yes," she said. "But I told her the plan and she agreed. She even helped us lift the planks."

"It's settled then," said Roza, and filled the rest of their group in on the plan. "We'll secure what we can for tomorrow, and then see what develops tonight. But we can't assume that Jakub or Tomasz will save us. I need everyone to think long and hard about alternative plans."

"We could kill Mira," said Estusia.

Roza nodded. "I've already considered that. If we're not able to secure anything from Henryk tomorrow, or figure out a solution for the rest of the five days, we may have to consider extreme measures."

"I can't be responsible for that," said Anna.

"For what?" said Roza. "Mira is a monster. She's been around since the start of the camp. She might be better behaved now, because times have changed, but I've heard the rumors about her. She used to strangle women at night just so she could keep their extra ration of soup and bread. It was a common practice here in the early days, and Mira was notorious about it. No, Anna, she's no innocent. If it comes to getting rid of her, she'll have received her justice."

"She's coming," Estusia warned. Mira had returned to the barracks and was moving down the long corridor between the bunks.

Anna spent a restless day in their building. There were ominous sounds outside, including a clear exchange of gunfire, but then everything died down except the occasional shouts of some Germans running along the rail line. Rumors swept through the bunks like wildfire: The Russians were here; the Germans were killing everyone in the camp; the *Sonderkommandos* had risen in a full revolt but had been put down. Each seemed as unlikely as the next. But as the day continued, it was clear that whatever was happening out there was over. Evening came and with it their thin soup and a little ersatz bread mixed with sawdust. There was no roll call that night, since nobody was supposed to have left the barracks at all. Anna was grateful for that, because they would have come up one woman short. Mira could probably cover that up, but there were no guarantees, and if the Germans found out someone was not there, there would be terrible retribution until answers were given.

Finally the long, terrible day was over, and Anna crawled onto the hard wooden slats with her bunkmates and spent a restless night trying to find some sleep.

Pop. She woke to the strange noise, shaking her head and fighting through the fog in her mind. What was that? The light was still low in the barracks, so it must have been just after dawn. Anna looked around and saw a head or two raised up, but most of the women were still asleep.

Pop. There was the sound again. The lights flipped on and then came Mira's voice, shouting at them to get out of bed. Anna rolled out and rose, arching, her limbs and back sore and throbbing from the rigid bunk. Estusia stepped out next to her. "What's that noise?" she whispered.

"What are you talking about?"

"That crack. There's some strange sound I've never heard before out there."

They heard it again. Estusia craned her neck. "I don't know what that is."

Mira interrupted them. "Get your breakfast and then form up inside."

"We've never held roll call inside," whispered Anna to Estusia. "Even in the dead of winter. What's going on?"

They lined up for their breakfast, which consisted of a cup of coffee made from ground-up acorns. Some of the women drew bread out of their dresses, which they'd saved from the night before, so they had a little food in the morning. Anna, still feeling ill, had given hers to Roza. She sipped at the coffee, trying to puzzle out what was happening to them. While they were standing there, the noise repeated several more times. Roza and her other friends joined them.

"What do you think that is?" Ella asked.

"It sounds like a gun to me," said Roza. "But that doesn't make any sense because the shots are spread out too much."

"Maybe it's something else," said Anna, hopefully. "It almost sounds like a sledge hammer on a nail."

"We'll have to wait until we can find something out," said Roza.

"Form a line near your bunk," said Mira.

"Maybe she's going to tell us now," said Estusia. They lined up, backs toward their bunks, in two lines facing each other down the long corridor of the barracks. It took a little time for everyone to move into position, since they had never been asked to assemble inside. Finally they were lined up to Mira's satisfaction, and she stood in the middle of the room.

"I have an announcement to make," she said. "Due to conditions in the camp, there will be no work today. We are confined to our barracks again." She stared up and down at them harshly. "But listen up! It won't be another holiday like yesterday. We will spend the day cleaning up this building. Every centimeter of it will be shining by the end of the day, or you'll stand at attention in here all night long. The SS will inspect us later. If they find anything out of order, you will be severely punished."

"What's going on outside?" a woman down the line asked Mira.

"Who spoke?" the block wardress demanded.

Nobody answered at first, but eventually the woman raised her hand. Mira stepped over in front of her and slapped her hard across the face. Then again, and again. The woman took the first couple of blows, but then began to duck, raising her arms. Mira kept hitting her until the woman fell to her knees, her arms covering her head. The block wardress kicked her hard in the stomach and she doubled over, coughing and gagging, her knees to her chest.

"Does anyone else have any questions?" Mira demanded.

The room held a stony silence.

"Good. Then get to work, you lazy sluts!"

The women moved away from the line. Some headed toward the barracks doors where buckets with mops had been placed. Anna moved to her bunk with Estusia, removing their thin blanket and crawling into the bunk to remove any scraps of fabric or smudges of dirt that might be apparent. She knew if anything was found by the Germans, they would use it as an excuse to punish them all.

Roza brought them rags dipped in water and they scrubbed the bunk, keeping an eye on Mira, taking a rest when they could to preserve their energy. Anna's mind was racing. What was she going to do? They were not going to work at the Union Factory today. She would not be able to ask Henryk for any help. If the camp was shut down, neither Jakub nor Tomasz would be coming tonight.

"I'm not going to be able to get anything for Mira," she whispered to Estusia. "What will she do to me?"

Her friend thought for a few moments, and then a smile came across her face. "This might be better than if we'd gone to work today. Think about it. Mira can't expect you to bring her something if the camp is shut down. This buys us another day. Tomorrow things should be back to normal, but if not, we're moving closer to the action day. Only four days to go right now."

Estusia was right. She hadn't thought of that. She should be safe today from Mira.

As if she'd materialized when Anna thought of her, the block wardress appeared at the foot of their bunk. "Anna, come with me."

"What do you want with her?" asked Estusia.

"That's none of your concern!" snapped Mira. "Unless you want my attention on you as well."

Estusia lowered her eyes.

"That's what I thought. Anna, with me. Now!" she repeated.

Anna climbed out of the bunk and followed Mira to the end of the hallway and through a door where Mira's private quarters were located. Anna had never been in here and she was shocked at the luxury. There was a private stove. Mira had a crude wooden desk and a chair. Her bed was a single tier and she had a mattress and a pillow. There were even a couple of books and a lamp on the desk. Anna hadn't seen anything like this in months and her eyes feasted on these objects that seemed like they came from another world.

"I didn't bring you here for a tour," said Mira. "Where are yesterday's valuables?"

Anna was shocked. "Yesterday? I don't even have today. How can I get you anything if we're shut up in here?"

"Don't lie to me, you little bitch," said Mira. "I know you hide things in this barracks. I told you yesterday that you would have to pay me daily, and that you'd better not miss a day. I want yesterday's payment and today's, no later than noon."

"That's impossible," said Anna. "You're mistaken about keeping things here. I . . . I can't bring you anything today. But tomorrow, I will bring you payment for all three days." She had no idea how she would manage that, but she had to say something right now.

"That's not good enough," said Mira, taking a step toward

Anna. "If you're telling me you can't pay today, then I'm taking you to Schmidt right now." She grabbed ahold of Anna's dress near the collar and pulled her toward the door.

"Wait!" shrieked Anna. "I'll bring it to you."

Mira paused, twisting Anna around so their faces were a centimeter apart. "I'm serious. I want all of it by noon today. Do you understand?"

"Yes."

Mira let go and Anna crashed to the ground, her back wrenching painfully. The block wardress stepped away and moved to her desk. "It better be enough for both days," she muttered, staring at the wall.

Anna struggled to her knees, her back on fire. She pulled herself up and hobbled out of the room. She was only able to take a couple of steps before she fell again. She could hear footsteps as Estusia ran to her side.

"Are you all right?" she asked.

"Get me away from here," Anna implored. Estusia helped Anna to her feet and then, one arm around her back, helped her limp back to their bunk, where she lowered Anna gently onto the wooden bed.

"What happened?" her friend asked.

"She wants payment now. For yesterday and today," Anna managed to whisper through the pain.

"Is she mad?" asked Estusia. "Where would you get that?"

"She thinks we have valuables hidden in the barracks."

"Where on earth would we have those?"

"I don't know," said Anna. "But she believes it, and she wants full payment by noon."

"That's impossible."

"That's what I told her, and she threatened to drag me to Schmidt now."

"What are we going to do?"

Roza came up at that point, and Estusia filled her in on what had happened. The leader shook her head. "We don't have anything. Well, not anything that would appease her."

"Then you do have something?" asked Estusia.

"A few zlotys," said Roza. "I keep it hidden in case of this kind of emergency. But Mira thinks we have gold and jewels. There's no way this would be enough."

"It's something," said Estusia. "We should give it to her and tell her we'll get her more tomorrow."

"I don't think that will work," said Anna.

"There's no other choice," said Roza. "Let me handle things. Mira and I have a certain understanding. She knows what I stand for. In the past, I haven't bothered her and she doesn't interfere with me. Perhaps I can convince her to wait."

"We'll have to try," said Estusia. "It's either that, or we dispose of her."

"It may come to that," said Roza. "But let's see if I can convince her. A dead block wardress will not be explained easily. They might liquidate the whole barracks. I'll get the money and go talk to Mira."

Roza departed and Estusia stayed with Anna, trying to rub away the fierce agony in her back. Roza returned a few minutes later.

"What did she say?" asked Estusia.

"She took the money but she wasn't pleased," said Roza. "I think she's accepting things, but we better watch her. Under no circumstances are we to let her take Anna again to her office. If she summons you, I'll go with you. Estusia, you follow along. If you hear a commotion and I call for you, charge in and we'll deal with her in her office. From there, we'll try to figure out what to do."

"You can't risk all of that for me," said Anna. "Just let her have her way with me if it comes to that. I won't let you all be liquidated because of my mess."

"This is all of our problem," said Roza. "We stick together.

And I'm not going to let that whore of a wardress kill you because of her greed and corruption. One way or another we'll resolve this together."

They went back to work on the cleaning. Anna was too injured to do anything, so Roza had her lie on her side with a rag in her hand, as if she was preparing to clean the vertical beams that held up the bunks. She kept an eye out for Mira, and when the wardress walked periodically through, she would nudge Anna, who would set to work scrubbing the beam, biting her lip from the pain, until Mira returned to her quarters again, and Anna could take a break.

In the early afternoon, Mira left the barracks to report to the SS about the morning labor. Anna was able to roll over on her back and close her eyes, trying to fight down the waves of throbbing fire in her back. She was thankful they weren't required to march to the Union Factory today. She had no idea how she would have made it. She could only hope that she would have healed enough by morning to make the walk tomorrow.

The door opened again. Mira had returned. Anna heard Roza gasp next to her and she opened her eyes, struggling to roll over to see what was happening. And then she saw it: Schmidt was with her. The wardress was pointing toward her bunk and she saw the SS guard's eyes following her finger until he focused on Anna. His face was red with anger and he rushed toward her bunk, hands out as if he would strangle her in her bed.

"You're coming with me right now!" he screamed, reaching for her. Roza tried to stop him but Schmidt backhanded her, sending her spinning out of his way. He reached into the bunk and seized Anna, dragging her out of the bed until she crashed to the floor. Her back wrenched again and she shrieked in pain. He ignored her, pulling her along the floor. She fought to get her knees under her, to get to her feet. Her hair was coming out at the roots and her head exploded in hot white light. Her eyes were blurred. She felt his hands on her arms and he dragged her to her feet.

"I know," he whispered to her. "I know what you did and you're going to pay for it like nobody in Auschwitz has ever paid!" He kicked the door open and shoved her out of the barracks. She crashed into the mud, her head banging hard against the ground. She was losing consciousness. She couldn't understand his screaming threats. Darkness closed in around her.

Chapter 32
The Interrogation

October 1944
Auschwitz

Anna spit blood. Another blow rang down on her face, and another. She blinked, her mind spinning. Through the fog she heard Schmidt's voice, asking her questions, taunting her, but she no longer understood the words.

She reached down and touched her stomach, tears running down her face. Her fingers burned where Schmidt had torn out her fingernails one after another. She was dying. She could feel it. She felt a terrible sadness for her future, mixed with relief that all of the suffering would soon be over.

"Please." She heard the words coming out of her swollen lips. "Please, kill me."

"Oh, I don't think so, my dear," said Schmidt, whispering in her ear. "Death is far too easy an ending for you."

"I'm sorry about Kamila," she said. "She was trying to kill me. I had no choice."

She could hear him laugh. "Do you think this is about

Kamila?" he asked incredulously. "I told you she had her purposes, but for me, she was no more than a dish to sample. Frankly, I'd grown rather tired of sampling the same thing over and over. That's why I'd turned my attention to you. That and the little cat and mouse game I was enjoying with your precious Jakub. No, Anna, that's not what you're here for. I want to know the plan."

"The plan? What are you talking about?" she managed to say.

He struck her again, hard against the cheek. She barely felt the blow.

"Don't lie to me, you little bitch. We know all about Jakub and the resistance. And we know that the women's camp was involved too. But we don't know who or how. That's what I want from you, my dear. The details of your involvement. I want to know that, and I want to know where the men are headed."

Where the men are headed? So there had been a revolt? Some of the men had fought, and some of them must have escaped the camp. Could Jakub be with them? He must be, otherwise why would Schmidt have brought her here? She felt the happiness surge inside her, giving her new strength.

"I don't know anything," she answered.

He struck her again, and again. She coughed and sputtered, trying to fight back the pain.

"Tell me everything."

"I'm sorry. Sorry about Kamila, sorry about everything. But I don't know what you're talking about."

He rained further blows down on her. She kept her arms crossed, protecting her middle as he slapped her over and over.

"If you tell me, I'll spare Jakub's life, and your own. Think about it, Anna. You have more at risk now than your own life."

Spare Jakub's life? Why would Schmidt offer that? Why would he expect her to care about Jakub after everything he'd told her? *He was lying all along*. She had never believed him, but now she knew the truth. Her husband would never betray her. It was Schmidt all along.

She heard a knock.

"Not now!" Schmidt shouted.

There was a murmuring at the door and the guard stepped away from her for a moment. She heard more whispering but she couldn't make out the words. Damn the buzzing in her head! The door slammed shut again and Schmidt was back.

"I'm sorry that I am going to have to leave you for a little while, my dear. It looks like we have your lover and his friends cornered, and I need to attend to things. If I capture him alive, I promise to reunite the two of you before the end. You've been a worthy adversary. So much steel in such a little body. It's a pity I was never able to sample your wares. Your illness and then this damned fighting has robbed me of a wondrous exploration, I'm sure. Ah well, I suppose it's too late for that now. I'll have to use you for other amusements. I promise you that what we've done so far here is merely an appetizer. I'll have the full feast for you when I return. Before the end, you will tell me what you know about the women's camp and this little revolt. Perhaps if we are lucky, Jakub will get to watch as I peel the flesh from your body, a little cut at a time. And that's not all I'll do," he warned. "I can take everything away from you before the end." He reached down and kissed her neck, his hand resting on her stomach. "Yes," he said finally. "A pity."

Chapter 33
Success and Failure

October 1944
Auschwitz

Hans paced in his office. It was well past midnight and he'd heard nothing for hours. How could a ragtag group of prisoners evade his men for so long, particularly when the Germans knew where they were headed?

What if Schmidt had been wrong? The sergeant was so sure of himself, so confident in his intelligence, but what if his informant had lied to him, and that message they'd found was meant to deceive them? Hans had put all his available men down to the south near where the rail line passed through the outer perimeter gate. That's where Schmidt said the prisoners were traveling. But what if they'd gone north instead, toward the river? Was there some way across that Hans didn't know about? He'd stripped the guards down to the bone up there. If a hundred men charged one of the northern gates, even without any weapons, they would be able to overwhelm the soldiers and escape the greater Auschwitz complex. That would be a disaster of momentous proportions. They would have to ask the SS in Berlin for assistance. Or even worse, the Wehrmacht. Kramer would be humiliated, and Hans knew where that blame would be squarely laid.

He checked his watch again. It was nearly one in the morning. Something was wrong. He placed his fingers on the phone receiver. He wanted to get Schmidt on the line. They would need to pull some men and reinforce the other gates out of the camp. Whatever the risk, they had to hedge their bets.

The telephone rang in his hand, and he jerked in surprise at the sudden noise. Taking a deep breath, he picked up the phone and pressed it to his ear. "*Jawohl.*"

"I've heard from my number two. We headed them off at the gate," said Schmidt over the line. "Just like I said they would be."

Hans exhaled in relief. "Your number two? You aren't there?"

"I'm on my way there now. I had another matter to take care of first, and the men had to get into position."

"Do they have them?"

"Not yet. They're in the woods a half kilometer away from our position. It looks like they're resting right now. They probably think they're in the clear, that we didn't see them. But they are wrong."

"Aren't they going to get away?"

"Not a chance, sir. I have men closing in from every direction. They will be in position in the next half hour. Then, with your permission, I'll end this charade and bring them to heel."

Hans was about to give the go-ahead, but then he paused. What about Dieter? He was confident his nephew was still with the prisoners. They hadn't found him among the bodies in the crematorium, nor in the woods near the camp. If he was with this group of escapees, in the pitch darkness, he could be killed by accident in the rush to capture them. He had to take precautions against that.

"I'm concerned about—"

"About Dieter?" asked Schmidt. Hans could hear a hint of a smile in the sergeant's voice. "I've already considered that, sir. I've ordered the men to shoot only in the air, unless they are directly threatened by return fire. That should keep those Jews busy with their heads down. If your nephew is still alive, he should be safe."

"I need you to make sure. Personally."

"I already planned that, sir. I'm going to be in the front of things, and I'll make sure the men don't get carried away."

"You're a good man, Schmidt. I'm sorry I haven't always recognized that. Let's finish this," he said.

"Yes, sir." Schmidt hung up on the other end. Hans checked his watch. It should all be over in an hour. He sat for a few minutes, his eyes flickering to the hands on his timepiece, over and over. What was he doing? He couldn't just sit here. He rose and put on his greatcoat, then shuffled down the stairs to the ground floor. Exiting the building, he called a driver.

"Where to, sir?" the man asked.

"The railroad gate."

Hans arrived a half hour later. SS were crawling in and out of the building near the gate like ants, a scrambling hill of activity. He stepped out of the car and marched inside, searching for the soldier in charge. He found a corporal sitting beside a desk, poring over a map of the area.

"Where's Schmidt?" Hans demanded.

The soldier looked up and then sprang to his feet, giving the Hitler salute.

Hans returned it, then repeated his question.

"He arrived about ten minutes ago. He's out there in the woods now, running the operation, sir."

"Isn't it over yet?"

"It should be," said the corporal. "They moved in as soon as Schmidt arrived."

"Was there any gunfire?"

The corporal nodded. "A little, but it came and went quickly. Since then, it's been quiet out there."

"Take me," demanded Hans.

"Sir, it would be better if we waited until they mopped things up. Some of those Jews had weapons."

"Take me now."

The corporal nodded and led Hans out of the building. The man flipped on a flashlight and they walked through the field, stepping carefully on the uneven ground. As they grew closer to the woods Hans could hear noises among the trees, the sharp clamor of his own language. He didn't hear any Polish. He smiled to himself. The Germans had things under control.

They reached the woods a few minutes later. There were more flashlights here. And bodies. Hans saw the corpses of a half dozen prisoners. *So much for firing in the air.* They'd been dragged into a row and one of the SS stood guard over them, as if somehow they still constituted a threat. Hans marched up to a cluster of soldiers who were standing and talking together.

"Where is Schmidt?" he asked.

One of the men looked up. "Farther along, sir," he said.

Hans stepped past the men and kept moving into the trees, the corporal tailing along with him. He could see prisoners in the distance now, ringed by SS with automatic weapons. The inmates were sitting down in a tight circle, arms around their knees. He found Schmidt, standing near the other guards, a pistol in hand.

"Sergeant," he said, getting the man's attention. Schmidt looked up and smiled. "We have them, sir."

"Where is my nephew? Have you found him?"

Schmidt's face flushed. "Not yet, sir. But he must be near.

We've verified with the prisoners that he's been with them and that he's alive."

Hans felt the relief wash over him. Dieter was safe. He just had to locate him. "Did you search the prisoners for him?"

Schmidt nodded. "He's not with this group. But a few of the Jews took off into the woods. Don't worry, they won't get far."

"Did you make sure they won't be shot?" asked Hans. "I don't want any mistakes. There were a lot more men killed in the initial attack than I wanted."

"Don't worry," said the sergeant. "I told them if anyone is responsible for killing Dieter, it would be their career. They won't take any risks."

Hans nodded. "Great job, Sergeant."

"Thank you, sir. Would you like some tea while we wait?"

"That sounds excellent."

Schmidt nodded and one of the men walked up, pouring some hot liquid into a metal cup from a canister. Hans took a few sips. The liquid was lukewarm and bitter, but it tasted better than anything he'd had in days. His nephew was all right and almost in their custody. They'd captured the inmates. Everything was going to turn out better than he'd imagined possible.

They waited for a half hour. SS men kept returning with additional clusters of prisoners. Each time Hans rushed to the group, looking over the prisoners and then asking about Dieter. But time and again his nephew was not with them. The inmates, who were interrogated on the spot, had not seen Dieter since the attack in the woods commenced. His nephew was still out there somewhere, and as the time passed his anxiety grew again. Two hours later, the guards stopped returning. The searches continued until dawn, but Dieter was nowhere to be found. Someone or some small group had escaped them, and they had his nephew.

The search continued as the sun peeked out over the horizon. Hans checked his watch. It was near seven. Schmidt walked up to him. "Sir, should we call off the search?"

"Absolutely not," he said. "We need to find Dieter."

"Sir, it's been hours. The men are tired and hungry."

"I don't want to hear about how difficult of a time they're having," he snapped. "Our brothers on the Eastern Front face these conditions every minute. They're up for days at a time and they have enemies who shoot and kill them. Real enemies. Tell the men if they don't like this, I'll arrange for them to join the Waffen-SS, and they can see how they like facing the Russians instead. Keep up the search, Sergeant."

"Yes, sir," said Schmidt, but Hans could tell the guard disapproved. *Let them grumble*, he thought. It was daylight now and the search would be easier. He just needed to find his nephew. Then they would deal with these prisoners and he could give the men a break. The whole staff was due a furlough for this, he reasoned. He would announce that when the operation was wrapped up and recommend the same to Kramer. They could let the men have a trip back home for a week, perhaps a fifth of the staff at a time. That should raise everyone's spirits and would be a fitting reward for a job well done.

"Sir, I need you." Schmidt had returned and was pulling on Hans's coat.

"What is it?" Hans asked irritably.

"The *Kommandant*," whispered Schmidt.

Hans looked up, and sure enough Kramer was there, marching up to him in front of a trail of underlings who followed him like baby ducks.

"Krupp. What do you have to report?" he asked. He looked over at the prisoners. "I heard the operation was over hours ago. Why are these Jews still out here?"

"We're still conducting a search," said Hans. "There may still be a few more out there. I wanted to wait until daylight to find any stragglers."

"To find your nephew, you mean," said Kramer.

Betrayed again. He looked over at Schmidt, but the man looked as surprised as Hans was. Had the sergeant reported to Kramer? Was he just playacting now? There was no way to know and it didn't matter. *Someone* had told Kramer what he was doing.

"Yes, Dieter is still missing. There are likely a few prisoners out there as well. I wanted to nab them all before I reported the success to you."

"How thoughtful of you," drawled Kramer. "I'm calling most of this off. The men are exhausted and I want to deal with these prisoners. You can keep a few men and continue the search out here. I want Schmidt to take the rest of them back to the camp."

"But, sir—"

"Those are my orders, Krupp." The *Kommandant* turned to Schmidt. "You heard me, Sergeant. Gather the bulk of the men and then march these prisoners back to the camp. I want them contained in the perimeter of Crematorium II, with a heavy guard on the gate and the electric wires hot."

"Do you want me to do anything else with them?" Schmidt asked.

"Not now. You can pull a few aside for questioning after I arrive."

"And the rest?"

"Execute them."

"Do you want me to use the gas?"

Kramer shook his head. "It's too good for them. I want them to expect it. Put them facedown in the yard. One bullet at a time to the back of the head. Space it out, so they can think about it. And, Schmidt, I want you to personally handle it. Each one."

The sergeant smiled. "Thank you, sir, that's a real honor."

"The first of many that will come your way, Sergeant."

Schmidt turned to Hans. "He deserves more than I do."

"We shall see," said Kramer.

Schmidt saluted and moved off to follow the *Kommandant*'s orders.

"Why do you think there are more inmates out there?" asked Kramer.

"Well, I don't know for sure. But it makes sense. Dieter wouldn't have run off by himself. If he's not here among the men, then he's got to be out there somewhere with a few prisoners who managed to escape."

Kramer nodded. "I guess you're correct about that. We can't have them get away, Krupp."

"Yes, sir, I know that. You've made that more than clear."

"This is a disaster enough to report to Berlin. If we can show we cleaned the whole thing up, we'll be far better off. I'm trusting you, Krupp. Get it done."

"Yes, sir. I told you I will."

The commander turned and stomped off, leaving Hans with a handful of men to continue the search. Dieter was out there somewhere. He had to find him while there was still time.

Chapter 34
Marek

October 1944
Auschwitz

Jakub slept fitfully on the floor of the former gas chamber. His body shivered and he couldn't shake the feeling that the victims had never left this place, that they were calling out to him for justice. He kept hearing a crack over and over as the Zyklon B canisters were dropped into the room and then the wooden trap door was snapped shut.

He woke with a start. It was morning. Light crept in through several holes in the wall. Tomasz and Dieter lay nearby, a meter apart. Both were still asleep. *Crack!* He jumped. There was that sound. He thought it was in his dreams, but there was a sharp pop somewhere out there in the distance.

He heard the sound again. This time it shook Tomasz out of his sleep as well. His friend looked around as if surprised by his surroundings, then he took a deep breath as he apparently remembered where they were. He looked up at Jakub. "Good morning," he said. "I trust you slept well."

"Horribly."

"Well, if you can't sleep decently in a gas chamber, where will you get your rest?"

Jakub laughed at the joke. Dieter was stirring now, and the SS guard pulled himself up to a sitting position. "*Haben Sie Frühstück?*" the guard asked, smiling at them.

"Not a thing for breakfast," said Tomasz. He turned to Jakub, glancing sideways at Dieter. "We're going to have to do something about him if we are seriously considering escape."

"I thought you wanted to go back and negotiate."

"Now that I've had a night to sleep on it, I think I'd like to get the hell out of here if that's a possibility." He leaned forward. "Which brings me to you, Jakub. I know there is a contact out here somewhere. A Pole. I think it's time we looked your friend up to see if there's anything he could do for us."

Marek. Of course. That was brilliant. He'd been so busy fighting for his life over the past twenty-four hours he hadn't thought of him, or what he might be able to do for them. Marek couldn't have helped the whole group, but now that it was just the three of them . . . "He lives in the town of Auschwitz. But how would we get there during the day? Should we wait until nightfall?"

Tomasz shook his head. "We don't have food or water. We'll get weaker by the hour. We'll have to go now. We'll keep to the woods and make our way toward the town. When we get close, we'll figure out some way to get to your friend."

"It's going to be tricky with Dieter," said Jakub.

Tomasz looked at the guard. "I've been thinking the same thing. We've kept him as a potential bargaining chip, but now that I'm not going to bargain, he's become a liability. We may have to make some hard decisions this morning about the boy here."

"Couldn't we just tie him up and leave him?" asked Jakub. He did have his own reasons for wanting the guard's silence. But the man had never done anything to him.

Tomasz shook his head. "It's too dangerous. We don't have

anything to tie him up properly with. Besides, if he got out, we'd be dead men."

Jakub knew his friend was right. "How are we going to do it?" he asked.

"Now I wish you still had that pistol. Look at that kid. He's tall as can be. Thank God he's not very muscular. I think you'll need to distract him, then I'll hit him as hard as I can from behind. He should go down, and when he does, you hold him tight and I'll strangle him."

"Do you know how to kill someone like that?"

Tomasz smiled grimly. "Trust me."

Jakub felt sick. He'd never killed anyone, and although the Germans richly deserved his vengeance, he wasn't sure this new guard who couldn't be more than seventeen or eighteen, really counted.

"Are you ready?" asked Tomasz, moving around behind Dieter.

"Stop!" shouted Jakub. He couldn't do this! He stepped forward and placed himself between Tomasz and Dieter.

"Are you mad? What in the hell are you doing?" Tomasz demanded, his fists clenched.

"I'm sorry," Jakub said. "But I can't do it. I can't kill an innocent man in cold blood." He turned away, tears in his eyes.

"You're a sentimental fool." Tomasz laughed. "What am I going to do with you?" He raised his hands in exasperation. "Fine, have it your way. We'll bring the big clod along. But if we get into any trouble, we'll have to dispose of him. Do you understand?"

"I do," said Jakub. His friend started to rise but he stopped him. "Thank you."

Tomasz looked at him and laughed again. "I don't know why I tolerate you. Honestly, I do not. First it was that insane obsession with Anna. Then you betray me and join the damn resistance. Now you want me to keep this Nazi alive, when he'll turn us both in and kill us as soon as he gets the chance. You're like some crazy brother. That's the only explanation. I may not like what you do, but you're my brother, come what may."

"You're a brother to me too, Tomasz. More than that, you've saved me in here. So many times. Without you, I'd have given up long ago."

Tomasz looked at him seriously for a moment. "You're right, of course. But it doesn't make dealing with you any easier." He stood up. "All right, we've got to get going. Do you want me to tend Dieter, or will you?"

"I'll do it," said Jakub. "You need to concentrate on where we're going."

"Right again, I suspect."

Crack! There was that sound again. "What do you think that is?" Jakub asked Tomasz.

"I don't know," his friend said. "But we'd better go and find out."

Jakub stepped over to Dieter. The German seemed to realize that something had just happened. That he was in danger. "*Kommen Sie*," Jakub said in the best German he could manage. "We aren't going to harm you."

Dieter looked at him, his mouth half open as if he was going to say something. After a moment's hesitation he simply nodded and followed Jakub. Tomasz turned and stepped to the door. "Let's go," he said, before opening the latch and striding out into the morning.

Jakub took the back of Dieter's tunic and moved outside. The morning was cloudless and fine, but very cold. He raised his head up to the sun, enjoying the light. He nearly lost himself in the moment, but he shook his head, forcing himself to concentrate. He was playing a dangerous game with Dieter. He had to keep a close watch on him, or he might take off at any moment. Jakub had no doubt that if the young German broke away, there was no way in their weakened state that they could keep up with him. He was surprised the youth hadn't fought free and made a run for it the moment they'd stepped outside, but for whatever reason, he stayed with them, keeping a few paces from Tomasz but following in the man's steps.

They moved out among the trees. As they walked out of sight of the little white house, it again struck Jakub as so bizarre that they could be so close to Birkenau. The woods were peaceful, with birds chirping, and the only other sound was their feet on the fallen leaves. They could be out for a Sunday stroll through the park.

They heard the sharp sound again, but this time it was closer. Jakub felt his heart drop. Out in the open, he knew exactly what it was. It was the sound of a pistol. Tomasz froze, obviously recognizing the same thing. "That's in the camp," he said. He turned to the left. "Let's go around."

"No," said Jakub. "I want to see."

Tomasz turned to him with sad eyes and a glance toward Dieter. "No, you don't. We don't need to watch this. We need to get away."

But Jakub was already moving forward. He suspected he knew what this was, but he had to see it with his own eyes. He was drawn toward the repetitive noise inexorably, as if he were in some sort of maelstrom that was pulling him ever closer. At first, he could merely see the forest, tree after tree, but then in the distance, he made out buildings and a fence, the familiar sights of Birkenau.

"Slow down!" hissed Tomasz. "It's not safe here! There could be patrols."

But Jakub didn't care. He had to witness this. He kept moving, slower now, a few trees at a time, and then he could see. He was standing on the edge of the woods on the far side of the rail, perhaps seventy meters from his old enclosure. The perimeter within Crematorium II was filled with SS, more than a hundred. They were clustered around lines of striped figures, all facedown in the grass. It was his *Sonderkommando*, or at least the survivors. They'd been caught out there, so close to escape, and dragged back to the camp. He recognized a face here and there. He searched hard among them and then he saw him. Roch was in the front row. Nearest to Jakub. His head down but looking up periodically. His face was angry and full of resistance. But there was a peace there too, an acceptance of fate—that he'd fulfilled his part and had no more to do.

And there was Schmidt. The arrogant little guard was walking along behind Roch's row of men, a gleeful smile on his face. He stepped up to a prisoner, three men over from Roch, and aimed a pistol a meter from the man's head. *Crack!* He pulled the trigger and the prisoner's body jerked, blood pouring out of a wound in the back of the man's head. The legs shivered for a few moments and then he was still, except for the dark red liquid spilling out all over the grass.

He felt a tug on his arm. "Jakub, we've got to go." Tomasz was holding Dieter's arm, but the man didn't seem like he wanted to run away. He was watching with a kind of sadness in his eyes as well, as Schmidt moved to the next man and fired. "Come on, Jakub."

"No, I have to see this."

Schmidt finished with another man and then moved to Roch. The guard lowered his head and said something to the resistance leader. Jakub saw Roch lift his head in response and Schmidt kicked him hard. He could see the blood flowing from his nose as the SS guard shoved his boot into the middle of Roch's back, raised his pistol, and fired.

Jakub felt the wound in his own mind. Tears welled up in his eyes and he couldn't see. He felt his body drop to the ground and he wept there, quietly, his fists beating the ground, as his friend, his leader, died a few meters away. Tomasz tried to pull him up but he lay there for some minutes. "Come on, Jakub, we can't stay here. If you want to honor Roch, it won't be by suffering the same fate. It will be by escaping. Let's go!"

Jakub stood slowly. A calm had come over him and a clarity he'd never felt before. He knew what he had to do.

"Let's get out of here and find your contact."

Jakub shook his head. "No," he said simply.

"Are you crazy? We have to get out of here."

"I'm not going."

"You will go. I'm not leaving you behind here, Jakub. It's suicide to stay this close to the camp. I won't allow you to kill yourself."

"I'm not going to kill myself," he said.

"Then what?"

"I'm going to save Anna."

Tomasz paused. "Are you mad?" he asked.

Jakub looked up at him. "I'm going to save my wife."

Tomasz sputtered. "Your wife? What in the hell are you talking about?"

Jakub told him about Anna's demand and his agreement. He explained smuggling in the rabbi, their ceremony, and their secret life as husband and wife.

"She tricked you," said Tomasz. "It was just her way to pull you in and keep you. Trust me, if anything better came along, she would have taken it. Maybe she already has. We don't know what happened between her and Schmidt. We have to go while we still can."

"Don't say those things, Tomasz! I did everything I could to save her from Schmidt. But if he did do anything to her, it was against her will. I know that. I can't leave her behind. I must try to get to her, no matter what happens. I have to try."

"There's no chance," said Tomasz. "You'll never get back into the camp."

"There has to be a way," said Jakub.

"We can't do it," said Tomasz. He paused, his head cocked to the side. "Then again, if there is any chance, maybe your Polish friend can help. Let's get to your contact and see if he has any ideas."

"But we're right here, right now," protested Jakub.

"You're not thinking," said Tomasz. "It's daytime. Anna isn't going to be in the camp. She'll be at the factory."

Tomasz was right. Although everything inside him screamed out to make the attempt now, there was no point if Anna was away at work. Then he realized there was another possibility. "What if we got her out of the factory?"

"I don't know," said Tomasz. "It's possible. That's yet more reason to visit your contact. He'd know better than us if there is some way in and out of that factory."

Jakub nodded. His friend was right. If they could make it into Auschwitz village and reach Marek, they would be able to rest and obtain food and water. Neither he nor Tomasz knew anything about the factory, but the Polish leader might. If they couldn't infiltrate Anna's workplace, they'd be no worse off resting in Marek's house for the rest of the day. Then at night, they could try to slip into Birkenau somehow, get Anna and be out again while it was still dark. With miraculous luck, they might make their way through the outer fence and be in hiding by this time tomorrow. It all sounded impossible, but while he drew breath there was a chance. "Yes, let's do it," he said.

Tomasz smiled. "Now you're showing at least a little sense. Let's go." Tomasz turned and led them away from the camp and the popping gunshots that still trailed them as they left.

By early afternoon they had made their way to the outskirts of the town of Auschwitz. They stood among the trees, watching the comings and goings of the hamlet. Something wasn't right, and it took Jakub a long time to realize what it was.

"There aren't any prisoners in town," he said.

"Bad luck for us," said Tomasz. "Perhaps we'd better wait

until nightfall after all before we try to get in there. We're going to stick out, particularly with Dieter in tow. I can't see how we would make it without somebody stopping us, and if they do, our young friend here is going to squeal."

"I don't want to wait," said Jakub. "We'll have to risk it. The factory is our best chance to get to Anna. We need water and food in any event."

"It almost makes me miss Birkenau," said Tomasz. "At least we knew what was going to happen there. There was something to drink and something to eat. Out here, it feels like certain death."

"Don't mention water," said Jakub, his throat burning so badly it was becoming difficult to talk. "Well, shall we try it?"

Tomasz shrugged, a grim grin on his face. "We might as well. I don't know how we are going to manage to stroll through the middle of the town without attracting attention, but we might as well get on with it."

"We're going to do what you always taught me to do," said Jakub. "Act like we know what we're doing and hope for the best."

"I hate when my words come back to haunt me. Well, let's give it a try. Keep Dieter close. We want him to look like he's guarding us, if that's at all possible. And pray they don't stop us for questions. If they do, you let me do the talking. Not that it will do us any good."

What if they were captured alive? Jakub wondered. What about Dieter? With everyone dead, it hardly mattered anymore.

They stepped out of the woods and moved step-by-step toward the town. Jakub had never felt more exposed. He expected every second to hear screams in German and guards rushing them from every angle. He followed behind Dieter, watching the young man closely. Now more than ever, he expected him to run as soon as he had a chance. But for some reason, he stayed with him, keeping their pace, following along behind Tomasz.

They made the first row of houses, then the second. The streets here were practically deserted. They had been fortunate to enter the town away from the main road, and thus they were not close to the vendors or the storefronts. Still, there were people in these houses, almost all of them German. Surely some of them knew about the escapes and would be on the lookout for anything suspicious. They continued walking through another row of houses.

"Stop here a second," said Jakub. He was looking around at the houses, racking his brain to remember what Marek's dwelling looked like. He felt a rising panic. He'd come here at night last time and from a different angle into the town. What if he couldn't find the house again? As he looked, he noticed a woman a few houses down. She was taking down some laundry she had hung between her house and one of the posts holding up her porch. She was watching them intently. Jakub scanned all directions and he spotted another woman, standing at a window, her hand pulling the drape back, peering at them.

Jakub turned his head to the left. Standing on the porch was Marek, watching him wearily. "This way!" he whispered frantically to Tomasz. The little group turned and moved toward Marek's house.

The Pole stared at them in surprise, eyeing Dieter. He started to turn away.

"Don't!" shouted Jakub. "We need you!"

Marek hesitated, looking around him at the adjacent houses. He hesitated, and then gestured them toward the door. They rushed inside.

"What in the hell are you doing here?" Marek asked, staring in horror at Dieter. "Are you mad!"

"He's our prisoner," said Jakub.

"Can that matter?" asked Marek. "It's the middle of the day!" Marek said.

"Water," Jakub murmured, not sure he could talk any further. Marek rushed to the kitchen and Jakub could hear liquid hitting glass. He returned with three full mugs of water and they each took one gratefully. "Out with it now," he said as Jakub gulped down the water.

"We were betrayed," Jakub finally said, fighting out the words.

Marek nodded in understanding, his eyes widening. "The explosion. The gunshots. We feared the worst but there was nothing we could do. Tell me everything."

Jakub relayed the whole story about the betrayal, the attempted revolt, and the near execution in the gas chamber. He explained their unlikely battle and the flight from Birkenau, the capture of the bulk of the *Sonderkommando* and their execution back at the camp. He had to stop several times as he battled back tears, but he eventually explained the entire story.

"I agree with Tomasz," said Marek, glancing at Dieter. "It was foolish to leave him alive. And now you've blown my cover as well."

"How can that be?" asked Jakub.

"You came to my house in broad daylight. Two prisoners with an SS guard? A day after the revolt. I won't last twenty-four hours. We're all going to have to make a run for it."

"Should we wait here until dark?" asked Tomasz.

Marek shook his head, stepping to a window and checking the street. "That's far too risky. The Germans could be here anytime. One of our wonderful citizens will have reported what they saw. It won't take long before they come here to search. I have no place to hide you, and I'm a Pole. They'll have half my teeth pulled out in a torture cell before they'll listen to any of my explanations. No, we are all going to have to make a run for it."

"I'm not going without Anna," said Jakub.

Marek looked at him in surprise. "What are you talking about?"

Jakub explained his decision, his relationship with Anna.

The Pole shook his head. "I agree with Tomasz. That's impossible. I'm sorry. I understand your loss, but her best chance of survival is to sit tight and wait for the end of the war. Hell, she has a much better chance of seeing tomorrow morning than we do." As he spoke, Marek moved back and forth in the kitchen, packing a small bag with some bread and a half wheel of cheese. He walked back in quickly and looked them over. "What am I supposed to do with all of you?" he asked. He tapped his head for a few seconds. "I could try to go as a prisoner, but nobody would ever believe it. I don't have time to shave my head and I'm in too good of shape. No, it looks like I'm going to have to join the Nazis after all."

He left the room, returning five minutes later. Jakub was surprised to see the Pole dressed in an impeccable SS corporal's uniform, complete with polished boots, belt, and pistol.

"What are we going to do with this one?" Tomasz asked, gesturing to Dieter.

"You said he walked on his own into the town?"

Tomasz nodded.

"Strange," said the Pole. "Well, he's either scared to death or he has some other plan I can't see. I guess we'll have to trust our luck for now. Let's take him with us. We can always deal with things in the woods before we reach the outer fence. I don't see at this point how we can trust him at the gate."

"I can't go without Anna," said Jakub again, half to himself.

Tomasz turned on him. "You heard the man, Jakub. Now you didn't listen to me, but you have got to listen to Marek. We are probably dead already, but if there's any chance of making it out of here, we must go, and go now. We can't go to the Union Factory and we sure as hell can't go back to the camp. We've got to get into the woods and then try to find some way out of the greater camp. We have a fighting chance now. We've got a weapon, another uniform, and some food and water. Marek, I assume, knows his way around here. If we make it out of the town alive, we might just escape Auschwitz after all, but we can't do it by heading the wrong direction." He raised his hands. "I'm sorry, my brother. I would do anything if it were otherwise, but we can't save her. Remember what you lost before. Remember what we've all lost. We have to live for them."

Survive. The word convicted him again. He shook his head, refusing to move or speak. He couldn't leave her. He had to fight for her. But other words conflicted with those. His promise to his father. Perhaps even more compelling were the words of Marek. They were in tremendous danger and would be even more so if they went back for her. Perhaps he was right. Perhaps she was in better shape if she stayed right where she was. After all, she had Schmidt for a protector now . . .

He nodded without speaking. Tomasz clapped him on the back and Marek smiled at him.

"All right, boys. I want both of you out front," said the Pole. "I'll walk behind our young hero here and keep an eye on him. Tomasz, you take the lead. We are going to go out the front door and we'll stroll right through town like we don't have a care in the world. When we leave the village, I want you to head off the road on my word, and hurry into the woods. Once we get in there, we'll run for as long as we can, and put some distance between us and Auschwitz. If we make it a few kilometers into the woods without being spotted, we might just make it."

Marek opened the door and they strode out into the street. Again, the eerie feeling of being watched washed over Jakub. Marek gave directions as they marched. Jakub was horrified to see the man lead them right into the main part of the village. They passed cart after cart of goods. Several guards walked past them, nodding to Dieter and Marek. Jakub was sure Dieter would run for it when they were so close to these SS, but again, for some strange reason, he kept walking along. Perhaps he feared that the Pole would shoot him before anyone could help? Whatever the cause, they were soon out of the hamlet and walking along a dirt road to the north.

"To the woods, now!" shouted Marek when they were a kilometer from the town. They turned and sprinted toward the trees, moving up and down a ditch and into the trees a few meters away. Once there, Tomasz settled into a jog and they shuffled away, weaving through the trees and the undergrowth. Jakub's heart was soon pounding, and his breath came in wheezy gasps, but he kept moving, his eyes following the bob of Tomasz's head. Finally, when he thought he could not possibly go any farther, the Pole signaled for them to halt. Tomasz threw himself down on the ground. Jakub dropped next to him, rolling over on his back, his eyes up to the sky.

"Is that all the farther you can go?" Marek asked critically, walking Dieter over and pulling him down to a sitting position. "Well, I guess it will have to do." He checked his watch. "We ran for about twenty minutes. We've got to be at least two kilometers from town. It should be enough for now." Marek sat down next to them and pulled out a canteen. He gave each of them a little water and then shared half of the bread and some cheese. Jakub tried his best to take slow bites, but he was too hungry and he was soon devouring it, finishing quickly and looking to Marek for more.

"That's enough for now," said the Pole.

"Where are we?" Jakub asked after he caught his breath.

"I don't know our exact position," said Marek, "but we're more or less northwest from the town."

"And where are we headed?" asked Tomasz.

"Nowhere for now. We'll sit tight here until dusk, then we'll move on. If we head north, we should hit a road in the next few kilometers. As soon as it's dark enough we'll make straight for that, then follow that in the tree line. There's a gate about five kilometers from where we reach the road. That's our way out, if there's any way."

Tomasz whistled. "That's a goodly way to go."

"I haven't told you the worst part. The road crosses the Vistula about two kilometers from the gate. It's guarded. We won't be able to cross the bridge itself. We'll have to wade through the water."

"Hell, we'll freeze to death after that," said Tomasz.

"There's no other choice. That's the best way out of here."

"We'll need all our energy if we're going to cross that river," said Jakub.

Marek nodded. "That's why we're going to rest right now. I want you both to get some sleep if you can. I'll stay up with our guest here. Besides, I have some questions for him."

Jakub froze. "I've already interrogated him," he said. "He only arrived at the camp a few days ago. He doesn't know anything."

"Well, I've got nothing else to do for the next few hours," said Marek. "It doesn't hurt to see if you missed anything."

Jakub laid down and kept his eyes closed, but listened closely to the conversation. His German wasn't perfect but he was able to understand enough, and Dieter essentially confirmed what Jakub had already told Marek: that he was a new guard and had barely worked at Auschwitz before he was captured. After a time, Marek gave up. Jakub heard Dieter lie down himself. Jakub breathed deeply in relief.

"You're still up, I see," said Marek. Jakub opened his eyes. The Pole was sharp. He hoped he hadn't raised his suspicions.

"Yes. I'm sorry," he explained after a moment. "I'm having a hard time getting to sleep. It's been the most frightening day-and-a-half of my life. I guess I just can't shake the situation."

Marek watched him for a moment and then nodded. "It's understandable, with what you've been through. You've done well—the two of you. The only thing that doesn't make sense is why you didn't crush this Nazi's windpipe in that cottage when you had the chance."

Jakub sat up, considering the question. "I can't kill an innocent," he said at last. "He's new. And so young. I don't feel like he's as responsible somehow."

"Give him a month," said Marek. "They're all the same. True believers and monsters."

"I don't know about him," said Jakub. "He could have betrayed us many times and he didn't."

"It's not honor. It's fear," said Marek. "He's trying to save his own skin and he figures we'd kill him before he could get away. But you watch, if he sees his chance, he'll escape."

"Perhaps. Perhaps that's it," answered Jakub. He laid his head back and closed his eyes. Images and thoughts swam through his mind. He knew he wouldn't sleep. In a few hours he would be putting everything on the line. They would either make it or they would be dead or tortured by morning. He desperately wanted to live, but if it came to capture, he hoped he would have the courage to attack the Germans, to force them to shoot him. Far better that than a slow torture. But if he was captured, was there a chance to avoid interrogation? Would Dieter intervene on his behalf?

He thought of Anna, and the guilt and uncertainty ripped through him again. How could he just leave her there? Even if there was no chance to rescue her. Hadn't they already witnessed miracle after miracle? Wasn't there some chance to retrieve her? But there was an end to luck, he knew. Tomasz and Marek were right, there was only death that direction, and after all, she was still safe in the camp and had Schmidt's protection from now on. The Russians weren't too far off. There was a chance she would make it.

He lay there for what seemed an eternity, his eyes closed, running his mind through the loss of his family, the months in the *Sonderkommando*, the fence, their escape, and again and again, about Anna. He was jolted when a foot nudged him. He'd slept some after all.

"Time to go," said Marek.

He was surprised that the sky had darkened considerably. His entire body ached from the hard, uneven ground, and he pulled himself to his knees, stretching. His head was groggy but his body felt rested, and he thought he would be able to walk the distance Marek had told them about.

The Pole handed him some more bread and cheese. Everyone else was already up and eating. "That's the rest of it," said Marek. "If we want more, we'll have to get it outside the fence."

"Or from the Germans," joked Tomasz.

Marek shot him a dark look. "Don't speak of that," he said.

They munched away in the growing darkness, each alone with his thoughts. Finally, Marek stood up and stretched, cautioning them to silence as he cocked his head to listen for a moment. "It sounds all right out there," he said. "Let's go."

They rose and moved out, the Pole in the lead this time, with Dieter directly behind him and then Jakub and Tomasz walking together. The light was already fading and soon it was just like the evening before, their pace slowing as they wove through the tree trunks, hands out, avoiding low-hanging branches. They stumbled along that way for an hour or more.

Marek raised his hand and they halted. Jakub couldn't see anything at first, but he stepped up next to the Pole and strained his eyes. There were a few more trees, and then a fifty-meter space of underbrush led to a ribbon of road in the distance.

"There is our path," said Marek. "I was growing nervous that we were not heading the right direction. Without any stars to guide us tonight, I was relying on my instincts to lead us."

Jakub clapped him on the arm. "You've done well."

"We're not out of this yet. That was the easy part. Now we

must make it to the river, and somehow through it and on to the gate. The water is dangerous, but the gate is death itself. We have to pray that it is lightly guarded tonight."

"How many Germans are there?" asked Jakub.

"If we're lucky, two or three. But I've seen a dozen there before as well, and no reason why it is one way or the other. The Germans seem to switch things up at random, likely to make it more difficult to plan an escape from here."

"A dozen. That would be fun," said Tomasz.

"That would be impossible. But everything you've done in the last day falls under that definition. So let's see if we can get one last piece of luck."

He led them off and they moved to their left, marching along the tree line. They were making faster time now in the better light and the thinner foliage at the edge of the woods. Twice they had to dive for cover as a vehicle passed. Jakub's heart raced and he expected at any moment that the truck would stop and a score of German guards would fan out and race in their direction, but they moved by at the same speed and disappeared in the distance, seemingly unaware of their presence.

Jakub heard the distant whisper of water. The noise rose as they kept walking until it was a steady rustle.

"Look there," said Marek. "The bridge."

Jakub strained his eyes through the darkness. In the distance, through the trees, he could see a dim arch.

"We must be quiet," said Marek. "There are always Germans here, watching the road."

They moved slowly now, creeping from tree to tree. Jakub stepped carefully, trying not to make unnecessary noise. They reached the bank of the river, the trees huddling over the water on both sides. The bridge was a bare fifty meters away.

"The Vistula," said Marek. "It's not too far across here, and it's only chest deep. But the current is strong. We must tread quietly and carefully or we'll lose our way." He looked at

Jakub and Tomasz. "Both of you hold on to Dieter while we cross. If he shouts, hold his head under the water and don't let him back up."

Marek lowered himself carefully down the bank, which was a few meters below the forest. Jakub followed, one hand behind him, clutching Dieter's tunic. The bank was muddy and he nearly faltered, but he held on to a branch and eventually made it to the bottom. He assisted Dieter and Tomasz, and soon they had all made it to the edge of the river.

"Careful now," said Marek. "Place each step carefully and make sure you have a firm footing before you move again. If the river carries you away don't panic, and don't shout out, just swim toward the opposite bank and we'll retrieve you downriver."

Marek took a step into the water, then another. The river was twenty meters wide here. Jakub glanced at the bridge. He couldn't make out the Germans, but he knew they must be there. Had they heard them rustling down the bank? He turned to the water and, keeping his hold on Dieter, he stepped into the river. The bed was muddy and slick. The filth threatened to pull his feet out from under him. He took another step, and another. The water was freezing and he had to fight down the urge to gasp. The water crept up to his knees, then his waist. The current tugged at him now and he nearly lost his balance. Jakub kept moving, willing himself forward. The water reached his chest. He felt himself being swept away by the water and he dug his feet into the mush below, battling for a hold. He took another step and another. The water was receding. A few more agonizing movements and he felt in control again, the bank only a few meters away.

He reached the ground and collapsed in the mud. His clothes were drenched and he was exhausted, his teeth chattering in the freezing air. Tomasz and Dieter collapsed next to him. How could they go any farther?

"We can't stay here," whispered Marek.

"We need a few minutes to catch our breath," said Tomasz.

"It's too dangerous," said Marek. "We've got to get a few meters into the woods."

Jakub fought to his feet. He grabbed ahold of Dieter again and followed Marek up the opposite bank. He made it up somehow and stumbled into the woods. The wind cut into him now, freezing him to the bone. They hobbled forward another fifty meters or so until Marek finally let them rest. They stayed there for an hour, shivering in the darkness, until they were finally able to move on.

Within just a few minutes of continuing their journey, a faint pinprick of light appeared on the far horizon. Marek pointed to it and whispered to the group. "That's the gate. We must be even more cautious."

He moved slowly now, stepping from tree to tree, taking frequent pauses to listen. In the distance, they heard a dog barking and the Pole waited for long minutes until the animal stopped before they continued.

The light grew in intensity and the outlines of a guardhouse grew against the fading sky. They were a kilometer away, then half that. Marek stopped them about two hundred meters away, still within the tree line.

They all peered through the darkness, trying to make out guards in the distance. The guardhouse had a window facing their direction and he saw at least one head moving back and forth inside.

"What do we do now?" Tomasz asked.

"We wait," said Marek.

"For what?"

"For confirmation of what we're facing. Look," he said, pointing toward the gate. "We won't be waiting long."

In the distance, past the gate, a pair of headlights was approaching. As the foreground was lit up, Jakub saw that a striped round pole barrier was suspended about a meter off the ground across the roadway. A guard stood on either side of the road, both with machine pistols. The guard nearest the house also held the leash of a German shepherd.

The truck halted and the guard stepped up, talking to the driver. The dog strained at its leash on the opposite side, and the guard moved around the truck, letting the animal sniff the contents in the back.

"Only two," said Jakub. "We're in luck."

"Not so fast," said Marek.

The door opened and an SS officer stepped out, accompanied by four more men. He moved around to the driver's side as the soldiers fanned out around the vehicle. From the guardhouse, Jakub could see at least two more men peering out the window. The gate was guarded by at least a squad of SS, well armed and on close alert. After all their sacrifices, there was no way through.

Chapter 35
Through the Gate

October 1944
Auschwitz

They stood there in the darkness, watching the swarm of Nazis in the distance carefully checking the truck before lifting the gate and waving it on.

"We can't go through there," said Tomasz.

Marek shook his head. "No, we cannot."

Jakub felt his heart crushed in his chest. "What then? Have we come this far only to fail at the end?"

"Quiet!" warned the Pole. "Give me some time to think."

They stood there for a few more minutes while they watched the guardhouse. Jakub was at the end of his wits. He was exhausted. He'd used all his energy to get here and he had no reservoir for another sustained march. They were out of food and water. Their clothes were wet and they risked hypothermia if they remained out here in the open. They had to go through this gate, or they had to fail in the attempt. And there was no way they could be successful like this.

Marek was not ready to quit. "We can't go through here," he said. "At least not tonight. We need to make our way back a bit and hole up here until tomorrow. We'll approach the gate again then and hope it is more lightly defended."

"You're out of your mind," said Tomasz. "Look at me. Look at Jakub. We can't go any farther. We have nothing to sustain us and why would the gate be more lightly defended tomorrow?"

Marek's face showed the truth. "It may not be. But I don't see anything else we can do. We have one pistol, and we have a prisoner who will betray us if we try to talk our way through."

"What if we disposed of him?" asked Tomasz. "Like we should have before."

Marek shook his head. "No good. I speak German but not well enough to get us through. Do you?" he asked them.

Both Jakub and Tomasz shook their heads.

"My plan was based on two Germans at their post," said Marek. "That way, if things fell apart, we could shoot our way out. With a dozen Germans, it will never work. No, the only chance we have is to wait and see what tomorrow night brings."

Jakub thought about this. It was as if God had brought this moment to him and was speaking into his heart. "I'm going back for Anna," he said.

"What the hell are you talking about?" demanded the Pole.

"We have a whole day now. There's plenty of time for me to go back and get her, and return in time for us to leave tomorrow night."

"You're out of your mind!" said Tomasz. "We've been over this again and again. There's no way to get her out."

Jakub turned to his friend, smiling. "I know I will probably be caught," he said. "But I have to try. Don't wait for me. If there's any chance to get through that gate, you take it. If I do make it back here and you've gone, we'll make our way out somehow."

Tomasz stared at him for long seconds. Jakub was afraid he

was going to attack him. Finally, he spoke: "If that's your decision then you're staying here with Marek and Dieter. I'll go back and get her."

"Absolutely not," said Jakub.

"Listen to me," his friend said. "Listen in your heart and you'll know that I speak the truth. I'm the only one with a chance to get back into the camp and out again. If you tried it, you would be arrested, tortured, and murdered. Hell, they might even get enough information out of you to track down the rest of us before we could get through the gate."

"You'll be caught yourself. They'll do the same to you."

"Maybe, but I doubt it. I've been in plenty of scrapes over the past couple of years here. I've always talked my way out of them. I'm sure this is the only way. I'll go get her and bring her back. You can wait until tomorrow night and get back out of here then."

"And what if there are a dozen guards then too?"

"One problem at a time."

"You're both out of your minds," said Marek. "We need to sit tight here and wait for the right moment to escape. Going back for some woman is suicide."

"She's my wife," said Jakub. "She's not just *some woman*."

"That is regrettable, but it doesn't change things. We need to leave while we can."

"He won't come with us," said Tomasz. "And I won't leave without him. I'll take off now. I'll enter the camp in the morning and have her back here by nightfall tonight." He started to leave.

"You're not going anywhere," said Marek. He was holding the pistol on Tomasz now. The inmate looked at the Pole, a grin on his face.

"Look at the mess you've landed me in now, Jakub. But don't worry, he can't shoot me. If he did, those guards would hear him and we'd all be dead. Isn't that right, Marek?"

The Pole refused to answer. "He knows I'm right." Tomasz bowed to him and then darted off into the trees. Marek stood for a long time watching him, then spat on the ground in disgust. "You've killed us all with your stupidity," he said at last.

"This isn't how I wanted it," said Jakub. "I wanted you to leave with him. I only was prepared to sacrifice myself."

"No matter what you intended, this is the result," said the Pole, turning his back to him and taking a seat. "At this point, there's nothing to be done but wait. I'll keep first watch. You'd better get some rest."

Jakub lay back down. Dieter sat down next to him, his head against the base of a tree. Jakub's mind was a storm of emotions. Had he just sealed all their fates? He'd not only refused to go with them when they had the chance, he had also allowed Tomasz to return in his stead. Was that because he truly believed his friend had a better chance of bringing Anna out, or because he was terrified of returning to the camp? He wasn't sure, and he didn't know if it even mattered anymore. If Tomasz was caught, they would be captured within hours in any event. He simply knew that he could not live with himself if he escaped and left Anna behind, regardless of what he'd promised his father, no matter what Schmidt had told him. He'd made an oath to Anna before God, and if he lost his own life in the process, he would try to save her.

The night passed slowly. He shook in the freezing cold and his teeth chattered. He wasn't sure he ever even slept. After a long period, Marek nudged him, and he took over the watch while the Pole lay down to rest. Jakub kept looking up at the sky, waiting for it to lighten, but it remained the same bluish black. Finally, when he thought he couldn't take it any longer, an almost imperceptible lightening grew in the eastern sky. A little later, the Pole arose, followed by Dieter.

"Any word from Tomasz?" Marek asked, stirring and pulling himself to his feet.

Jakub shook his head. "Nothing so far."

"Well, he said he wouldn't be back until tonight. At least the SS didn't scoop us up yet. That means he at least made it back to the camp."

"Do you think he has any chance?" Jakub asked.

The Pole shrugged. "You would know better than me."

"I've never seen anyone cleverer than Tomasz. Nor braver, for that matter," Jakub said. "He faced countless guards who questioned him when we were bribing our way through the gates. I've never seen him falter. He's been around a long time, an old number, he has connections everywhere."

"Well, you've answered your own question and perhaps your own doubts. If he's the most capable person to get through the camp, then he had the best chance of bringing your Anna out. So, all we can do is sit back and wait."

The day passed even more slowly than the night. With no food and without knowing what might be around them, they had nothing to do but sit quietly in the woods and wait. *At least my clothing is finally dry,* Jakub thought. He hoped that at any moment they would see Tomasz and Anna coming through the trees toward them, that by some miracle they'd been able to make their way here during the day, but he knew that was incredibly unlikely. Tomasz was too smart to risk it. If he had made his way in and out of the camp, he would have found a safe place to bed down for the day, and he would make his way here after nightfall. All the possibilities ripped through Jakub's mind. Tomasz might have been captured on the way back, or at the gate. If so, it would be best if they had killed him outright. What if he and Anna were caught on the way back out? He couldn't force the images of torture out of his mind. He just hoped they would talk quickly. No matter that if they did talk, he would be captured at that point as well. At least their suffering might be over.

His throat burned like he'd never experienced before. His

tongue felt like a swollen block of sandpaper in his mouth. It no longer seemed a part of his body. He wondered if Tomasz and Anna did make it back if he would even have the strength to get up and continue on. They didn't need food, but he knew they needed water. He hoped Tomasz would be able to bring them some when he returned.

"I'm thirsty," he managed to mumble to Marek through his strained, parched throat.

The Pole nodded in understanding, then shook his head. "We must wait. The Germans will have water and we can get it if and when we take the gate."

Of course, the guardhouse would have supplies. If they were lucky and there were only two guards again tonight, they could overpower them with the element of surprise. Once the Germans were incapacitated, they would have weapons, ammunition, food, and most blessed of all, an ample supply of water. What would happen then?

Jakub tried to imagine life outside Auschwitz. Would they find Poles to help them? Did Marek have contacts who could help them escape to a safer place? Was there even such a haven in German-occupied Poland? He could hardly believe in life outside the camp. Every scrap of his existence over the past few months had focused on staying alive. His life before the camp seemed like a misty dream.

Finally, the sky began to dim again. Jakub felt more awake. His thirst bothered him less. He focused on the anticipation of Tomasz and Anna coming to them. His Anna. What would he say to her? How would they recover from what Schmidt had done to her? He had to get past that. Anna had no control over anything Schmidt had done to her. They would start a new life together, and try to forget about the past.

"They should be here soon," he said finally, as darkness fully settled on the forest.

"I don't think so," said Marek. "It will be a couple of hours at least. If Tomasz is as smart as you say he is, he won't have risked starting out until about now. He may have to work his way along until he finds the road. That will take time as well, and even if he traveled quickly yesterday, he will be some kilometers away from us. I'd say it will be midnight before we see him."

That wasn't the news Jakub wanted to hear, but it made sense. He looked over at Dieter. He was not sure how much the German understood, if any. He'd borne himself quietly all day, keeping his eyes closed, his back on the ground and his face to the sky. Why hadn't he betrayed them? Was Marek correct that he'd been afraid for his own life? He was a new guard after all. Perhaps that was it. But there were moments when he could have run away and there was nothing they could have done to stop him. Didn't he realize that? Jakub wondered again why he had stopped Tomasz from killing the man. Certainly, it would have been prudent to do so. What would they do with Dieter if they did make it out? Jakub shook his head. That was in the hands of God.

The night moved on. Marek checked his watch. "It's near midnight."

Jakub strained his eyes in the pitch darkness. He listened intently, hoping for the sound of a broken twig or the rush of undergrowth somewhere out there. Time slowed down again in the darkness as they sat there waiting. Another hour passed, then two. The Pole kept looking at his watch.

"I don't think they're coming," he said at last.

"We have to wait."

"We will for a little longer, but you need to prepare yourself that we may have to go on our own."

"I won't leave without them."

"Don't be a child," said Marek. "You've put us at risk enough. You may have cost your friend his life in the attempt." The Pole rose. "If they aren't here soon, we will have to leave.

You keep a lookout here. I'm going to see what we're facing at the gate. Pray that you didn't waste our only opportunity last night." Marek stepped into the woods and his shadow was soon lost from sight.

Jakub sat there next to Dieter. The German sat up and was watching Jakub intently. He opened his mouth as if he was about to say something, but he stopped abruptly.

Jakub heard a rustling in the distance, coming closer toward him. Tomasz! He pulled himself to his feet, ready to greet his friend and his wife. He took a step forward, the excitement overwhelming him.

A figure stepped past a tree. It was only Marek. "We're in luck," he said. "There are just the two guards there, and tonight no dogs. They won't see us until we're right on top of them." He checked his watch again. "We have to go, Jakub. I'm sorry. But it's time."

"We have to wait," said Jakub again.

The Pole looked at him, shaking his head. "I have hard news for you, my friend. They didn't make it. Something happened along the way, and they were captured or killed."

"We don't know that."

"You're right. But we can't risk it. If Tomasz was captured alive, under torture he'll tell them where to find us. They could be on their way right now. Worse yet, they will alert that gate. One radio call and we lose the element of surprise. They'll mow us down when we're fifty meters away from them. The only chance we have is to go now."

This was it then. Marek was right. Tomasz had been right. He'd sacrificed his friend for nothing. In Auschwitz, there were no good choices. You took the small chance to save yourself or you sacrificed everything. In trying to use Tomasz to save Anna, he had lost them both. There was only one more thing he could do. *Survive*. He would escape and he would live for them. He would spend the rest of his life making up to Tomasz for recklessly gambling with his life.

"All right," he said at last, surrendering the last fraction of his hope. "Let's go."

"Good man," said Marek. He stepped over to Dieter and reached a hand down, pulling the young guard up to his feet. "Let's move."

They followed behind the Pole. It was much more difficult to move tonight. His muscles had tightened up and his legs kept buckling, threatening to topple him over in the darkness. His mind was numb. He couldn't think of Tomasz or Anna right now. The danger ahead pushed those terrible thoughts from his mind. Everything was focused on making it through the gate. *Survive.*

They reached the edge of the woods. The gate was there in the distance with its pinpricks of light. They were no more than two hundred meters away. Marek moved his head back and forth along the line of the road, searching for any vehicles or even foot traffic, improbable as that seemed.

"We're good," he whispered. "Remember, I need to get as close to them as I can. If Dieter makes any sound or movement, tackle him to the ground and I'll take on the guards. We must hope and pray he remains passive. If not, we'll take care of him after I take out the guards. Are you ready?" he asked.

"Yes," said Jakub.

"Leaving without us?" A voice from the darkness jolted Jakub. He turned. Tomasz was there in the trees. He could just make out a Cheshire grin on his face. "If you don't mind, we'll come along with you."

Jakub stepped forward, his eyes searching the trees. She must be there.

"Anna!" he cried, too loudly.

"Quiet!" Marek insisted.

But he didn't care. He rushed forward, his eyes searching the darkness. There she was, standing in the shadows behind Tomasz. He rushed toward her, and froze.

"Bak. How nice to see you again."

It wasn't Anna, it was Schmidt. He had a machine pistol fixed on Jakub. A mischievous grin stretched his face and his eyes twinkled.

"I'd feared I'd lost you," he said. "And look what else we have here," he said, eying Dieter. "The long-lost nephew. But who is this other SS guard?" he asked silkily. "That's no German, I think. This must be our local Polish resistance member. How nice of you to join our party as well."

Marek raised his pistol but other Germans rushed out of the trees. Marek fired wildly and darted away, sprinting into the woods. A German cut him down with a burst of machine-gun fire. Marek's body rattled and shook as it absorbed the rounds. He fell forward and crumbled to the ground.

Jakub turned to Tomasz in shock and amazement. His friend returned the gaze, sadness covering his face. "I'm sorry, but I had no choice."

An SS soldier moved up to Jakub, raised his machine pistol and whipped it around, crashing the butt of the weapon against the side of Jakub's head. He spun around and hit the ground hard, his head on fire. He tried to rise but his stomach was heaving, and he couldn't focus. He crumpled to the ground and remembered nothing more.

Chapter 36
Saved

October 1944
Auschwitz

Hans waited impatiently at the main gate to Birkenau, checking his watch every few seconds. What was taking them so long? He resisted the temptation to phone his wife. He wanted to make sure Dieter was truly safe before he made the call. Finally, in the distance he could make out twin points of light, far away at first, but growing as they bounced and flickered toward the camp. Soon he could make out the dim outline of a truck as it rumbled closer. He felt his pulse quicken in excitement. Against all hope, everything was coming together.

The truck reached the gate. Hans pushed through the guard and rushed to the driver's window. Schmidt was in the passenger seat and he leaned over to speak with Hans, shouting to make himself heard over the roar of the engine.

"We've got them, sir!"

"Where is he?"

"Who?"

"My nephew!"

"He's in the back with the guards and the rest of them."

Hans rushed to the covered vehicle, throwing open the heavy canvas flap. He was greeted by the barrel of a machine pistol from one of the SS guards. The man lowered his weapon immediately and Hans shined a flashlight around the bed of the truck. There were two prisoners inside. In the far back, he saw with horror the body of a guard, blood filling the entire front of his tunic. On the other side of the backseat his nephew sat.

"Dieter!" he cried, losing his composure for a moment. His nephew looked back at him with a grim, sad expression. What had these bastards done to him over the past few days? He felt his anger rising. Well, they would pay heavily for this, as all the rest of them had. Schmidt joined him as the two guards at the end of the truck began picking themselves up and moving to jump out of the bed.

"Who was killed?" Hans asked. "Do you know the man?" The commander's words echoed in his mind. He'd wanted no more losses of any kind. But still, was that realistic? Hans had saved his nephew, captured all the prisoners, and put down a significant rebellion. Surely one more dead man wouldn't count against all he had done.

"Rest easy, sir. That's not one of ours. This was some Polish scum they were working with. He was trying to lead them through an outer gate. Nearly made it too. I wanted to capture the Pole alive, but he fired at us and tried to escape. We had no choice but to shoot him."

"That was careless of you!" Hans snapped, secretly delighted that the dead man was a Pole, and not one of his own. "Still, it cannot always be helped. We should be able to get plenty out of these two."

"Just the one," Schmidt interjected.

"What do you mean?"

"The other man is Tomasz Lis. He's the one I told you about and the one who led us to Dieter," explained Schmidt. "But this one," the sergeant said, gesturing to Jakub. "He's a real prize. Bak was on the inside of the whole operation. He'll know plenty about who was involved, how they obtained the weapons, everything we'll want to know."

"Excellent. Well, let's get them all inside. I'll bring Dieter with me and you take care of the prisoner. We'll begin questioning him after I've taken care of my nephew."

Schmidt nodded. Hans reached out his hand to Dieter and his nephew took it, not looking at him, as he helped him out of the truck. "Your mother and aunt have been terribly worried. And so have I."

Dieter did not put his arms around Hans but stood there stiffly, without responding. Hans felt his anger boiling over again. He wanted to pull out his pistol and shoot this Jakub on the spot. But he restrained himself. If Schmidt was correct, he would lead them to many more arrests.

"Don't you worry about things right now," Hans whispered, pulling back. "We'll get you taken care of and rested. Later this morning, after you've slept, you'll get a visit from the family, then you and I will be able to sit down and talk about what happened. Is that all right?"

Dieter merely nodded.

Hans gestured to some SS orderlies that were waiting and they hurried up to assist Dieter to the hospital. Hans watched them escort him away, wondering what was going through his nephew's head. *Well, at least he's walking. He doesn't seem to be physically harmed. He's probably just exhausted, and in shock from the ordeal he just went through. He'll be better after they treat him and he gets some rest and a warm meal.*

He watched in cold silence as the guards unloaded the prisoners. The prisoner Tomasz tried to approach him, but he was pulled away by the guards and Hans refused to look his way.

He would deal with this man later, after he'd talked to Schmidt further and had some time to think about it. As for this Bak: "Take him to solitary confinement," he ordered. "Give him a little water and nothing else. No lights, no blankets, no bed. I want him to be in the proper mind to consider his future. But keep him alive. I want guards watching him every moment. I'll attend to him later today."

A car arrived and Elsa and Hannah rushed out. "Where is he?" Hannah demanded.

"They just took him to the hospital," said Hans.

"Where is that?" she asked, starting to move past him. Hans held on to her. She fought him, but he wouldn't let her past.

"Let me go! I'm going to see my son!"

"You can't just yet."

"You won't stop me, Hans!"

Hans refused to release her. "Your son is fine," he said. "I just saw him. He walked out of the back of this truck. He's just exhausted. He needs some food and rest. We can visit him in a few hours."

"I want to see him now," Hannah whispered, but she had calmed down and she was no longer trying to push past Hans.

"I know. And I would let you if I thought it was best for Dieter. But your boy is fine. He's safe, and later today everything will be all right, you'll see. Even more than that, he's a hero now. He helped put down this revolt. Kramer promised me a promotion for Dieter."

"And transfer to Berlin?" Hannah prompted.

"And a transfer to Berlin. If he wants it."

Hannah burst into tears, Elsa moving to comfort her. "This has all been too much," she said.

"I know it has," said Hans. "But it's over now. Go home and get a little rest. You can come back in a few hours."

Hannah nodded and they turned to leave. Elsa shot Hans a look of gratitude, and of love. Somehow, by a miracle, his plans had worked out in the end. He'd saved his nephew, put down the revolt, and assured his position at Auschwitz, and with his family. He owed everything to Schmidt, he knew, and he would be putting in the strongest recommendation possible for the man's elevation to the number-two position in his department. Schmidt was the true hero of the hour, and he would be forever grateful to him. What a great man, and here he had always distrusted him.

His wife and sister-in-law departed. They would go home and make the flat perfect for Dieter's return. Dieter would have to spend some time debriefing, but they'd have a fine celebration when he was released, and the commander had already granted his nephew a weeklong leave to rest and recover.

Later in the morning, Hannah and Elsa returned to see Dieter, who was now awake. Hans stayed out of the hospital ward, drinking tea and chatting with one of the guards while they visited. They came out an hour later, and thanked him with tears in their eyes.

He entered the ward after they'd gone and found his nephew much recovered. Just as he'd thought, the sleep seemed to have done wonders for his nephew. He was smiling now and sitting up with a plate of breakfast. Hans took a seat next to him, a notebook in his hand, and asked Dieter to relate every detail about the events that had unfolded over the past few days.

Kramer stopped by about noon. By that time, Hans was nearly finished. He had a dozen pages of closely written notes. He was amazed at some of what he'd heard and alarmed at how organized and knowledgeable the *Sonderkommando* members seemed to have been. But he would deal with that later. He knew he had to find out more, so he couldn't leave his nephew just yet.

The commander chatted with Dieter lightly for a few minutes, joking about the adventure he'd just been on. Then he opened an envelope, reading out Dieter's promotion for gallantry in the face of the enemy. He stood and saluted, motioning for Hans to join him outside.

"How is the boy doing?" the commander asked, genuinely concerned.

"He's going to be fine," said Hans. "Physically he's remarkably recovered."

"Oh, to be nineteen again."

"Indeed. I have detailed notes from his experience. They are alarming. I'm going to finish up here and then I'll have my staff get to work on typing them up. I'll have a report for you early this evening."

"Will you have time to go over it tonight?"

Hans hesitated. "I was going to have a little celebration dinner with my family, but—"

"Of course you will. Take care of your family first. Let's meet first thing in the morning."

"I appreciate it, sir."

"You're the one who hasn't been appreciated," said Kramer, looking Hans over as if with new eyes. "You've done miraculous work here. And Dieter won't be the only one who wins promotion from this."

"Schmidt was the real hero."

"Yes. Who would have believed it? Well, he'll get his due as well. I'm going to follow all your recommendations."

Hans gave him the Hitler salute. "Thank you, sir."

The commander returned the gesture. "No, thank you. Now, finish your interview and then please get to the prisoner. Do we know anything from him yet?"

Hans shook his head. "I haven't started. I wanted to find out what was going on with Dieter before I set to work on him."

"How long do you think it will take?"

Hans smiled. "Not too long, I think. I'll bring you updates on information as soon as I've collected any."

The commander extended his hand. "Good work, Hans. I'll

meet with you when you're ready and we can review what you've learned and also talk about your recommendations for Schmidt, and for yourself."

Hans smiled as the commander left. He could not believe his good fortune. He said a farewell to Dieter and then stopped by the dining hall to put together a couple biscuits with salami and cheese. He wolfed them down. He hadn't realized how hungry he was. While he ate, he hummed a little tune, his mind running through the questions he would have for this Bak. Should he give the man a chance to answer or just start in with the torture first? Perhaps he should ask Schmidt, or this Tomasz? Hans considered the informant. Schmidt recommended he be saved and inserted with the new *Sonderkommando* when they formed it. It wouldn't be the first time. The man had been in Auschwitz almost since the beginning. But these low-numbered prisoners were causing him no end of headaches at this point. Perhaps he should just put a bullet in him? Well, he would see what he could get from Bak, and then decide how to deal with the snitch.

He slurped down some tea and grabbed a pastry for dessert, taking bites as he walked back into the camp and headed toward the penal barracks. He passed a few prisoners as he strolled along, and they stood at stiff attention, eyes at the ground, cowering as he moved by. He paid them no mind. They had nothing to fear from him. Not this morning at least.

He reached the building a few minutes later. Schmidt was there, and so was Tomasz. The two of them were talking and drinking tea. They both nodded to Hans when he arrived.

"Are you ready?" Schmidt asked.

Hans nodded. "Any thoughts on how we should start?"

Schmidt turned to Tomasz and asked the same question. The man paused for a second and responded in broken German with a thick Polish accent. Hans had trouble understanding the man.

"What did he say?"

"I'm not sure," said Schmidt. "Let me clarify." The guard switched to Polish and the two of them rattled off for a few minutes. Hans only caught a word here and there.

Schmidt turned back to him. "Tomasz suggests you let him talk to this Jakub first. They've been friends in the camp and he thinks he might be able to get the information without torture."

"Would it be reliable?"

Schmidt nodded. "I've known Tomasz for a long time. He knows he has to be honest if he wants to save his own little skin."

"Fine enough then. I agree. Let's hold off on the more direct methods until they've had a chance to chat. How long do you think it will take?"

Schmidt turned back to Tomasz and asked the question in Polish. "An hour or two, he thinks. He's wondering if he could bring a little food and water in to the prisoner? He thinks it might help. If he doesn't get anywhere, I'll take some more persuasive steps."

Hans nodded. "That's fine." He thought about remaining here, but if it was going to be that long, he had other things to do. "Call over when you're ready for me," he instructed Schmidt. "Don't get too far into the direct interrogation without my presence. I want to see this happen." He relished the thought of watching this little Jew squirm.

"Yes, sir."

Hans strode out and returned to his office. He sat down at his desk and began the after-action report. He found it difficult to concentrate. The future streamed through his mind. The war would be over soon. It would be hard on Germany, but they would get through. He would be a decorated member of the SS, with a proven track record of performance. He should be able to find a senior position in a police department. Perhaps even the top job in a smaller community. He would hire Dieter and bring him along slowly. They would live a few houses down from each other. Soon enough his nephew would settle down and there would be grandkids eventually. He would never have his own children, but he would be a surrogate grandfather for Dieter's. Yes, just like after the last war, Germany and his family would go on.

He started his paperwork, trying to concentrate on the details, but he'd been up far too many hours. His eyes grew heavy and he stood up and closed his door, returning to put his head down on the desk for a short nap.

An hour passed. A loud knock disturbed his rest. He looked up, his eyes blinking. His head felt like it was full of sand and he shook it, trying to drive away the weariness. "What is it?" he finally managed to mutter.

The door tore open. A guard was there, his face ashen. *What was the problem now?*

"Sir, I need you to come with me right now!"

Chapter 37
The Interrogation

October 1944
Auschwitz

Jakub lay crumpled in the corner of the cell, his body shaking from the cold. He was in total darkness and he didn't know if he'd been here for hours or for days. The guards had given him half a cup of water and nothing else before they'd thrown him in here. The liquid had done little to assuage his thirst, and his body begged for something to drink. He felt a fever in him, and he wondered how he could stand up to even a little of the crucible that awaited him.

He thought of Anna. He hoped she was safe. They knew nothing about her involvement in the revolt. If there was any justice, they would have left her alone after they captured him. But this was Auschwitz, and justice here meant little unless it was twisted and coiled. And if they found out what she and the other women had done for the insurrection . . .

He faded in and out of consciousness. The shivering increased and his teeth chattered loudly in the blackness. He wasn't sure how much longer he would even be alive. He hoped his heart would just give out and they would find him dead in here. If he was gone, there was no chance he could give up Anna or anyone else in the throes of torture. What if he had sacrificed everything for her, only to damn her by revealing her role in gathering gunpowder?

Tomasz. His *friend*. He'd betrayed him. His anger helped burn away some of the cold. How could he have done this? It was to save his own life, of course. When Jakub had refused to take their best chance to escape, then Tomasz had resorted to what the ghetto thug considered the next best option. Preserving his own future, no matter what the cost was for him.

He heard footsteps in the corridor and a fumbling of keys. His door flew open and a stabbing light burned his eyes. Bodies strode into the room and hands reached for him, violently ripping him upright and half dragging him out of the cell and into the hallway. He heard himself screaming from pain and terror as they carried him a few doors down and shoved him into another room. This space had a concrete floor and brick walls. A single lightbulb swung from the ceiling. There were no chairs, no beds. The door slammed behind him and he lay facing the back wall, shivering more from fear now, tears running down his face.

"Jakub." He heard the word and couldn't believe the voice. "Jakub," it repeated. He rolled painfully over and there he was, standing over him. Tomasz.

"You bastard," Jakub managed to say. "You betrayed me."

"Quiet!" said Tomasz, leaning down quickly. "I have water. You need to drink." Jakub wanted to refuse but he was too weak, too thirsty. He lifted his head slightly and Tomasz held it as he drank out of a steel mug. He didn't stop until he'd finished all of it, then his head fell back and he closed his eyes, not wanting to look at his friend.

"You betrayed me," he repeated.

"That's not what happened," he said, leaning down to whisper into Jakub's ear. "I made it back to the camp and was able to talk my way inside to Canada. Some friends loaned me a little gold and I bribed my way into the women's camp and found Anna. I made it into her barracks but she wasn't there. That's when Schmidt caught me."

"What do you mean she wasn't there?"

"Schmidt took her. A couple days ago. Apparently, there was a murder in the latrines during our revolt. It was that skirt of Schmidt's, Kamila. The block wardress turned in Anna for the crime and Schmidt stormed in and dragged her out. Nobody has seen her since."

"I don't believe you."

"Look, I don't care what you think of me. I've done what I had to in this, to save myself. I'm trying to save you too."

"How can you even say that?" Jakub demanded.

"Quiet! We don't have much time and you must listen to me. You left me no choice. You brought this on yourself, Jakub. I never believed in this escape business in the first place, but I tagged along and I was ready to leave with you. If you'd just agreed to escape when we had the chance, we would have made it through and we'd all be free now. But you wouldn't. You insisted on bringing Anna out. When you refused, you doomed us all. I tried to save her but I was caught myself. I took the only option I had left. Cutting a deal."

"You saved your own skin, and cost Marek his life."

"I don't give a damn about Marek or anyone else. I care about you, Jakub. It's always been about you. And I would sacrifice a thousand Polish resistance leaders to save you. I've never told you why, have I?"

"Why?"

"I lost my real brother here. His name was Dominik. He was only twelve."

"You've never said anything about him."

"I haven't. I couldn't. They pulled him into the bad line. I tried to get to him, but they beat me, they led him away. If I'd only had something to give them, something to bribe them with, I could have saved him."

"You can't blame yourself for that, Tomasz. You'd just arrived. You didn't know the rules. There was no way to—"

"It doesn't matter," said Tomasz, his hand wiping a tear away. "I learned to live with it. I survived here—even learned to prosper. And then you came along. You were young, innocent like him. You even look a little like him. So you see," he said, looking up to face him, "I couldn't save Dominik, but I could save you."

"But you didn't, Tomasz. I'm here and they're going to torture and kill me."

"It doesn't have to be like that," said Tomasz.

"What do you mean?"

"Tell them what you know. Everything you know. I've already spoken to Schmidt. He hates you but he knows you have critical information. You were on the inside, Jakub, even if just for a little while. You must know more—some of the information about other leaders, how they got weapons. If you tell me everything you know, I have Schmidt's promise that he will spare your life. He will reassign us to the new *Sonderkommando*. I'll be in charge and you can be my assistant. It means food, safety. We'll survive the war."

"You don't really believe that, do you?"

"About leading the next group I do. They need people who know what they're doing. At least one or two. As for surviving, that's the lie they always tell us, isn't it? But if we can survive this and keep a supply of food coming our way—keep up our contacts with the SS—who knows? It's never been more than a flicker of hope, but at least it's a chance!"

"There's nothing I can do to help," said Jakub. "I don't know anything." But that was a lie. He *did* know something.

Something about Anna and her friends. Where the gunpowder came from. Would that information be enough to save his life? It might, he realized. He felt the old tug, his father's word. *Survive.*

"There must be something you can give me. I only have a little time before Schmidt comes in. And then I can't protect you anymore."

He had to have time to think. "Could I get something to eat? I'm so hungry."

Tomasz looked like he was going to argue, but then he relented. "I understand. You must be starving. Let me see what I can find you." Tomasz rapped on the door and left. He came back a few minutes later with a loaf of camp bread. He handed it to Jakub, who tore into it, devouring the food in a few moments.

"Thank you," he said. "I want to know about Anna. Is she here? Is she safe?"

"She's in another cell, on the other end of the building," said Tomasz. "If you won't save yourself, think about her."

"What do you mean?"

"They beat her up pretty bad, Jakub. I won't lie to you. After Schmidt caught me and I told him I would lead him to you, I demanded to see her. Her face is badly bruised. They pulled out her fingernails and I think they broke her arm. But she's all right, Jakub. I got them to promise to stop—at least until I had a chance to talk to you."

"The bastards," said Jakub through gritted teeth. He tried to rise.

"Stop it!" said Tomasz. "There's nothing we can do about that right now. There's something else I must tell you. The most important thing of all."

"What?"

"She's pregnant, Jakub. She's pregnant with your child."

Pregnant. How could that be?

"She told me," he continued. "She's known for a few days now. Schmidt took her out of line on the way back into Auschwitz the night after he tortured you. He was going to have his way with her, but she was too ill. He took her to the hospital. They examined her there and found out she was pregnant. Schmidt wanted to have her liquidated right then and there, but some of her friends used their influence to get her discharged out of the hospital and back to her barracks. Kamila must have heard about her and Schmidt going off together and confronted her. Anna wouldn't talk to me about that, so she must be protecting some of her friends."

Jakub's mind reeled. Anna was pregnant with his child. She had never been with Schmidt, forced or otherwise. He had a family. A future. But all of that was gone now . . .

"Please, Jakub. Please, for your sake, for Anna's, tell me everything you know. I promise to protect you both, but you must give me something to work with. Otherwise they'll start in on both of you, and it will be too late to cut a deal. You'll lose her, and your baby!"

What was he going to do? If he told Schmidt about Anna's friends, about the gunpowder, he would be sacrificing other lives to save his own. He thought of his father, his mother, his family. They were honorable people. His father had forced him to promise to survive, but had he meant at any cost? He conjured an image of Anna. So frail. He thought of her resistance to him, her demand that they marry. She had held on to her integrity in this hell, regardless of the cost. He knew what she would tell him. That he couldn't sacrifice others to save her, to save an unborn child. Roch would say the same. The resistance leader would never let others suffer to save himself. Only Tomasz would advise to do whatever it took to make it. Tomasz, who was going to survive this-while the rest of them died.

But truthfully, was he any different from Tomasz? He thought of Dieter and remembered approaching the guard. He'd promised the young man information about the *Sonderkommando* in exchange for Anna's protection. But he wasn't going to betray his friends. Just pass on some things that couldn't get anybody hurt. When he'd heard about the hidden pistol and uniform, he'd thought he had the perfect item to tell the guard. They couldn't be traced to anyone. But would he have stopped at that? Would he have given more if it was required? He didn't know. He'd never had a chance to even go that far, because someone had betrayed them all. Now he had the chance to save himself, to save Anna and their unborn child. All he had to do was tell Tomasz about the gunpowder.

"I don't know anything." The words came out almost of their own accord. He wasn't sure it was what he wanted to say. And Tomasz responded as if he knew the same, as if he could hear each and every thought.

"You know that's not true, my friend. You're following the wrong voices. Listen to your father, listen to me. We are in hell here. I can keep you alive. I can save your wife and your baby. But I need your cooperation now. I can't go back to Schmidt with nothing, and time is running out."

"I can't do it. I don't know anything that will help them. I'm so sorry."

His friend looked at him for long moments and then he clapped him on the shoulder. "Farewell, my friend. God protect you. You're my brother forever."

Jakub felt the tears running down his face. Tomasz had betrayed him but he'd done it out of his own need for redemption. He'd tried to protect him the only way he knew how. He thought about dozens of times when Tomasz had taken care of him, fed him, saved his very life. He was a brother. Perhaps closer even than that. In some ways he was closer even than Anna. He couldn't find himself angry with Tomasz. He said a little prayer for him as his friend stood to leave. He hoped he would survive the war. That everything he'd done, the sacrifices he'd made, would in the end be worth it.

Tomasz walked to the door and rapped on the wood again. A guard opened and Tomasz whispered to him. He took a last look at Jakub, smiling sadly, and walked out the door. In a moment he was gone.

He lay that way for some time. At least he could see now. He knew what was coming. There were no more chances. The only thing he had left was to somehow resist them. He thought of Anna, of their child. Everything was lost except his honor.

The door opened and he heard another familiar voice. "Bak, my friend. So nice to see you. Thank you for coming for a little visit. I'm going to check in on your little friend Anna for a few minutes, then I'll be back for a chat with you. I hope you don't mind if I spend a little time with her before we begin. I miss her." The guard laughed and slammed the door behind him.

An hour later Schmidt returned, dragging a stool with him. Jakub was in the corner now, his back against the wall. The sergeant had a smile on his face. "That was fun," he said, chuckling. "For me at least. I must say she didn't enjoy herself. But I had a wonderful time."

"What did you do to her?" Jakub demanded.

"I'm afraid that's between her and me," said Schmidt. "But don't worry. I have enough energy left for you. I'll reunite the two of you in a little while. I have some things I want you to watch, but for now, I need to have a little chat with you." He stepped over to Jakub and sat down a half meter away from him, studying his features as if examining a new project. "I understand you didn't tell your friend Tomasz anything."

"I don't know anything."

Schmidt shook his head. "That isn't the proper attitude. Tomasz wanted to see if you would tell him what you know without my involvement. I gave him that as a reward for his good behavior." He peered intently at Jakub, his grin widening. "Tomasz has been a very good boy for a very long time. But you don't know about that, do you?"

"That's a lie," said Jakub. "You caught him bringing Anna out. He had no choice but to give you information."

Schmidt laughed. "Is that what he told you? You're a fool, Bak, and you always have been. Tomasz has been informing us for years. How do you think he's managed to have his little trips to the women's camp? Did you think he was just bribing his way through? That we would take valuables from him and let him walk around the camp? That was for your benefit. He's been feeding us everything we've needed to know. He thought he could bring you along to do the same."

"I don't believe it," said Jakub.

"You know I'm speaking the truth. Think about yourself. You've been protected all this time because Tomasz insisted I leave you alone. I would have killed you long ago. I don't know what it is, Bak, but there's just something about you that has always worn on me. But Tomasz intervened on your behalf. I acquiesced, but only reluctantly." Schmidt smiled. "That's why I was so delighted to discover your little affection for Anna. That was a way for me to get back at you. Although it would have been far more satisfying without her little complication."

"Leave her alone!"

"Still protective, are you? There's not much left of her to protect now."

Jakub felt his anger rising. If he wasn't so weak, he would have attacked Schmidt then and there, whatever the consequences. He tried to lunge at him but all he managed was a flinch of his limbs. The guard watched the gesture and laughed out loud.

"That got to you," he said. "I'll never understand your interest in that little slut. Is it because she's carrying your bastard?

Well, they're both going up the chimney, and so are you, unless you sing now."

Jakub didn't answer.

"So you already knew about the pregnancy, I see. Did Tomasz spill the story? Well, no matter. To each their own, I guess. What matters now is her life, and your own. I told you that I'm going to kill her. Your child first, then her. I'll do it over a week, and you'll get to watch every second of it. You can stop it and you can save your own life as well. But it will cost you everything you know."

"I told you, I don't know anything."

Schmidt shook his head. "That's a naughty boy. Well, if I can't talk you into it without any assistance, I guess I'll have to choose other methods of persuasion. Should I start with you or with Anna? Maybe I'll see if you can grow more talkative with some direct methods first." He tapped his cheek a couple of times as if considering what to do next. "Let's see, I guess I could give you a choice in the matter. What do you think, Bak, a finger or a toe?"

Schmidt drew his SS dagger out and turned it over and over. "Have you seen one of these up close?" he asked. "This is a prized possession of the SS man, given to him to commemorate his acceptance into the order. Many organizations have such tokens, but fortunately, this one has a practical application as well."

Before Jakub could respond, Schmidt lashed out with the knife. Jakub saw the flash and felt a fire in his forehead. Blood poured down his face and into his eyes. He screamed with the pain, his hands flying up to try to stem the flow of the wound, but he had nothing to stop it with. He fell backward, the back of his head hitting the ground hard, his back arching from the pain.

"Now, now, Jakub. Surely, you're not going to react so violently to such a little cut. Why, we've only just begun." Jakub felt his wrist gripped and pulled away from him. He tried to fight, but Schmidt pinned his chest to the ground with his knee. He felt a sharp press on the base of his little finger. "Now, the first thing I did was just to get your attention. It stings, I'm sure, but it's nothing permanent. Before I go further, I need to ask you again to reconsider the information I need. I'll give you a few seconds. Otherwise, I'm afraid I'm going to have to deprive you of a digit."

Jakub's heart nearly beat out of his chest. He was terrified, but what could he do? He'd made his choice. He thought of Anna, of Roch. He couldn't let them down. "I don't have anything for you," he repeated.

"Too bad," said Schmidt. He felt a tug and a million needles ripped up his wrist. He screamed in agony. Bright lights filled his mind.

Frozen water woke him. He coughed and sputtered. He must have passed out from the pain. The water washed out his eyes and he could see now. He looked down at his left hand. A bloody rag was stuffed on the end. A fiery throb tore up his arm over and over. The bastard had done it—he'd cut off a finger. Schmidt was standing over him, watching him carefully, that self-satisfied smirk beaming from his face.

"Did that bother you?" Schmidt asked. He chuckled to himself. "Are you ready to talk now or shall I move on to the next one?"

"Jakub, please, tell him what he wants to know." Jakub turned his head. Tomasz was there, his face pale and full of misery. "Please. He'll stop as soon as you tell him. He's promised me."

"Yes," said Schmidt. "Listen to your friend. He's always been smarter than you. He sings when I ask him to, and because of it he's going to live." He looked down on Jakub again. "You can do the same, but you're going to have to hurry. There's nothing more useless in Auschwitz than a one-handed man."

What could Jakub do? He saw the imploring eyes of Tomasz. How could his friend have betrayed him? Was it true what Schmidt had said? That he'd always been working for the Germans? He had to know.

"You betrayed us, Tomasz," he whispered. "You were always working for the Germans."

"That's a lie," his friend responded, but Jakub could see in his eyes that it was the truth.

"How could you have?"

"Fine," said Tomasz, shrugging. "So it's true. I did what I had to for myself, and for you." His friend took a step forward. "What's done is done. I can live with myself. But don't let this have been all for nothing. Tell Schmidt what he wants to know. He's a reasonable man. If he says he'll spare your life, and Anna's life, then he's telling the truth."

Schmidt returned to him. Reaching down, he pulled up his left arm again and pressed the dagger to his ring finger. "What will it be, Bak? I'm out of patience."

"Tell him, Jakub. Please just tell him."

Jakub closed his eyes. What could he do? The agony clouded his mind. He realized at some point Schmidt would break him. He heard Tomasz's voice in his mind, begging him to submit. *Survive*. His father's promise returned to him at this last desperate moment.

But he knew in that moment that his father was wrong. It wasn't enough to simply survive. Roch had been right all along. If he didn't live for others, then there was no point in living at all. He knew Anna. She would never betray her friends. She would die, and he must die with her. "I don't know anything," he managed to mutter. He closed his eyes, waiting for the ripping pain.

Minutes passed. He was too weak to open his eyes. He fought the throbbing pain, trying to gather his strength.

He heard the door open again.

"Jakub!" He heard the voice and his heart coursed with emotion. He opened his eyes. Anna was there, next to Schmidt. Her face was bloody and bruised. She held her right arm with her left. Schmidt threw her to the ground and she shrieked in pain.

"Anna!" he shouted, reaching for her.

"Jakub! I never betrayed you!"

"I'm so sorry!" Jakub shouted, barely able to see her. "This was all Schmidt's doing! I never left you!"

"I know that!" she cried, her words stumbling out between the sobs. "I'm carrying your child!" she shouted.

"I know, my dear! I love you!"

"How touching," said Schmidt, giving Anna a kick to the stomach.

Jakub screamed, trying to rise, but he didn't have the strength.

The German turned to Jakub. "Now, my friend, what shall it be? Will you tell me what I want to know, or do you want me to proceed? I promise this is your last chance."

"Tell him what he wants to know!" implored Tomasz.

Jakub looked to Anna. She was lying on the wooden floor but her eyes were on him. She smiled and mouthed the words: *I love you*.

Jakub closed his eyes and shook his head. His whole soul cried out for the end of his life, for the loss of Anna and their child, and for the agony he would endure until it was all over.

"Too bad," said Schmidt. "I thought you were wiser than all that, Bak. Ah well, let's finish off these fingers, and then we'll call one of our physicians in to dig that little bastard out of Anna." He felt Schmidt's hands on his wrist again and he braced himself for the pain.

An explosion echoed through the cell. He opened his eyes in alarm. Schmidt was standing over him, knife still in his hands, but his mouth was open and blood was trickling out of it. His hands reached up involuntarily to a gaping hole in his chest. He collapsed to the ground. Jakub blinked. Tomasz was still there, but he had turned his attention to the doorway. An SS guard was standing there, a smoking pistol in his hands. It was Dieter.

The young man was staring down at Schmidt in surprise, as if he didn't understand what he'd just done.

"Dieter, you've saved us," Tomasz managed to utter, his arms in the air. He took a step toward him. The guard looked over at Tomasz, a stern look on his face. He raised his pistol.

"I speak some Polish," the guard said, surprising them all. I grew up not so far from the border, so I knew both languages."

The guard aimed his weapon at Tomasz.

"No!" shouted Jakub.

"Don't feel so sorry about your friend," said Dieter. "Why don't you ask him about Urszula."

"What are you talking about?" demanded Anna.

"He had her killed. I saw the report at headquarters. She caught Tomasz meeting with Schmidt. When she confronted him, he had her arrested. She was executed the next morning."

"How could you have!" demanded Anna.

"I had no choice. She was going to ruin everything!"

"How could you have, Tomasz?" asked Jakub.

His friend looked at him with a deep sadness in his eyes. "I didn't want that to happen to her. Schmidt promised to transfer her. He lied to me."

"That's not all you did, Tomasz," said Dieter. "I know full well what you intended to do to me in the cottage. You tried to kill me, and you would have succeeded if Jakub hadn't stopped you."

"Wait," said Tomasz. "I can explain. We were only trying to escape!"

Dieter fired, taking Tomasz in the chest. His friend flew back and crumpled against the back wall, his body tumbling to the ground, blood pumping out of the wound. The guard moved forward, assessing Tomasz for a moment before he turned his attention to Jakub, the pistol aimed at his forehead. Jakub closed his eyes; this was the end.

A shot fired. He opened his eyes, trying to understand what happened. Dieter was lying over next to Schmidt, blood flooding out of the side of his head. He'd shot himself.

Jakub crawled toward Tomasz, landing hard on the ground next to him. His friend lay on his back, his eyes wide, tears streaming down his face. The circle of blood on his chest was rapidly spreading.

"Tomasz," whispered Jakub. There was no answer.

"Tomasz, can you hear me?"

The ghetto thug turned his head slightly, his eyes straining to focus. "Jakub, is that you?"

"I'm here."

"Jakub . . . I'm sorry. Forgive me. I did it for myself, and for you. I tried to protect you."

"You betrayed all of us."

Tomasz shook his head. "You've never understood. There's no way out of here. Look at me now. I sold my soul. It was worth nothing. I'm still going up the chimney." His head fell back and his eyes rolled into the back of his head. Blood spilled out of his mouth, his body shook for a few moments, and then he was still.

He held his friend's hands for a few seconds. "I forgive you," he whispered. He let go and rolled onto his stomach.

Anna was kneeling over Schmidt. He realized she had his pistol in her hand. Jakub heard groaning. The guard was still alive. The guard opened his eyes, staring up at Anna in pain and in fear.

"For my family and for me," she whispered. She put the barrel against Schmidt's forehead and fired. The German's body bucked one time and then was still, a pool of blood growing under his head.

Anna dropped the pistol, her body falling away. Jakub crawled to her, pulling her to him. He held her that way, desperately clinging to her. "I love you," he whispered. "I will always love you."

He heard boots pounding in the corridor. He raised his head toward the door. An SS guard, pistol raised, was staring at the scene in horror. Jakub tried to speak to him, but the man rushed him. The last thing he remembered was the bottom of the German's boot as it crashed down on his head.

Chapter 38
The March

January 1945
Upper Silesia

The snow was deep, the air frozen. The long line of prisoners shambled along, with nothing but their thin, striped uniforms against the cold. Many had no shoes. Every few minutes a figure would fall out of line. A guard would scream at them. A shot, and the line moved on.

There was no food, no shelter. They'd walked for days. They had no idea how much farther they were going. The Nazis told them nothing.

Anna marched along with the rest of them. Her mind was as numb as her feet. She thought of Jakub. She wondered if he lived—or if the last part of him was growing inside her. She touched her stomach again, feeling her baby. She didn't know if it would survive, if she would live long enough to bring it to the world, but she would endure anything, fight anything, live through anything to make sure Jakub's child survived.

She was beyond hungry. They'd tortured her for weeks. Beat

her, starved her. She'd told them nothing. Every moment she was sure they would kill her. How could there be any other ending? But by some miracle, they did not. Somebody talked. Her friends were fingered, and had endured the same as her. She remembered the morning when she'd watched them hang. Somehow, her name was never revealed. God had reached down and sheltered her through the fire.

Now she marched through another valley of death. She would survive it. She said the words over and over. Nothing would stop her. For her family, for her Jakub, for her future.

Chapter 39
A Meeting

August 16, 1945
Kraków

Hans sat across the table from Elsa. They hadn't spoken in months but she'd agreed to meet him. She was thin and her face was drawn. He knew what she'd been through and his heart was broken. He wanted to reach out to her but he knew that would only upset her. How had it all come to this? She searched his features and he wondered what she might be thinking. Was there anything left for the two of them? Anything he could say to her to change the past?

"How is Hannah?" he asked, not sure how else to start the conversation.

Elsa's face darkened. It had been a mistake for him to bring that up. "She's trying to survive. She found a job with the government. She's a typist in the new identification department. They are requiring everyone to bring their old papers in, to prove who they are and that they have no connection with the Nazi Party, or the SS. If they do—"

"How did she get that job? With Dieter—"

"I don't think his paperwork had even gone through before he . . . before the country collapsed. In any event, they don't seem to have a record that he was affiliated with the SS. So Hannah's in the clear."

"How about you?"

She stiffened. "Well, I'm the wife of an SS officer, aren't I? They won't issue me new papers. I can't even get a ration card. I have to depend on friends for food and housing."

"Where are you living?"

"You remember Frau Heinemann?"

"The baker's wife?"

Elsa nodded. "Her husband was killed on the Eastern Front. Her two sons also."

Hans shook his head. "How awful."

"Yes. Well, she didn't have anyone living with her and she offered to take me in. She can't spare any food but I've got other people helping with that."

"Has the SS assisted?"

She scoffed. "The SS is gone, Hans. I don't know about everywhere, but in our town, everything has been disbanded and anyone involved with the Party is trying to escape, or pretend they never were a part of anything."

"It shouldn't be like that," said Hans. "We were a legitimate part of the national government. All we did was follow orders. We weren't some kind of rogue agency."

"They don't care about that," said Elsa. "I don't think you understand, Hans. It's not like the last war—where things were hard but we were basically left alone. They've come in and taken over everything."

"That can't last," he insisted.

"I think it will—perhaps forever. They've divided the whole country up and given a chunk of it to the Poles. I'm just thankful our city was left in Germany. At least we didn't have to pack up and move."

"I refuse to believe it is as bad as all that."

"Well, that's convenient for you, since you aren't having to deal with it."

"And I'm better off?"

"That's not why I came here."

This was what he was waiting for. "Why did you come?"

"Hans. I had to see you."

She had to see me. So, she did miss him after all? There was still something there. Some scrap of a future to cling to.

"I've wanted to see you too," he said. "I've missed you desperately. I know it might seem impossible, but I want us to start over. I don't even know how that would happen—if there is a future for us to consider. But if there is, I want you by my side. I want your forgiveness. Please, Elsa, you're all I have left in the world." He reached for her hand but she pulled it away. She looked at him for long moments and he held his breath, praying God would soften her heart.

"Hans, you don't understand me. I . . . I struggled with this for a very long time. But I saw no choice but to move forward." She reached into her purse and removed a small stack of documents. "I petitioned the new government for a divorce from you. I cited your wartime position, your involvement with the SS, your current *situation*. It took a few months but the government granted my request. We're divorced now."

Divorced. She'd cut the last bond they had together. All this time he'd waited to hear from her, for her to come to him, and while he was waiting, she was destroying their marriage. So, there was no future, no flicker of possibility that if all went well, they would be together again, in a new Germany, or perhaps in America. He wanted to scream at her, but he couldn't cause her any more pain. Of course, it was within her rights to do this. He just didn't want to let go. "I understand," he said at last, his voice shaking. "Quite right of you to do." He looked up at her, tears in his eyes. She was crying too. "I'm so sorry for everything," he said.

She stared back at him and nodded slightly. "I know, Hans. I know you did what you thought was right. But all of this must be over. I must move on and see if there is any future for myself out there. I hope you will forgive me too."

"You don't even have to ask," he said. "Please tell Hannah how sorry I am also. I know she would never talk to me. And give my best to my parents, if you ever see them."

"I will." Her hands shook and she placed the documents on the table. She slid them toward him.

There was a shout and the door whipped open. A Soviet soldier was there, rifle in hand, screaming at both of them. He reached down and picked up the papers, throwing them violently at her and waving his finger in her face.

"I'm sorry," she said, not understanding the soldier's words. She put the documents back in her purse. The Russian glared sternly for a few seconds more, then stormed out of the room. "I'm sorry," she repeated. "I didn't know that would happen."

"There is no worry," he said. "They won't let you give me anything. I understand what's in the papers. I don't need a copy. Not now at least."

"What will you do?" she asked.

"Who knows," said Hans. "I had hoped if I was ever let out of here that we might try to build a life together again. Without that . . . I'll manage. I've spent the last six years alone. We both have. After everything we've been through, we will go on somehow."

"Yes," she said. "Much has happened. The Russians were not gentle when they arrived in our town."

"What do you mean?" he asked.

The door opened again. A Soviet officer came in this time.

"You're not allowed to discuss propaganda, Frau Krupp," he advised her in thickly accented German.

"But it's not—"

"Your time is up," said the lieutenant, glancing at his watch.

"But I was told I would have an hour."

"Policies change, *Frau* Krupp."

She looked at Hans. He nodded, knowing it would do no good to argue. Despite everything, he didn't want any more harm to come to Elsa.

She started to rise. "I guess I'll be going now," she said.

"Thank you for coming. Please know that I understand, and I forgive you."

She smiled a little. She smoothed the fabric of her dress, looking at him and at the officer watching them. She took a step around the table toward Hans as if she would embrace him.

"No touching," said the officer.

She nodded and stepped back. "Goodbye, Hans."

"Goodbye. I'll always love you."

Tears filled her eyes again. "I loved you too. I'll always care about what happens to you."

That would have to be enough. The officer led her to the door. She took one more look back and then she was gone. The Russian returned. "Let's go, Krupp."

He led Hans out of the room and down a hallway through another door until they reached a set of bars. The officer fumbled with some keys and opened the iron door into a long corridor filled with cells on both sides. Hans's door was about halfway down to the left. The officer unlocked the cell and Hans walked in. There was a cot with a brown blanket and a thin pillow. Two buckets sat across the room, one for water and the other to relieve himself. Otherwise the cement walls and floor were gray and bare. Hans remembered the prisoner barracks at Auschwitz. The food the prisoners were forced to try to live on. He was still far better off.

"I have some news."

He'd forgotten the Russian was still there. "What is it?"

"The tribunal met again considering your case. They've reached a decision."

This was it then. "I don't suppose you have better news for me than my wife?"

"I'm afraid not. I'm sorry, Krupp, but you're to be hanged."

The news swept through his body like electricity. "When?"

"Tomorrow, at dawn."

"Why did you let my wife come then?" he asked. But he knew the answer. They had hoped she might say something incriminating to him. Something that would provide new leads, new information for other cases. But she hadn't. Hans had never shared anything with her. Their distance, even when living together in Auschwitz, had saved her.

"Do you want anything special for dinner? We don't have much, but I can see what we have."

"A little schnapps?" He hadn't tasted alcohol in months now. It would dull the pain.

"I'll see what I can do, but I doubt it. Would vodka serve as well?"

"Yes, that's very kind of you. Perhaps some sausage and bread, and as much vodka as you can give me."

"I can give you a little. It's not a party. If you're sick in the morning, there will be hell to pay for me."

"Anything would be a kindness."

The officer looked at him closely. "Are the things they say about you true?" he asked. "You were the head policeman in that murder camp?"

Hans nodded. "I cannot deny it. I had no choice. A refusal to obey orders would have meant death for me."

"That is no excuse. You realize that, of course."

Hans was silent.

The officer nodded. "I'll attend to your meal. I will see you in the morning."

"You'll be there then?"

"*Da.*"

The officer left and Hans sat down on his cot and closed his eyes. So, this was the end of him. He would face God soon and must account for his actions. What happened to people who died with the souls of thousands, perhaps a million, on their conscience? He would find out soon.

Chapter 40
A New Road

September 1, 1945
Detention Center, US Zone of Occupation, Germany

"What is your name again?" The American lieutenant stared at him across a bare folding table. The office was cramped and stuffy, with no windows. He'd waited most of the day to finally get in here and have his turn.

"Jakub Bak."

The lieutenant, who spoke Polish, scanned a file he had in front of him. "It says here that you were in the Auschwitz concentration camp." The man, a skinny, gum-chewing American with red hair, in his midthirties, looked Jakub over with compassion in his eyes. "I've heard a little about that place. I'm sorry for what you went through."

"Thank you," said Jakub, not wanting to think about that. "I've been here in this camp now for two months. When is my application going to be approved to relocate to America?"

The lieutenant raised his hands up in an expression of dismay. "I've told you that it will be at least six months, if not a year."

"But I'm a special case."

"Look, Jakub, I know you must have gone through a lot, but everyone thinks they deserve preferred treatment. You're not the only person out there who suffered. I'm dealing with many concentration camp survivors. Not only that, I have thousands more that were in slave labor camps." He smiled at Jakub. "We are doing everything we can. This camp isn't anything like what you dealt with before. You know that. I just need you to wait your turn with the others. Before you know it, you'll be cleared to travel and you'll be in the United States, where you can start a new life."

"I know everyone has suffered," said Jakub. "But I'm not like everyone. I want to tell you about what I've been through."

The lieutenant looked at his watch, stifling a yawn. "I don't have time, Jakub. There are dozens more applications I have to get through today."

"Just give me five minutes."

"I don't see how that is going to make any—"

"Five minutes. That's all I'm asking."

"Very well."

Jakub told the lieutenant about his time in Auschwitz, the loss of his family, Tomasz, Schmidt, Anna, Roch, the revolt, and the capture. He explained the months of imprisonment and torture, the certainty that he would be executed. He told him about the day he was retrieved from his cell and forced to join a terrible death march through the snow. The first new camp, then the second and third one. How he was left to die with thousands of others, only to be liberated by the Americans in April 1945. He talked for an hour, and the lieutenant never asked him to stop.

When he was done, the soldier was quiet for a long time, staring at the ceiling, tears streaming down his face.

At last the man spoke. "You're right," he said. "You are a

special case. I can't promise anything, but I'll do my best for you. If there's any way to speed things up, I will do it."

Jakub shook his hand. He knew this man would do everything he could for him. "Thank you, sir."

"Thank you. For all of us. For humanity. For everything you endured."

Jakub rose and left the office. He walked down the long rows of refugees, men and women, an entire people from every corner of Europe, who were all here fighting for a new life, a new world, in America.

He stepped out of the building and through a checkpoint. The guards looked at his pass. There were no bribes here. No electrified fences or threats of death. But the camp *was* fenced in and guarded. He was still a prisoner, even if his life was no longer in jeopardy. He slogged through the mud, tramping along the row of temporary houses until he found his own. He stepped through the door and into his little apartment.

Dinner was already cooking. He could smell the chicken and the cabbage soup. She was smiling at him, his treasure, his life, his Anna. In those terrible months after Auschwitz he'd given up hope of ever finding her again. When his camp was liberated, he'd gone through the motions of finding her. All of the survivors were trying to find their loved ones. But for almost all of them, the truth was, that everyone they had ever loved, ever cared for, all of their fathers and mothers, husbands and wives, sisters, brothers, and children. All of them were gone.

After the war, he was living in a displaced person's camp. He was at a table, drinking coffee, and poring through a list of other survivors when he'd heard her voice. She was there, against all odds, standing before him, arms reaching out to touch him, hold him. They were one flesh, one person forever.

He smiled as he remembered that miraculous reunion. As he watched her now, she was still tiny, still fragile, but she no longer looked starved. The haunted shadows creased her eyes, but they were receding slowly.

"Is there any news?" she asked.

"Maybe a little," he said. "I got the lieutenant to listen to me today. I told him my story, and yours. He let me tell all of it. He said he would do his best for us."

"Do you believe him?" she asked.

"I do." It was a different world for them to put their trust in a man in uniform. That this man would help them get to America, would look after their best interests, instead of working with every part of his being to kill them. That took some getting used to as well.

Anna crossed the room and held him closely. He could feel her trembling and her tears covering his shoulder and chest. "It's going to be all right," he whispered.

"It will be, and it never will," she answered.

Of course, she was right. They had each other. They had this future, but their families were gone forever. Auschwitz had taken that and just about everything else. They both had terrible nightmares. They clung to each other in the darkness, fighting their way to dawn. He hoped that would change someday, but for now, they battled the demons that devoured their sleep.

A cry rang out. It was the baby. Anna started toward him but Jakub intervened. "Go ahead and finish dinner, my love. I'll take care of him."

Jakub stepped into their bedroom. Next to the bed was a little crib with faded paint and a worn blanket. Their baby was there, born in the ashes of the war, their future and their hope. He picked their little boy up and the infant nuzzled against him, eyes closed, trying to nurse.

"That won't work for you, little Dieter," Jakub joked. "You'll need Momma for that. But right now, she's a little busy."

The child squirmed and cried, wanting his mother. Jakub took him into the kitchen and he stepped behind Anna, a hand on her shoulder, watching her finish their meal. They were together, and despite the terrible scars, they were a family, a future. He smiled and said a little prayer for all those they had lost, who he hoped were looking down on them from heaven.

Author's Note

Information About Places and Characters

KL Auschwitz

The Auschwitz concentration camp system (Konzentrationslager Auschwitz) was the largest labor/extermination system in the Holocaust. At least 1.1 million people perished there during its operation.

The camp started in a small converted army barracks within the town of Auschwitz itself in 1940/1941, about thirty miles from Kraków in Upper Silesia. The camp began modestly and housed about 1,000 male Polish prisoners. The Germans imported thirty German criminals to serve as the first *Kapos*. There was no initial plan for Auschwitz to expand into the mega death-factory and labor complex that it would later become. The camp grew organically as the SS over time refined the purpose of their concentration camp system, and as policy evolved regarding what to do with what the Nazis referred to as "the Jewish problem."

The first gassings at Auschwitz occurred in the penal block,

Block 11, when the barracks was sealed up and a group of Soviet prisoners were killed there using Zyklon B. The operation took quite a bit of time and was messy and inefficient because of the building structure. Eventually the morgue at Auschwitz I was converted into a gas chamber with an adjacent crematorium. This gas chamber is the only one at Auschwitz still in existence today, the others having been destroyed by the Germans at, or near, the time they evacuated the camp.

A much larger camp was designed and built in 1941 and named "Birkenau" after the birch trees that were adjacent to the constructed area. This camp, built from scratch, housed tens of thousands of prisoners. The Germans initially utilized two small cottages near Birkenau, the "little white house" and the "little red house" for continuing their gassing operations.

Birkenau was expanded on an industrial scale. A rail spur was built, allowing trains to bring the passengers directly into the camp beneath the arched "Death Gate," the most famous symbol of Auschwitz, along with the sign over the entrance to Auschwitz I: *ARBEIT MACHT FREI* (Work will set you free). Four new buildings were designed that housed large gas chambers, crematoriums, and housing for the *Sonderkommando*s, all in one structure. These structures were called Crematoriums II, III, IV and V. These buildings were located at the west end of Birkenau and were placed in separate perimeters away from the camp and shielded by trees and enclosed fences. The new crematoriums were true killing factories, designed specifically to undress, gas, and cremate thousands of people a day.

The greater Auschwitz camp structure eventually would encompass a huge area, with 40 sub-camps including a large industrial area at Auschwitz III.

For approximately 90 percent of those brought to Auschwitz, life would end within an hour. SS doctors carried out selections as the prisoners came off the trains, and only the young and strong were typically selected for work. If you were not put into the labor group, the Germans would escort you either along the rail line to Crematorium II or III, or through the middle of the camp and then west to Crematorium IV and V. You would be brought into a large room to remove your clothes and then moved into the gas chamber and gassed with Zyklon B. The killing process lasted about twenty minutes.

For those selected for labor, they would be tattooed with a number on their arm and assigned to a barracks and to a *Kommando* for labor. Work was backbreaking, from dawn to dusk, and the prisoners had inadequate clothing and grossly inadequate food. The average worker was only able to be productive for about six weeks, before they became so thin and ill that they too would be selected for liquidation. Those in Auschwitz who survived either had contacts among the camp elite, were lucky enough to be assigned lighter labor, or had access to extra food from service in the *Sonderkommando* or working with the clothing and other items in the huge storehouses called "Canada."

After the massive influx of Hungarian transports in the summer of 1944, the gassing operations at Auschwitz slowed substantially. In January 1945, with the Soviets closing in, the camp was abandoned by the Germans, after they destroyed the gas chambers and did everything that they could to cover up the operations. The SS herded most of the remaining prisoners away to camps inside Germany. Sick and frail prisoners died by the thousands.

The Soviets liberated the camp on January 27, 1945. There were approximately 7,500 survivors who had been too ill for the Germans to take with them. The Russians also discovered some of the Canada buildings intact, with hundreds of thousands of sets of clothing, tens of thousands of shoes, and tons of hair.

Rudolf Höss, the camp commander of the overall complex, was hanged in Auschwitz on April 16, 1947. Only about 15 percent of the Auschwitz personnel were ever tried for their actions associated with the camp.

The Auschwitz Revolt

The Auschwitz revolt is a true event in the history of the camp and occurred in October 1944. A few women, at the ultimate personal risk to their lives, smuggled trace amounts of gunpowder into the camp from their labors at the Union Munitions Factory, a slave labor operation located outside of Birkenau.

The revolt was intended as a camp-wide effort, in conjunction with members of the Polish resistance. The intent of the leaders was to entirely liberate the camp. Unfortunately, the SS, through informants, learned of some of the elements of the plot and decided to liquidate the *Sonderkommando*s. Members of the *Sonderkommando* at Crematorium/gas chambers II and IV revolted when it became apparent they were going to be killed.

The *Sonderkommando* members in Crematorium IV were Hungarian. They blew up part of the building in a pitched battle with the SS. Ultimately the Germans gained control of the area and they executed the prisoners who were not already dead. However, the crematorium and gas chamber were permanently damaged and the Germans abandoned this location. This gas chamber never functioned again and no more lives were lost inside the building, because of the heroic resistance of the Hungarian *Sonderkommando*.

The *Sonderkommando* members in Crematorium II also revolted and fought against the Germans. A notoriously evil guard was pitched into a crematorium oven alive during the fighting. The Germans quickly closed in on the perimeter and the prisoners fought their way out of Birkenau and sought to escape the Auschwitz camp complex itself. Unfortunately, they chose to move to the south toward other sub-camps instead of to the north in the direction of the Vistula, where they might have found opportunities to hide and continue their escape. The bulk of the *Sonderkommando* members were rounded up, returned to Birkenau, and executed.

The Auschwitz revolt, while ultimately unsuccessful, survives as a brilliant flash of light and hope amidst the ultimate despair that humans can conceive. These prisoners, who were without weapons, surrounded by hundreds of guards, electric wire, and hostile civilians, and hundreds of miles behind the German lines, fought and freed themselves, even if just for a moment, from the camp that many historians would consider the most infamous murder factory in world history.

In terms of escapes, during the history of Auschwitz there were over 900 attempts to escape. Less than 200 made their way to freedom.

Sonderkommandos

The *Sonderkommandos* or "Special Commandos" were groups of prisoners that operated most closely with the murder process not only at Auschwitz-Birkenau, but at other concentration and extermination camps in the Nazi camp system.

These men were pulled out of a transport and set to immediate work removing the dead from gas chambers, often with their first exposure to this work coming from having to handle their own relatives and friends who were on the same transport. They were forced to welcome people in undressing rooms, encouraging them about the process and making sure they folded their clothing and put a string through their shoes. The job these men were forced to do is unimaginable.

Despite the horror of the work, *Sonderkommando* members were often considered among the most fortunate at Birkenau, because their access to the clothing of the dead gave them opportunities to find food, valuables and money. They were supposed to turn everything over to the Germans, but inevitably some of the valuables and most of the smaller food items were kept by the prisoners themselves. The gold, jewelry, and money were traded with guards and other prisoners for more food, allowing *Sonderkommando* members to supplement their woefully inadequate camp rations. These men therefore tended to survive longer than the six-week average in the camp, and by working inside and laboring in the same building where they slept, were not generally subjected to the same physical deprivations that the general camp population suffered.

The *Sonderkommando* members still faced a terrible ultimate reality. As the closest witnesses to the murdering process, they were a significant liability for the Germans, particularly as the war turned against the Nazis. For this reason, the *Sonderkommando*s were periodically liquidated, with the members forced into the very gas chamber that they had serviced for those months or years. As a result, very few *Sonderkommando* members survived the war.

After the war, particularly in the first couple of decades, *Sonderkommando* members were viewed by historians as a partially guilty group, because of their direct involvement in the killing process (only the Germans administered the actual Zyklon B or carbon dioxide gas). Some felt that they should have allowed themselves to be killed, rather than participating in the duplicitous process of assisting people in undressing and helping them into the gas chambers. Over time, this attitude has changed. These prisoners had no choice in the matter. If they wanted to survive, they were forced to fulfill the role that the Nazis gave them. Their suffering is not unique in the camp system, and is merely illustrative of the myriad of horrors, and terrible decisions, forced on the victims of the Holocaust.

Estusia Wajcblum

Estusia (or Ester) Wajcblum was nineteen when she was brought to Auschwitz along with her fourteen-year-old sister Hana (or Anna). Their family was murdered and they only had each other. They went to work in the Union Munitions Factory. They became friends with Ala Gertner and Regina Safirsztajn, as well as Roza Robota. They began smuggling gunpowder into Birkenau, in tiny amounts per day, hidden in secret pockets in their clothing. At times there were searches, and the women would be forced to dispose of the gunpowder and grind it into the dirt or mud with their shoes.

This smuggled gunpowder was used by members of the *Sonderkommandos* to create grenades. The women were part of the larger camp-wide plans for a revolt to free the camp with the assistance of the Polish resistance.

After the failed *Sonderkommando* revolt, some of the men involved were kept alive and tortured. Someone, or several men, revealed the source of their gunpowder and Estusia, Roza, Ala, and Regina were arrested. The four women endured months of terrible torture and rape, but none of them ever revealed anyone else involved in the plot or in bringing gunpowder into the camp.

On January 5, 1945, the four women were hanged at Birkenau. Estusia's sister survived the war. She wrote an autobiography detailing her life before, during, and after the Holocaust, called *Never Far Away*. This book was published on November 30, 2001 by the University of Calgary Press, and is an excellent read. The book is available on Amazon.com and likely at many bookstores and other online vendors.

Josef Kramer

Josef Kramer was the camp commander, *Lagerführer*, of Auschwitz II-Birkenau from May 8, 1944 to November 24, 1944. Kramer oversaw Birkenau in the summer of 1944 when the Birkenau camp saw its most significant influx of inmates, and during the most frenetic timeframe for gassing in the camp's history.

The reason for this was the opening of Hungary for the removal of their Jews. Hungary during World War II was a semi-autonomous ally of the Nazis. During the war the Jews in Hungary were discriminated against and terrorized, but the leader of the nation, Admiral Horthy, would not allow the Hungarian Jews to be transported out of the country and into the general German concentration camp system.

This all changed in 1944 when German troops occupied Hungary. SS Obersturmbannführer Adolf Eichmann arrived in the country and began mass deportations. In the summer of 1944, over 400,000 Jews were deported from Hungary, with the vast majority of these being transported to Birkenau. Almost all these Hungarians were immediately gassed. Ironically, for the inmates of Auschwitz this was known as a time of prosperity when there was ample food and valuables because of the transports, and because during this time the Germans were too busy handling the massive influx of trains to focus on mistreatment of the semipermanent camp populations.

This time of "paradise" for the camp came to an end at the latter part of the summer, when the Hungarian transports ceased. The guards again turned inward into torturing and punishing the inmates of Birkenau, and with the Soviets creeping ever closer in Poland, the prisoners could see that doom was closing in. This change of conditions was one of the factors that led the *Sonderkommando* teams to organize for a future resistance, before they were all liquidated, as the camp ceased its full operation and the Germans prepared to evacuate the prisoners at some juncture and move them west into Germany.

Kramer was the perfect commander to handle this situation. He had a reputation for cruelty. He took an active part in the selections at the train stops and was aggressive and strict with the SS staff.

In December 1944, Kramer was moved to the Bergen-Belsen concentration camp. He remained in the camp when the British arrived.

Kramer was tried for his actions during the war and several former inmates testified against him. He was hanged at Hamelin prison on December 13, 1945.

Jakub, Roch, and Tomasz

Jakub, Roch, and Tomasz are all fictional characters. Jakub represents so much of the Auschwitz experience. First, he battles with survivor guilt. Jakub feels unworthy to have survived the initial selection when his family arrived at Auschwitz. He knows he survived only because he was young and able to work. All his family is dead. In addition, as a member of the *Sonderkommando*, he is watching hundreds or thousands of people a day be murdered in the gas chambers of Crematorium II. This gas chamber, according to historical accounts, was the one used the most on a daily basis in Birkenau. Jakub came to Auschwitz and became a member of the *Sonderkommando* before the bulk of the Hungarian transports to Auschwitz in the summer of 1944.

Jakub is faced with the same ethical problems forced on the Auschwitz inmates. He is stealing food and valuables from the dead in order to survive. The more people are run through the gas chamber, the more he has to eat and to trade for other food and privileges. He suffers from ongoing waves of guilt about this, throughout the book.

He is also dealing with a crisis of who to trust. He is a prisoner, although he has committed no crime. The guards, unlike the vast majority of officers in a regular prison system, are sadistic, murderous, and there to perpetrate the maximum agony on the inmates. Jakub is forced to choose between Roch, an idealistic leader who preaches self-sacrifice, even the sacrifice of one's life, for the good of the group; and Tomasz, a pragmatic survivor, who wants to protect Jakub, but uses bribes and information to carve out safety for himself in Auschwitz.

Jakub also must choose to save himself or risk his life for others. This was a common theme in Auschwitz, even if it was as simple an issue as fighting for a greater share of food. Prisoners were set against each other by the Germans. There were informants everywhere. The fifteen-hour days of backbreaking labor left little time for social interaction, or for individual prisoners to take care of each other.

Jakub ultimately chose to risk his own life to save Anna. While this may be a satisfying result for the reader, the reality in Auschwitz was that in the vast majority of instances, it was nearly impossible to save yourself, let alone anyone else. Holocaust survivors over and over in their testimonies discuss this very issue, and how grappling with these ethics have haunted them for the rest of their lives.

Hans and Dieter

Hans represents an SS officer that one could certainly encounter in the concentration camp system. Because of wartime conditions, ideological education, and general human pragmatism, there is a massive disconnect between his concern for his family and the way he treats prisoners.

The reader will note there is nothing sadistic about Hans. He takes no pleasure in the mass murders in Auschwitz, or in playing games with individual inmates. Instead, he sees his position as a part of Germany's struggle against enemies without and within. This was pure Nazi doctrine. The Nazis followed a pseudoscientific philosophy that the Aryan people, including Germans, were the superior race in the world. Other races, like the Slavic people of Russia and Poland, for example, were considered *Untermenschen* (under people). The Jews were a special race, who the Germans theorized were a threat to all humanity. In this theory, the Jews lived in community pockets throughout the world. They were clever, rising to important positions in medicine, law, the arts, and finance. According to the Nazis, the Jews used this power and money to further secret aims, to the detriment of the individual nations. The Germans particularly blamed the Jews for betraying the German people at the end of World War I. Although there was no evidence of an actual betrayal, a large number of right-wing German organizations including the Nazis accepted this as truth and vowed never to allow this again.

Hans was following this philosophy. The Germans, particularly the SS, with Hitler's permission, had segregated the Jews into isolated ghettos and camps, and then moved them into the concentration and extermination system with the intent of eradicating the Jews from Europe, and potentially from the planet. Hans sees the Jews as an enemy of his people, and that their extermination is a horrendous but necessary action.

He also has highly personal motivations for his actions. Hans has a broken marriage. He is in trouble with his commander and in jeopardy of losing his position. Desperate, he brings Dieter to the camp in hopes of making his wife happy, and with the idea that Dieter could obtain information from prisoner contacts and help him with his work problems. When everything falls apart, Hans acts in his self-interest, to save his future career and his nephew.

Dieter is another case altogether. He is young and has the idealism of a German who has waited for years to serve his country. He is furious that his uncle has taken this away from him. He reconciles himself to the reassignment to Auschwitz, but then is horrified by what they are doing there. He is more sensitive than Hans, and after witnessing the gassing of a transport of Jews, he is secretly desperate to get away.

After his capture by the Jews, he witnesses their heroic fight and escape, and their ultimate execution by Schmidt. When Jakub saves his life, he decides he will not try to stop them from getting away. When they are ultimately captured, he cannot live with what he's seen over the past few days. He decides to kill Schmidt and Tomasz, and then take his own life.

Dieter, more than Hans, sees past the propaganda he's been indoctrinated with for a lifetime. When he is confronted with what his own people are doing, and what they are capable of, he is so ashamed that he cannot live with the truth. Unfortunately, in Germany during World War II, there were plenty of people like Hans. People willing to go along with things either because of their beliefs, out of fear of reprisal by the authorities, or for their own personal gain.

Anna Siek

Anna, also a fictional character, faced many of the issues women dealt with in the camp. Many of the women in the Union Munitions Factory sought out male protectors who would furnish them with food and goods.

There are no statistics about unequal relationships and/or the rape of women prisoners by SS men at Auschwitz. Such relationships would have been officially illegal, particularly with Jewish women. However, it is well known that such relationships existed in significant numbers, with the men providing protection and food to the women. All these relationships were based on the worst possible abuse of power and would have placed the women in an impossible situation where they were forced to trade affection and physical relationships for survival.

Anna became pregnant at Auschwitz. Pregnancy was often a direct death sentence, with pregnant women sent to the gas chambers or euthanized by injection in the camp hospital. Stanisława Leszczyńska, a Polish woman, was a midwife in Auschwitz who was supposed to murder newborns, but instead delivered and saved perhaps three thousand babies in Auschwitz. Her story is a fascinating and heroic tale in and of itself.

Anna was a woman of integrity. She would not be involved with Jakub until they were properly married. She resisted other men's attempts to form a relationship with her, particularly Sergeant Schmidt. Anna risked her life smuggling gunpowder and was willing to sacrifice her life for something higher. She begins the novel where Jakub ended it, willing to give up her life for others and even for an ideal.

Acknowledgments

I want to thank my wife, Becky, for always assisting me with a read-through or two. Thank you to John at Kensington for his continued support and to Evan, my amazing agent.

A READING GROUP GUIDE

BEYOND THE WIRE

James D. Shipman

ABOUT THIS GUIDE

The suggested questions are included to enhance your group's reading of James Shipman's *Beyond the Wire*!

DISCUSSION QUESTIONS

1. Why as readers and as humans are we so drawn to the tragedies of the Holocaust?

2. Is Tomasz a hero or a villain? Is he both? What drives Tomasz and what motivates him? Did Tomasz ever intend to assist Jakub in escaping, or was he plotting all along to betray him to the SS?

3. Schmidt is a fictional character and yet his personality is seen in many true stories. In the book *Unbroken*, a sadistic corporal in the camps is respected and feared, even by his superior officers. Why would we, as humans in such a setting, revere and respect someone like Schmidt?

4. The members of the *Sonderkommando* were criticized after the war for having access to better food, better living conditions, and for "assisting" the Nazis in the killing process. Is this a valid criticism? What arguments can be made for and against this?

5. Is Kamila a "bad person" in the book? What drove her motivations and is there an argument that she was simply a victim of her circumstances?

6. Why did Roch want Jakub to be part of his resistance group? What did he see in Jakub? Why did he trust Jakub so quickly?

7. What drove Dieter to take the actions he did? How did he go from the brave German preparing to fight for the Fatherland to the desperate and hopeless figure at the end?

8. Hans is a husband who works at his job and comes home to try to deal with his personal problems. Is Hans partic-

ularly sadistic? Is he particularly evil? How did someone like Hans, a policeman from a small town, end up in the position he was in, doing the things he was doing?

9. If you were in Auschwitz in the *Sonderkommando*, what would you do? Would you have stolen items from the dead to save your own life? Would you lie to people about to enter the death chamber?

10. Could this happen in the United States? Whites against other races? Citizens against immigrants? Left against right? What about other "sophisticated" countries in the world today? Are we beyond the Holocaust or does it wait in the shadows for us, lurking just below the surface?